BEAUTIFUL SONATA

The third of the *Sonata* novels

Helen Weygang

The *Sonata* novels

Chance Sonata

Fractured Sonata

Beautiful Sonata

Pagan Sonata

Dark Sonata

For Becca, whose courage and determination are a forever source of hope and inspiration in dark times

For Becca, whose courage and determination are a forever source of inspiration and of hope in dark times.

Franz Xaver Gruber & Joseph Mohr – *Stille Nacht, heilige Nacht (Silent Night)*

Franz Schubert – *Sonata for Arpeggione and Piano D. 821*

J.S. Bach – *Partita in D minor for solo violin, BWV 1004*

Edward Elgar – *Concerto for cello and orchestra in E minor, Op. 85*

Jim Steinman – *Bad for Good*

Dmitri Shostakovich – *Piano Trio no.2 in E minor*

Bedřich Smetana – *Piano Trio in G minor, Op. 15*

Arnold Schoenberg – *String Quartet No. 2, Op. 10*

Wolfgang Amadeus Mozart – *Sinfonia Concertante for violin, cello and orchestra in Eb, K364 (320d)*

Anton Webern – *String Quartet, Op. 28*

Franz Xaver Gruber & Joseph Mohr – *Stille Nacht, heilige Nacht (Silent Night)*

It seemed to Kathy that the year 1982 was going on for ever. The weather got ever colder as the year crawled towards its end. Alison closed her café for the season, Kathy carried on knitting the brown and grey striped sweater and Piers worked hard on the piano parts for Jean-Guy's recital in between his flights to New York. The others hadn't failed to notice that the airline hadn't put him back on-call yet but nobody was sorry. It meant Piers' working life was much more regular and Jean-Guy was happy as he could plan some kind of rehearsal schedule now.

It seemed a lifetime ago to Kathy that Sarah had had her triplets but the babies were still less than a year old when the first blast of the really icy weather hit the east coast of Suffolk. They had had a few frosts since mid-November but as the year got ever closer to Christmas the ferocious east wind that would take your breath away as you walked the coast path came whipping in off the sea but Kathy refused to give in and drive to the village. Sarah didn't see much of her husband as he spent so much time in London these days but she was perfectly content with her parents and Alison helping her with the triplets, and watching her waistline become ever larger until she wondered if her skin would stretch that far. To the relief of those concerned with Sarah's care and with her health, she was blossoming in this pregnancy and had none of the persistent sickness she had had with the triplets. Kathy had become quite a regular visitor to the house beside the shop now and always got a warm welcome from Sarah and Alison and she even managed to convince herself the triplets recognised her voice if not her face and seemed to be pleased to see her too.

Kathy missed Piers on her walks to and from the village, but it was getting very close to the time she and Jean-Guy had to be in London for his Wigmore Hall concert and then the three of them would travel up to Suffolk together and stay there until two of them picked up their working lives early in the new year. To keep Kathy from worrying during that final run-up to the holidays, Piers had rung her a few times and she encouraged him to explain about Yule, the winter solstice and the turning of the wheel, then told him he was going to be expected to eat turkey and pull crackers with the rest of them. He knew when he was beaten but they had several long conversations on how they could combine the Pagan Yule with what would one day be the traditional Christmas at the farmhouse. Kathy thought it all sounded rather fun with its emphasis on nature and the turning of the wheel rather than the blatant consumerism she had come to hate about that time of year.

Kathy and Jean-Guy drove to London late on Sunday nineteenth of December to give them a day's breather before the recital on the twenty first, and, to their relief, the maroon Aston Martin was already in the car port. They realised Piers could only just have got back from what was his last flight before his break as he was still in his uniform in the kitchen, sifting through the post while the coffee machine warmed up.

Kathy gave him a hug and a kiss on the cheek in greeting as she always did and he smiled as he handed her quite a clutch of cards.

"Here, these are for you," he told her. "I didn't know you had so many friends."

Kathy remembered the Christmases when, thanks to her ex, she had been lucky to get half a dozen cards and they were the ones that had been sent to her old childhood address. Now she had quite a healthy collection of envelopes to open and it made her thankful yet again that she had left that awful period of her life behind her. She flicked through the envelopes then looked at Piers and returned his smile. "I am a woman of many surprises. You mean you haven't got dozens of cards too?"

"No I haven't," he told her and almost sounded cross. "People who know me know I don't celebrate Christmas. One or two clever ones find a Yule card for me, or make one, but mostly they don't bother." He shrugged and made himself some coffee without offering to make some for them. "I don't send cards either. Nobody to send one to But I did send one to Roisin after all these years. Seemed rude not to."

Kathy was glad to hear he was keeping in touch with his sister. "Not even Dacre?" she teased.

"Me, Dacre and Mick spend a lot of hours shut up in a very small cockpit together. Why the hell would we want to exchange Christmas cards? Quite frankly we're glad to see the back of each other for a few days at this time of year."

"Really?" she asked cynically,

"Well, almost," he admitted and necked his coffee. "Right, me for some sleep. See you in the morning."

"Yes, in the morning," Kathy agreed. "I'll just get a shopping list together, is there anything you want me to get?"

"We're low on bread," he said vaguely. "But is it worth it if we're away for Christmas anyway? No! Don't go down there for a piece of paper, that's all mucky in there."

Kathy had just fished what looked like a clean piece of white card out of the bin and was faintly surprised to hear the urgency in his voice. "This one looks fine," she reassured him. "I've learned with you that when I want a piece of scrap paper, the best place to start looking is in the bin." She saw his hand reaching to snatch the card away from her so she turned her back on him and flipped the card over to read it. There weren't many words on it but those few that there were made her pause before she turned to look at him.

"Were you going to tell us about this?" she asked and waved the card under his nose.

He gave up any attempt to get it back from her now it was too late. "No."

"What is it?" Jean-Guy asked curiously as he had never seen his landlord in such a state before.

"Tomorrow. Memorial for Chantal," she told him, her eyes never leaving Piers' face as he stood so defensively beside the door to the stairs. "It starts at ten thirty so what time are we all going to leave?"

There was a short, heavy silence in the kitchen. "I'm not going," Piers said and the other two could tell he was beginning to lose his temper.

Kathy hesitated but she wasn't going to back down. This was Piers and he would never hurt her. "It's an open invitation so you can't stop us going if we want to," she pointed out as kindly as she could.

Her soft words were wasted on the man who was clearly torn between conflicting emotions of anger and grief. "Just butt out of my life for once, will you? If you want to go, that's fine. You're right, I can't stop you. But don't expect me to come with you."

Kathy bit back her own temper, not liking to be spoken to like that. "I think you should," she said gently, hating to see him so obviously upset.

"Why?" was the hostile demand. "Why the hell should I? She's gone. She left me a year ago. I couldn't cope with it then so what makes you so sure I'll cope with it now?"

"Because you have to," she told him simply. She looked at him as he stood there at the foot of the stairs, somehow looking small and frail as he had when she had coaxed him into playing the Wigmore Hall gig in the first place. Hoping Jean-Guy would understand, she stepped across the kitchen and took Piers' face in her hands. "A year ago, you couldn't bear to say goodbye to her. You tried to follow her across the Samhain bridge but you turned back and now it's time to say goodbye to her from this side of the veil and let her go. Jean-Guy and I will stand one each side of you and we'll say our goodbyes to her too. We didn't get to do it last year and I'd like to have the chance."

"It's not that," he said and his voice was suddenly heavy with sadness. "Her brother and her pastor have asked me to give a eulogy at the memorial. I have tried so hard to write it. But I can't do it. Even at the very end, my very last chance to prove myself to her, I've failed."

Kathy had never been asked to give a eulogy at a funeral but she could understand why he would find it so difficult. "Would it help if one of us had a look at it for you? How far did you get?"

Piers sniffed a bit. "I, um, kind of wrote a poem but it wasn't any good."

"Still got it?"

"No."

"Will I find it a bit further down the bin?"

"No. I put it in the sink and set fire to it. You're too late anyway, I rang Pascal and told him I couldn't do it. He was disappointed but said he understood."

Kathy tucked her arms round him, not even thinking what Jean-Guy might make of that gesture. "Recite it to me."

"What?"

"I know what your memory's like. You'd learned every single word by the time you put that match to it."

He moved out of her embrace. "I can't."

Jean-Guy had been watching the two of them. "Don't push it," he advised Kathy. "Piers has said it is too hard to speak his words of grief and we must respect that. If you still have your poem, even if only in your mind, perhaps you could write it down and ask the pastor to read it for you? He is used to people who are grieving and I'm sure he will understand more than anyone else how hard you are finding all this."

Kathy wished she'd thought of that too and felt a bit crass now. "Yes, could you do that? Do you think he would?"

Piers sounded a bit brighter at that thought. "Yes, I'm sure he would. Thank you, Jean-Guy. Sometimes you are remarkably sensible." He half smiled. "Ironic really if you think about it. The only visitor I had while I was in hospital was a Pentecostal pastor."

"How did that happen?" Kathy asked curiously. "We couldn't even find out where you were."

"His wife is a doctor in the A and E at Hillingdon and she recognised me from the funeral. So she told her husband I'd been brought in with self-inflicted injuries, the pastor just phoned them up, said he was my priest and as I wasn't expected to survive at that point the hospital agreed he could come in if only to give me the Last Rites. Couldn't get rid of the bugger after that. Hospital wouldn't allow anyone else near me but he just wouldn't go away. Dacre hung around until I was off the critical list but then he had to go back to work but that bloody pastor just wouldn't let me go. We'd got to know each other pretty well caring for Chantal and for a bloke with a faith like he's got, we had some pretty intense conversations during the early days of my recovery."

Kathy had to smile at the lightness of his voice. "And did he manage to baptise you in the end?"

Piers' smile was the lovely one she had missed so much. "Nope. But he knew he wouldn't. Still, he had fun trying. Yes, you're right. I'll ask him to read it for me."

"And you'll come with us as we walk up to the veil and say goodbye for one last time?" Kathy asked gently. To her profound relief, Piers wrapped gentle arms round her and rested his face on top of her head for a moment.

"Yes I will," he promised and Kathy could tell he had found some peace in his heart at last.

"And you won't try to cross the bridge this time?" she checked and hugged him back.

"Not with you two hanging on to me," he reassured her. "Now please can I go and get some sleep or are you going to watch me do that too?"

She reached up and gave him a kiss on the cheek. "In your dreams. I'll send Jean-Guy in to share with you, shall I?"

"Piss off, Piglet. We'll leave about half past nine. And don't wear black. It's a celebration of a life."

Somehow Kathy wasn't surprised by how many people there were at the celebration of Chantal's life. She looked at all the people gathering at the church in Tooting and guessed there were several hundred there. Chantal's brother and his family were waiting at the door of the church to greet the arrivals and to thank them for coming, and the whole family hugged the ex-husband of the woman whose life they had come to celebrate. It was a quiet hug of shared grief, nothing was said except Piers politely declined the invitation to join the family for the celebration. He introduced Kathy and Jean-Guy to the family and they too were joyfully welcomed into the congregation and she couldn't help but notice Chantal's brother had the lovely, warm smile of his sister. She wished she had known them years ago but instead it was to be a fleeting acquaintance as she guessed Piers had no intention of keeping in touch with the family now Chantal was no longer there to bind them. They had let him back in to honour the wishes of the dying woman but, without her there, he was just the adulterous ex-husband who had destroyed the marriage.

She vaguely remembered the pastor from his brief visit to the farmhouse back in the spring of 1981 and she thought the service was so beautiful and dignified. The pastor pointed out that the hymns had been chosen as they were Chantal's favourites but Kathy wasn't surprised Piers was silent when those around him sang the joyous hymns. It was after one of the hymns that Pastor Stevens told the congregation he was going to read them a poem, a very short poem, that had been written for Chantal by the man who had been married to her in the eyes of God and who had seen her through the darkest times of her life and been with her when she had gone to join her Lord.

We met and danced in the sunlight
And faced all the storms in our lives
We climbed the hills of happiness
And walked silently in the dark valleys
Together.
You had a soul and a spirit of such beauty
But the scars in your heart couldn't heal
You are with them now in your heaven
With your God and your love in your soul.
You crossed the bridge with your heart full of sunlight
Dance in the light for us all

There was a profound silence in the church as the pastor finished reading then he moved seamlessly on to the

Lord's Prayer and it was only then that Kathy realised she couldn't speak as she had tears blocking her throat. She tucked a silent hand into that of the man sitting next to her and gave his cold fingers a squeeze, but neither of them said a word. It wasn't a perfect poem but she could understand why Piers hadn't felt able to read it out loud himself.

Outside the church, there was another round of hugs from the family and Kathy saw Chantal's brother say something to Piers that nobody else could hear. She didn't like to ask as he didn't look best pleased by the remark and she wondered vaguely if he had been warned off in some way.

Fortunately for her curiosity, once they were back in the car and the doors were shut so nobody would hear, Piers said to his passengers, "Well, that went better than I expected. But if either of you make one comment about that bloody awful poem I put together then you're getting left outside the Tube station. At least that's one career I won't have to worry about." He was thoughtful as he put the key in the ignition. "I was sure they'd tell me to go home on the first bus. Seems I misjudged them."

"What did Pascal say to you?" Kathy asked and hoped he wouldn't mind.

Piers half-smiled as he started the car. "Silly sod told me that they weren't going to make this an annual event, it was just a one-off as so many people had asked for it as the funeral had been family only, but he said I wasn't to bugger off and never speak to them again. In fact, I was told in no uncertain terms, that they hope Chantal's granny will make her hundredth in 1987 and I'm expected to go out to Jamaica with them for that if she's still with them."

"Oh, that is so sweet," Kathy exclaimed. "Can I come with you? I've never been to Jamaica."

"Me neither," Jean-Guy put in. "So you now have to take both of us as well. I have never met anyone so old. But I think you won't like the heat out there."

"Too bloody right I won't," Piers agreed and was glad he had these two with him now. "Right, if you're OK with it, I'd just like to go along to the cemetery for a couple of minutes as, even if I do get coerced into going back to the West Indies, there is no way I am coming out here again until they bring me in a hearse." Kathy shot him a hard look but he just smiled vaguely at her. "You'll see."

It was only a short drive to the cemetery and the three presently stood in a group, looking at the simple, elegant tombstone where Kathy put some flowers in the vase and then paused for a moment looking at the words on the stone and was thankful Chantal had gone to her God with no bitterness and no regrets any more. She took Piers' hand when she saw the inscription gave the name as Chantal Emilie Buchanan (née Montgomery) but other than that it just gave her dates of birth and death.

"That's how she wanted to be named on her grave," Piers told her softly and sounded oddly unemotional. "It was the last thing she ever asked of me."

Kathy looked further down the stone and saw right at the bottom in quite small writing the line from one of her favourite carols. *Sleep in heavenly peace.* With a shock she realised the space on the stone was for Piers' own inscription and he had already chosen his burial place, probably not long before he had so nearly needed it. She put her arms round his waist and hugged him tight through his indigo coat. It was a curiously intimate moment as Jean-Guy had come to the same conclusions. He wrapped his arms round the pair of them and nobody spoke but slowly, quietly, they all came to breathe as one.

By contrast to the icy winds blasting across that bleak cemetery, the atmosphere at the Wigmore Hall was refined and excited in the evening of Jean-Guy's latest recital with his chosen accompanist. Jean-Guy still hadn't stopped trying to get Piers to agree to the 'penguin suit' as it was such a formal occasion but once it was clear that yet again the pianist would give up the gig and the fee rather than wear the white tie and tails, Jean-Guy admitted defeat. Even Kathy's now-legendary skills of persuasion would not budge him on that one. Jean-Guy cussedly wore the tie and tails but Piers and Kathy were in full black. Kathy didn't like that arrangement as she felt it gave Jean-Guy some kind of superiority over the pianist, but Piers genuinely didn't seem to mind. They had eventually reached a compromise that Piers would at least walk across the stage with shoes on his feet, but after that was free to do what he liked which meant, the others were quite aware, that those shoes would be under the piano stool while Piers was still sounding the tuning notes for Jean-Guy.

As always, Jean-Guy got them to the wings of the stage early so he could listen to the audience arriving and try to judge the atmosphere. Tonight it felt good. It piqued him slightly that he was dressed formally and what he considered correctly for such an occasion but his pianist was far more striking in his full black. He was in the same clothes he had worn for their first recital at Snape just over a year ago now, but this time the clothes fitted him properly and weren't hanging loose on a body that had already lost over three stone in weight and was still going to lose another two. Those hollows had gone from his face and although just sometimes there were still shadows in his eyes, tonight he looked quite calm and peaceful as he always did backstage. Jean-Guy had often wondered if the child Piers had been so quiet before going on stage with his sister and for the first time he understood why Kathy always asked Piers if he was feeling alright. On this occasion he had done as he always did and assured her he was fine, but Jean-Guy still sometimes wondered why the other man showed no sign of nerves or excitement as the other two of them did, but just stood placidly with his music held almost defensively against his chest.

Jean-Guy looked thoughtfully at him and suddenly commented, "You're very quiet."

"Sorry," was the distracted reply. "Just thinking."

"Nice thoughts?" Kathy checked before Jean-Guy waded in and upset the other man.

Piers shrugged. "Kind of." He looked at the other two as though realising something for the first time. "It's what I do," he explained. "Going through my head right now is every note of every piece we are playing tonight. Kind of mental preparation, I guess. Don't you two do the same?"

"Well, I do," Kathy reassured him. "Sometimes. But aren't you just the slightest bit excited about this gig?"

Piers looked across the stage as he had done at Snape. "Not that I would ever show," he said quietly and the other two thought that was the most tellingly sad reply he could have given them. The shutters had come crashing down again so they knew it went back to his childhood and that hungry and terrified little boy who knew if he wasn't note perfect then he would be punished. Concerts were just something he had to get through and then, if he did well, he would go to bed unbeaten and fed.

Kathy and Jean-Guy exchanged a look and didn't know what to say for a moment.

"One day," Jean-Guy told Piers just as they were about to step onto the stage, "you will tell me the whole story of the penguin suit and why it means so much to you.

For tonight I will be happy just to hear you play the right notes."

The dark mood and memories had clearly passed. "Cheeky bastard," Piers muttered much to Kathy's amusement.

If Jean-Guy had genuinely had any concerns about the other man's playing for this first solo cello concert since he had been so sick in the new year, there were none left by the end of the recital. Piers easily proved he could still play as an equal to the impressive Jean-Guy Dechaume and they enchanted their audience for the whole evening. Kathy dreamed her way through the perfect music as she turned the pages until she realised that she had turned the last page of the Fauré as the anticipated encore had been demanded and it was all over. The celebrated soloist quite properly acknowledged his accompanist and the two took a bow together, then the accompanist pulled the page-turner forward and gave her a round of applause too. The cellist glared but the unrepentant pianist simply pushed his shoes back on and the three were cheered off the stage.

Jean-Guy gave Piers a slight hug when they were out of sight of the audience. "Thank you," was all he said.

"My pleasure. Now I am going to go home and sink half that bottle of vodka I've got in the freezer."

"I'll join you," Kathy challenged. "Then tomorrow it's back to Suffolk for Christmas. Oh, hang on, that means one of us shouldn't drink tonight."

"You drink tonight and I'll get hammered tomorrow," he told her with one of his lovely smiles. "When I've got the Yule garland made. Do you think the Prof will let me put it up in the sitting room?"

"I'm sure he would if only I knew what it was," Kathy replied.

"Show you tomorrow," he promised.

"Look forward to it. And then when we've got your Pagan Yule sorted we can get on with our own variation on Christmas."

Piers returned her smile and cheered ironically. "Lots of food with spices in it. Just what I can't eat."

"There must be one thing in Christmas dinner you like," Kathy persisted, seeing he was in a good mood.

Piers seemed to consider that very carefully. "I like the sprouts," he told her, the corners of his mouth just lifted in a smile.

"Nobody likes sprouts," Jean-Guy assured him. "They are the strangest vegetable I have ever met and I don't understand them at all. We had cabbages in Czechoslovakia and my mother knew many ways to cook them. But sprouts? What is the point of them?"

Piers shrugged on his coat. "The point is they give you the best farts ever." The other two hadn't been expecting that and just looked at him. Piers looked back, faintly puzzled. "Were you expecting some grim tale of my past? Sorry to disappoint you, but I've been told several times recently that I need to lighten up a bit so please will you just stop trying to wrap me in cotton wool all the bloody time? I'm not an invalid."

Jean-Guy saw the quick flash of temper in Kathy's eyes and hurried to stop her antagonising Piers. "Good, because we don't have enough cotton wool to wrap someone your size. You may have double sprouts but don't give Audrey your turkey or you will make her sick. And I am happy to hear you have to be more of your Tigger self. You make a very bad Eeyore. It doesn't suit you."

"Silly sod," was all Piers said.

The three arrived in Suffolk early on December the twenty second, much to the Prof's relief as he had half-expected one of them to make up some kind of excuse and back out at the last minute; refusing to be with them even if he wasn't running off to Tokyo. But this time there were going to be four people in the house and Audrey was one of the happiest cats there unlike she had been last year.

Piers went out after they had had coffee and the others realised they were going to have to trust him and let him go alone but they all felt as though they were waiting for something until he turned up after about an hour with quite a lot of greenery in the bucket he had taken out with him.

"Right, Piglet," was his abrupt greeting to the woman so cosily curled up in an armchair in front of the fire. "Watch and learn. Should have done this yesterday on the first day of Yule, but today will have to do."

Kathy looked up from the book she was reading as Piers sat cross-legged on the floor and his nimble fingers started weaving together the cuttings he had brought in. Kathy saw he had holly and mistletoe, some strands of ivy that he was using almost as a kind of string and some sprigs of fir trees.

"Where did you find the tree bits?" she asked curiously.

"Oh, round and about. I went along the posh houses on the other side of the caravan park as they've got lots of trees. And I didn't nick any of it either, I knocked on the doors and asked. People were curious so I told them what I wanted it for and they were OK with it."

Jean-Guy stopped his cello practice to watch too as Piers quite quickly made up a snake of greenery about three feet long and then looked at it. "It's not as sparkly as Kathy's little tree was last year," he commented not unkindly.

"Probably not. But this is just the leaves and some mistletoe and holly berries. What I really need are some fruits. If I'd thought about it, I'd have dried some apples or something back home before we came here."

"Oh! I know," Kathy told him. "We can slice up some oranges and put them in the warming oven for an hour or so and stick some cloves in them to make them smell nice. Won't take long." A thought crossed her mind. "Are you OK with the smell of spices? It's just eating them that makes you throw up?"

"So delicately put," he remarked. "But, yup, pretty much." He couldn't help smiling at her. "Do you know what? I think I'm bloody glad I didn't have you as a little sister when I was growing up if that's the way you would have talked to me."

Kathy loved it when he smiled at her like that. "Ah, the dreaded middle child. It would have suited you."

Piers paused in his garland-making and looked at Jean-Guy. "She's done it again, hasn't she?"

"Done what?"

"Made some crack or another and I don't know whether I've just been insulted or paid a compliment."

"Oh yes, she does it to me too."

The two exchanged a smile and Piers went back to his garland until he was happy with what he had done with the greenery. "Orange rings?" he asked Kathy.

The atheists among them just watched with amusement as those two got on with drying some orange rings and then set about putting up the little artificial tree on the piano and this time Audrey left it well alone.

By the time they settled to work on some trios without much enthusiasm but with the first of the eggnog made up by Kathy making them a little more relaxed than usual, the orange slices had been added to the garland which was now draped along the mantelpiece above the fire in the sitting room and the whole room smelled of cooked oranges and spices. Kathy had found some cinnamon sticks which she had added even though Piers told her they weren't traditionally part of Yule but she pointed out that she didn't follow traditions but liked to put her own interpretation on things and he very sensibly hadn't argued with her.

The Prof had met all his editorial deadlines by the beginning of December so he was feeling quite mellow as he sat in one of the chairs with a purring Brno on his lap and listened to the sounds of the Dodman Trio, now all slightly the worse for alcohol, but still showing they were one of the best piano trios on the circuit.

Kathy felt she was on edge for the whole of the next day and didn't want to let Piers out of her sight. She didn't dare ask him more than twice if he was feeling alright especially as he got a bit snappy with her the second time. After lunch Jean-Guy and Piers went into the sitting room saying they were going to play cello sonatas but in fact to drape themselves one in a chair and one on the sofa and fall fast asleep within ten minutes.

Kathy stayed in the kitchen and helped the Prof with the lunchtime washing up. "Are you as nervous about tomorrow as I am?" she asked.

He seemed genuinely surprised she should have asked, "I don't see why you should be," he told her rationally. "I survived the first anniversary of my wife's passing with maybe some sad memories but nothing more than that." He stopped her with a smile. "And, no, I am not going to have a deep conversation with you about is it better to lose the one you love slowly and have time to prepare but also to have to watch them go, as Piers did, or to lose them unexpectedly in a bomb blast but with no suffering, as I did."

Neither he nor Emma had ever spoken of how Emma's mother had died. All Kathy had ever known was that it was the event that had brought about the Prof's decision to leave the country of his birth and take his infant daughter with him.

"I, I didn't know," Kathy faltered.

"Why should you? I told Emma about her mother when she was still a very young child and, as children do, she wanted to know what had happened. Then she never spoke of it again so nor did I. But every year on the anniversary when Emma was at home, we would raise a glass to her." He smiled at a fond memory. "The glasses went from orange squash to Coke to wine but we always raised a glass to the memory of Duska."

"Oh, what a lovely name," Kathy couldn't help saying.

"Yes, it is an old Czech name. Emma is hoping her second child will be a girl as she has always said she will name her daughter after the mother she doesn't remember."

"Well I hope it is," Kathy sympathised. "Or she'll tell Derek they've got to keep popping them out until he gets it right."

The Prof almost laughed at that idea. "Poor Derek. I know Emma always said she'd like more than one child but, yes, let's hope they have their daughter fairly soon." He decided to tell Kathy what she wanted to know. "I had been at work in the Conservatoire, just an ordinary summer day. In those days we lived in a small house just outside Prague so I suppose it was a blessing that we didn't live in a block of flats or maybe more people would have died. I wasn't supposed to be working that day as it was during the holidays but I needed to use the library for a few hours. I don't know the details, I don't even know really who planted the bomb, but I had been working with those you might call the Czech Resistance for years. Nothing major. Just trying to do my bit to stop the total Soviet obliteration of our history and culture. I came home and our house was on fire. At first I thought I had lost both my wife and my daughter but then one of the neighbours saw me and came rushing across to tell me that they had heard the explosion and had come round to see what was happening but the whole of the ground floor was on fire. Duska had run upstairs with the baby as she couldn't get out and the neighbour had told her to throw the baby down and then some of them would hold out a blanket so she could jump too. So she did as she was told and the neighbour caught the baby and passed her to his wife but just as four of them were holding out the blanket there was a second blast and the whole house disintegrated. We were lucky that none of those trying to help was injured." He thoughtfully put the last of the clean plates into the draining rack. "My only consolation is that she would have known nothing about the second blast and she would have seen her baby was safe."

Kathy had frozen in her drying up. "But... but..." she started and didn't know what to say.

He put a comforting hand on her arm. "Kathy, it was twenty-six years ago. Yes, I still miss her but I have learned to live without her and my life has grown and moved on although she is always with me. I have talked for hours with Piers about his loss and I have reassured him that he will learn to accommodate the pain into his life and just because he celebrates Yule, or suddenly remembers how to laugh it doesn't mean he loves her any the less."

Kathy sat at the table twisting the tea towel in her hands. "But, I don't understand how you could ever come to terms with something like that. Either of you."

Petr Mihaly looked at the miserable woman and wished he hadn't told her. "Give me a minute," he said and went out of the room.

Kathy thought he was going to go and fetch a photo of his late wife or some other memento of the life he had lost and she was not expecting Piers to come into the kitchen, sit next to her at the table and gather her into a gentle hug.

"Piglet," he told her fondly, "you have to be one of the nicest people I know. You can make me feel like a miserable, selfish bastard any day of the week. The Prof is now worried about you worrying about me so he's asked me to come out here and tell you that there isn't going to be a repeat of last year. Yes, I got in a mess. It was my own fault as I wouldn't listen to anyone. Not you, not Pascal, not Dacre. Nope. Thought I knew better than all of you put together. Told myself and everyone else that I was fine, it wasn't going to be a problem and I'd accepted that I was going to lose her." He paused. "I was an idiot. Again."

"No you weren't...."

"Haven't I told you before not to argue with me? Give it up, Piglet, you know you won't win."

She looked him in the eye. "Like I didn't with the Wigmore recital?"

"Got to give you that one," he agreed perfectly seriously. "Anyway, tomorrow, yes, you may find I'm a bit quiet. You might even find I don't want to eat much, I almost certainly won't want to play music. And that's where you and Jean-Guy come in."

"We do?" she asked, confused.

"Yes," he told her firmly. "Now, we need to establish a few more ground rules which are nothing to do with how we feel about each other even though we have a connection in our souls and…"

"I feel the same." She took his hands and smiled but she could feel there was a sadness in the smile she gave him. "Yes, we are in love with each other. But I think it's best if we agree to keep it a spiritual love rather than a physical one, don't you? You're married and I'm spoken for. I tried a fling with a married man once and it's something I've vowed never to do again."

He gently took his hands from her grasp. "Piglet, I didn't come out here for us to discuss our love lives. Although yours has no doubt been a lot more interesting than mine. So, back to where I was before you distracted me so successfully." He paused and got his thoughts back on track. "Right. Ground rules. Firstly, if I say I don't want to play the piano at any time then don't take it at face value. Call me a miserable old git and tell me it's good for me. Don't back down until I swear at you and go off in a strop."

Kathy thought to herself that this man was only too aware of his own faults but she didn't interrupt.

"Secondly, the Prof says I'm to tell you that if you ever think I'm not eating sensibly then you're to bollock me and feed me peanut butter and grape jelly sandwiches until I'm too full to move. So there you go. Unless you've got any ground rules you want to establish too?"

"Not right now," she smiled as she got to her feet. "I think we understand each other too well. Go on. Go and play the piano until tea time. Are you going to see Sarah and the kids while you're here?"

"Oh, yes. Apparently I'm expected for the night tomorrow so we can wait for Father Christmas to deliver the stockings. But I'll be back here for lunch the next day as I've been told your turkey giblet gravy is not to be missed."

Just for a brief moment Kathy wondered if Father Christmas would be coming to the old farmhouse any time soon but she didn't say anything. She was a bit startled when

Piers stood beside her and said quietly, "Hey, you'll be hearing those sleigh bells here soon enough."

She realised the close bond that held the two of them together was still strong. The raven was still her guide and this man was a closer friend than her husband could ever be.

"Sorry. Does it show?"

"Not so anyone would notice. What do you want me and Jean-Guy to play for you?"

Glad to have the mood lightened, she smiled. "Something mad and a bit crazy. Something new and modern with notes that clash and harmonies to set your teeth on edge."

"Suits me. Anything except bloody Christmas carols."

In spite of all her misgivings, Kathy enjoyed her Christmas that year. As he had said he would be, Piers was out of the house Christmas Eve night but he came back to the farmhouse just as the others were finishing a late breakfast. To Kathy's annoyance she didn't catch what Jean-Guy said to Piers as the arrival sat next to him with a cup of coffee but suddenly the one who had just arrived in the farmhouse snorted with laughter at the wrong moment and inhaled coffee which made him cough and wheeze until his eyes ran.

"I can't believe you said that," he told Jean-Guy when he could finally breathe again and he mopped his face with a piece of kitchen roll.

The Prof and Kathy exchanged a look as neither of them had heard the remark that had caused such hilarity but it had warmed their hearts to see it.

"What did you say?" Kathy asked, with no great hopes of a reply.

Jean-Guy looked genuinely bewildered. "I have no idea. I just asked him if Sarah's stockings had all been opened and he nearly choked on his coffee."

Piers shook his head and said pleadingly. "Don't. Please don't mention Sarah and stockings in the same breath ever again. You can have no idea. But, yes, the triplets had Father Christmas come to visit them. I'm not sure they had a clue what was going on but at least Sarah didn't waste money and got them sensible things. Made me realise something too. The last time I bought a Christmas present for anyone was in 1976 which was the last year Chantal and I were together."

Kathy was determined to derail his thoughts before he got onto the woman he had lost. "You mean you've bought me something this year?"

He gave her a lovely smile. "Of course. And I'm sorry, Jean-Guy, but I haven't bought her stockings."

Jean-Guy finally got the joke. "Oh, that is a shame," he said as seriously as he could. "I would have liked to see her in those."

Petr Mihaly saw the look the two younger men exchanged. "Out!" he told the pair of them. "Go and play music, entertain the cats, anything. But keep your smutty jokes away from my ears. Kathy and I have a turkey to cook." He caught the fleeting expression on Piers' face. "Please tell me you eat turkey?"

"Yes, I eat it. Never been a huge fan. Probably because I got it thrown at me too often."

His smile told the others that this wasn't some horrible memory from his childhood.

"Oh?" Kathy asked. "Go on. You can't say something like that and not tell the whole story."

"RAF tradition," he explained. "The officers serve the erks their Christmas dinner and then get out before the food starts flying. Sometimes we weren't quick enough."

Kathy saw the look in his eyes. "Do you miss it?"

"What?"

"The RAF."

"Not really," Piers told her and sounded as though he was speaking the truth. "Just sometimes. A bit. Maybe."

Kathy knew to divert that train of thought too, "You should have joined the Navy."

"Why the hell would I want to do that?"

She gave him her most wicked smile. "Colour would suit you better. RAF blue is far too pale for you. I bet Annette would back me up on that."

"Hmm. So I should have chosen which service I went into based purely on the colour of the uniform?"

"Oh, yes. I mean you'd look terrible in Army camouflage."

"OK, I promise not to run away and join the Army." Piers was still smiling as he got to his feet and picked a sprout out of the bag on the table. To the astonishment of all the others, he calmly peeled off the outer layers, bit off the end and then ate the rest of the sprout raw.

"Gross!" Kathy told him. "They're bad enough when they're cooked."

A second sprout followed the first. "Told you, I like sprouts. Just don't overcook them like you English always do. I think Sarah's mother started cooking hers last night."

Kathy handed him a third sprout. "Go on," she told him more kindly. "Go and put my present under the tree and if you're very good I'll let you cook the sprouts yourself."

Jean-Guy watched as this extraordinary man duly ate his third raw sprout. "And that is something else I don't understand," he remarked. "Crackers. What is the point of crackers? They just make a noise, have a joke in them that I don't understand and you get some silly toy you don't want."

"That is the point," Piers told him. He looked at Kathy with the widest smile they had seen for a long time. "Please tell me you've got crackers?"

She almost cheered. "Yes! At last someone who understands sprouts and crackers. We'll educate these two Philistines yet."

1983 finally came in with a hard frost on the east coast of Suffolk with snow in the sky and Emma rang on New Year's Day to tell the others that, just as she had said she would, she had given birth to her second child at half past four that morning. She sounded tired but delighted even if the baby hadn't been the hoped-for daughter and she and Derek had decided to name the boy Charles Henry in honour of the dim-distant relative who had left the family his house and estate. In the evening of that day, Piers took the Yule garland off the mantelpiece and threw the whole thing on the fire where it filled the room with the scent of burning fir trees and oranges.

"Why did you do that?" Kathy asked as it had taken him quite a while to make that garland and it was still a few days before traditionally the Christmas decorations had to come down.

"The twelve days of Yule are over," he told her simply. "The wheel is turning and it won't be long before the ground starts to wake again."

The very next day, the first anniversary of Piers' attempt on his life just slipped quietly by in the calm, cosy atmosphere of the farmhouse where there was always at least one purring cat and the last few raw sprouts to be eaten by the only person who genuinely liked them. The day after that anniversary had passed, Piers left the sanctuary of the farmhouse to go into the village to visit his daughters for their first birthday but otherwise he stayed quietly indoors with his cat for company.

It was a bitterly cold day with Piers due to go back to London the next day after his Christmas break from flying. He had put in the hours helping Jean-Guy to prepare for his concerts that year, but then it had got to the point where Piers had flat-out refused to play any more. No matter how Jean-Guy cajoled or yelled at him, he wouldn't budge on the matter so that day they had been playing trios and Jean-Guy had reluctantly realised that his experienced accompanist had been quite right. They had played their works and sorted out any problems, but still Jean-Guy wasn't satisfied then, as he had done with Kathy before the recital in Yorkshire, Piers had told him they had done enough. Sometimes, Piers pointed out to the internationally famous cellist, he could overwork his music and ruin it like an artist who kept working on a painting long after it was finished.

They played trios for a while more after lunch but hadn't been playing long before Piers stopped altogether pleading a backache and pointing out he had to go back to work and the flight deck seats on Concorde weren't the best for his back anyway. So he settled himself as he had done quite a few times before, lying flat on the floor in front of the sofa trying to get a bit of relief from the nagging ache in his spine. The other two decided a break was a good idea and as it was nearly time for the Prof to go and put the kettle on for tea, they settled companionably in the two chairs by the fire and got on with other things. For a while the only sound was the hissing and spitting of the logs on the fire and Jean-Guy could feel he was falling asleep. He hated sleeping during the day as it meant he didn't sleep properly at night so he put down the book he had been reading and looked round the wing of the chair to see if maybe Piers was ready to play again. Kathy was curled round in the other armchair in front of the fire and was sewing the striped sweater together and Audrey was sitting attentively on the piano wondering where the music had gone.

"How's the back feeling?" he asked trying to find out if the other man was still awake as he hadn't moved for quite a while.

"About the same," was the unhelpful reply. "I think that piano stool is too low for me which doesn't help. And it won't go any higher."

"Put a cushion on it," Kathy commented only half listening.

"Seriously thinking of taking a cushion to work with me," came the grumble. "Except I know those buggers will make jokes about piles."

Jean-Guy sighed and looked at the clock again. Still at least half an hour to go until tea and it didn't look as though Piers was going to get up any time soon. "So, Piers, if you didn't play the instrument you do, what would you choose?"

"Something small," came the surprising response from the floor. "Something I can put in my pocket and take with me. Are you so bored you're playing the 'what if' game?"

"Pretty much. I was just thinking how much do we really know about each other?"

"OK but no questions on love lives, past or present," Piers requested, deciding to play the game too in case anything interesting popped out and at least it would distract him from his back pain. "I'll pick either a mouth organ or a recorder. What about you?"

"Bagpipes."

That got Kathy's full attention. "Really? I'd have had you down for the harp or something quiet and intellectual."

"You see how little we do know. No, I fancy something wild and loud. Kathy, your choice?"

"I'm like you, I fancy something really loud. Maybe I should have tried the trombone like Sarah did."

"Bagpipes and trombone. What a combination," Piers put in. "Here's one for the two of you. What would you have done if you hadn't been a musician? I'm exempt from this one as I'm not a full-time musician anyway."

"You can't exempt yourself," Kathy protested. "Just for that you can choose first. You can't fly and you can't play the piano. So what would you do?"

"Right now I'm thinking I'd be a lot more use to myself if I was a physiotherapist."

"Give you that one," Jean-Guy allowed. "Kathy?"

"My parents always thought I'd be something like a teacher. But I always quite fancied the idea of being a novelist. I used to write stories when I was a kid and really enjoyed it. But I threw them all on the bonfire when I was about seventeen after I'd read them through and they just made me cringe." She looked across at Jean-Guy.

He smiled and sounded suddenly rather wistful. "I'd like to have been a ski professional and then retired to be an instructor."

Realising this game was indeed throwing up some revelations, Kathy looked at the man she thought she knew so well and Piers sat up on the floor with his legs out in front of him.

"You can ski?" she asked.

"Loved it. Haven't done it for about ten years but up until I was about twenty three I spent as much of my winters as I could at the Czech resorts teaching and helping in the ski chalets."

Piers slowly stretched forward until he had wrapped his hands round his feet and his head was on his knees so his voice sounded all upside down and funny. "Ski instructor, huh? I've heard about them."

Jean-Guy peered round the corner of his chair. "How the hell do you do that?" he asked. "I can't even touch my toes." To his unspoken envy, the older man pulled himself upright again then casually crossed his legs with his feet on his thighs.

"Always could." He clasped his hands behind his back and bent forward again until he had doubled over his own legs and his head was on the floor. "Come on, you can't just give us half a story. What did you get up to in the ski chalets and how many women did it involve?" The other two watched as he slowly started to bring his clasped hands over his head until there was an audible crunch from his spine. "Thank Christ for that," he said and carefully unrolled himself. He looked straight at Jean-Guy. "Well?"

"Sorry, your gymnastics have just totally distracted me. What else do you do?"

"I'm not a bloody performing seal. I've just always had a very bendy back and some rather dodgy joints and every so often one of them kind of pops out a bit and one of the RAF medics taught me some tricks to realign them. Is this why you wanted to know how many women I've slept with? Just to see if you can beat my record?"

"We said no questions about love lives," Jean-Guy reminded him. "It was like being a teacher and a chambermaid all in one but at least I got to ski in the evenings when everyone else was in their chalets or at the restaurants."

"I've never tried skiing," Kathy mused. "Tried ice skating once and hated it. I'm really not a sporty person."

"Oh, I don't know," Piers teased her. "I bet you looked really cute in your netball outfit."

She was pleased he hadn't lost his sense of humour, but she wasn't going to let him get away with that one. "And I bet you looked pretty daft in your football kit with your lily white legs sticking out from your shorts."

"Hey, I'm Irish. Hurling was my game. But he's letting us get side-tracked. Come on, Jean-Guy, tell us more about being a chambermaid."

"You are a dog with a bone," Jean-Guy grumbled. "OK, I admit it, there were some women. I was young and, well, very hot-blooded."

"How young?"

"I did my first season when I was sixteen. Want to swap loss of virginity stories?"

"No I bloody don't."

A guilty look passed between the two men and Kathy thought she should spare them any awkwardness. "I was fifteen," she told them. "He was another violinist in the youth orchestra. We were on a week's course using one of the local schools in the holidays and it started out with a bit of fumbling and groping in the loos then we kind of didn't stop and then we went back to the rehearsal like nothing had ever happened. That was one triumph I had over my ex as he always thought he'd deflowered a virgin. But he hadn't. Far from it."

"Go, Piglet!" Piers approved. "And in the school bogs too. You little tart."

"Fifteen?!" Jean-Guy squeaked, genuinely appalled that the woman he loved had had her first sexual experience so young. He couldn't understand how Piers could take it so lightly and wondered for a brief moment if the other man would feel the same when his own daughters got to be fifteen.

Kathy was pleased she had managed to shock the pair of them and playfully went off at a tangent by asking Piers, "Do you bend as far backwards as you do forwards?"

"Yes. But I've just got myself straight and I'm not putting it out again. Anyway, this game is turning out quite interesting after all. So, Piglet, first was the violinist in the bogs, then who?"

"Would you believe me if I said the next was my ex?" She met the challenge from those cornflower eyes.

"Not for one second. I can imagine you and Emma as the class slappers." His smile was at risk of being its old wicked self as she didn't reply. "Can't deny it, huh?"

The Prof came in from the kitchen which effectively stopped the conversation. "I have made the tea. Sorry, I am interrupting something. Have you three been telling secrets?"

"Not really," Kathy said a bit too quickly. "But Piers has been showing us some quite impressive gymnastics."

"Thank you," he replied. "But I can't ice skate, come to that I don't swim or ride a bike either, and I certainly can't ski. I'm just double-jointed and that's something I was born with. So how good were you at this whole skiing thing anyway?"

"Ah, Jean-Guy's skiing," the Prof smiled. "He was good in his day. National Junior downhill champion I believe and runner-up in the slalom at senior level?"

"Something like that," Jean-Guy mumbled, trying so hard not to give in to the thoughts of Kathy and the unknown violinist in the school toilets. "And then I broke my neck, my parents and my cello tutor had seven thousand fits and that was the end of that."

"You broke your neck?" the other two said in a rather comic unison.

"Well, cracked it."

"So no more skiing?" Piers asked. "That must have come hard."

"I'd go back to it tomorrow if I thought I could but several months in a neck brace kind of puts me off a bit."

"Can't you brace your neck before you ski just so you could go back to it?" Piers wanted to know.

"Let's not talk about it any more, please. Let's take the game back a bit. Where were we?"

Not wanting the Prof to think they had been talking on immoral topics, and certainly trying to protect Emmas's reputation with her father, Kathy quickly thought of another topic. "Worst ever job? I used to have a Saturday job in a shoe shop in Wimbledon when I was at school and did some waitressing and busking when I was at college. But I really hated that job in the shop."

They settled at the kitchen table with three of them eating mince pies hot from the Aga.

"I was a postman in my student days," the Prof offered joining in. "Hard work and probably the job I enjoyed least. I did bar work and being a waiter too but never minded them quite so much."

"Did my father ever tell you about the summer I worked in the steelyard when I was still studying at the Conservatoire?" Jean-Guy asked him. "I only did it for a bet. I think I must have smelled of sulphur for six months afterwards."

"Which part of the process were you?" Kathy asked trying to imagine her gentle Moly involved in hard manual labour.

"Smelting. Molten metal everywhere and so hot.it was like being in hell. And the smell of the factory is something I will never forget. But a college friend of mine betted I'd never manage it so I stuck it out for the whole summer. I was one of the ones moving the vats of metal around and helping to pour it as part of the extraction process. It was I think the hardest I have ever worked in my life. But I got on well with the other workers and they taught me a lot about not being a privileged kid with educated parents and a cushy career in music. So, Piers? Your worst job? Then we must go back to our music, you've had long enough to sort your back out."

"I never went to proper college or university," he replied, sounding wistful as though he envied the others the younger years they had had. "Although the RAF put me through something like it so I could get my commission. Like you, I did once do a job for a charity bet." He broke a piece of crust off a mince pie and ate it. "I'd not long been made up to captain and one of my cabin crew betted me I'd never stick at her job for a fortnight. And, as these things do, it all snowballed until in the end a lot of the air crew and even some of the ground crew said they'd sponsor me and so the airline got involved and then one of my old buddies in Air France heard about it so they got involved too, and it turned into such a publicity opportunity for both airlines. Buggers threw the lot at me. Spelled my name wrong on my badge and turned me into Pierce with a CE, gave me the worst of the Benidorm rowdies to deal with. Right down to taking away the calculator so I had to do the duty free with mental arithmetic. Put me on a couple of Air France flights just to make me speak French and finished me off with a long-haul overnight to Sao Paolo." He shook his head at the memory. "Hardest work I have ever done and great respect to them for doing the job they do."

"Did you survive the fortnight?" asked a highly amused Prof.

"Just about. I think I was on my knees by the end even though I wasn't working as flight crew for that time as well. But the NSPCC got a handsome donation as a result.

Three of us flight crew did it in the end, including a senior captain, so the charity did pretty well."

"And I should imagine you three also won the respect of all your airline colleagues," the Prof declared, "if the way Jean-Guy was treated by the steel workers in Prague ever afterwards was anything to go by. I am glad you three are talking like this. It will help your music no end."

Kathy looked at Jean-Guy and still couldn't imagine him working in a steel foundry. But then, she couldn't imagine Piers pushing a trolley up and down the aisle of an aeroplane either, and having to smile and be nice to the rudest of passengers. She realised Piers was looking at her. "What?"

"I want you to promise me one thing," he said to her so seriously the Prof and Jean-Guy began to get a bit worried.

"I'm not promising you anything until you tell me what it is," was the best she was going to offer this man who had proven his wicked sense of humour hadn't been completely wiped out by grief and despair.

"Good point. All I want is for you to promise me, no all of us, that you will never consider yourself anything less than an equal partner. Musically, socially, whatever."

"But…"

"No, Piglet. Just for once you shut up and listen to me. I've got my big brother hat on right now and it's the job of all little sisters to listen to their big brother. Isn't it, Jean-Guy?"

A profoundly relieved Jean-Guy half snorted with laughter. "You met my little sister, remember? I can't remember one single time she ever took any notice of anything I ever said to her."

Piers had to smile. "True. But Piglet is a good little sister who does as she's told. And I saw the look on your face just now. OK, so Jean-Guy has wheeled vats of metal around and I've done time as cabin crew. You could do either of those jobs, it's just that you've never had the chance."

Kathy started to feel a bit foolish now. It seemed this man could still judge her moods and her feelings far better than the one she had chosen to share her bed.

"And don't look at me in that tone of voice either. I've married Sarah and I haven't cheated on her, nor do I intend to. Especially with the girlfriend of my best mate."

She managed to look him in the eye. "Don't flatter yourself. I could have had you any time I wanted to."

He laughed then. "Do you know what? I think you're probably right. Thank Christ I didn't know you when you were a teenager. I wouldn't have stood a chance."

Petr Mihaly sighed fondly at his three 'children'. "Just go and play music," he told them. "And spare my ears from your nonsense."

Kathy had two gigs early in the new year so she went back to London with Piers the day after Twelfth Night, both of them envying Jean-Guy who had no bookings for the month and could stay on in the farmhouse, being spoiled by the Prof and able to practise his music.

They hadn't been in the house at Earl's Court more than an hour when there was a phone call from Annette's office to remind them they had a fitting session and a runway walk-through next week. Two days after that there was a phone call from Danny to ask if he could have a lift as he had to go to the runway walk-through too.

Kathy was genuinely pleased that this year was starting out so much more optimistically than the last one had. They had one more day of peace and quiet in Earl's Court then Piers went on his on-call shift that month. It was the first one he had done for a year and he half-hoped he wouldn't be called in as he could even be put on a long-haul as he wasn't due to go back to his regular Concorde line until next week but his luck was out and he got called in as captain on a diplomatic flight to Beijing. He was looking forward to taking Concorde that far, but the laws that prevented her flying supersonic over land meant it wouldn't be any quicker than going in a Jumbo Jet. Kathy just laughed when he grumbled to her and told him that at least Concorde would look prettier. The scheduling meant he would be back the day he, Kathy and Danny had to go to Vauxhall where Annette had her London base so two of them could have a proper fitting session and they all needed to be drilled in runway etiquette. Kathy knew the airline always liked it when Captain B was on-call as he could be showered, shaved, dressed and at the airport within half an hour of being paged but it did seem to mean he didn't often get away with an on-call shift and now he was getting Annette's fees as well, she wondered why he still did it.

Franz Schubert – *Sonata for Arpeggione and Piano D. 821*

Danny took one look at the empty room downstairs and said to Kathy, "Great music room. With that high ceiling the acoustic must be amazing. Where's your piano?"

"Um, upstairs in the living room," she had to admit and wondered why they had ever bothered putting the piano in through the upstairs window when Danny had worked out in seconds what hadn't occurred to any of them in months.

"You could get a full concert grand in here and the rest of our octet too, no problem. Can the Stretto borrow it for a London rehearsal room? I mean we'd pay for the space, we rent various places now anyway."

"Don't see why not. There's a bathroom on the other side of the sliding door and a kitchen just through here so you'd have everything you need. There's even a small garden out the back which is lovely for sitting in. And smoking in," she added pointedly. "I'll have to ask Piers, it's his house really. Jean-Guy and I are just the lodgers."

"Hell of a lot of space considering you're borderline Kensington. Bet the rent sets you all back quite a bit."

"Piers bought it. He took out something crazy like a ninety-eight per cent mortgage about five years ago and he charges us well under the going rate in rent, which is why he's glad of Annette's pay packets."

"Where is he anyway?"

They were in the kitchen by this time and Kathy glanced at the clock. "Well, unless something's gone wrong he should just about be landing the inbound flight from Beijing and will be here in about an hour and a half depending on how long the post-flight checks take."

Danny sighed and shook his head. "You make it sound like he drives the 39 bus to Fulham. Is that a coffee machine I see?"

Kathy took the hint and the two settled to musical chat and coffee but neither could ignore the time for too long. She liked the silence even less than she had enjoyed the rather vague conversation, not quite sure whether she was more anxious about Piers being late or worrying about what Annette was going to do with her.

"Must have been a delay," Kathy offered when Piers was nearly an hour overdue.

"Annette is going to kill the lot of us."

"Want to ring her? Phone's up the first stairs in the living room."

"Good idea."

So Danny rang the less-than-happy Annette and explained what was going on. He pulled a face when he rejoined Kathy in the kitchen. "One cross fashion designer is now waiting in Vauxhall and getting crosser and crosser by the minute. How many floors does this place have? You've got stairs everywhere."

"Three working ones plus attic and cellar. It's a lot of stairs to clean but at least there aren't any carpets so we can just mop everywhere. More coffee?"

"Better not, I'll be peeing all evening."

They both gave up looking at the clock and conversation didn't last much longer either.

"That'll be him now," Kathy said thankfully, hearing the distinctive engine in the street and feeling the relief wash over her. She did look at the clock then and realised Piers was getting on for two hours late. Which meant he would be in a foul mood and probably hungry as it was nearly lunch time.

"Thank Christ for that. Let's go." Without another word, they raced back through the empty room and out into the street where Piers was just lining up the Aston Martin to back it into the car port. Danny spared a split second to admire the car then he and Kathy almost hurled themselves into it.

"Don't even think about stopping." Danny said abruptly "Go on, move it. Annette is already issuing death threats."

"Jesus! Don't ever do that to me again," came the protest from the driver. "I thought you were some nutter with a knife. At least give me five minutes for a shower?"

"No chance. You can shower there and she'll let you have something to go home in. Just go."

"If we're that late already, what difference will five minutes make?"

"If you turn up this late, stinking of soap and with your chops shaved smooth as a baby's bum she will verbally flay the skin off you. Turn up all sweaty and smelly as you are and she'll love you."

Piers just swore under his breath and put the car back into first gear. "Seriously? You're that scared of her? And I'm not sweaty or smelly, thank you very much. We do have air conditioning on the flight deck, you know."

Danny didn't answer that and his silence didn't do anything to calm Kathy's nerves. "Know the way?"

"Not a clue."

"Just head for Waterloo. She's got an office and studio round Vauxhall way."

The London traffic was bad for a weekday and Danny had to admit the other man could handle it in this most unsuitable of cars.

"What made you choose an Aston?" he asked Piers curiously.

"I just liked the look of it."

"Take the right lane at the junction. Jean-Guy said you used to have a Ferrari."

Piers smiled. "That seems like a lifetime ago now. Yes, black 208. Total beast but good fun."

Danny looked at the impressive array of instruments on the dashboard and missed his Saab. "Why was the flight delayed today? According to Kathy you should have been in two hours ago."

"Luggage loading delay at Beijing. Annoying but not life threatening."

"Suppose. So what happened?"

Piers smiled in that way he had and Kathy caught it in the rear-view mirror. "I leaned out of the cockpit window and bollocked the luggage handlers in Chinese. That made the little buggers jump."

Kathy and Danny had to laugh. "Did they understand you?" Danny asked.

"Probably not as they would all have been Mandarin speakers and I speak mostly Cantonese. So for all I know I told them that their great aunts are camels. But at least they sorted out the problem with the baggage and it made the other blokes in the cockpit laugh anyway."

"And you called their grandmothers camels?" Kathy asked, amused.

"Not intentionally. I hope I told them to get a shift on or we wouldn't get home before midnight. But, who knows?"

Danny was curious to learn more about what he had assumed would be a glamorous career choice. "Ever had a baby born on board?"

"Fortunately not, but that would be in the remit of cabin crew to deal with. My job in such circumstances is to find the first safe airport to land in. Landed in some bloody crap places in my lifetime."

This sounded more promising. "Worst ever?"

Piers didn't have to think about it. "Narsarsuaq in Greenland. One of the most difficult bloody airports on the planet and we had to do an unexpected landing as the weather closed in. Forecasting has got a hell of a lot better in the last few years, wouldn't happen now."

Kathy remembered the hints dropped by the blond pilot in Amsterdam but before she could demand details, Danny had continued. "So what's worse? Landing in Greenland or doing whatever Annette has in mind for you?"

"I don't know what she's got in mind. Trying not to think about it too much. Let you know afterwards. Where am I going at the Vauxhall Cross? Hate this bloody junction."

"You and everyone else who drives through it. Hang a sharp left then we're nearly there. Office block's got an underground car park."

Annette was waiting for them in the car park and was almost on the point of going home but she hoped someone would have rung her to say if there was going to be much more of a delay. She watched the three get out of a very sleek Aston Martin, and saw how her most promising acquisition was dressed. She caught hold of one of his sleeves with the braiding on the cuff and told him abruptly, "You have probably got no idea just how hot you are in that uniform, have you?"

"Actually, yes I have but Danny says you'll let me have a shower. I've got spare clothes."

"You know what I mean. Anyway, I need to see you stripped off so I can work round your tattoo. I didn't see it properly in Stockholm but it seemed to go a long way down.

Am I likely to be breaching any decency laws by showing it off on a public runway?"

"It's not meant for public display," Piers warned her gently.

"Trust me, if I'm paying your wages I get to say what the public sees. Sure you won't consider an ear piercing like Danny's got?"

"I'd lose my job."

"OK, let's see what you've got on offer under that sweaty shirt. Can't believe they make your wear all those synthetics. Still I suppose it doesn't need ironing and you finish your flights wrinkle-free. Kathy, you smell a lot sweeter than this one does so I'll get you all measured up first. But I wish you wouldn't wear polo shirts, you're far too feminine. Is it true you and Danny used to be an item?"

"Um, yes," she said, surprised Danny had ever felt the need to pass that information on even if Annette was a close friend, and not sure why it mattered. "Quite a few years ago now."

"Never mind how long ago. So I'm guessing you won't mind stripping down to your underwear in front of him? Good, right, come on then, I was supposed to be back in Berkshire half an hour ago."

Annette led the three of them into the office block and Kathy was surprised that a company as eminent as House of Viola didn't have something grander. She guessed Annette was used to visitors thinking that.

"This is just a very small London base," Annette explained for the benefit of the two who hadn't been there before. "I do most of my design work at home and the manufacture is done in a small family-run factory in Huddersfield. I like to pay a fair price for my raw materials and I make sure it's those directly involved in the process who get the money and I won't give it to the fat cats and multinationals. Those are my ethics and there are a hell of a lot of people in the fashion industry who don't like them."

Kathy was silently impressed but guessed nobody interrupted Annette Delaney in full flow.

"My cottons and silks are prepared, dyed and woven by local co-operatives. Wool is from Yorkshire mostly although I have had some from Ireland and, oddly enough, someone put me in touch with a supplier in the Falklands. Again, all prepared, dyed and woven as few miles as possible away from the shearing sheds and I want natural dyes as much as possible so we keep the chemicals out of the environment. Much to Danny's disgust, I will work with leather and a very limited number of fur pelts but they all have to be by-products of the meat industry."

"I've told you…" Danny started.

"But," Annette cut across him, "thanks to a hostile anti-fur campaign by someone not three feet away from me, no future collections will have so much as a whisker. I'm still thinking what to do about leather. Right, this is my bit of the building." She grabbed a towel from a pile on one of the tables and held it out to Piers. "Shower's in the loos just through that door there. I rent them as part of this space and I don't think the soaps will have been nicked. It's only us three left and we all promise not to barge in on you. If you're feeling modest you can put your knickers back on but no more than that as I want to see this tattoo. But if you're OK with me taking the towel off you and measuring you in your birthday suit, I'm sure none of us will mind. I promise I'll warm my hands up before I do the inside leg."

Piers took the towel from her and gave her a filthy look. "Would you talk to a female model like that?"

"Oh, yes," she assured him. "I don't discriminate. Off you go."

"You didn't say it to Piglet."

"Who the hell is Piglet?"

"I am," Kathy explained.

Annette gave the disgruntled Piers a wide smile. "Ah, yes, but Kathy didn't turn up here stinking like a baboon's backside. But if you're quick in the shower, you may catch her standing about in her underwear."

Piers picked up on the joke. "I'll be less than a minute."

"And put your pants back on," Kathy told him. "I don't want to see what you've got on offer."

"Are you going to spoil all my fun?" Annette queried, laughing.

Piers treated her to the smile she knew was going to earn her a fortune. "Maybe." With that he went off to find the shower.

Annette shook her head. "They certainly broke the mould with that one. Come on then, Kathy, I refuse to call you Piglet, let's have a look at you."

Thankful she was wearing some fairly new, plain underwear, Kathy let Danny have a look at her again after a few years.

"Looking good," he complimented her approvingly.

Annette wasn't interested in her models in that way. She wrote down the results of her measuring, whisked what looked like a pile of dark green fabric off a table and dropped it over Kathy's head.

Danny gave her a raucous wolf-whistle. "Nice."

"Turn round," Annette instructed.

Kathy lurched a bit as the other woman was clearly pulling some lacing tight along her back and she looked down to realise she was wearing the most gorgeous dress she had ever known. She could feel the fabric against her legs was pure silk and she didn't mind too much when

Annette ruthlessly dug down the bodice to sort her out with what finished up as quite a decent cleavage.

"Now that," Annette told her, "is what you're supposed to look like."

Kathy twisted round in front of the nearest mirror to see what the rest of the dress was like. "Not for washing floors," she commented as the sequins on the skirt sparkled and flashed in the overhead lights.

"True. Danny, help me get her out of this then go and hoof the other one out of the shower. He's been gone so long I'm beginning to think he's gone to sleep in there."

The dark green dress came off, a short, royal-blue cocktail dress went over the unprepared Kathy's head and Annette ruthlessly pulled the hem down. "Nope. You've got shoulders like a blacksmith. No spaghetti straps for you. OK, good. I know what I'm working with. Right, pop your stuff back on and grab yourself a drink from the machine over there if you'd like one."

Kathy did as she was told, even though she was a bit miffed about the spaghetti straps. The machine obligingly turned out a cappuccino for her and by the time she'd got that in her hand, the two men were back.

Annette didn't ask Piers if he had put his underwear back on but briskly took the towel off him. "Damn," she said and sounded quite upset. "Hoping you wouldn't bother with the boxers." She was brisk and efficient as she measured the showered and sweeter-smelling Piers and she took a lot of notes as she realised he wasn't as slight as he looked. There was no fat on him but he was definitely chunkier on the chest and arms than the more lightly built Danny and had the most ridiculously long legs.

Kathy couldn't take her eyes off the man in his underwear even though she knew it was rude to stare, but for all the years she had known him, she had never seen Piers in such a state of undress before. She jumped as Danny nudged her in the back with his elbow and turned to see he had obviously been eyeing him up too. They exchanged a conspiratorial smile and didn't even try to pretend they weren't looking. The thing that struck Kathy the most was just how pale Piers was. She had thought that when he had first shown them the tattoo, but in the harsh office lights of that room, he looked quite unreal. Unlike her lovely Jean-Guy, there was nothing soft and middle-aged about Piers and apart from the cutest line of dark fluff running down from his belly button, his upper body was perfectly smooth.

"That is one hell of a tattoo," Annette commented as she quite impersonally looked down the back of his pants. "The only way I can get trousers on you low enough to show that off is to make them so tight they'll cut your circulation off." She rolled his waistband down as low as she needed to expose the tattoo then checked what the front view was like. "Just about get away with it," she decided. "But that bloody scarring you've got is going to be a pain in the arse. How the hell do you get scar tissue down there?"

Realising she expected a reply, the unhappy Piers said simply, "I got burned as a child. It's kind of moved a bit as I got older. Started out on my hip."

"Thank Christ it moved down and not up," was Annette's unsympathetic response and she turned him round again. "Right. I really want the whole design on show or it doesn't make sense. We'll just have to run with the scar tissue showing a bit at the front if we have to. How old were you when you had the tattoo done?"

"About twenty-six, twenty seven. Something like that."

"It's lasted remarkably well. The outlines are still so clear it could have been done last week."

"It bloody hurt."

The other three were quite shocked when Annette lifted up her blouse to show a surprisingly feminine tattoo of a cobra apparently winding in and out of her rib cage with its head finally emerging near her belly button. "Tell me about it. I had this done when I was thirty-two and it hurt like buggery. Then, about five years later I met and married a minor member of the British aristocracy and although he loves it, I'm not allowed to have it on show outside our bedroom. So, yes, I love tattoos as works of art and as body ornamentation. I hunt down tattooed models but they're like hen's teeth, especially the women. If I knew you better, or I was totally paralytic, I'd show you where I've got a rose. Danny refuses to get one. So I'm glad you've arrived on my lists. Anyway, back to the problem of your circulation."

Danny was sitting on one of the tables in the design room and getting over the shock of what Annette had just shown them as he had known her for years and hadn't had a clue. But it had distracted him from envying the other man's physique. He had to spend hours in the gym to look half as good as that and he was ten years younger. "You could put him in leather. That's kind of stretchy."

"Do you have a problem with animal skin?" Annette asked Piers. "Like that other one does."

"Well, I wouldn't buy the wife a mink," Piers hedged, trying to be diplomatic in front of Danny. "But I suppose as long as I eat it I'll wear it. Haven't really thought about it."

"Thank Christ for that, someone with a bit of sense. God, you in leather cut to show off that tattoo. That really will breach the decency laws. Would you consider getting inked again? No, don't get me going down that route now. Another time. Go and find yourself something off that rail of last season's seconds to wear home and I'll give you all your runway lesson as none of you has done it before. Kathy, I'm not putting you on the runway just yet, but it won't hurt for you to join in today. At least these two can learn to walk with you, well Danny can, I'm running Piers out on his own, and that way I won't have the pair of them mincing along together in practice." Annette watched Piers pick the two least assuming garments off the indicated rail. "And I'm not giving out your name at the show and I don't want you to come on at the end either," she told him.

Danny understood far better what that meant. "Trying to stop the opposition poaching him?"

"Just for a couple of collections, then I guess it'll be open season on you. In spite of your age. The irony of it is you are exactly the age of the market that usually buys the designs." She looked at Piers and sighed, then hauled the shirt out from inside his trousers and pulled it straight. She organised cufflinks in his sleeves, and flicked the collar upright before taking a striking jacket of a very dark hunter green off another rail and adding it to the shirt and trousers he had already thankfully put on. "You really have no idea how to dress yourself, have you?" she remarked. "You're another one just like Kathy. Hopeless, the pair of you. Like a couple of mannequins in a charity shop window. Right, come on. Out to the corridor and let's pretend it's a runway. Danny, bring the cassette player. Piers can you bring a torch and a chair please, I need one of you to be an overhead spotlight."

Kathy was glad she hadn't left for her evening gig when Piers got back from work the next day. He had had a classroom training session that day so he had gone out of uniform, just in an ordinary suit and tie but by the time he got back, his top shirt buttons were undone and the tie was in his pocket.

"How did it go?" Kathy asked. She watched as he made himself some tea and banged the tea caddy and mug rather too loudly. "That bad, huh?"

He pulled a face and opened the pantry door in search of food. "It was OK. More legislation coming in. We won't be able to fart in our own cockpits soon." Piers fished the tea bag out of his mug and sipped the tea. He hadn't cooled it with water and Kathy saw him flinch.

"You OK? And don't lie to me."

"Made the tea too hot. Stung a bit, that's all. Really not been a good day."

"Not like you to get in such a tizzy over a training course. You do enough of them."

"No, it's not that. Well, yes it is. I've told the airline I'm now dairy intolerant and they've always had my spice allergy on their records for any training or flying catering so what did the buggers provide today? Coronation chicken which I can't go near or a cheese and broccoli quiche. So I got bloody hungry as that just left me with a bread roll and some orange juice for my lunch. So, yes, I got, um, well. Let's say I maybe upset the tutor a bit which never goes down well."

"Oh dear. So then what happened?"

Piers sat at the table with her and spoke between gobbled mouthfuls of peanut butter and grape jelly sandwich. "I apologised before a major incident kicked off."

"Well done. And you really didn't eat the chicken or the cheese?"

"You have no idea how close I came."

His smile convinced Kathy he was being honest with her. "I'll believe you this once, but I'm watching you. Any stomach aches or anything and I'm calling the ambulance."

Sandwich finished, Piers put the water in his tea and necked it. "What are you playing tonight?"

"Haydn and Mozart at the Queen Elizabeth Hall."

"Do you know what, I'm just in the mood to come with you and buy myself a ticket after the day I've had. I'll drive us there in the Aston."

"And I bet you know of somewhere to park."

"Of course. Shall we stay out for a meal after your gig or go to our favourite all-night grocery like we used to? I'm not working for a couple of days so we've got the time."

"Oh, let's stay out for once. Sounds like you've earned it. I'll take you to our local Lebanese."

Piers had heard a lot about the place where Jean-Guy had once worked. "Isn't that a bit spicy?" he asked suspiciously. "I've never dared try it."

"Feeling brave? I'm sure the chef will tone it down if we explain it to him, or he may have some recommendations for you. He's a nice bloke and always asks after Jean-Guy."

"Today I'm not feeling brave. I'm sure you're right and I will go there one day but not tonight, huh?"

"OK, we'll fight off the Australians in one of the local greasy spoons instead shall we?"

Kathy had been out and bought herself a newspaper the next morning and was reading it over her breakfast cereal when Piers wandered sleepily into the kitchen.

"And why are you up so early? You said you weren't flying for a few days."

She was a bit worried when he looked at the coffee machine and clearly decided he couldn't face his habitual espresso.

"Bit unwell in the night," he admitted. "Must have been something in that meal last night." He wouldn't meet her steady gaze. "OK, I admit it. I threw up some blood along with my supper. But it was only a bit."

"Where's your nearest A and E?"

"Charing Cross. It's nothing to worry about."

"Don't you tell me what I can and can't worry about. When are you next flying?"

"Back to JFK day after tomorrow."

Kathy watched horrified as Piers gagged and instinctively put a hand up to his mouth but the blood ran through his fingers before he could get to the sink. Without thinking, she grabbed the keys for the Aston Martin. "Bring a bucket."

They were back at the house by tea time, one of them grumpy and a bit sore from the endoscope and the other rather pleased with herself for driving an Aston Martin through the London traffic. The doctor in Casualty had diagnosed a minor tear to the oesophageal lining, and asked him what he'd been doing to cause it. Realising Piers wasn't going to say anything, Kathy had grassed him up without remorse and the doctor had admitted to being a bit flummoxed so he had consulted a colleague from the Gastroenterology department. They had had another, longer, look with the endoscope, and the specialist had told the patient that the linings of his oesophagus and stomach were badly scarred and still very fragile. The Gastroenterology specialist had clearly never dealt with anything like it before and rang Hillingdon hospital to ask about this particular patient. Kathy was told she could go and get something to eat while they waited for the notes to come through as although they now had a fax machine it wasn't the quickest thing in the world. Kathy didn't think it would be a good idea to leave a cross Piers with the medical staff so she said she was fine and could wait.

The notes came through more quickly than the medical team had been expecting and they had a long consultation among themselves, apparently not even thinking to involve the patient which didn't do anything to improve his temper. Conclusions reached, all they told him was that ideally they wanted him to drink milk to dilute the acids but because he couldn't he would have to experiment with dairy-free alternatives. They repeated what he had been told in the first place that his best weapon was anything ice cold but really, they finally admitted, they didn't have a clue. He was booked in for a review in three months' time and discharged as the bleeding had stopped. Although he was thankful he hadn't had to be admitted, Piers still sulked all the way back to the house even after he had bad-temperedly let Kathy buy him a very late lunch in the hospital café.

"I'm not going to apologise," Kathy told him firmly as she closed the door to the car port behind them. "I'm just glad that there's going to be someone keeping an eye on you, especially now you've admitted that wasn't the first incident. I don't know how it ever got left a year in the first place."

"I don't know either," he snapped at her. "I was admitted to Hillingdon when it happened and they never said there would be any follow-up. I'm sure Charing Cross won't leave me alone now they've got the notes." It was as though the energy suddenly left him and he slumped at the table with his head on his arms. "So is this it for me from now on? Living like a bloody invalid? I really hope I don't lose my job and get slung out on my pension over it all."

"I don't see why you should," Kathy told him practically. "You've survived best part of a year back with them. But it might be a good idea to take a packed lunch on any future training courses." She was interrupted by a rattle of key in the car port door and Jean-Guy and cello arrived in the kitchen.

"What are you doing here?" Kathy asked delightedly and gave him a hug, totally forgetting she and Piers had been in the middle of a conversation.

"Minor crisis. Need an accompanist in a hurry to brush up for an audition. I tried to ring but nobody answered the phone." He noticed the man still with his head buried in his arms at the table. "What's the matter with him?"

"Minor crisis of his own," Kathy said briefly and hoped Jean-Guy would understand her sign language that it wasn't up for discussion. He totally missed the point of her signals.

"Oh?" Jean-Guy sat opposite Piers and grabbed his hair so he could lift his head up from his arms. "What happened?"

"Nothing," Piers growled and dropped his head down again. "Go away."

"No I won't go away. We are under instructions to make you play the piano and all I want is a run-through of the *Arpeggione Sonata* as it is always a good one for an audition. I don't need you for anything else as we play unaccompanied at the auditions. When are you flying again?"

"Day after tomorrow." Piers was getting curious now and his self-pity faded away. "Why is it a crisis? And since when did you do auditions?"

"Haven't you heard? There's going to be a candlelit performance of *The Planets* in Ely cathedral at Christmas time, conducted by the composer's daughter. I'm auditioning for the orchestra."

"Wow," Kathy commented. "Is that going to be the standard that someone like you has to audition?"

"Everyone has to audition. What are you going to play?"

"You mean I'm auditioning too?"

"Jane should have rung you today. She's got us both in the auditions."

Kathy felt the old thrill of an exciting gig running through her. "When are they?"

"Week after next, so you'll be needing our tame accompanist too. Haven't you answered your phone at all today?" Jean-Guy paused and looked at them. Discretion told him maybe he shouldn't ask but a stronger sense of curiosity won. "Just what the hell have you two been doing?"

Piers got to his feet and poured himself a glass of water from the tap. "Sorry, my fault. Bit of a health thing and been at the hospital all day. But all good now so let's go and play music. And if you two get in to this gig I'm going to expect a ticket."

"Best in the house," Kathy assured him. "Sure you're feeling better now?"

"Much, really. One day I'll thank you. But there is no way I'm ever letting you near that bloody car ever again. If I hadn't had my head in a bucket I'd have taken the bloody keys off you."

They hadn't got very far with the practice session when the phone rang. Piers, as the nearest, took the call and told the others, "That was Danny. Three of five Strettos have invited themselves to use our music room as they're auditioning for *The Planets*. What music room?"

"Ah," Kathy commented. She was about to tell him when the phone rang again. This time she answered it.

"Kath! Finally you're answering your phone. Where the hell have you been all day? Please tell me you've been in bed with your delicious landlord. No, haven't got time for that now. I need to come and stay for a few days. I've got an audition for the first time in God knows how long and don't have anywhere in London to stay any more."

Kathy didn't dare make any comments about her landlord and she really hoped he hadn't heard. "Hi, Emma. Nice to hear from you too. Don't tell me, you're auditioning for *The Planets?"*

"Of course. I don't expect I'll get in after all this time. But anyone who's anyone is going for it."

Kathy beamed at the others when Emma had gone again. "Sounds like we're going to have a houseful."

"What music room?" Piers repeated. "Piglet, what have you and Danny cooked up between you?"

Just for a moment she thought she had got away with it. "Come downstairs and I'll explain."

"Uh-huh. Is this before or after you tell your boyfriend about our day in bed together?"

Kathy felt her face getting hotter and hotter. She hardly dared look at Jean-Guy but to her relief, he smiled at her.

"You need to tell Emma not to shout at you when she's on the phone," he said kindly. "Even I heard that one."

Three people stood in the empty room at the front of the house and could quite see Danny's point of view. Kathy and Jean-Guy had played their instruments in the room and, as Danny had suspected, the acoustics were perfect. The room had blinds and not curtains, there was no carpet so the sound could ring out and not be muffled by soft furnishings.

"Now all we need to do is get the piano downstairs," Kathy remarked.

"No we don't," Jean-Guy told her. "Now we get Jane to earn her fees and see if we can borrow us a full concert grand. Most of the piano manufacturers are always happy to loan an instrument to people like us. My father never bought a piano in his life. It's a bit late tonight but I'll ring Jane in the morning and see what she can do for us. Do you have a preferred make of piano?"

Piers smiled, it appealed to his sense of the absurd that he had been put in the category of 'people like us' by someone as celebrated as Jean-Guy, so he thought he may as well aim high. "Well, I grew up learning on a Bösendorfer Imperial Grand with its ninety seven keys. God knows where my family got it from but it was way past its best by the time I knew it. Great piano though. Played all sorts in my career. So if I couldn't have a Bösendorfer I'd go for a Grotrian Steinweg, or a Blüthner from the technical point of view."

The other two were impressed. "Not sure Jane can swing you a Bösendorfer, that's a bit like asking to borrow a Rolls Royce when you could easily make do with a Ford," Jean-Guy told him. "You may have to settle for a Bechstein or a Steinway. But on the other hand she does like a challenge."

"Either of those would be fine too. Just so long as it's not a bloody Yamaha. They're good pianos, but they don't suit me."

Jean-Guy had often wondered why Piers had a 'thing' about Yamahas but knew this wasn't the time to ask. "OK, I'll tell Jane nothing less than a Grotrian Steinweg or a Blüthner."

"Good luck with that," Piers laughed and wandered off to the kitchen in search of coffee.

Piers went to bed early that night, happily setting off for his tiny single room at the back of the house so the other two sat in the kitchen drinking hot chocolate and eating shortbread.

"What happened today?" Jean-Guy asked, just to clarify in his mind that Kathy and Piers really hadn't spent the day in bed.

Kathy had her mind full of a concert in Ely cathedral. "Oh, that. Yes. Piers sicked up blood this morning so I took him to A and E. You'd have been proud of me driving that beast of a car of his through the traffic."

The relief, if Jean-Guy had admitted it, was overwhelming. "I'm always proud of you. Was it a bad attack?"

"Looked bad enough to me. The medics were fascinated by his history."

"You mean you told them what he'd done?"

"Well he wasn't going to and I thought they ought to know. He's in a bit of a grump with me as the Casualty doctor referred him to Gastroenterology and he's now well and truly on the radar with a check-up in three months. They were threatening him with a colonoscopy too at one point, poor sod. But it didn't come to that."

He kissed her softly across the table. "You are going to make a great mum."

"Fat chance," she said rather bitterly. "Do you think we maybe should think about talking to a doctor?" She knew she had to tell this man the whole truth but she still hoped there may be some way round it. It was too painful a story to tell. "I mean, I know it doesn't happen overnight for most people and maybe I'm just impatient. Doesn't help when I think how easily Sarah and Piers got on with it. Twice."

Jean-Guy was thoughtful. Just for a moment he wondered if Kathy was casting a slur on his fathering abilities with her mention of Piers and Sarah but then he saw the look in her eyes and knew her words had been genuine. She looked away from him and it occurred to him for the first time that maybe there was something she wasn't telling him. But he had learned that Kathy, like Piers, would keep her secrets. If they didn't want to share whatever it was then they wouldn't. This woman that he loved so much, and wanted to be the mother of his children, wasn't telling him something,. If he were to be honest, he was afraid of what they might learn if they went to a doctor and he hoped it was the same for Kathy. That her darkest fear was that they might be damned to childlessness as Piers and Chantal had been, which had in part broken their marriage. She had told him about Chantal's stillborn baby and the miscarriages and he hadn't known what to say to her. And he had certainly never mentioned it to Piers. All he knew was he would rather live childless with Kathy than lose her but have a swarm of children. He realised she was waiting for him to speak and probably thinking very similar things. If there was one thing he was not going to do it was run any risk of fracturing the beautiful relationship they had right now.

"I think perhaps we should wait for maybe a little longer. Although we have a good sex life, at least I hope you think we do, we have had so many other things to worry about in our lives that maybe even if our minds think we are ready for children, our bodies don't agree. But I don't want to leave it until it is too late as Piers did with Chantal. I often think that perhaps if they had had children then maybe he wouldn't have had the affair and ended their marriage. It was all so sad for them and I think too many 'ifs'."

Kathy could see the sense of his reasoning but she knew that below those surprisingly sensible words, he was frightened of something. She couldn't believe it was as simple as learning they weren't going to have children. There were ways now for couples to have babies if they couldn't conceive naturally and she was prepared to give that a go if that was their only option, but she hoped it wouldn't come to that. She closed her fingers round his hand. "Not sure I agree with you as from the little he's told us I got the impression the marriage was on the skids anyway and the affair just hurried up the ending a bit. But in the meantime we'd better get in a lot of practice so if it ever comes to it we can shock the fertility doctors with how many ways we've tried."

He smiled into her eyes and was glad she hadn't made any remarks about maybe they should ask Piers and Sarah for advice. He still wasn't totally sure he trusted the other man to behave himself with Kathy. They had told him there was nothing physical in the relationship between them and most of the time he believed them. What he really wanted to do was secure Kathy's hand in marriage so he knew she would commit to him. But he didn't dare ask her. Not yet. He had to be sure of her, and himself, first.

Auditions for *The Planets* were being held at the Guildhall School of Music and it seemed only a few days after Jean-Guy and Kathy had had their talk about children that the house in Earl's Court was invaded. Piers had left the house early as he always did when he was taking the morning Concorde to New York and he had arranged his lines so he would be away for the three days the house was full of people. He had reassured the other two that he wasn't avoiding the musicians but he wouldn't be auditioning for Ely and that way they had an extra bedroom free. Kathy wasn't convinced. She thought he was just keeping well clear of Olga, and in some ways didn't blame him.

With Piers gone, Kathy had one last walk round the house to make sure everything was ready for their guests. They hadn't had proper guests before like this and all the rooms were going to be in use including one of the attics so she hoped everything would work out. She thought the rooms all looked very welcoming with their patchwork bedspreads and at least the bedrooms all had curtains now, even if they didn't match the bedding, but it was a pity that they hadn't managed to get a few more rugs to put down over the bare floorboards.

She had just come down from the attic room when the phone rang in the sitting room so she rushed to answer it before Jean-Guy felt obliged to get out of bed.

"Kathy, hi. Alison. Is Piers there, please?"

Kathy fought down the rising panic. "No, sorry, he's on the early flight."

"Oh well, never mind. It's nothing urgent. Sarah's asked me to ring him to let him know they're keeping her in. She had a check yesterday and they said they'd rather keep an eye on her now until the birth."

"Goodness. Problems?"

"No, not at all. But it is quins and they know she's already got triplets at home who can be looked after by her parents and partner and they're really just being on the safe side about it all. No, she's still being her bloody awkward self and saying she wants to keep them inside as long as she can because she thinks it'll be better for them. She's less than a month off her due date as it is so she's done bloody well to stay at home this long. Anyway, if you'd pass the message on when you see him, please? Tell him there's no point in chasing down here, even supposing he would. I'll let him know if there are any developments."

Thinking that no matter how hard she tried, Alison still really didn't like Piers, Kathy just said politely, "Yes, of course. Please give our love to Sarah and tell her we'll be down to Suffolk soon anyway so I'm sure we'll pop in to see her. Sorry, there's the doorbell, we've got people coming to stay for a few days so I don't know when I'll see Piers again. Probably not until Friday now. But I'll certainly let him know."

Phone call concluded, Kathy raced down the stairs even though she had heard Jean-Guy on the move and she flung open the car port door to be greeted by a remorselessly grinning Emma.

The two friends exchanged a hug and Emma dumped her violin case and her bag on the kitchen floor so she could take her coat off. "You have no idea how stupidly excited I am about all this," she declared happily. "I've left the kids with Derek and the in-laws and I have this totally ridiculous sense of freedom. Am I a bad mother? Poor old Chas is only a few weeks old but I've left him loads of milk in the freezer and Derek's great at giving him a bottle." Her smile was the one Kathy remembered from her teenage years. "Oh, what the hell. I need this. I hope you've put me with your delicious landlord?"

"Not quite," Kathy laughed trying very hard not to decide if she would dash off to a rehearsal leaving behind a baby less than a month old. "He's taken himself off to New York but as you're on your own he said I can put you in his room as we don't have any furniture in the second attic. So you can now live out your fantasy of sleeping in his bed and thinking things you shouldn't. Come on, let's get you sorted out before the contingent from Sweden gets here."

"Oh, yes," Emma gasped as she puffed up the stairs behind Kathy. "I believe I'm now going to meet your driving instructor at last. So at least we'll have one delicious man in the house."

"Who is coming with his wife," Kathy pointed out as her oldest friend thankfully sat on the narrow bed and looked round the room which she had only glanced at briefly once before.

"Ooh, diaries."

"Pilot log books. Just behave while you're in here or I'll put you up in the empty attic. On your own without so much as a teddy bear. Just count yourself lucky Piers said it's OK for you to use his room. So he, and I, are trusting you to respect his privacy while you're in it."

Emma sighed and thought how much the irresponsible Kathy had grown up these days. "Of course I will. I know I'd hate it if someone was using my room and went down my stuff. Will I be sharing the bathroom?"

"It's going to be a bit of a free-for-all with the bathrooms, I'm afraid. But I've put Danny and Olga in the front bedroom on this floor so you'll be sharing with them and Gisela will be all the way up in one of the loft rooms so she'll have to pop down to use it. But, as it's you, you're welcome to use our en suite if you need it. We've got three toilets, two baths and three showers in this place so I hope we'll cope. You have no idea how mad it's been in here trying to get it all organised. I think we all got sick of scouring *Loot* and the small ads for furniture, but we did pretty well in the end."

Emma was slightly horrified that they had been buying yet more second-hand furniture when Jean-Guy and Piers were both earning good money now, but she could see the towels that had been put out for her were new. "I hope he doesn't mind me pushing him out of his bed, in a manner of speaking," she said as she brushed her hand over the faded yellow candlewick bedcover. "I didn't realise people still used candlewick on their beds. Takes me back to when I was a child."

Kathy smiled to see Emma still had good memories of her childhood. "No, he didn't mind. But the poor sod is fed up with staying in hotels for so much of his life."

"Do you know, before you lived with one I'd have said being a pilot, especially on Concorde, would have been pretty glam."

Kathy's smile became wry. "So would I. But it's just a job like any other. Funniest thing is I'd swear he has no body clock whatsoever."

"Kathy!" Jean-Guy yelled up from two floors down. "There's a man here with a piano. He wants to know if he can take the front door off."

"No he can't!" Kathy bellowed back. "It's extra wide as it is."

She and Emma exchanged a look and huge smiles, then raced down the stairs to see what was going on.

It was rather unfortunate timing that the group travelling from Sweden arrived while the men were still installing the piano in the downstairs room so all was chaos for a few minutes until Kathy got her guests upstairs to the sitting room, leaving Jean-Guy to deal with the removals men. Emma had been upstairs phoning Derek when the others all walked into the room and she saw Danny Tarling for the first time. She had never met him when he had been teaching Kathy to drive so the first time she met him it was as a celebrated model and film star whose first film was due for release in the UK in the summer. It had been heavily trailered in cinemas and on the TV and Emma couldn't help but feel a little star-struck when she was introduced to him. Which annoyed her a bit as she had never felt like that about anyone before. She had seen photos of him as a model and hadn't realised he wasn't over six foot but was almost exactly the same height as her at five foot ten and was much more slightly built than she had thought. She remembered vaguely that at the time Kathy had been quite worried about him as she was convinced he was anorexic as all he seemed to eat was Marmite and oat cakes. He wasn't as gorgeous as Piers, Emma decided but he was still quite handsome and he had the most enticing smile she had ever seen in her life.

She was almost taken in by it until she turned her attention to the woman at his side and saw the look she was getting from a clearly very jealous and possessive wife. And also a very pregnant wife.

"Hullo," she said cheerily to Olga. "When's the baby due?"

The Russian woman gave her a grudging smile. "Soon I am glad to say."

Kathy managed to get control of the situation before Emma made a fool of herself with a married man who was standing next to his wife. "Right, Danny and Olga, you're up on the next floor with Emma. Are you OK with all these stairs, Olga? Or would you rather have my room which is on this floor and Jean-Guy and I can go up into the spare room for the couple of nights you're here."

"Oh, that would be kind of you. My knees do not like all these stairs at all," Olga said and gave her a thankful smile. "If you're sure you don't mind?"

"Not at all," Kathy said quickly as she realised she had been out manoeuvred and Olga now had her husband well away from the charms of the tall, willowy Emma who was still annoyingly lithe in spite of having had two children. She hoped Jean-Guy would be as understanding.

"Yes!" Emma declared. "Best idea ever. Then we can stick Jean-Guy in Piers' bed and you and I can share the other room and sit up all night gossiping like we used to."

"Kathy!" Jean-Guy called up from the front room. "The men have gone now so do you all want to come and see the piano? I think he's chosen a good one."

So they all trooped back downstairs again and admired the very imposing Blüthner full concert grand, originally built in the early part of the century from a maple wood that now glowed with the patina of age.

"How did he come across that beauty?" Gisela asked and the others watched as Olga plonked herself down right in the middle of the double piano stool and started to play some simple finger exercises.

"Our agent put out word that Jean-Guy Dechaume's chosen accompanist was in need of a practice piano in his Kensington home," Kathy laughed. "We had no great hopes but it worked like a charm. Seems our Piers has got a bit of a reputation now after their gigs at the Wigmore and the Festival Hall. Good response from manufacturers and retailers and Piers went all over the place trying all sorts of pianos which he said was a novel experience as he'd always just played whatever he'd been given. He found this one in a very high-class retailer in Bayswater and the story was that when its original owner passed away the family didn't want it any more so they sent it back to the shop he'd bought it from and said they didn't want any money for it but none of them was likely to play it and it took up too much space in the house. So the shop tried to sell it but nobody wanted as it's old-fashioned and second hand, and they were so glad to get shot of it when Piers turned up they not only waived any kind of loan fee but also arranged its delivery and tuning as soon as they could. So they pretty much gave it to him. There's certainly no agreement in place for its return."

Having heard the story, even the unimaginative Emma felt a bit sorry for the piano that had been left to one side of the room so the pianist would be close to the window to maximise light on the music yet still have a good view of other people playing.

Olga finished running through the exercises on the piano which hadn't responded to her touch and she was quite dismissive of it.

"As I thought, he clearly knows nothing about pianos," she declared. "Personally I would have gone for a brand new Steinway."

"Yes, I'm sure you would," her husband told her. "But you weren't the one who picked it out from dozens of possibilities so it might be a better idea to trust his judgement on this one."

"True," she agreed. "He is good player and I love the colour of it. If it is alright with you, Kathy, I'll unpack my bag and have a rest now for a while. I think you have too many stairs in your house."

"There are a lot," she agreed. "Still, it keeps us fit going up and down them all day."

Gisela hadn't said much so far but she was smiling as she joined the others in the kitchen and had worked out the coffee machine in less than a minute while they could all hear Olga stumping up the stairs and crashing about in the front bedroom. "You're so good with Olga," she complimented Kathy. "I don't know how Danny puts up with her. I just want to smack her half the time."

"She's alright," Kathy said loyally. "Just another grumpy East European, isn't she?"

Jean-Guy knew when he was being got at. "Of course. Personally I blame it on the weather."

The two women joined in his joke against himself. "How very English of you," Gisela teased.

By the time Piers got back to Earl's Court, the auditions were over and the guests had all gone. Kathy and Jean-Guy had done the laundry and restocked the kitchen and felt quite pleased with themselves when their landlord came back to a clean and tidy home. Somehow Kathy wasn't surprised he seemed almost relieved to learn that it had been Jean-Guy who had slept in his room while the two women gossiped in the spare room and he just laughed when Jean-Guy told him he really needed to get a new mattress as that one would give a gymnast backache.

Piers listened to Alison's message when Kathy gave it to him and he thought about it while he made himself a sandwich as he had come in hungry as he often did when he had been flying.

"Sounds as though she's in the best place," was his first reaction.

Kathy had been sure he would go belting off to Suffolk if only to stake his claim with his wife before Alison got there first and told the hospital he'd been banned.

"You're not going to go up there?" she asked, feeling a bit disappointed.

"Not yet. Sarah and I talked about this. I tell you if Alison ever heard half the conversations Sarah and I have when she can't hear us, she wouldn't be so confident of her position in that household. I'm bloody sure she bullies Sarah but I can't find any evidence of it try as I might. But that wife of mine is sufficiently stroppy that she won't let Alison dominate her completely. So Sarah and I talk. I have to be careful not to be too anti-Alison as that would just drive the two of them back together again. And we're ready for this one. Sarah made sure my name is on her notes as the father and she got that all organised before any mention was ever made of Alison being her birthing partner. If that's what Alison wants to do then she's welcome to it. I've got no great ambitions to watch Sarah delivering babies even if it is by C-section."

"Now I'd have thought you would," Kathy replied before she could stop herself.

"Why the hell would I want to do that?"

Kathy genuinely couldn't understand his reluctance to be there for the birth of his children. "Doesn't Sarah want you there?"

"Um, yes," he admitted. "But she got over-ruled by Alison."

At that point, Kathy got totally exasperated with him. "Oh, screw bloody Alison! They're not her children your wife is about to have and I really think you should be there when she does have them. You're their father and they need to know that from the moment they take their first breaths. I've told Jean-Guy that when we have ours he's going to be there with me right from the first signs of labour to when I pop it out hours later all knackered and sweaty. And do you know what? He said he can't wait. Just what is your problem?" Piers didn't answer her and Kathy felt awful as she realised the only time Piers would have been in a labour ward was when he and Chantal had been told that their baby would never live. He hadn't known what it was like to hold his child as it took it first breaths. "I'm so sorry," she started but he cut her short.

"It doesn't matter. We've traded our dark secrets and I'm not going to relive mine. What happened to Chantal is nothing like what is happening to Sarah."

Before Kathy could think of a diplomatic way to make sure Piers really had managed to separate the two in his mind, Jean-Guy put his head round the kitchen door.

"Ah, here you both are. Piers, you are in your uniform so does that mean you are going to go and sleep now?"

Piers looked at the clock. "Just for an hour or so. If I stay in bed now I'll be wide awake at 2am and that's never a good thing."

"Good. I want to hear what the sound is like in the music room now we have your piano."

Piers looked accusingly at Kathy. "You have kept me out here wittering on about bloody babies and all the time there's a piano in the music room? What did you want to go and do that for?"

She had to smile at his tone. "Silly me," she admitted lightly. "I'd had this rather naïve idea that your children might be slightly more important to you than some old piano or another."

He gave her a fond kiss on the cheek. "Silly you indeed. Right then, Jean-Guy, let's make sure I've got the one I picked then I really am going to have a bath and a snooze."

And that, Kathy thought as the two men left the room, was the only time she had ever known Piers not go straight upstairs after his post-flight snack.

That evening they tried out the new music room for a proper trio rehearsal and Kathy and Jean-Guy understood why Piers had chosen that particular piano as, under his touch, it had a beautiful tone with a warmth and depth to it that Olga hadn't been able to produce.

"Fantastic piano," Kathy complimented. "We all had a go at it and it just sulked."

Piers smiled quietly at her and said perfectly seriously, "That's because when I saw it stuffed out of the way in a corner of a back room of that shop I heard its spirit. You have to learn to listen to the silence."

"You are very strange," Jean-Guy told him.

Kathy knew exactly what Piers meant. "No, it's true. We all have to learn to feel the music and our instruments, not just play. I bet you're devoted to that cello. You chose to bring it with you when you ran although it would have been so much easier for you to leave it behind."

Jean-Guy looked slightly shocked at that suggestion. "I couldn't leave it behind. It belonged to my great grandfather and I first played it when I was eight."

"So if you had been told you had to leave it behind, would you still have run?" Kathy asked him.

He thought for a while, then made up his mind that the time had come to speak out. "I was," he admitted. "And I refused. I would never leave it behind. It came in useful on my travels across France as I could use it to busk for money when I had none. Some nights I was sleeping rough and I worried that the weather might damage it as it only had that thin case in those days. It was my sputnik, my travelling companion. It is my past, my present and my future. I couldn't leave it behind."

"So," Kathy persisted. "Freedom or cello? Which would you have chosen?"

Jean-Guy looked at the other two who were waiting for his reply. "I don't know," he finally had to say. "I genuinely don't know."

Piers closed the top of the piano. "Anyone for a cup of tea?"

Kathy gave him what she hoped was her winning smile. "Any chance of some hot chocolate, please?"

He looked from her to Jean-Guy. "Two hot chocolates coming up. Come on, Jean-Guy, out to the kitchen. From the look on your face you're finally ready to tell us your story."

Jean-Guy gently put the cello on its side on the floor. "Yes, finally maybe I am. I still say you are odd with your talk of spirits and silence but I have to admit I know what you mean."

"Go and find the biscuits and tell us all about you and your sputnik. Good name, by the way."

They all sat in the kitchen, two of them drinking hot chocolate and the third having to make do with cool tea as he still hadn't worked out a way to make a chocolate drink that was palatable without milk.

"So," Kathy prompted. "Sputnik?"

"I had known for years I couldn't stay in Czechoslovakia," Jean-Guy began. "Then back in 1980 my father told me he had sent the message across to Petr Mihaly to let him know I had to go. So for a while I had had all I needed to know but the Czech authorities were suspicious of me by now and also I knew the Soviets and the KGB had me on their radar as well. They never left me alone. Every concert, every tour, there was someone from the diplomatic with me. But I had a booking to play with a French orchestra who were giving a concert in Stuttgart. They are a famous orchestra and it was a compliment for them to ask me to play and so Czech authorities had granted me a visa to travel to West Germany just for that concert. Three weeks before I was to travel they… let me just say they called me in to talk to me. That is too dark a part of the story for me to tell you right now but I mentioned a little of it to you last Christmas." He paused and looked round the kitchen of the house where he had made his home. "I knew that there was an extreme risk they would punish my family but my parents told me they would forfeit their freedom or even their lives if they had to so I could be free."

Kathy took his hand and held it as he continued.

"They didn't trust even my father for this trip so I was escorted to Stuttgart and met the orchestra. We had time for one run-through and then there was about an hour before the concert. My chaperones stayed with me the whole time as they knew I was now in the West and dangerously close to the border with France where I could so easily pass as a native. One of the other cellists was a man who looked a bit like me. Same kind of brown hair and eyes and about my height. I will never forget the name. Jacques Sébastian de

Caulincourt. I played my concert and, as all good orchestras do, they took me to the local bar afterwards where they systematically got my chaperones very drunk by spiking their drinks and then Jacques gave me his French passport and told me to get on the bus with the rest of them.

"I guessed this was the switch and asked him what he was going to do. He just said not to worry. He had a perfectly good American passport in a different name which would get him out of the country the next day and if I would excuse him he was going to catch a night bus out to the airport before anyone started looking for him. It was all, I don't know, unreal and easy at the same time. We crossed the border into France in the small hours of the morning while my chaperones were still sleeping off their drink and the border guards didn't bother too much with a returning French orchestra. They checked passports and counted heads and that was it. I was through. But the orchestra was playing next in Strasbourg and couldn't keep me with them. So I was on my own. My knowledge of French geography wasn't good and all the orchestra could do was give me a map and wish me luck and then I started walking. I knew the name of my first contact and the address and that was all. Each one told me the next and then, I have no doubt, disappeared or changed names so if ever I was taken and tortured they couldn't be found. Some days went well and I got lifts, other days not so good and it was bad weather or I was hungry or tired as I hadn't found anywhere safe to sleep that night. I knew to stay off the main roads as that was where they would look for me and I knew to stay away from buses and trains as they would be looking there too. So I walked all the little roads of France. It took me weeks, months maybe to get to Paris and the contact I had there on the outskirts in Fontenay-aux-Roses. They kept me in Paris for a while but it was expected I would go to a big city so they moved me on to the coast out in Brittany where I stayed most of the winter. But the Soviets were still looking for me and we all knew I had to leave France as that is where they would expect me to stay. Eventually the people helping me managed to get me on a lorry out of Roscoff to Plymouth and I had a long crossing in the back of a lorry which was full of electrical goods. No food and just one small bottle of water, nowhere to pee and I was locked in so if anything had happened I would have been trapped until they found my dead body."

Three drinks had grown cold in their mugs by this time but the story hadn't quite finished. "The driver let me out of his lorry in the middle of the night in an all-night truck stop somewhere near Okehampton. Finally I got to use the toilet and the driver bought me a meal and a drink but then his instructions were to leave me there. He had only been paid to bring me that far. My knowledge of English geography was nil so I didn't know what to do. But about an hour after the lorry driver had gone, a lady trucker came into the café and told me to come with her as she was the next stage of my journey. This time I was able to travel in the cab. But she never told me her name and there was no writing on her lorry. If a policeman had asked me, I couldn't have identified her. Truthfully, sometimes on that journey I wasn't convinced it was a 'her' so I thought maybe it was the ultimate disguise and I didn't ask any questions. She was going to Felixstowe, allegedly, and left me in the car park of Manningtree station where I slept on a bench on the platform then used the ticket the lorry driver had given me to catch the first train of the day one stop to Ipswich as those were my instructions. And there Emma, and you, met me. And my life hasn't been the same since."

There was a long silence in the kitchen after Jean-Guy had finished his story. Kathy looked at Piers who just gave her a smile and said quietly, "Go to bed, you two. I think you both need some sleep after that. When do the audition results come out?"

"Wednesday," Jean-Guy sniffed and wiped his eyes. "Sorry."

The other two went one each side of him and gave him a hug until he had got some of his composure back. Then Kathy took him by the hand and led him upstairs, leaving Piers to clear up in the kitchen.

Two letters arrived at the house in Earl's Court on the Thursday and then all the phone calls started. By the Saturday evening Kathy knew that she was leader of the second violins and would be sitting next to Emma. She had originally been put near the back of the first violins with Emma as deputy section leader of the seconds but, much against Jean-Guy's advice, she had rung the organisers to ask if she and Emma could be seated together. Jean-Guy couldn't understand why she would accept a position in the second violins when she already had a place in the firsts but Kathy genuinely didn't mind. Just to be playing in the concert was enough and she was looking forward to it even more now she would be sitting with her oldest friend. Danny was in as principal viola and Jean-Guy, unsurprisingly, was principal cellist. Olga had not been accepted but it was very carefully explained to her that this was not a reflection of her abilities but purely an administrative issue as she was still a Soviet citizen and her UK work permit was lapsed so they were very sorry but they couldn't accept her. Gisela hadn't made the final cut either but her letter had been much more to the point and just said they were only looking for eight viola players and wished her luck in any future auditions she may have.

Piers was glad to escape to the comparative peace and quiet of a large international airport on the Tuesday morning after having spent the weekend with two madly excited musicians. Because of the high standard of the players there was only going to be one rehearsal of the orchestra and that would be in the middle of December. Two days before the concert they would have one rehearsal with the choir which had been similarly hand-picked. All musicians involved had been sent their music and also a note of where they would be staying for the night after the concert. Kathy and Emma were together in a bed and breakfast in Ely and Jean-Guy would be in a small hotel on the outskirts of the town. They were left to make their own travel arrangements. That was another round of phone calls and it was arranged that Danny and Emma would go to the farmhouse the night before the concert and they would all travel together in the Land Rover. Which meant, Kathy realised, Professor Mihaly would finally get to meet the elder nephew of David Tarling; something he had been wanting to do since he had first learned the eminent Donald had an older half-brother. She guessed he could hardly wait.

J.S. Bach – *Partita in D minor for solo violin, BWV 1004*

February arrived oddly mild in the middle of London but by the time Danny came back to the house in Earl's Court one evening in the second week of the month to snatch a night's sleep there the mornings at least had become still and frosty again. It was quite cold when he and Kathy got up at some ridiculously early hour so they could catch a train to St Albans while the morning light was still clear and slightly frosty and House of Viola could get their fashion shoot out of the way before too many people arrived in Verulamium Park. They got up so early they nearly beat Piers out of the house and he was almost startled to find them in the kitchen when he came through the staircase door to make himself some coffee before setting off for work.

"So how come you're not on the shoot?" Kathy yawned at the man who looked annoyingly handsome even at that hour of the morning.

Glad not to have to wait for the machine to warm up, Piers had the time to be pleasant for once. "Apparently I'm a closely-guarded secret."

"Doesn't make sense. She stuck you in front of the cameras in Stockholm."

"True," he admitted as he added some cold water to his drink and necked it. "I think I took her a bit by surprise and now she's had time to plot. Not going to worry about it. She's putting me on the runway in a couple of days so I'm sure I'll find out more then."

Danny came in from the garden where he had been having a cigarette to accompany his morning coffee. "I've seen the sketches," he told the other man. "And I'm just bloody glad it's not me she's doing that to."

"Don't start winding me up," Piers cautioned him lightly. "Not when I've got to go to work. Right, behave yourselves, you two. I'm on a same day turnaround so I'll see you about midnight."

"Have a good flight," Kathy called after him as he closed the car port door behind himself.

Danny looked at the closed door and sighed. "That bloke really has no idea has he?"

Privately Kathy thought Piers had lots of ideas so she wasn't sure what that remark was supposed to mean. She looked at the clock. "Come on or we'll be late."

The two set off for the Tube station not used to being out and about on the streets of London in the morning darkness. "How do you manage it?" Danny asked as he followed Kathy into the lift to the platform to catch a Piccadilly Line train to King's Cross.

"Manage what?"

"Living with him? Especially like this time when you're on your own with him as Jean-Guy is in Halifax or somewhere."

"Harrogate," Kathy corrected automatically. She thought it prudent to nip this one in the bud before it went anywhere. "OK, let me explain something to you. Piers and I are friends. Yes, we are close friends and maybe we flirt a bit together sometimes. But it's not going to go anywhere."

"You're kidding me, right?"

"Stop it," she hissed at him as they boarded a nearly empty Tube carriage. "Just stop it. I've had this conversation with Piers, with Jean-Guy and with the Prof. And I'm not justifying our friendship to you as well."

Danny snorted and realised she hadn't chosen one of the smoking carriages on the train. "Suit yourself," he said grumpily. "But I still say the pair of you are kidding yourselves if you think you're going to stay just friends much longer."

"Want to tell me why you've got an unsuitable wife?" Kathy challenged him. "Hmm. Funny that. Suddenly you've run out of things to say. So maybe we should just agree to butt out of each other's love life, huh?"

"OK," he laughed. "But I'll be watching you. And I still say you'll have slept with him before I ever split from Olga."

She held out her hand. "Deal."

"Prize or forfeit?"

"Forfeit. Loser has to get a tattoo. Of the winner's choosing."

Danny looked at her quizzically. "Tattoo, huh? You find someone's butterflies as much of a turn-on as I do?"

Kathy felt her face flush. "I never said that." She forced herself to look into those clear, grey eyes that did nothing to hide Danny's amusement.

"So if he offered, would you say 'yes'?"

"Would you?" she flashed back, enjoying the joke.

"Hell, yes."

She didn't believe him. "Oh, shut up. So, tattoo? Agreed?"

"Agreed."

They shook hands and the bet was sealed. The two friends joked about it for a while in their innocence but the whole thing was forgotten by the time they got to St Albans.

Kathy wasn't quite sure what to expect from a fashion shoot especially as Annette was photographing her summer collection on a bright but cold February morning in Hertfordshire. She had only recently caused another scandal in the fashion world by publishing a photoshoot using a female model who clearly had a prosthetic arm and in some of the shots hadn't even been wearing the prosthetic, but that day she had only the two models as the emphasis was on her new petite range. And, she had found, petite models as shapely and beautiful as Kathy were very hard to come by. So her one petite model had to work hard that day and the dashing film star wasn't much more than a prop for the lovely woman on his arm. Annette was pleased with her choice. Kathy and Danny were totally relaxed in each other's company which made for good photos but Annette had watched the three who had come to that fitting session and she had almost seen sparks between Kathy and Piers which was missing from the way she reacted to her former lover with her this morning. These two were old friends. It was lovely to see and made for some stunning photos in the early morning mist with the leafless trees cleverly hidden from shot. But what Annette really wanted was to get Kathy and Piers for one of her collections so she could try to capture whatever it was that fizzed between them. It was just she had a horrible inkling that the two of them would look faintly ridiculous together as he was so much taller than her.

For the last photo in the shoot, Annette had her two models sitting on a big log by the lake. Danny in his smart dark blue suit was straddling the log like a horse but Kathy was sitting in front of him more side-saddle to show off the needle-thin six-inch heels of her silver shoes that went so well with the floating white and silver dress that she had a bad feeling was actually going to be marketed as a wedding dress and it didn't help that the stylist had given her a small bunch of pink and apricot flowers to hold. The bark of the log was rough on her legs through the thin fabric of her skirt and she had her unglamorous duffle coat over her shoulders as long as she could as she was getting cold by now and a blue-lipped model wasn't quite the look Annette was after. So Kathy sat patiently holding her flowers and the front of her coat to try and keep warm and looked out across the park. The fashion shoot had attracted a small audience as it always did and she suddenly realised what it must have looked like.

"Do you think they think we've just got married?" she asked Danny who was having a quick cigarette while the photographer changed films.

"Probably," he laughed. "I'll have to ask for a copy of the photo so I can show it to Olga."

"Did you two have a nice wedding?"

"No, not really. It was organised in a hurry by the KGB. But that isn't the story to tell you in a public park. Let's just say it was more of a political union than a love match but we're working on it because I sure as hell don't want a second divorce on my records."

"No," she agreed. "I don't suppose you do. Tell me some other time when it's not so cold and uncomfortable. Don't you find all of this a bit strange? Sitting about in public places wearing clothes that cost thousands of pounds."

"I did at first. But then at the very first Annette's clothes didn't sell for anything like that much. Then she got picked up by some very influential people and it all just took off. I was genuinely happy for her."

It was beginning to make sense to Kathy now. "Ah. So is Annette another one of your exes?"

"What? No she bloody isn't. We're just friends."

That did surprise Kathy. "Uh-huh. So you and she can be friends but when I say the same about me and Piers you don't believe it?"

"Not for one minute. I see Annette maybe three or four times a year. You and Piers are living in each other's houses and... Never mind. That bet still stands."

Annette looked at the two on the log and still wished she had had a different male model for the photo. Maybe one day. "Right, you two. Kathy, get the coat off and I want the two of you to look very cosy. You can do cosy, can't you?"

"Isn't that something to do with teapots?" Danny muttered in Kathy's ear and made her laugh as he shuffled closer to her on the log.

Kathy reluctantly handed the coat to Annette so it wouldn't be seen and let Danny put careful arms round her so he didn't spoil the line of the dress. His embrace was comfortingly familiar and she leaned against his chest, breathing in the smell of the cigarette smoke on him, now mixed with an unfamiliar aftershave and some strong hairspray keeping him looking neat and tidy. She tucked one arm inside his jacket for some very welcome warmth and felt him rest his cheek on her head. Funny how these tall people always did that to her she thought and allowed herself a little smile.

"Oh! That is just perfect," Annette yelled at them. "Don't move."

Kathy wished she could have been wrapped in Jean-Guy's arms at that precise moment and she lifted her little bouquet to her nose as the flowers smelled sweeter than stale cigarette smoke and industrial-strength hairspray.

Annette Delaney looked at her two models and began to think maybe she ought to put Kathy's fees up. But she really was going to have to get that petite beauty in a photoshoot with the drop-dead gorgeous man, even if she had to do the whole thing with the pair of them horizontal to hide the height difference.

The petite range wasn't extensive as it was a bit of an experiment for the designer and the shoot was over before the park got too busy. Kathy and Danny were thankful to be back in their own comfortable clothes and cheerfully let Annette treat them to breakfast in a town centre café while the rest of those involved in the shoot packed up the van and went back to London.

"So," Annette said as she sipped her hot chocolate. "First shoot over and done with. Hope it wasn't too terrible for you in those skimpy dresses?"

"No, not at all," Kathy lied and was glad she had come to the event wearing her warmest sweater and her blue duffle coat. "And thank you for letting me keep the blue dress."

"My pleasure. Going to wear it to the runway show the day after tomorrow?"

"Oh, I suppose I could. But I'll need a warm coat."

Annette smiled at her. "It'll be pretty hot inside. And very noisy once the sound system gets going. Most people don't expect the noise. Where's Piers today?"

"Day trip to New York," Kathy replied. "He's arranged a same day turnaround so he can catch up on his sleep tomorrow."

"Good. I hope he's been eating sensibly?"

"Oh, yes. He's still looking saleable."

Annette loved the other woman's well-defined sense of humour. "Glad you're protecting my investment for me. Of course, he'll hate me by the end of the runway show but what the hell. The fee I'm paying him to do what I want him to, he'll just have to put up with it."

"Sneak preview?" Danny smiled. "I've only seen the preliminary sketches."

"No bloody chance. Just be glad I'm not doing it to you." Annette looked at Kathy who was innocently finishing off her own hot chocolate. "How much shorter than Piers are you?"

"Nearly a foot," Kathy replied, wondering what this was all about. "I'm five two and he's six one."

"Hmm. It's too late for the London show now. And I won't get it all organised in time for New York next month. But, yes. I think I know what I'm going to do with the pair of you."

Kathy looked at Danny who had known Annette so much longer and wasn't consoled to see his delighted grin.

"It's what she does," he told Kathy. "She gets ideas. Scares the crap out of me when I hear that."

It was a bitterly cold, raw February morning when the two men met at the small café on Tooting High Street. It was near Tooting Broadway Tube station so it was always busy but most of the customers were taking away their coffees and teas as they were dashing in and out on their way to work. The two men ordered their breakfasts then found themselves a table half-way between the window and the counter so they were out of the way of the main throng of people.

Pascal put a small box on the table. "Good to see you again," was his opening comment as he looked almost warily at his ex-brother-in-law.

"And you," was the polite, instinctive response from Piers as he cautiously sipped his coffee and guessed it was a fairly cheap instant. But it didn't taste too bad and wasn't too hot as the lady at the counter had done as she was asked and put some cold water in it. "Is it all done then?"

Pascal nodded and sighed. "I had no idea she had so much stuff in that small flat. Gina was a big help but there were some things in Chantal's Will that took us a while to sort out. How are you coping these days?"

"Oh, better, thanks."

Pascal and his family had been so shocked when they had learned what Piers had done in the aftermath of Chantal's death, they had gone rushing round to his house in

Earl's Court as soon as the pastor told them he was home again after his long convalescence in Suffolk and they had stayed for nearly the whole day. It had been a hard, emotional day but it had helped all of them to move on after their bereavement. Now it was just over a year later, Chantal's brother and sister-in-law had finally finished clearing out her flat and disposing of her possessions as she had asked and Pascal was meeting up with Piers in this less-than-ideal place as he and his family were flying out to Jamaica for a month and Piers was on a day off between a day trip to New York and his first runway show.

He tapped the box. "This is what she wanted you to have," he said a little awkwardly as the waitress brought across their breakfasts. "There's not much. Gina thought you might like some photos so she took copies of a few family ones, including that one of Grandma Aurelie that you'd always liked so much.

Piers found a smile from somewhere. "You mean the one where she's getting in a total mess with the mango?"

"That's the one. You never could look at that one and not laugh."

"True," replied the man who didn't laugh much at all these days.

"She also wanted you to have her jewellery."

Piers paused in buttering his toast. "What? Why the hell would she do that?" He hadn't been able to get to the Will-reading after Chantal's death and the first thing Pascal had had to tell him was that the first condition of it was that he wasn't to know anything about the terms of it.

"She didn't say. But she did say you're to keep it for your daughters and you mustn't sell it. There's not much."

"I never told her Sarah was expecting what turned out to be triplets. I mean she knew I'd remarried but that was it."

Pascal wasn't surprised to hear the defensiveness in Piers' voice. "I know. Didn't make much sense to me either. Anyway, that's what she wanted. She'd said Gina and I could keep what we wanted from her belongings. We didn't keep much. The photos, couple of ornaments. Gina thought you might like a couple of mementos so we put them in the box for you. You can pass them on to a charity shop if you don't want them. There were some books that were obviously yours so they're in the box too. One of them looks like one of your flying log books."

"Yes," Piers had to agree. "I was kind of annoyed with myself for leaving that behind as I hadn't quite finished it and had to buy a new one. So thanks for that." He finished his toast and licked the remains of the marmalade off his fingers before wiping his hands on his napkin.

Pascal remembered how that licking habit had always irritated his sister but she had never been able to stop it. It made him smile to think of it again. "The flat's sold," he said bluntly. "But the whole of the money has gone to Rita."

Piers had been about to finish off his coffee but he paused with the mug in his hands. He hadn't been expecting any of the proceeds from the sale of his ex-wife's flat but he hadn't been expecting that. "Rita?"

"Yeah. That's why it's taken so long to get it all sorted out as we had arrange for the money transfer out to America for her."

"Funny, I'd have thought she'd either have left it to you or to her church or a charity or something."

"No. Whole lot to Rita along with a sealed letter that went from her solicitor to Rita's attorney out in Chicago and none of us has a clue what it says."

Piers had never really got on with Chantal's younger sister but they had tolerated each other on the rare occasions they met. By the time he had lived out in Jamaica after he had left the Air Force, Rita was already working in neighbouring Barbados and she had left for Chicago about the same time Piers and Chantal had moved to Paris for his work with Air France. These days he could compare his rather scratchy relationship with Rita with the one he now had with Alison but he had never been able to work out why it was Rita didn't like him. She'd made it quite clear that she hadn't approved of her sister taking a husband with the pale skin and blue eyes of his Irish heritage but they had never had the blazing rows Alison tried to stage with him.

"Have you any idea why she would do that?" he asked curiously as he habitually tidied up his crockery for the waiting staff to collect.

"No," Pascal had to admit. "Gina's best guess is that Rita's going to use it to buy a house out there."

Piers looked at him sharply. Something about Pascal's tone of voice caught his ear and he knew a half-truth when he heard one. "Uh-huh. And what's your best guess?"

Pascal hadn't forgotten how shrewd the other man was. He could pick up on the slightest inflexion of voice or facial expression and he didn't miss much. Pascal checked his watch. "Sorry, but I've really no idea. Anyway, I'd better be on my way as we've got a plane to catch and so have you." The two men got to their feet and Pascal handed over the box. "Been good to see you."

"You too," Piers said automatically as he tucked the box under one arm. "Have a good holiday and give my regards to Grandma Aurelie."

"Thanks. Will do. What time's your flight?"

"Oh, no. Going home now. Not flying today."

"Still on Concorde? My kids still don't believe they've got an uncle who can fly to New York in under four hours."

Piers smiled slightly to realise he was still 'Uncle Piers' to Pascal's children even though they must now be well into their twenties. "Yup. Tell them to let me know if they're ever heading out that way and I'll see if I can get them a jump seat ride."

Pascal so nearly laughed as both men knew that was something that wasn't very likely to happen as all three children had always hated flying even though they often went out to Jamaica to visit family. "Still going all over the world?"

"Goes with the job."

The two stepped out into the raw wind whipping along Tooting High Street and shook hands in farewell.

"Gina or I'll give you a ring when we're back," Pascal told him. "Give you all the news from Grandma."

"Thanks. Appreciate it."

The two parted ways and neither looked back to watch the going of the other one. Piers had parked a couple of streets away and he looked at the road of Victorian houses that were nearly all flats now and he wondered if his ex-wife had lived in one of them. It was a slow journey back to Earl's Court from Tooting and although the Aston Martin had a good heating system, even it struggled against that cold London air and he was almost shivering as he let himself into his house and put the box on the kitchen table.

Fortified with an extra sweater, he went back to the box, knowing he wouldn't be able to settle until he had at least looked inside it and rescued the log book that had been missing from his collection for years. He made himself a mug of coffee from the machine and took a deep breath then ripped off the Sellotape. To his relief, Gina had thoughtfully put the log book on the top so he could take it out and have a quick flick through it. A photograph fell out of its pages and he picked it up from the table without thinking. It was as though someone had stabbed a shard of ice through his heart and he heard his own breath catch in his throat. It was something instinctive that made him put the photo up on the shelf behind the coffee jar with its image turned to the wall. He wondered if Chantal had done that on purpose in some kind of final act of spite. He certainly would never have put a photo in a log book like that. But it did explain why he hadn't been able to find that book when Chantal had granted him one day to take his stuff out of their house while she was out at work.

Two pages on from where the photo had been hidden was a postcard of Trafalgar Square. He'd forgotten just how neat Chantal's writing was.

Piers, here is your log book back. And the photo we both liked so much. Please forgive me as I forgave you all those years ago. Chantal xx. 21.06.1981

Grief was forgotten as conflicting emotions ran through the man who sat at his kitchen table as though transfixed. "Oh, Chantal," he sighed out loud. "What have you done?"

He put the postcard back in the log book and looked inside the box hoping to find a clue in there. But all he found were a couple of aviation books that he hadn't wanted to keep but it had been good of Gina to give them back. The photo of Grandma Aurelie made him smile as it always did and then all that was left in the box was a smaller box that he guessed contained Chantal's jewellery. Feeling quite brave, he tipped out the contents of the smaller box and consciously quashed his emotions. She'd kept the opal engagement ring and there was her wedding ring. The silver hoop earrings she had only ever taken out of her ears when she was at work. Her silver cross on a chain that she never took off from round her neck. And two tiny silver bangles obviously for a baby or a young child.

Piers picked them up and looked at them curiously. He'd never seen them before and they were quite new and shiny so he guessed it was maybe something she had bought for Gina's daughters and never got round to handing them over. But Gina would have seen them and she had clearly boxed them up to hand over with the instructions he wasn't to get rid of any of the jewellery. He smiled slightly as he put the bangles back as he had no idea how you were supposed to divide two silver bangles between triplets. Something for Sarah to sort out in the future. He put the books back in the larger box too and got to his feet to go into the music room to do some practice. He could have sworn he caught a slight scent of the perfume Chantal had always worn. Common sense told him it was just a lingering aura left on the things that had been in her flat but it still spooked him.

He looked up at the photo on the shelf and said quietly, "What have you done, you scheming witch?" Somewhere in his memory he heard her laugh and he knew that his ex-wife had somehow, subtly, taken some kind of revenge on him.

Danny hadn't stayed a second night in the house in Earl's Court as he was due to meet up with his wife at Annette's London flat in Eaton Place. He would far rather have stayed in the welcoming, rambling house that always made him feel at home rather than in the upmarket flat that belonged to Annette's husband, but Olga had pointed out that the flat had a lift and as he had got her pregnant again it was only right that they should stay in the place that didn't have stairs. But he went off without complaining too much and told the other two he would see them at the runway event next week.

Kathy was even less sure what to expect from a fashion show in a posh London hotel than she had been for a photoshoot but the whole experience was almost surreal right from the moment Piers hailed a taxi in the Earl's Court Road to take them to the hotel. Kathy never travelled in black cabs as she couldn't justify the expense but Piers didn't want to drive and wouldn't go on public transport unless there was absolutely no alternative, so the pair of them arrived at the hotel just a few moments before Annette and her party joined them. It made Kathy feel a bit better that the designer had come by cab too so it didn't seem such an extravagance after all. Besides which, Piers had paid the driver and given him a very generous tip.

Kathy hadn't met Annette's husband before and Sir Giles Delaney reminded her rather of a friendly teddy bear as he was quite plump and had a very low, rumbling voice, and it was hard to believe Danny's description of him as a shit-hot QC who nobody ever messed with. Olga was extremely pregnant by this time and made a show of having to take first her husband's arm for support then, when Danny and Piers were taken away by Annette to be prepared for the show, Olga clutched Giles' arm instead. Funny thing, Kathy thought, as soon as Danny was out of sight his wife stopped grumbling quite so much and seemed to be walking a lot more easily.

The three were shown to seats at the end of the runway but not as close as the press who were hard against the walkway itself with a barrage of cameras waiting at the far end, and Olga claimed the middle of the three seats without asking the other two first. Kathy knew what Annette meant as the audience began to fill the seats and the temperature in the room rose until it felt stifling. There didn't seem to be any air circulating and the atmosphere was heavy with the mingled scents of expensive perfumes and fur coats recently released from mothballs for the occasion. She had tested the weight of Piers' indigo coat and felt rather sorry for him if he was going to be wearing something like that under those lights. She hoped he wouldn't have a thick woollen sweater under the coat as well. It crossed her mind that perhaps the pregnant Olga was finding it all a bit much, but the she seemed perfectly relaxed as she chatted with Giles. But Olga had taken Annette's advice more seriously and was in a very fetching maternity dress that was almost summer wear and the dark olive green colour flattered the tones of her skin and hair. Kathy hadn't paid enough attention to Annette's words of warning and although she had put a dress on, it was quite a warm needlecord and she could feel the sweat between her shoulder blades even before the sound system was switched on and the relentless noise of the introductions and the blaring music somehow made the whole place even more oppressive.

    The first fashion house started its show and Kathy forgot she was hot and thirsty and had the beginnings of a headache. She looked at those women and men strutting along and was so glad it wasn't her on that runway. She couldn't quite forget that Annette had threatened her with it but the more she watched what was going on, the more she was convinced it was something she was never going to want to do. Sometimes it was bad enough just walking onto a stage with a violin tucked under her arm and she had recently been grateful to Piers who would walk on beside her. It hadn't taken her long to work out that when he had been a child he would have walked on a few paces behind Roisin and would just have slipped quietly onto the piano stool with no expectation of acknowledgement from the audience. Now he walked beside the violinist as her equal, even if the two of them were behind the renowned cellist, and it suited the pair of them to do that. Kathy looked briefly away from the runway into all those flash guns going off and she felt rather sorry for the models, some of whom looked quite dizzy when they turned from the end and walked back again. She thought she would rather do another sonata recital in Yorkshire than ever have to go on a fashion runway, but had a bad feeling that if Annette told her she was going to be posturing down the catwalk like that, then she would meekly do as she was told rather than get in a tangle with the other woman.

Viola was the fourth fashion house to be showing a collection and Kathy's first thought was how Annette's models were nothing like the professionals they had just been watching.

"They look so different," she managed to communicate to Olga over the noise of the heavy metal music that Annette was using for this show and Kathy had to admit it suited her designs that were somewhere between Victorian melodrama and New Romantic with a lot of metal and lace and jagged hemlines.

"It's what she does," Olga explained, struggling in her turn to be heard above the loud music. "She says it's showing her clothes as they should be worn. A lot of the other fashion houses don't like her attitude and people she uses. But I do love her designs. Oh, here's Danny now."

Kathy turned her attention back to the runway and had to admit she would never have expected her driving instructor to finish up looking like that. She couldn't see that thin, scruffy man who had done so much to help her get over the mess with her ex. If he had been sexually attractive then, he was way off the scale now and a tiny, treacherous, part of her wished that maybe they had stayed together. But they had known even at the time that it wasn't going to be long-term between them and even though Danny had assured her many times he wasn't in the habit of going to bed with his pupils, she was never totally sure she believed him. Annette had sent him out with a grey fedora hat to finish off his first outfit and the way he stopped at the end of the runway and looked at those cameras from under the brim made her regret more than ever their relationship had been so brief. Danny's clear grey eyes held a raw promise in them and his smile had never been more alluring. Her body remembered the feel of him and the smell of their passionate times together, which was a bit unnerving as his wife was sitting about three inches away from her. Kathy could quite see how that smile would sell a lot of designs and she understood why Olga had said her husband was good at his job.

Annette's collection wasn't as big as some and she had two black women modelling, something none of the other houses had done, and two white men. One was Danny and the other a younger man who, according to Olga, was Scott who had done two previous collections for Annette and had refused all other offers from fashion houses as they wanted him to give up his teaching job and lose three stone in weight. So he stayed with Annette and with his blond, dark-eyed looks was an impressive contrast to Danny.

There was still no sign of Piers after the four had done about three turns each and the outfits, especially those of the women, were getting to be almost borderline bondage now. Certainly not something Kathy would ever consider wearing in public and she began to hope that maybe, just maybe, Annette wouldn't like the photos from the park and she could just quietly be dropped by House of Viola rather than have to parade around in clothes like that. But that maroon dress on the lady with the long plaited hair was incredible. Kathy sighed inwardly and wished she had the confidence just to put on something like that with its skirt barely covering the model's behind and the top half of it an incredibly intricate leather lacing over a shimmering sheer under-dress.

"I can't understand why we haven't seen Piers yet," Kathy remarked with no great hope either of her companions would hear her.

"Could be anything," Giles explained, his bass tones barely audible above the throbbing music. "Most probably a fault with the garment, although she was so excited about this new discovery of hers I can't think she won't use him."

Olga leaned a bit closer to Kathy so she didn't have to shout at her. "Danny says word on the vine is that she's paying Piers five figures to do this so she will use him if she has to glue the clothes on him because the manufacturer got the measurements wrong. Apparently it's quite theatrical." She sounded a bit miffed that her husband seemed to be in danger of being knocked off top spot.

"Isn't she always theatrical?" the fond husband asked.

"Oh," Olga exclaimed, sounding disappointed. "There is Annette now. That must mean it's the end and she's decided not to use him for some reason. Wonder if he still gets paid?"

Kathy looked at the back of the runway. Danny and Annette were standing each side of the entrance but the centre was in total darkness which was unexpected as even Kathy had worked out that each house finished its show with the designer and all the models on stage together. The audience was already on its feet applauding although no models had come out yet, but it certainly felt as though the Viola show was over. With a suddenness that nobody was expecting there came a bass thump through the sound system, so loud and so low Kathy wondered for a moment if her heart had stopped. She jumped when Olga grabbed her wrist.

"Here we go," Olga breathed as there was a second thump.

Kathy didn't take her eyes off the back of the runway. On a third bone-jarring beat a blinding overhead shaft of white light hit a solitary figure standing where only a second before had been total darkness, and Kathy genuinely didn't recognise him at first. With so much light on so pale a skin there was something unreal, almost mystic about the lone figure. Stripped to the waist with his arms crossed on his chest, Piers' head was bowed and his hands were on his shoulders covering the panther and swallowtail. All Kathy took in was that he was wearing only a pair of very well-fitting dark brown trousers that looked as though they were made of leather, there was heavy jewellery in shades of brown and glittering with silver round his wrists and his feet were bare.

"She's got the wedding ring off him," Kathy mouthed at Olga.

"Five figure fee," she said rather bitterly.

The heavy metal music began pulsating louder than ever before, hypnotic in its volume and the dull throbbing bass, and every single eye in that audience was transfixed as two hidden dressers got the coat on Piers and he finally raised his head showing more leather and silver round his throat. Kathy couldn't believe that was the scruffy man with the filthy laugh who started to walk down the runway, totally alone unlike the other models had been, with the coat buttoned and his hands in the pockets. The stylists had given him the longer hair again and the features of his face were obscured behind make-up that owed a passing resemblance to the Mexican Day of the Dead. They had put sparkling studs at the tips of his ears, he had an ornate copper-coloured hoop attached to the septum of his nose, and a dark copper-coloured ring on the second toe of his left foot which

Kathy thought was probably very tickly. The coat itself wasn't indigo like the one he had at home but a deep forest green with coppery gold where his own was grey velvet and the whole effect looked as though it belonged in some fairy tale world of woodlands and sprites.

Kathy barely heard the audience noise any more and the heat she was feeling was nothing to do with her warm dress. She felt as though she was barely breathing as Piers stopped at the end of the runway and slowly unbuttoned the coat using just his right hand then let the coat fall open. A well-practised tweak of the collar and lapels gave the fashion media a tantalising glimpse of some markings on his chest and Kathy wanted nothing more than to touch his smooth skin and feel where that the cute line of belly fluff had been shaved off. She wondered if he had minded. For maybe half a minute he waited, looking without blinking through his carefully mussed-up fringe into the lenses and flash guns of the world's fashion press. If the well-known Danny had stood in that spot and got her all excited with his promise of delights untold, this unnamed, unrecognisable figure was all the more seductive with his calm, impassive pose that said he really didn't care if nearly everyone in the audience now wanted to leap onto the runway and get their hands on him. Kathy made herself think a little more rationally as she looked at him and couldn't recognise the man who had slumped at the kitchen table just over a year ago, bereaved and wretched. That figure on the runway was a superbly self-confident man, teasing and tantalising and standing just out of her reach which was in itself some kind of exquisite, sexual torture. But that was all it was, she had to tell herself. A pose. An act. He was never going to be hers and she had to accept that no matter how hard it was.

She guessed Piers must have been counting the beats of the music as at the exact change of tempo he turned with a dramatic swirl to show off the inserts in the coat, and began his walk back along the runway as though he was now bored with the whole thing. As he came level with Annette and Danny, with his back to the entire audience, the two stepped forward and neatly stripped the coat off him, letting it fall to the floor. Then he was back in that brilliant shaft of light and looking even more out-of-this-world with the whole tattoo exposed right down to the skull. Timed to absolute perfection, on the first heart-stopping beat he defiantly raised his arms out to the side with fists clenched and the light glittered and sparkled on the silver of the wrist bands. On the second beat he tilted his head back in a classic gesture of rebellion. The floor shook for a third and final time with the heavy bass beat as the light went out, and the darkness was complete.

Kathy realised she and Olga were physically clasping hands and Giles had gone very quiet. She let go of Olga but didn't take her eyes off the stage. Danny had picked up the coat and he and Annette were now centre stage and the other models grouped round in the expected finale to take the applause of the audience, but there was no sign of Piers. It was as though Annette had presented this unreal figure, paraded after everyone thought she had finished. Not seen all evening and now apparently gone back to the faerie world he had come from. Kathy didn't need Piers' hearing to know questions were flying round the room.

"Wow," was all Olga said. "No wonder she paid him five figures. Just look at all those people round order books."

"If the story about the fee is true," Giles commented, "and it may well be, I would guess that she will recoup it twenty times over looking at the way they are writing in the order books. In fact I would wager the coat and trousers are sold already, straight off the runway to somebody far less suitable."

Kathy hadn't realised. "You can buy off the runway?"

"Oh, yes," Olga told her, amused by her naivety. "By the time Piers got back from his little walk just now she will have sold outfit probably for about what you or I may earn in a good year. Among rich elite there is quite a cachet to be had getting designer clothes off models. I wouldn't mind betting they tried to buy model too if what Annette has told Danny is true."

The three remained in their seats for the showing by the next two fashion houses but after that finale from Viola the designs were uninspired and the models appeared to have all the personality of half a dozen telegraph poles. At the end of those showings, Giles checked his watch then got to his feet. "Come on then, ladies, I believe the rest of our party should be waiting for us outside by now."

"Are they not coming in for the rest of the show?" Olga asked as she hauled herself up with a bit of help from Giles.

"Not this time. She's keeping Piers well away from the opposition for the time being."

It took a while to work their way out of the building through the crowds. The night air struck cold after the heat inside the hotel and Kathy was glad to see the other three were already waiting for them on the pavement. Annette looked elegantly fashionable in a long black cape over her electric blue dress but the two men were happy and shabby again in jeans and sweaters and sharing a cigarette.

"Well done," Kathy greeted them, but although Danny smiled wearily at her Piers didn't seem to have heard. To her amusement, Danny nudged the man sharing his cigarette and pointed to his own ears. Piers suddenly grinned, handed the cigarette back and fished in his ears before putting something in the pockets of his jeans.

"Sorry," he said to Kathy. "Had plugs in as all that noise was making me feel sick."

Kathy realised there were more downsides to having such acute hearing than being woken up every time someone flushed a toilet at night. But now she knew why he had been counting at the end of the runway and probably just feeling the beat through his feet.

It was gone midnight by the time Kathy and Piers got back to the house in Earl's Court and she was slightly appalled at the night-rate premium apparently charged by black-cab drivers but she guessed they deserved it. It wasn't a job she would like to do.

Kathy made them some tea as they were both too high on noise and lights to go to sleep just yet. "Did you enjoy that?" she asked curiously. "I must admit you looked pretty impressive up there."

"Thank you. It was one of the strangest things I have ever done. But it was like Danny told me, it's acting. Like you and the Quartet or all of us and the Octet. Your reality is playing your violin in a sensible concert and mine is sitting at the flight deck of an aeroplane."

"So you're not doing it again?"

He took a few sips of the black tea which Kathy had made to the right temperature. "Yes, I'm doing it again. I'm doing it purely for the money which I am first using to clear the mortgage on this place and then anything left goes into a trust fund for however many children Sarah and I end up with, to be held until the child reaches its twenty third birthday."

"That is so thoughtful of you. What does Sarah think?"

"Haven't told her yet. I'm letting the money go into my account first as it still seems unreal that I'm going to get paid so much. Then Annette's husband is going to sort out the legal niceties." He smiled into his mug of tea. "Funny thing about Sarah, she's never once asked me what my income is and she's certainly never asked for any of it. But I set up an account for her to draw on for the kids anyway and I can see she does use it." He looked at her. "How can you still look so awake? Mind you, I'd never have thought walking up and down a runway could be so tiring. Annette has said she'll courier over the photos tomorrow morning so if it's OK with you we'll wait for them then go back to Suffolk."

"Sounds good to me. Jean-Guy's away until tomorrow too and the Prof is picking him up at Ipswich so he'll be happy. What are your plans?"

"Getting my fingers round that sodding Mendelssohn first of all. Back to Heathrow on Tuesday when I pick up my line again. Annette doesn't want me for a while so Mr Mendelssohn will have my undivided attention." Piers finished his tea and drank two mugs of water without stopping. "Well, I've had enough excitement for one day. You off to bed yet?"

Kathy helped herself to another biscuit. "In a minute. Were those leather trousers she put you in?" She was going to mention the missing fluff and the toe ring but thought his pride had probably taken enough of a bashing over things like that so she didn't.

Piers resigned himself to sitting up a bit longer although he was craving some sleep. "Yes. Leather trousers and a wool coat under those lights. I think I sweated off half a stone just walking up and down for two minutes. They'd fixed the face paint with something that smelled like yacht varnish, if I'd smiled I'd have cracked, and I'd swear they took it off with a chisel. And still people bought the whole outfit off runway. Piglet, please can I go to bed now? I have a backache, a headache and I'd swear I've got sweat rash on my head from that bloody wig."

Kathy felt really guilty and gave him a hug and a kiss on the cheek. He smelled very strange, probably something to do with whatever the make-up people had used to get the paint off his face, and she wondered how many people in that audience would want to swap places with her right now. "Sorry, you're quite right." She had seldom seen him look so tired and washed out. "Bed."

Round blue eyes looked at her and she had never seen him smile quite like that before. "You made that sound like an invitation."

They were woken in the morning by the ringing of the bell at the street door. Kathy got downstairs first, in her nightdress and dressing gown and with her hair all over the place, wondering who on earth it was as people who knew them always went to the side door.

She had totally forgotten the photographs were due and peered blearily at the visitor. "Oh, hi. Sorry. What's the time?"

"Nearly nine. Looks like the two of you made a night of it."

Kathy stood back and let the visitor in. "So sorry. We sat up talking far later than we should have done. Please go and help yourself to some coffee or something."

Annette had to smile at the sleepy woman in front of her. "Well, I would but I've never been here before and don't know where your kettle is."

"Oh, God. Sorry. It's this way."

Annette looked at the room with its handsome piano, music stands and piles of music everywhere. She was a bit confused to see there was a wet room at the far end. "Funny sort of a room," she mused more to herself than out loud.

"Mm. The previous owner was in a wheelchair so this was his main room. It was Danny's idea to turn it into a music room. This way."

Annette followed her into the kitchen. "Oh, my goodness, you've got an Aga."

"It was here when Piers bought the house. Are you OK to use it? There's an electric kettle somewhere and a coffee machine."

Annette put a couple of photo albums on the table. "For pity's sake go and have a shower and sort yourself out," she said kindly. "I'm sure I can manage."

Up on the first floor landing, Kathy met an equally sleep-fuddled Piers just coming down from the second floor. "Who the hell was that?"

"Annette with the photos. I've left her making coffee in the kitchen."

"Shit. Totally forgotten."

"Me too. Got a feeling she thinks we're an item."

"Silly cow. Need a shower."

"Yup. Me too. See you down there."

Annette Delaney was quite happy looking round the kitchen while the coffee machine cranked into life, it reminded her of the one she had at home but was at least five years older judging by the design of it. She couldn't see a cooker or a microwave so guessed they did their cooking on the Aga or ate out. A cursory look round made her think they did a lot of cooking at home as there were shelves of dry goods and herbs and an old-fashioned pantry that was well-stocked, as well as some very well-used utensils and pans on the Aga. She reached up to take down the jar marked "Coffee" from the shelf but the deep sheepskin cuff of her coat just caught a piece of card that had been propped up behind it and she guiltily picked it up to put it back. Curiosity got the better of her so she turned it over and felt almost shocked when she realised it wasn't the shopping list she had assumed.

First of her hosts to arrive was Piers, still looking deliciously half asleep and Annette was almost sorry he had found time to dress himself in shirt and jeans and hadn't wandered down the stairs with that tattoo on view.

"Morning," she greeted him. "How do you take your morning coffee?"

"Straight double espresso," he told her. "Thanks." Annette watched as he added some cold water to the drink she gave him then downed it in one go. "Sorry. Don't think I've got over yesterday yet. And just to put you straight, Piglet and I aren't sleeping together."

"Refill?" she asked amused and didn't say anything else, mostly because she didn't believe him.

He shook his head and filled a glass from the tap. "No, thanks. Now I switch to water."

Remembering this was a man who didn't drink milk, she guessed he wasn't going to have any more coffee straight after the hit of that double espresso. "Where's the best place to sit and look at photos?"

He had to think about that. "Here probably. It's the only table in the house."

"Well, having seen the first room on the way in I'm guessing you're not very big on furniture."

He smiled then and took a drink of water. "Never been able to afford any. Managed to get a few second-hand bits now, but it takes most of my wages just to pay the mortgage. Best thing I ever did was take in a couple of lodgers and agree to your indecent fees."

"Thank God for that. I'm stripping you off in New York next month and if my idea pays off it will be a higher fee as you'll have more to do. So that'll pay for the odd lampshade."

He was a bit taken aback by the sudden brutality of her statement and was glad his brain was starting to get back into focus. "Oh, OK. What date? It's just that I'll be in NYC anyway as Jean-Guy is giving some concerts at the Lincoln and I've sorted my lines so I can fly those two out there and bring them back."

"Twenty sixth."

Piers looked at a calendar hanging on the wall next to the Aga. "Yes, I'll be there on the twenty sixth using the lines I've got, so can you get them a couple of tickets for the show, please? Piglet really enjoyed the one last night."

Kathy joined them in time to hear that. "Certainly did. Good morning, Annette, I'm a bit more awake now. Are you parading Piers again soon then?"

Annette noticed the other woman was still wearing her habitual polo shirt and dark trousers but this time had made herself look even worse by throwing on a beige mohair cardigan that made her look like a hamster. Without making any remarks on Kathy's dress sense, Annette made her some coffee too now she had sussed out the machine. "Next month in New York. We've just worked out you and Jean-Guy can come along too. In fact, while you're out there I can organise a street shoot using both of you." She looked at Piers. "Not sure what I'm going to do with you though. I don't want to put you on display on the streets until after the second runway show then I'm afraid I'm going to have to let you go so the rest of the houses can fight over you."

He sat at the table feeling oddly disappointed. "Why?"

To distract herself from Kathy's awful cardigan, Annette gently touched Piers' unshaven cheek. "Because you would earn way more than I pay you just by going to an agency and letting them all have a piece of you. By the time you come off that runway in New York you will be a celebrity and everyone will want you on their chat shows, and the women's magazines will be fighting over you for photo sessions. You could earn a bloody fortune."

Kathy tried not to be too envious as she sat with them with her coffee and really wanted to look at the photos. "Why can't he stay with you like Scott has?"

"Because Scott is a carthorse next to this thoroughbred."

"Yeah, I was talking to some of the others while I was sitting around for hours backstage last night. I don't want to be famous, I certainly don't want to finish up as some kind of, I don't know what, whatever it is you're implying. So, if it's all the same to you, I'd rather you kept my runway identity a secret, I can go on flying my aeroplanes with nobody any the wiser but if it keeps you happy I'll sign an exclusive contract with Viola like Scott has."

Annette looked at him as though he was mad. "What? Even Danny's gone freelance and has worked for nearly all the big houses now. Plus the amounts he earns from advertising and voice overs which are indecent even to my mind and I can get pretty gross."

"Yes, but Danny's only other income, after Olga made him stop driving, is his music and he is still having physio on his hand. In case you haven't noticed from all the writing on that calendar over there, I earn quite a good living flying between London and New York with the occasional trip somewhere else, and pick up the odd pound or two with the Dodman Trio when they let me and the last thing I want is another job."

"So I have you and your tattoo all to myself?"

"You do. But if there's a diary clash the airline and trio to come first. And while I really couldn't care less if you want to get me covered in ink, I must stick to the airline dress code on tattoos and piercings so nothing that will show when I've got a shirt on, even a short sleeved one. So all ink stays well above the elbow. OK?"

Annette held out her hand and couldn't believe that she had finally got someone who could bring to life some of her more extreme designs. "Agreed. But I'd still love to get some metal in those ears of yours." Piers just laughed and the two shook hands. "And that puts a whole different perspective on things and I will gladly put you on the streets of New York with Kathy and Jean-Guy. But that will just be you, no face paints. I'm saving that for the next runway show." Annette took a sketchbook from her bag and made sure both the other two could see her drawings. "Right, this is what I'm putting you in for New York. Not dissimilar to the London show but it'll be different make-up and accessories. I don't want the forest fairy look you gave me so beautifully last night. I want you to pack aggression and a lot of menace. Can you do that?"

Piers looked at the picture and hoped she was going to put his fee up. "Not easy when you're mostly naked," he remarked. "Nakedness in itself implies vulnerability."

"Oh, God," Annette groaned. "A clothes horse with brains. I don't need one of those. Kathy, tell me, does that look imply vulnerability to you?"

She looked a bit harder at the drawing. "I think you're selling every red-blooded woman's fantasy."

"Good. That's the idea. It's just a pity it'll be sold to bored housewives trying to spice up their overpaid and probably overweight husbands. But, OK, take your point. Must admit when I sketched this one out I hadn't met your tattoo and it would be a shame to lose it under the strapping. I'll work on it."

Piers just shook his head as though he didn't quite believe this was all happening, and Kathy could sympathise with that. He happened to look towards the coffee jar and noticed something.

"Where is it?" he asked Kathy a bit sharply.

"Where's what?" she replied innocently. She looked in the same direction. "What?"

He was starting to sound annoyed. "I put a photo up there and now it's moved. Where is it?"

Annette cut in. "Sorry, that was me. I knocked it with my cuff when I was getting the jar down." She showed it to him. "Is that your wife?"

"First wife," he said rather tersely, obviously trying to be polite to the guest, and physically turned away from the image.

Kathy put a consoling hand on his arm. She hadn't noticed the photo on the shelf so she guessed it had been turned face to the wall. "May I?" she asked gently and he didn't say she couldn't. "That's Chantal," she explained quietly to Annette. "She died of cancer just over a year ago."

Annette saw she had touched a raw wound which she couldn't understand as, so far as she knew from Danny, Piers had been married to someone called Sarah for nearly two years so there was something about the dates that didn't add up. She silently handed the photo to Kathy who took one look at it and didn't know what to say. Piers and Chantal were standing cuddled together, her back was to the camera and her arms were round his neck. He was holding her very close with his pale arms folded across the dark skin of her back and the contrast was dramatic. She was tall and slim, and Kathy could see from the angle of Piers' shoulders that he didn't have the tattoo in those days which looked odd. Their faces were touching and they seemed to be dancing barefoot although there were no other people in the background, just a sun-drenched shoreline. It was beautiful and intimate and Kathy felt the tears sting the back of her eyes as she finally understood the words of the poem Piers had written for the memorial.

"It's not as pornographic as it looks," Piers explained now he had got his emotions under control. "I didn't have a shirt on but she actually had one of those backless tops on with a neckband but you can't see it under her hair. We'd got married that morning and then after the party one of our friends asked if he could take some photos that weren't the official ones. It was the only one that survived the bonfire she had during our divorce. Her brother came across it when he was clearing out her flat. God knows why she kept it."

"Where were you?" Annette asked curiously.

"South Africa. There are some penguins in the background if you look hard enough. We got married on an RAF station and had to be careful where we took the photos because of their apartheid laws."

"It looks so sweet and innocent," Kathy couldn't help remarking. She picked up something in the silence and looked at Piers. "Sorry, have I said something I shouldn't?"

He smiled then but his eyes were clouded with a deep sadness of memory. "We were. We'd only got married that morning and still had the wedding night to go." He saw the way two incredulous women were looking at him and the sadness was replaced with something much lighter. "What? It was the fifties and we were in the military. We'd have been dishonourably discharged if we'd behaved the way you all do these days."

Kathy thought of that confident man striding down the runway last night and beguiling the fashion media, then looked at the two innocents dancing on the beach in a sun-soaked Africa. "Shall we look at some fashion photos?" she asked before it all got too involved and emotional, and got up to refill her coffee cup.

In the afternoon Kathy and Piers went back to Suffolk and she only knew how unsettled Piers was as he agreed she could drive the Land Rover but he didn't seem overly unhappy to have been reminded of his first wedding. Just rather quiet. He looked out of the side window in silence until they were north of Colchester.

He sighed just once. "I suppose it makes the most sense to drop in on Sarah while we're almost passing the door," he said as though he didn't want to go.

"Yes, it would really. Did you ever hear any more from Alison?"

"No," he replied shortly. "I rang her back after you'd given me her message but I got a definite brush-off. She didn't quite tell me to butt out as she was the father now but it was in the sub-text."

"So for all we know Sarah's had the babies?"

"I'd guess not. She's stroppy enough to tell that cow to ring me again after the birth."

"Does their relationship bother you?"

"In more ways than you could imagine. What do you mean exactly?"

Kathy knew she had to tell him the truth. "It's just some of the things Sarah says. They remind me too much of what I used to say to justify my relationship with my ex."

He knew what she meant. "You think Alison's abusing her?"

Kathy back-pedalled a bit. "That's a very strong word. I don't know. Can't put my finger on it. but there's no doubting Alison is the one in charge. What do you think? You know the pair of them much better than I do."

"I think they have a very odd relationship. I don't have a problem with gays, men or women, don't even care if people are bi but I'm thinking like you. There's something wrong with that relationship but I can't work it out. If I try to talk to Sarah she just gets defensive and the one time I tried to say anything to Alison she totally lost it and yelled at me for being a 'bloody homophobe' and said if I didn't take that back she'd get a court order banning me from ever seeing the kids again."

Kathy was appalled. "Can she do that?"

"Like to see her bloody try."

"What are you going to do?"

"At the moment? Much as I don't like it, nothing. I've seen Sarah naked enough times to know there aren't any bruises on her so there's nothing physically violent going on. Can't pick up any evidence of anything more psychological. And, know this sounds hard, but not sure Sarah would side with me if Alison carried out the threat of the court order. That woman is devious enough to cut and bruise herself then tell the police that I'd done it."

Kathy swung the Land Rover into a handy layby and stopped. "Whoa. Hang on. What?"

Piers looked at her properly then. "Can I be brutally honest with you?"

"Of course. I promise not to be offended."

"Right, well. You are," he sighed again. "No, I'm going to say this. You are probably one of the most beautiful women I know. You must have had the men sniffing round you for most of your adult life and I'd like to think that if you told them to back off then they respected you enough to do that and went off after someone else."

Kathy thought guiltily that she hadn't told many of them to back off but she didn't want to tarnish her reputation right at that moment. "OK, well, kind of. What's your point?" she asked gently.

"My point is… Like you, I get the sniffers. Like you, I tell them to piss off. First I had Chantal, then I didn't want anyone at all after I'd let that other bitch destroy my marriage and then Sarah turned up. But some of those I told to piss off didn't like it. I have no idea why, I tried to be nice about it. And quite a few of them got vindictive and made accusations against me. I've had to learn over the years that I must never be alone with people I don't trust. Sadly of both sexes but particularly women. And because of the past accusations I have to be very, very careful. If Alison rips her clothes and cuts herself then goes rushing off to the police and tells them I did it, they will easily find out that I have a past littered with such things. So how long have I got before one police force or another decides there can't be that many accusations without there being some truth in it?"

Kathy sat at the wheel of the car and watched the A12 traffic whizzing past. She felt incredibly flattered that this most stunning of men had called her beautiful but she couldn't deny her own vanity had been fed by the attentions of others until Richard had mentally crushed her and then physically attacked her at the end, leaving her self-confidence and sense of self-worth destroyed. But none of her rejected admirers had ever done to her the things Piers was saying had been done to him. It was all too easy, she supposed, for a slighted woman to accuse the man who had rejected her hoping for some kind of revenge. As Marianne had done to her Russian lover when she had been sixteen.

"I don't know what to say," she admitted after a long silence. "I feel I owe you a huge apology on behalf of my sex. I can't believe anyone would do that. Well, yes I can, but it's horrible. I mean it's not as though you're the kind of bloke who puts it about and carves notches on the bedpost is it? Sorry, I'm talking in clichés. You don't deserve that. Nobody does. But I have to be honest with you too. You are a hell of a flirt when you get going so I can see why some people got hopeful."

He looked down for a few moments then his eyes briefly searched her face before he spoke again. "Do you remember that time you sat on the sofa and told me the worst thing that had happened in your life?"

"Yes," Kathy replied. "I know I need to tell Jean-Guy but…"

Piers interrupted her, still speaking quietly, hesitantly. "Well, I suppose I owe you the courtesy of telling you about one of the worst times in my life. I've told you I had an affair. And how that finally broke up my marriage. Well," he paused again. "Well, after I'd ended the affair with her, the conniving little bitch went to the police and said I'd raped her."

Kathy wasn't sure what to say. His very use of the words brought memories washing to the surface of her mind and for one frightening moment she thought she was going to be sick. She certainly gagged and she knew he had seen her.

"I'm sorry," he said softly. "I know for you it was real. I was never going to tell you."

Kathy swallowed the rising vomit but her voice was colder than she had intended. "So why now?"

"Because it's the kind of thing Alison will do. She'll tell it to you and Sarah first hoping one of you will go to the police with her to give her lies more credence. I know Sarah won't believe her for one minute but for you, well, you know about it from what you went through." He didn't try to touch her. "But, please, believe me, I didn't. She was hurt and angry and lashed out at me in the only way she could think of. But unlike nearly all the other allegations, this one got serious. I was arrested and suspended from my job. The police held me in custody. Chantal walked out on me the day after the police released me. She told me it was what I deserved and she left." He stopped and was clearly battling with some very painful memories.

Kathy could tell that this time he wasn't lying to her. Falsely accused by a woman who had beguiled him into an affair and then abandoned by the wife he had loved, his life had been torn apart in a way he couldn't have imagined. Her heart went out to him and she put her hand over his as he sat so perfectly still next to her. "Were you charged?" she asked gently.

He shook his head. "No. I was lucky in a way that she didn't know the flight I was on had been delayed so she said I'd done it to her at a time when I was going through post-flight checks with my captain and flight engineer and they made statements saying I was with them at the time. We'd had a cow of a flight and went to the bar for an hour or so before we all went home. So she said maybe it was the next day. That had been a day off between flights for me, so the police talked to Chantal and she had to tell them that I'd been with her all day. When my accuser tried a third date the police got a bit suspicious and in the end I was released without charge. But my name is probably still on police records. And if Alison says the same thing then I don't like to think of the consequences." He looked down at her hand but didn't move his own from under hers. "Why would she do that? I tried to be nice about it."

She couldn't tell him. Could not tell this beautiful, broken man that with looks like his it was inevitable women would expect him to be some kind of stud who would help them to live out their fantasies. Men who looked like he did weren't expected to be devoted, faithful husbands and fathers who genuinely didn't want to shop around. She gently squeezed his hand and gave him her nicest smile.

"Let's keep it simple for now shall we and just say there are some mean and horrible people in the world. But if any of them dares to even think about doing anything like that to you ever again then send them to me and I will not only tell them that you are one of the nicest human beings I know, but I will also beat seven bells out of them on your behalf."

To her relief he sounded relieved and amused at the same time. "But then you'll get accused too."

"Never," she laughed. "I'm five foot nothing of pathetic woman. Who'd ever believe that of me? So there you go, I'm now officially your bodyguard."

"I shall sleep safer in my bed for that," he assured her and gave her a kiss on the cheek. "Thank you. I still don't know how you can condense all my neuroses into six words of common sense." He paused for a moment. "I'm sorry. Perhaps I shouldn't have said anything."

"No," she said truthfully. "I'm glad you felt you could. I'm guessing you don't want it made common knowledge?"

"Not in the slightest." He looked away from her for a moment, then took a sharp breath and got control. "Right, do you want to go and see Sarah?"

"Yes," she said firmly, realising the conversation had moved on. "For one thing you're probably worried silly about her and for another at least I'll be on full bodyguard duty if Alison is with her."

"True. When did you last see Sarah?"

"Oh, quite a while ago now. Why?"

"She's, um, expecting quins and, not sure how to put this. Oh hell, she's the size of a small barrage balloon and very conscious of it."

Kathy thought again just how adorable this man was to be so concerned about his very pregnant wife's feelings that he was warning her not to be too surprised when she saw her. She couldn't believe anyone could ever be so spiteful they would have accused him of the worst of crimes. "I will be as discreet as ... whatever is discreet." She reached across and gave him a soft kiss on the cheek before starting the engine and pulling out into the traffic on the A12.

In spite of Piers' warning to her, Kathy was shocked to see the size of a woman very close to giving birth to quins. She felt so sorry for Sarah who was sitting half propped up on her bed wearing just a loose cotton nightgown and, Kathy hated to admit to herself, bearing more than a passing resemblance to the metaphorical beached whale. To Kathy's unspoken relief there was no sign of Alison but she knew she had to ask.

"Oh, she'll be along later I expect," Sarah replied and tried to get more comfortable. "She's been along every day so far but it's usually easier for her to come in the evenings as that's when Mum can look after the girls for an hour or so as she's got some cover in the shop. Anyway, it's lovely to see you both but you do look very tired. What have you been up to? I've been stuck in here so long I don't even know if it's raining."

The other two couldn't quite see the logic of that but with Sarah there often wasn't any logic. Piers sat in one of the chairs beside her bed and gave her a gentle kiss.

"Daft woman," he told her fondly.

"Well, I know what I mean."

Kathy had to smile at those two exchanging their quiet nothings and then Sarah cupped Piers' face in her hands and had a loving snog with the man who had got her into this state in the first place and she still loved him madly.

"We've brought you some photos to look at," Kathy offered. "From the fashion shoot in Stockholm as well as me and Danny in the park. To say nothing of this one on the runway last night."

"Oh, yes," Sarah remembered. "I really wish I could have seen that. Oh well, maybe next time. Come on then, let's see." She winced and put a hand on her belly. "Sorry. There's at least one footballer in there," she told them. "Or maybe they're just having a party. Five good strong heartbeats at the last count so the consultant is now quite hopeful it'll be a successful birth for all of them."

Sarah was the only patient in a tiny side ward in the maternity unit so Kathy pulled up a second chair on the other side of the bed and handed the first album to Sarah so she could rest it on her bump and start to look at the photos. "Oh, that's your purple coat," she exclaimed. "You never told me it's a Viola design. Mum said she thought it was when she first saw you in it but didn't like to ask in case you'd spent a lot of money on it. She says that it really is one of the top English fashion houses now but the lady in charge will use all sorts of odd people to be her models."

"Like me, you mean?" Piers asked amusedly.

"Well, yes. I mean you've got a job anyway and you're way older than a normal model."

He gave her one of his odd looks. "Thanks for reminding me. Just turn on a few pages and you'll see the coat in green. And the coat was a gift from Annette. It didn't cost me anything."

"I think you'll look better in green," Sarah agreed without passing any comment on the gift of the coat, and flicked through the book. "Oh my God!" she shrieked when she got to the photo of her husband at the end of the runway with his face obscured by the make-up and his eyes half-hidden by that fringe of hair. But he had undone the coat and the panther tattoo was on show so she knew it was him.

The other two thought that was quite an extreme reaction but it was rather funny.

Sarah gasped a bit and clutched her side. "Please," she panted to Kathy, "push the red button for me."

Within five minutes, Kathy was on her own in the single ward and trying to imagine how Piers was coping as he had now found himself in exactly the place he had sworn he would never be. With his wife while she gave birth to quins. She had no doubt that Sarah would be fine with it all and Kathy spent a few amusing moments trying to decide if the reluctant father would either faint or be sick in the delivery room. Although she hoped for Sarah's sake that he would be a lot more use than that. With nothing else to do, she sat back in the chair and looked through the photos again and wondered if she dare stray in search of a cup of tea. It seemed like an age and yet no time at all before Piers came to join her. His smile told her all had gone well and she gave him a hug.

"All five landed safely?" she checked, just in case.

"Yup, all five. The midwives and doctor couldn't believe just how fit and healthy they all look."

"So, tell me. Did you faint or throw up?"

"Be proud of me. Neither." He caught her knowing smile. "OK, I'll admit it. It was nowhere near as bad as I thought it was going to be."

"Ah-ha! Go on, say it. You're really glad you were there with her."

"Oh, go on then. Wasn't too sure when they put a gown and a pair of gloves on me and kept handing me these bloody bundles to hold. And I do mean that literally. But with five of the little buggers coming out they ran out of people to hang on to them."

Kathy gave him another hug, delighted to hear the love in his voice. "You are so adorable, do you know that?"

"You're as daft as the other one," he told her and unhooked her arms from behind his back. "Anyway, Sarah's just being tidied up a bit and she's sent me to ask you if you'd like to meet the quins? They're not looking their best but they have only just been hauled out."

"You put it so nicely," Kathy told him. "Yes, I would love to meet your children. Thank you."

She was a bit embarrassed to find the babies were all in wheeled cots next to their mother who was still being attended to by the medical staff but Sarah really didn't seem to mind one bit.

"Are they in order?" Kathy asked and kept her attention on the cots rather than the mother for now.

"Yes," Piers told her as the staff said they could have a few minutes alone together. He arranged the blankets over his wife to give her a bit more modesty and explained to Kathy. "Left to right. Girl first, then three boys and the second girl last. And my foolish wife said I could name them as I got over-ruled on the last lot. So, phonetically in order you have Ethneh, Akan, Eearlah, Kailaun and Doonlee. Now look at the labels on the cots and see the spelling."

Kathy looked and had to smile. There, lined up in the order of the minutes that separated them, were Eithne Francesca, Eachann Guy, Iarlaith Robert, Caolan Thomas and Dunlaith Kathleen. "Trust you. Nobody will ever be able to spell them."

"Or pronounce them," he laughed and helped Sarah to get settled and comfortable in the wheelchair a nurse had left for her as the newly-delivered mother was too sore from the operation to walk anywhere. "Right, Piglet, we now have the logistical problem of getting one mother and five babies back to the ward. Then I'm going to give the mother-in-law a ring before we leave and we'll probably pass Alison on the A12."

Kathy and Sarah realised that was his way of saying he didn't want to be there when Alison arrived and started crowing over the babies as though she had been somehow physically responsible for them.

"Tell you what," Sarah said to him. "Don't ring her just yet. Why don't you two come back to the ward with me for a while and we can all have a bit of a rest. The nurses have promised to bring me some tea and toast anyway and I'm sure they can find some for you too."

"Are you sure you want me there?" Kathy checked, feeling oddly proud to have been included in this little family.

"Oh, yes," Sarah assured her. "This one is in far too much of a state to be any use. I mean, he's supposed to be the clever one and it hasn't occurred to him yet that if he rings the bell someone will come and help me and the babies."

Kathy caught the new mother's smile and her heart warmed to her. "True. Put him in the cockpit of Concorde with an engine fire, a blizzard and a bird strike and he wouldn't turn a hair. Stick him in a birthing suite with his babies and he turns into a useless heap of mush."

"I know," Sarah said fondly. "I think that's why I love him so much."

Piers leaned over her in the chair and they exchanged a few short kisses. "Love you too," he told her. "Even if you did just call me a heap of mush."

"Actually, that was me," Kathy pointed out.

"You're right," he agreed. "I think I have just turned to a heap of mush. Oh well, they train us to deal with engine fires and bird strikes. Nobody trains you to deal with this."

Kathy and Piers were still with Sarah when Alison turned up in the late afternoon and when she arrived in the doorway to realise there were eight people in the room she just stopped dead and stared.

"Oh my God," she intoned. "Why the hell didn't anyone ring me?"

"We were going to," Sarah protested. "But we all got chatting and, oh I don't know. I didn't realise it was so late. You two had better be on your way or you'll have the Professor and Jean-Guy thinking you've got lost."

The two visitors looked at each other and Piers finally thought to check his watch. "Oh, shit," he said. "We'd better run for it before they call out the Coastguard. One or both of us will look in tomorrow." In a pre-emptive strike he gave his wife a kiss on the lips and her partner a kiss on the cheek as he passed her in the doorway. "Congratulations," he said to Alison without a hint of mockery in his voice. "Take good care of them."

"Oh, I will," she said and to the surprise of the others gave him a spontaneous hug. "Thank you. I'll be round with dairy-free cake tomorrow."

Kathy didn't speak until they had driven away in the Land Rover this time with Piers behind the wheel. "That was very magnanimous of you."

"Not really. It was meant as a warning."

"I think she missed the point."

"Trust me, she knew exactly what I meant. So I don't think we need to worry about her, at least for a while."

The Prof hadn't quite called out the Coastguard but he and Jean-Guy were waiting anxiously in the sitting room when the other two arrived in the house. They were delighted to learn that Sarah was safely delivered of her babies and forgave Kathy and Piers for being so engrossed they had totally lost track of time.

After a quick, late meal for the two arrivals, Piers went into the hall to ring his mother-in-law to give her the news. Kathy really wanted to know if Piers had known her full name was the Kathleen of her great-aunt and not the Katherine everyone assumed or whether it was a coincidence and she was flattering herself his youngest child had been named in her honour.

While Piers was still on the phone, Kathy and Audrey went into the sitting room where Jean-Guy was not playing his cello for once but was quietly looking through Annette's photographs. He glanced up and watched as Kathy came into the room but thought she seemed a bit lost and confused somehow. "Good photos," he complimented her. "It is hard to recognise Piers under all that make up."

"That's the idea," she replied vaguely, still trying to get her thoughts in order. She saw he was looking at the photos of her and Danny in the park and it made her feel a bit odd to realise her current lover was looking at photos of her with one of her exes. A tiny voice whispered in her ear that maybe he would turn the page and would look at photos of her future lover and it frightened her. "Can I talk to you?" she asked him before she changed her mind.

"Always," he assured her as she sat next to him on the sofa. He closed the photo album and realised something had upset her so deeply she was almost trembling in his arms. "What is it?" he asked anxiously. "Just tell me. In any words you can think of. We will make sense of it at the end."

"Piers told me something in the car on the way home," she began and saw the look in his eyes. "Oh, no, not what you're thinking at all. Something far more shocking. But he asked me not to tell anyone. Only I want you to know. I should probably ask him before I tell you. But you told him about me and my ex. Oh, help. I don't know what to do."

Jean-Guy was consoled that the other man hadn't tried to woo her away from him. "Tell me," he invited gently. "He need never know you spoke his secrets but if it is so bad, he may feel better knowing we all know. Secrets can be so hard to keep sometimes."

So she told him exactly what Piers had said to her in the car, how she could see how much it still hurt him and how he was so afraid it would come back to him if Alison ever decided she wanted to accuse him of something similar too.

Jean-Guy saw Piers' confession from a different point of view and he thought about it for a while. "I am not handsome as Piers is," he reassured her and put a hand on her lips to silence her. "No, don't try to tell me I am, I am not going to be fooled by that, even if it is nice of you to try to say so. Looks like his are very rare and he makes people fall in love with him just to see him. No, not fall in love but they desire him. Maybe some men would like that and take advantage of it, I don't know why he doesn't but he has his reasons. No, what I am trying to say to you, without boasting I hope, is that once I had a reputation as a cellist and I too had the people who flattered me and complimented me and, yes even asked me to take them to bed." He paused. "Maybe I was not as restrained as Piers and maybe I took up some of the offers but that was in another life. Yes, I hope I still have a reputation as a cellist and, yes, maybe there will still be some people in our world who will say nice things to me in the hope I will help them in their careers. But that is all over for me now. I have chosen you, I am lucky that you have chosen me too, and knowing I have you means I am now deaf to those words people say to me. So I can see why Piers has still these problems. He is so much older than me and still has such looks he can turn heads in the street. He can't help it. I used to wish I was that handsome but now he has made me glad I'm not. Does that help you to understand?"

Kathy looked up into his dark eyes and gave him a soft kiss. "Yes, I think so. Funny isn't it, we all like to believe that beauty is the answer to everything, but it's really not."

Jean-Guy looked at the woman in his arms and didn't know how she could not see her own beauty. It filled his heart with love and joy that she had chosen him every time he looked at her. "Play some music," he advised her softly. "It will help you to get your thoughts into order. And please don't worry about Piers. Maybe a long time ago he was guarded by Chantal but he has us and Sarah now and we won't let anything like that happen to him ever again."

Kathy was glad she had told him and she rather liked the idea of the three of them looking out for the predators who desired the beautiful man who didn't want them. She took Jean-Guy's advice and quietly played some Bach Partitas until her tired mind settled down and she smiled at the man on the sofa who was looking at the photos again.

"Hey, you," she said softly and he looked up. "I think it's time for bed."

Jean-Guy closed the album of photos. "Yes," he agreed. "I think it is."

Edward Elgar – *Concerto for cello and orchestra in E minor, Op. 85*

Piers went to visit his wife and quins the next morning, remembering Alison was more likely to be there in the afternoon, and the others were quite surprised when he wasn't back by lunch time. They had just finished their meal when Alison arrived at the back door and politely knocked before coming in.

"I've brought the cake," she said and put a foil-wrapped bundle on the table.

"Well, thank you," Kathy said and looked hard at the other woman. "What's wrong? Another row with Piers?"

"Let me get you some coffee or something," Jean-Guy offered and got to his feet. "It won't be as nice as yours but you look in need of something."

Alison sat at the table and gave Jean-Guy a smile of gratitude. "Thanks. I'd just finished making the cake when the hospital rang to say there's a problem with one of the babies and they asked me not to visit today."

The others with her thought that was a bit unusual as she had been with Sarah all through the pregnancy and had been on the notes as the preferred birthing partner again.

"A serious problem?" the Prof asked as all three remembered how Piers had told them that they were statistically likely to lose at least two of them.

"I don't know," Alison admitted. "I mean even Piers wouldn't be so unkind he told them not to tell me anything, would he?"

"Unlikely," the Prof assured her and tried to believe it. "I would guess that the usual administrative wheels are in motion and as they have both parents at the hospital it didn't occur to them that anyone else would need to know. So what do we all do now?"

"We wait," Alison said heavily.

To the profound relief of the four of them the phone rang before Alison had finished her coffee and the Prof, as the nearest, answered it.

"Oh, hullo, Piers. Yes, she's with us.... Oh. Oh that is good news. OK, I'll pass it on. Are you coming home tonight? ... Yes. Hang on a second." He held the receiver out to Alison. "Piers," he said rather unnecessarily. "Wants to talk to you."

"Me?" she said in surprise. "He can't stand the sight of me." Alison took the phone rather as though it might sting her and the other three discreetly left the kitchen and went into the sitting room.

"Why would he talk to her?" Kathy asked. "I mean, she's right. He can't stand her. And it's mutual."

"Yes it is," Jean-Guy agreed, "But Alison is Sarah's life partner if that's how you want to put it and in some ways, in many ways, he feels that he is the intruder in that relationship. He doesn't like it but for Sarah's sake he tolerates it."

Kathy sat in the armchair and thoughtfully got on with some knitting. "Do you think he feels the same about our relationship? That he's the spare part to us too and doesn't really belong anywhere?" Nobody answered her question although she hadn't meant it to be rhetorical. "Anyway," she remembered. "What was his good news?"

The Prof smiled. "The problem was with Dunlaith. Her body temperature kept dropping and they didn't know why. They wrapped her and monitored her but her core temperature remained very low." He could guess what was going through Kathy's mind. "Yes, they thought to check the parents as they had both of them there and it seems the babies' father also has an abnormally low core body temperature. But it is not bad news for Dunlaith. They said she is anaemic which is what has caused it in her so she is being treated. And that was all Piers would tell me but he had that sound in his voice that means he is unhappy about something. But he reassured me at least twice that Dunlaith will be absolutely fine. And the other four apparently are fit and healthy and eating enough for a small army."

"Poor Dunlaith," Kathy sympathised. "Oh, well, I'm sure he'll tell us all about it when he gets back. Did he say when that will be?"

"Um, no. He said he is going straight to London as he is back at work in a couple of days." The Prof paused as Alison arrived in the doorway.

"Hi," she said vaguely. "Thanks for the coffee and sympathy. I'd better be off now as Piers has to go to London and Sarah's mum has got cover in the shop so I can go now and she can mind the triplets."

"And Dunlaith really is OK?" Kathy checked.

Alison smiled. "Yes, she'll be fine. It was just a bit of a panic and it didn't help that they thought it might be something more serious hence the check on the parents. But once I'd explained I used to be a nurse before I became a baker Piers got a bit more technical. Basically it's a touch of anaemia. They don't know why Piers' core temperature is so low and he wasn't going to tell them once he knew the kid was OK."

The other three trusted the former nurse to know not to be worried about a slightly anaemic baby but they could tell something wasn't adding up.

"So is Piers anaemic too?" The Prof asked. "I would be surprised as he has been eating very well recently."

"I have no idea. I did ask as politely as I could and I'm not going to repeat what he said in reply. Based on what

Sarah's told me I have some ideas but, not for me to speculate."

"Please speculate," Kathy requested. "Or I at least will be worried silly."

Alison sighed. "OK, but this is just my opinion, alright? Piers has let a few things slip to Sarah and she's asked me my opinion in case it was something she needed to make him go and see a doctor about. To put it bluntly, he was abused pretty much from birth and he spent most of the first fifteen years of his life in a state of advanced malnourishment, borderline starvation. Coupled with the fact his mother seems virtually to have kept him outside, especially if it was wet or cold which it often is in western Ireland, until the kid passed out from hypothermia. So put those two factors together and his brain got so screwed up trying to regulate his body temperature it's kind of settled for accepting a few degrees lower than most people are."

"But he's fit and healthy now?" Kathy checked.

"Oh, yes, as much as he can be what with that and his damaged joints. He won't come flat out and say anything but every so often he lets Sarah have a glimpse of the truth and I can tell that under that handsome exterior he's as hard as nails."

The Prof didn't want this conversation to continue. He knew far more than the others did about the man who had just become a father of quins and he also knew what Kathy's keen sense of curiosity was like. "Thank you, Alison, for your common sense. I think we will all worry a little less now."

After the fuss over Dunlaith, nobody was surprised that Sarah was told she would be in hospital for at least a month while the medical staff kept a very close eye on her as well as the babies. She didn't mind. Her parents and Alison were quite adept at coping with the triplets and it gave her time to get used to the idea that there were now eight children in her life whereas only two years ago there hadn't been any and she had given up hope. Then a handsome Concorde pilot had walked into her shop and somehow everything had turned out just the way her grandmother had said it would. Sarah had never really worried about the fact she was attracted equally to women as to men. She had known Alison a long time and didn't even mind the way the other woman treated her sometimes. In a way, she had thought Piers would be the same; that he would outwardly tell her she was his equal, that her opinions mattered and listen to her for a while. Then remind her she had been the dunce in her class at school, she had never had to do a proper day's work in her life and she had never had to worry about anything as she knew that one day she would inherit the shop which would be worth a lot of money when she sold it. Piers had never done any of that. He had always told her that she wasn't stupid but just needed her own time to process the information. He would ask her opinion on things and if he didn't agree he wouldn't yell at her and tell her she didn't know what she was talking about but he would ask her gentle questions until he understood why she had that opinion but he never told her she was wrong. She liked the way Piers treated her. He stood back from her work in the shop, sympathised when she had had a hard day and had never, ever mentioned selling the shop when it was hers. He wasn't perfect, she knew. Sometimes he got a bit scratchy with her but he would never let it escalate into an argument as Alison did. He would just smile and tell her they had to agree to differ. Or sometimes he would go and sit in the garden for a few minutes until he had recovered his good mood. And for that, she loved him. She had come to love him far more than she realised she had ever loved Alison but she didn't know how to get out of that relationship. Most of the time she was perfectly happy with Alison. But, just sometimes, she wondered.

The quins stayed in hospital long enough to have their six-week check and then, with no reason to keep such a healthy mother and babies with them any longer, the medical team reluctantly had to say goodbye to the little family and let them go home. They had all got quite fond of the infants whose father flitted in and out to visit as and when he could working away from home so much, and the grandparents came quite regularly. The medical staff weren't too sure of the relationship between the mother of the quins and the woman who visited her every day, unless the father was there, but Sarah assured them that Alison was an old friend. It was one of the junior doctors who spoke to a social worker about it and asked if perhaps they could look into things a bit. The social worker had a heavy case load but she agreed that she would have a catch-up with Sarah at some point. Then somehow the papers got filed, more cases piled in and the concerns of a junior doctor got lost in the workload of a stressed social worker.

By the time the quins came home towards the end of March, Jean-Guy was monopolising Piers at the piano to polish up the pieces he was playing in New York. Then the end of March arrived and almost before he and Kathy were ready they were in the Aston Martin and Piers was cursing the traffic on the M4 as they went to Heathrow to catch the morning Concorde to New York.

Jean-Guy had asked if he and Kathy could travel on Concorde expecting if not to be laughed at, then politely declined, but the New York Philharmonic administrators hadn't batted an eyelid. They knew how much they were charging for tickets to the Czech cellist's concerts and a contribution towards a couple of round trips on Concorde was just a drop in the financial ocean. And it also meant he would arrive in their city much more refreshed than if he had come long-haul. In a way they didn't blame him wanting to travel on the supersonic plane and it would make a more spectacular arrival anyway which would keep the voracious press happy.

Piers dropped Kathy and Jean-Guy off at the departures area then went to park the Aston in the staff car park telling them that he would try to see them briefly before take-off but at least one of them was to make sure they visited the flight deck during the flight.

Kathy and Jean-Guy soon found out that travelling on Concorde was quite a different experience from being an 'ordinary' passenger. Check-in was expedited and they were taken to the Concorde lounge where the passengers for the morning flight were already gathering and if Kathy had thought Jean-Guy was slightly famous, he was nothing compared with some of the people who were in the room with them.

All the passengers for that morning's flight were enjoying the refreshments on offer when the air crew came through the lounge having prepared for the flight so they could welcome the passengers to the aeroplane they could see was waiting for them.

Piers took a moment to stop with the two he had brought to the airport that morning. "Don't eat all the biscuits," he told them cheerfully. "You'll be fed a banquet on board."

Kathy couldn't help thinking how being in his home environment suited him. The first officer and the flight engineer had also stopped for a brief word with some of the passengers but it was obvious to her eyes that most of them, especially the women, really wanted to get the chance to talk to the dashing captain and it rather appealed to her sense of humour that he had come straight across to talk to them and seemed quite oblivious to the room full of rich and famous people.

"No wonder you don't eat at home," she told him and pretended to straighten his already perfect tie. "If you ate like this every time you flew, you'd be fat as a barrel."

"Cheeky cow," he said fondly and kissed her on the cheek. "See you the other end."

She watched him join the rest of the crew and they all went to make their final preparations for the morning flight. "Now he makes sense," she said half to herself.

Jean-Guy knew exactly what she meant but didn't like to admit it. "Whole new world," was all he said.

Kathy was a bit disappointed that the inside of the celebrated aeroplane seemed quite small but she and Jean-Guy settled in their seats and looked round finding it odd to think that the man they knew so well was sitting the other side of that closed door at the front of the plane quietly doing his job. It made them realise just what a responsibility it was to be captain of such a craft now filling up with some very well-known people.

The captain gave the welcome announcement over the PA system with the names of the morning flight crew, assuring the passengers all three of them looked forward to welcoming some of them to the flight deck. In the meantime they were invited to sit back and be prepared for a rather noisy take-off. He sounded so calm about it to a madly excited Kathy that she had to remind herself that for him it was just his job. By the time the captain had finished speaking, Concorde was taxiing along to the runway and Jean-Guy sitting by the window could see that the people on the ground had all stopped what they were doing just to watch the beautiful aeroplane going about her business on a rather unremarkable drab March morning. He thought it was very gracious of the other air traffic to let Concorde jump the take-off queue until he remembered that the other planes would have been told to do that as Concorde burned a lot of fuel just trundling along the ground. But it made him feel slightly important which surprised him.

Kathy was looking across him to see what was going on and it came as quite an exciting surprise when the third and fourth engines were fired up to join the two taxiing engines and they felt the full power of the plane as it paused at the end of the runway like a greyhound straining in the trap. Now they understood why Piers had liked driving a Ferrari. Concorde thundered down the runway with an ear-splitting roar and they knew the exhilaration of hitting over two hundred miles an hour in just a few seconds. Then they soared into the sky and, just as the captain had explained, banked quite sharply to the right and the display at the front of the cabin told them they were already at 800 feet. It made Kathy think of the time she had looked above the raven on her balcony and heard this plane telling her to run. The first officer of the flight came over the PA system to explain that in another thirty miles they would be going supersonic and the passengers should expect to feel a couple of slight pushes. She wasn't quite sure what the 'pushes' were supposed to feel like but she felt the power of the acceleration in her soul as well as her body and it wasn't until Jean-Guy said "Ow!" rather loudly next to her that she realised she had been gripping his hand so tightly his skin had gone quite white. She gave him an apologetic grin and let go of his hand, watching the display at the front of the cabin that looked as though it was never going to stop. The height indicator was still rising as the cabin crew started serving the food but Kathy was too thrilled to eat.

A very pleasant young flight attendant called Henry quite understood when she said she wasn't hungry and he quietly spoke through the intercom to the flight deck. He returned to Kathy with a broad smile on his face.

"Captain B's compliments, Miss. He says would you like to visit the flight deck now and then maybe you'll calm down enough to eat breakfast."

Kathy returned the smile and got to her feet. "Thank you," she said politely. "But I have already had breakfast."

"Come on," Henry said. "I'm afraid you won't get long as there are a lot of people on this flight wanting to visit." He gave her a slightly unprofessional wink. "There always are when we've got this particular captain on board." He led her along a narrow corridor beyond the passenger cabin and showed her to a seat at the back of the flight deck. Piers was sitting immediately in front of her with a grey-haired man on his right. A third man was occupied with an impressive panel of instruments and he didn't even seem to notice she had been parked in the spare seat behind him. It was surprisingly cool in the air-conditioned cockpit and she saw the flight crew weren't wearing the jackets they had had on when walking through the passenger lounge but the first officer and the flight engineer looked smart in short sleeves while Piers had rolled up the sleeves of a long-sleeved shirt which suited him so much more. It had also been quite a low doorway into the cockpit which went a long way towards explaining Piers' back problems.

"You can leave the door open," the man at the instrument panel said vaguely to Henry. "It'll save you all from roasting back there."

"Thanks, guys," Henry said then turned his attention to the passenger in the jump seat. "Just sit yourself there and don't touch anything," he told her then left the cockpit to resume his cabin duties.

"And especially don't touch the crew," said the grey-haired man. "Hi, I'm Dacre." He twisted round in his seat so they could exchange an awkward handshake.

Kathy was pleased to be able to put a face to the name and thought it was a nice, friendly face too. Not sure how to express what she really wanted to say, she settled for a non-committal, "Oh, nice to meet you. Piers has told us about you being his emergency backup."

Dacre smiled, and silently blessed her for her discretion. "He still owes me a bottle of Scotch."

Piers finished the radio conversation he had been having. "Piglet, welcome to my world. See you've met Dacre and this is Mick, best flight engineer in the business."

"You're not the pilot I met in Amsterdam," Kathy said to Dacre as Mick gave her a distracted wave and made some adjustments to his controls. "He said something about an unpronounceable place in Greenland then didn't finish the story."

Dacre was clearly amused. "That would have been Jake Hollander. We call him Dutchman which isn't very original but he does fly. Sadly I missed that one as it wasn't one of my flights. Heard about it though. Gone down in airline history, if not aviation history. You need to get Mick to tell you the story; he tells it like something out of a Hollywood movie."

Mick fairly shouted with laughter. "Disaster movie if not downright horror. The boss over there doesn't talk about it, but it's one that nobody who was there will forget in a hurry."

Piers looked slightly annoyed as the radio claimed his attention again. "This is Speedbird Concorde One," he confirmed then listened for a while before glancing at his watch. "Yes, ETA in about two hours fifteen." Another pause and a slow smile spread across his face. "Well you'll just have to go a bit faster, won't you? I'm not slowing down just to save your reputation." Whoever it was on the radio was definitely amusing him now. "No, you've got the bloody Tornado, you do the handbrake turn." Another pause to listen. "Oh, piss off, Uncle Tom, bored with you now."

"We just outrun your mates again?" Dacre asked cheerfully, seeing their captain had finished speaking.

"Yup, damn but they hate us." He was still looking at the sky as he explained to Kathy, "We're going just as high, just as fast and we're sitting here in our shirt sleeves drinking coffee while they sweat it out in full flying suits."

"I'd swear they listen in so they know when you're flying this bus," Dacre laughed. "Nobody else gets raced so much by the military."

"Probably. I don't know so many of them now, but that was one of my old buddies. Surprised they're letting old fossils like him still fly now he's a Group Captain."

Much as Kathy liked to listen to the men chat as they instinctively kept control of the plane hurtling a hundred people faster than the military jets could catch them, she was getting ever more curious about the untold story. "Back to Greenland?" she asked hopefully.

"Nothing to tell," Piers cut in. "We had to make an unexpected landing in a bit of snow."

"Oh, come off it, Buchanan," Mick told him. "Men aren't awarded the QGM for landing in a bit of snow." He gave Kathy a lovely lopsided grin. "Queer Gay Male."

"No it's not," Dacre laughed. "Stop winding the poor woman up. Kathy, our esteemed Captain B was awarded the Queen's Gallantry Medal for that 'landing in a bit of snow' as he will insist on putting it. Mick and Dutchman got Queen's Commendations. Shut up, Piers and let Mick tell her the story. Not only the best flight engineer in the business but the best storyteller too."

Seeing he was outnumbered, Piers just sniffed a bit and acted as though he had found something fascinating to look at outside. Mick grinned hugely and continued in his gentle Scottish lowlands accent. "We were on a normal scheduled night flight USA to Heathrow, not in this bus thank God but a relic of the past." He looked at Piers. "I'm sure you remember that old thing."

"Engraved in my worst nightmares," he confirmed. "Bloody thirteen year old VC-10. Probably doesn't mean much to you," he said to Kathy. "It was usually a good aircraft but that particular bus left the States with at least two issues flagged in its maintenance log and one crew member short as there were no more available."

Mick interrupted lightly. "I don't suppose for one minute that she cares. I'd been over the flags with the maintenance crew and we'd all agreed she'd get us home. Mind you, the hours that thing had put it, it should have been in a retirement home long before that flight. Anyway, I'd been put on with Dutchman, it was my last job before I started my Concorde training, and the boss over there got it as an on-call job even though he was supersonic when he joined us from France. But he'd still got a valid type-rating and there weren't many of us left. First time we'd flown together. Weather wasn't too bad at the time although there was a storm building up over the North Atlantic. Forecasting wasn't as good then as it is now even though it wasn't that long ago and they basically told us to stop whining and get on with it. We were past the point of no return when we heard on the radio that all flights in the area were to find a place to land as the storm was faster and worse than forecast. So we heard all these others turning back or landing and it wasn't long before we were the only poor sods in that sector still looking for a landing place. We'd thought we could make Reykjavik but, well, let's just say that wasn't looking likely. So the boss took the decision to call Narsarsuaq as we were that desperate by now, and request landing permission. My God but we were desperate even thinking of putting down in that place with mountains, volcanoes, slick ice and that's without the blizzard, total darkness and crosswinds off the Richter scale we'd got by then. But we called them up and they asked us what the hell we were doing in the air. Last they'd heard was all flights grounded so it was only the emergency crew there. But once they'd realised we were going to put down at their airport as we had no choice they got into gear and they were brilliant.

"So the boss played it by the book, quietly alerted the cabin crew to expect a messy landing and calmly told the passengers we were diverting to Narsarsuaq because of the weather and he was very sorry but it was going to be a bit of a rough ride for a few minutes so it was belts on, fags out and everything stowed away. Then we had to circle back into the teeth of that bloody storm to line up for our approach with the windshear so bad we were being blown sideways and that old aeroplane was shaking so much I thought it was going to fall apart with all of us in it. But we made it to our final descent, outside temperature so cold our instruments were giving us false readings at that low altitude and the volcanic ash had scoured the windscreen so we were blind as well. They'd got runway lights on but with the snow and with the screen so useless all we could see was one big mass of diffused light. No idea what was where or anything. But we ran through our checklists and I just hoped my bowels wouldn't let me down." He paused his narrative and looked at the pilots but although Dacre was enjoying the story, even if he had heard it many times before, Piers didn't appear even to be listening but was still watching the sky outside and occasionally checking the instruments on the flight deck.

"I could spin it out for an hour, but I won't as there are other people wanting to sit in that seat. Temperature by now heading for minus forty, warning lights and bells going off as everything iced up. Ailerons and elevators stuck in the wrong place, landing gear frozen solid so we were coming in on skids and not wheels. We had no checklists left to help us by now, flying totally blind on manual like something out of the 1920s. Then Dutchman and I thought our Captain B had lost it as he asked the pair of us and control to stop talking as he needed to hear what the plane was saying to him. So we worked with him and he had me doing things to those engines that weren't in any rule book I'd ever read. From the sound of Dutchman's voice as he said back the instructions he was being given he was holding his bowels in too. I'd swear Captain B was listening to hear what the engines needed doing to them, and how close we were to the ground. We had nothing left except his instincts and experience. Then, very quietly, like it was no big deal, he turned on the PA and gave the order for passengers and cabin crew to brace for a rough landing as we were going to be coming down in a lot of snow. And when your captain gives that command you start to believe you won't survive the landing. But down we came, engines throwing snow everywhere, wheels jammed up, and reverse thrust going so hard we should have been going backwards. Then we were sliding on the ice but the good thing is that much snow made one hell of a brake. We could hear Ground Control cheering their heads off as they could see our lights shining through our bow-wave of snow. Couldn't see us, just some ground level aurora borealis of coloured lights ploughing along in the snow on their runway. But we came to a stop and realised we were all still alive and didn't appear to have hit anything. Then that cheeky bastard over there switched on the PA system like it was a perfectly normal landing and welcomed the passengers and crew to our unscheduled stop in a slightly snowy Greenland where the temperature on the ground was currently minus thirty eight Centigrade and would passengers please remain in their seats and would cabin crew please check everyone was OK and wait for further instructions."

Kathy leaned forward and peered round at Piers who finally looked at her and smiled. "Tells a good yarn, doesn't he? It really wasn't that bad and we are very highly trained for such eventualities."

"It was that bloody bad," Mick corrected. "And a lot worse. We'd got nothing left to work from except your gut instincts. Anyway," he continued, warming to his tale as this was a very attentive audience and the hero of the story hadn't actually told him to shut up yet, "best bit was the, what do you call them? Greenlanders? Greens? They told us to keep light and heat on until they'd hooked up the GPU but give them a few minutes to get that sorted then they'd work out how to get us out. So the boss gave the order for cabin crew to serve any hot drinks we had left and while we were doing that they got the power unit connected as they'd somehow ploughed a path through to us from their terminal building and got some steps out. So we disembarked the passengers, ran the checks, did a sweep of the plane and then had the most embarrassing walk into a terminal I have ever done in my life. Bloody passengers all cheering and applauding and I've never been so kissed and hugged by people I don't know in all my life. I'll tell you, when I looked back at that aeroplane in a snowdrift up to its wings and positioned so beautifully on that runway I could have rushed out there and hugged it for looking after us. Whatever it said to the captain, it certainly knew what it was telling him and thank Christ he listened to it." Mick gave the slightly-scowling captain an unrepentant grin. "And just how much frozen Greenland vodka did you sink that night?"

Piers unsubtly dodged the question. "Vaguely remember I was so bloody tired I fell asleep on the floor cuddling some kid's teddy bear he'd insisted on giving me. But probably not as much as you."

"No idea. You and the bear were sitting on the floor but still upright when I last looked at you before I crashed out. So we spent three days in Narsarsuaq terminal eating boiled seal and turnips. No, they looked after us remarkably well considering we hadn't been expected, but the Greens worked hard and defrosted us, got the runway just about navigable although the airport was still officially closed, and told us if we could land in that state we could certainly take off again even if the volcanoes were still rumbling. We did the checks and the boss didn't argue when I said the old girl should see us home. The only thing they hadn't been able to sort out in time was the bloody useless windscreen as it needed replacing but the boss was OK to basically fly on instruments. It was that or we were going to be stuck there until the snow stopped as there was no way they would have risked trying to get a rescue aircraft out to us. Got back to London only about ninety two hours late and landed in torrential rain with zero visibility through the windscreen but they knew we were coming in damaged and the emergency routines were in place but it was a picnic in the park by comparison. Landing was so smooth, nobody even realised the boss was flying it on instruments and instinct until we were at the gate and people saw the state of the windscreen and then all hell broke loose. Maintenance told us it should never have survived the winds and the ash before it landed in Greenland never mind being able to bring it home with us and probably one pilot in a million could have handled it. But the good old Greens know what they're doing with frozen aeroplanes out there far more than we do. And thank Christ for a pilot trained by the military to fly blind in the dark. The big cheeses wanted to bollock us but couldn't find anything to bollock us about as we hadn't crashed their aeroplane and we'd even brought it back with us. There was an enquiry, of course, as we'd all been put in mortal peril, as the legal teams put it, but the blame got laid on the weather forecasters in the States. Anyway, story got out and the three flight crew got called in to Buck House for gongs."

Kathy was silent for a moment, trying to take it all in but realising that the passengers on that flight would never have known just how much danger they were in. She wondered if they had seen the useless windscreen when they were boarded at Narsarsuaq and she hoped not. "When was this? I don't remember hearing anything about it at the time."

"December 1978," Mick told her. "It was a one-day wonder on the TV news, a three-day wonder in the aviation world, and you were probably still at school."

Her smile was wry and without thinking she said out loud, "Actually I was on the run from a violent ex-boyfriend and wasn't really paying much attention to the wider world." There was an appalled silence in the cockpit but she had enjoyed the story, even allowing for Mick's poetic licence and she said to Piers. "Sorry I missed your big moment. Did you have to go and meet the Queen?"

He knew she was thinking of his reaction to learning about Emma's father-in-law becoming an earl. "She only does posh things like knighthoods. We got the Duke of Kent."

"And there was one heck of an after-party," Mick laughed.

Piers suddenly smiled in that way he had. "But do you know the darnedest thing? I'd just crawled home from our little trip to Greenland and had gone to the local shop to get something to eat when some rotten cow nicked the last packet of custard creams from under my nose."

"I'm sorry," Kathy said instinctively. "I thought you looked completely exhausted that night. I felt really sorry for you and so nearly asked if you were feeling alright. But you did say I could have the biscuits."

"Ah-ha!" Mick exclaimed delightedly, "Finally we get to meet the mystery blonde he used to go on about."

"You certainly do," Piers agreed.

Mick laughed. "Well, you can steal my biscuits any time, darlin'."

"Oh, shut up, Mick," Piers cut in and this time he meant it. "Piglet, go back to your boyfriend, you've occupied that seat long enough. I'll meet up with you in arrivals when we've all cleared immigration."

Kathy went back to her seat realising that nobody argued with the captain of an airliner but she really hadn't minded Mick's teasing at all. She was also feeling a bit guilty about the custard creams although at the time she had genuinely thought he was being nice and letting her have them. It was the first time since running from Richard she had realised there were still some kind men in the world who didn't expect her to go to bed with them. It was the first time in a long while she had felt any hope.

Jean-Guy was looking out of the window. "I thought it was getting dark," he told her. "But apparently that's space out there. What's it like in the cockpit?"

"Surprisingly cramped, it's no wonder Piers gets backache. You'll have to go and see them before we land. I've now met Dacre who saved his life and also Mick the flight engineer who told me a lovely story about Narsarsuaq."

"About where?"

"The unpronounceable place in Greenland the pilot in Amsterdam mentioned."

"Good story?"

"If only half of it was true it was pretty incredible. And now I know where Piers got that teddy bear from that's in the living room. Did you know he's got a medal?"

"I've seen the ribbon. Never really thought about it. I suppose I assumed it was something he'd got for flying Concorde or becoming a captain or something. So what is it?"

"Queen's Gallantry Medal. I'd never even noticed the ribbon."

"On his jacket, just below the wings."

"Remind me when we get there, I'll have a look."

What they had not been expecting at Kennedy airport was the reception from the enthusiastic New Yorkers for the "brave Czech defector" who had so generously agreed to share his talent with their own beloved Philharmonic Orchestra. The media were waiting for them as soon as they had cleared immigration and they were whisked off for a quick press conference before they had had a chance to meet up with Piers. Somehow Kathy wasn't surprised that he tracked them down and was patiently waiting for them outside the conference room.

As Jean-Guy was the hero of the hour, Kathy let the cavalcade sweep past the man in the corridor. She got behind the crowd and gave Piers a smile of greeting then tucked her hand through his arm as she had done so many times before so they could follow the others. "Bit easier than landing in Narsarsuaq, huh? They're putting us in a limo to our hotel. Apparently we have a suite. I've never been in a suite in my life. Can we offer you a lift?"

"Welcome to the USA," he told her happily. "Nah, you're fine. I'm staying in the same hotel as the rest of the crew so I'll get a cab across to your hotel later. Bet you don't have the Tsar's grand piano in your suite."

Kathy, now she was looking for it, noticed the small ribbon on his jacket below the pilot's wings which she had never thought about before. She gave it a gentle poke. "Why didn't you explain that to us?"

"Didn't think you'd be interested."

"You can be so annoying," she chided him fondly.

"Come on, you two, stop gossiping," Jean-Guy called to them sharply. "Some of us have a rehearsal to go to."

"And who are you?" one of the reporters asked Piers.

"Me?" he laughed, his eyes twinkling with amusement under his correctly positioned hat. "I'm just the chauffeur."

Jean-Guy sighed as though at the quirks of a child. "This is Piers Buchanan. He's the pianist of our trio and also piloted Concorde on our flight here."

"Can we have photos of the three of you, please?" some of the reporters asked.

So they obligingly posed, but, Kathy noticed, Piers didn't take off his hat and in fact pulled it slightly forward to hide his face a little. But it was part of his formal uniform so nobody said anything about it. Out at the arrivals area they parted their ways. Jean-Guy and Kathy were taken away in their limo by a representative from the orchestra and Piers went to catch the airline crew bus to take him to his hotel. Kathy watched him go and couldn't help thinking about a dark, snowy airport in Greenland where many lives could have been lost but weren't and there had been no enthusiastic press reception then. She guessed Piers would have hated such a fuss anyway. But she did now feel really bad about the biscuits.

Kathy and Jean-Guy were scheduled to attend a dinner at the Juilliard School that evening as a welcome to New York which they didn't really want to go to as they knew Piers was flying back to London the next day and they had been looking forward to seeing some of the sights of New York with him. They had invited Piers to join them at the dinner but he had laughingly declined saying for him it was just a normal turnaround and he needed to get in his rest period.

It took a while to get checked in to their hotel as so many people wanted to greet Jean-Guy and congratulate him on coming to the West. They were all so enthusiastic and effusive it was a relief to finally escape to the sanctuary of their suite and collapse on the enormous bed.

"That's one thing I like about the English," Jean-Guy said wearily. "They really just couldn't care less. In a nice way. I don't think I'd like to be famous."

Kathy propped herself up on his chest. "News for you, you already are." She looked round the room and suddenly shrieked with delight. "Oh my God! There is a piano in the suite!"

"Yes, I asked for one. I've got used to Piers as accompanist now and, I know it's a bit selfish, but I didn't want to use the ones at the Juilliard they were offering me."

"But they would be offering you people who could teach Piers to play the piano. Can't you give the poor chap a rest?"

He idly rubbed her back and wondered if he had the energy to make love to her. "I've also asked if you can borrow a violin. I think there's a Guarnerius on offer for you."

Kathy sat up next to him and shoved the hair back off her face. "What?" she breathed.

"A Guarnerius. Please don't drop it, it's probably worth more than Piers' car." She still sat there just looking at him but he could feel her excitement as a tangible heat where their bodies touched. "I thought it would save you having to bring yours."

"But I wasn't expecting to play while we're out here."

He pulled her back down on top of him. "Can I explain later?"

Jean-Guy knew he still had a smile on his face when he opened the door of the suite in answer to the knock. To his relief, their pianist was looking casually, if annoyingly, handsome in his outfit of Viola clothes and wasn't in his habitual scruffy jeans and shabby unironed shirt with a moth-holed sweater.

"Good. Presentable you," was his greeting. "Kathy's just getting changed, come and tell me what you think of the piano."

Piers came into the room and had to smile. "Might have known you'd have a piano."

"I asked for one. Come on, get your shoes off and tell me what you think of it."

Piers walked all round the piano but didn't attempt to play it. "Why have you got a piano? You don't play. And you're out tonight and I'm off again tomorrow."

Kathy came wandering out of the bathroom wrapped in a towel and realised they had a visitor. "Oh, excuse me," she said and felt rather embarrassed but thankful that at least she had wrapped a towel round and it was only Piers. "Just wanted to grab some underwear."

Piers chivalrously turned his back but Jean-Guy could see he was smiling. He heard the bathroom door click shut again. "Didn't waste much time, huh?"

"We agreed not to make comments on love lives."

"Sorry. So why the piano?"

"Wait and I will tell you."

Kathy didn't take long to dress and soon joined them in a flowery Laura Ashley dress she had got in the sale and which was really too long for her but she liked it and she had seen that the men were quite nicely dressed for once.

"OK, so what's the secret?" she asked, hopping on one foot so she could pull on her shoes.

"I was asked to take a masterclass on the *Arpeggione Sonata* at the Juilliard in a couple of days. It was tempting until I found out that only last month they had had a cello masterclass with Rostropovich. There is no way I can compete with that so I said we will run a masterclass on a trio. Would you rather the *Dumky* or the Mozart B flat? I've brought both sets of parts so feel free to choose either. All I want you two to do is play as and when asked. I am taking the class and there will be three trios attending as well as an audience. They will provide us with two pianos so we won't waste any time with instrument changes and we have to go to pick up Kathy's violin."

Kathy and Piers accepted they had now stepped into Jean-Guy's world and this was the redoubtable cellist who had defected from his homeland to further what had already been a phenomenal career so far.

"Well, I'd vote for the Dvorak," Piers offered without protest, realising he and Kathy weren't going to get much say in the matter now the autocratic cellist was in his element.

"Me too," Kathy agreed as she really didn't have a strong opinion either way. She just wanted to get her hands on a Guarnerius, play it, and then let Emma know she had played it. To be playing one in a masterclass at the Juilliard was more than she could ever have hoped for. "So how do we get to the Juilliard?" she asked.

Piers smiled. "Well, in a hotel like this you go downstairs and the doorman will hail you a cab. There'll be half a dozen yellow cabs circling the entrance waiting for fares."

"Sounds a good plan," Jean-Guy approved. "The school said they will give us lunch too when we have picked up the violin and checked out the classroom."

They were met at the Juilliard by a very enthusiastic Professor of Music who instructed them to call her Judy and then set off at a cracking pace along the corridors. The coveted Guarnerius was in her study and Kathy nearly wept to see it. Judy explained it belonged to the School and had been bequeathed at the end of the last century by a rich benefactor who had wanted it to be used by visiting violinists who needed an instrument in an emergency. Otherwise it just sat in the school repository and it hadn't been used for a while as violinists didn't seem to have emergencies any more.

Kathy looked at the instrument sitting unloved in its case and felt so sorry for it. "It's beautiful," she said without thinking.

"It'll need some playing in," Jean-Guy remarked. "Smells as though it hasn't been used for years."

Judy's face was all smiles. "I have been in touch with the benefactor's descendants and they have said they would be delighted if you would use it for the whole of your stay and also if you would consider using it on an indefinite loan from the Juilliard. I understand your trio is getting quite well known now, and all we would ask is that there is a credit in the programme or on any recording notes to say the violin is the property of the Juilliard School. Should you no longer need it for any reason then it will have to be returned."

Jean-Guy was looking critically at the violin so it was Piers who gave Kathy a quick shoulder hug. "Lucky cow," he muttered in her ear. "Go on, grab it before he gets hold of it."

Kathy realised she was shaking as she reverently took the violin out of its case and held it in her hands. "Wow," was all she said. "I don't know what to say. 'Thank you' doesn't seem enough." As though in a dream she tensioned the bow and applied some rosin before the Guarnerius was allowed to speak for the first time in many years. Its tone was warm and clear and just the basic scale of D major made Kathy want to weep. She ran through some of her warm-up exercises and was amazed by the fullness of the low notes and yet still the very high sound was just as effortless and made her own violin sound like the shrieking of a squeaky wheel. The notes were perfect and the sound sang so beautifully up to the roof of the rather small study.

"It likes you," Piers told her and ignored the filthy look Jean-Guy gave him.

"May we see the recital room now, please?" Jean-Guy asked. "And then if there is anywhere to get a coffee I think we would all be grateful."

"Oh, no, coffee first. The staff are all looking forward to meeting you."

So Kathy had to tuck the precious violin in its broken case under her arm and go with the others to a faculty room where there were a dozen assorted professors and tutors, all of them eminent in their field of music, waiting to greet them and press coffees and pastries on them. Judy was quite distraught to realise the pianist couldn't eat any of the pastries as they were all dusted with either cinnamon or nutmeg but he charmingly assured her that he didn't eat cake anyway so it really didn't matter. Kathy wasn't at all hungry having eaten on the flight over but she thought Piers would be wanting something by now.

"Did you eat on the plane at all?" she asked him.

"No, don't usually."

"So have you eaten at all today?" On getting no reply, she nudged him in the ribs. "Well, have you?"

"I'm fine. I'll eat lunch."

"I'll be watching you,"

Kathy was quite sorry to leave the musical chat but Judy was all set to whisk them off to inspect the recital room where they were to give the masterclass. Privately, Kathy thought she had played in concert halls smaller than that recital room and she knew the violin would sound superb in those acoustics. There were two pianos in the room, one was a rather elderly rosewood Steinway and the other a very smart new Yamaha.

"The Steinway is an early one from the 1920s," Judy explained. "Given to the School only five years ago and completely rebuilt. The Yamaha we purchased new in 1980 and all the students who use it say it is a dream to play." She beamed at the pianist who was looking a bit confused. "Do you have a preference? Please do try them both." She couldn't quite believe it when Piers used Kathy's shoulder to steady himself and calmly took his boots off. She watched as he padded off barefoot to the Yamaha and idly ran through a few warm-up exercises.

"Does he always do that?" Judy asked Jean-Guy.

"Always. We've given up trying to stop him."

"May I ask why?"

Jean-Guy answered her question with another. "Do you play the piano?"

"Yes, of course. I performed Rachmaninov Three with the School main orchestra as part of my PhD."

"Have you ever worked as an accompanist?" Jean-Guy guessed from Judy's lack of reply that she was trying to think of a diplomatic way to express her loathing of the idea. He spared her having to be polite. "Piers is a trained accompanist and he doesn't do solo work. He has what you might call an unconventional technique, part of which is he doesn't wear shoes. Ask him why and all he says is that it helps him to feel the pedals. All I know is that he is without a doubt the most brilliantly talented accompanist I have ever worked with. So I don't say anything any more about how he does what he does. I think the Steinway will suit him better."

Judy wasn't sure what to say after that. But if Jean-Guy Dechaume described this accompanist as 'brilliantly talented' then, she supposed, he must be. But she could certainly see what he meant about an unconventional technique.

Piers left the Yamaha and sat at the Steinway instead. Again a few exercises and Judy paid particular attention to his technique. She watched very carefully as he treated them all to a breath-taking performance of the last couple of minutes of Liszt's second *Hungarian Rhapsody*. Seemingly oblivious to the effect on his audience he asked calmly, "Can I use this one, please? That other one has no soul."

Jean-Guy sighed and wished Piers wouldn't say things like that in front of strangers. But if that was the standard of his playing these days, he was allowed to get away with remarks like that. And bare feet. In public. "OK, that's the piano sorted. What can you tell me about the musicians I will be teaching?"

Judy recovered her wits after that performance and wondered why the hell this man didn't play as a soloist.

"Oh, easily among the top students of their instruments. They've formed their own trios and have all been rehearsing both the Dvorak and the Mozart we corresponded about."

"I'd prefer to teach them on the Dvorak," Jean-Guy announced.

"I'll let them know. Is there anything else you'd like me to show you, or shall I take you to lunch now? Some of the staff will be joining us there too as well as the students you will be coaching in the masterclass."

"Oh, then I am happy to go and meet them now." Jean-Guy looked across at the other two. Piers had got his boots back on and the pair of them were obviously chatting about the Guarnerius again. "Then we must go back to our hotel for our own rehearsal as Piers is flying back to the UK tomorrow."

"He has a concert to play in?"

Jean-Guy was surprised there was anyone left in the musical world who didn't know. "No, he is an airline pilot. But he will be back in time for our class."

"Yes, I suppose it is hard for him as he doesn't play as a soloist."

Jean-Guy detected something in her tone and was annoyed on behalf of his friend. "Please don't make the mistake of thinking that just because those two don't work as soloists that they aren't capable of doing so. I have heard Kathy play the Shostakovich One for practice many times and you could put her in front of the New York Phil tomorrow and she wouldn't disgrace them." To his horror, Judy seemed quite taken with that idea.

"I'll speak to the conductor. Unfortunately we can't work it into a concert while you're here but she can certainly run through it in rehearsal with them. In fact, I think that would be a nice gesture as she's borrowing the Guarnerius."

Privately Jean-Guy thought Kathy was probably going to throttle him, but he wasn't going to back down now. "Kathy," he called across to her. "Did you bring any music with you?"

"No," she responded, sounding rather surprised. "Should I have?"

"Um, how do you fancy running through the Shostakovich with the orchestra while we're here?"

Kathy didn't think for one moment that he meant it. "Yeah, right. I haven't even memorised half of it yet and I'm certainly not going to make a fool of myself in front of the New York Phil. But thank you for the offer."

"Mr Dechaume and I were just saying it would be a nice gesture if you were to play the Guarnerius with the orchestra while you're here. If not the Shostakovich, then what would you choose? Whatever it is, we will have it in the library if you want to refresh your memory."

A blend of sheer panic and absolute joy engulfed Kathy and she looked wildly from Jean-Guy to Piers. "No. Are you kidding me? You really are serious, aren't you? I've never had any ambitions to be a soloist."

"We're not asking you to do a public performance," Judy encouraged her, thinking maybe it was asking a bit much of an ensemble player to stand in front of such a renowned orchestra and play a concerto. "We just thought maybe a quiet run-through, just you and the orchestra with the rehearsal conductor would be a nice way to say 'thank you' for the loan of the Guarnerius."

"Can I think about it tonight, please?" Kathy asked, starting to remember how to breathe even if she didn't feel much less panicked at the idea. At least there wouldn't be that many witnesses. Apart from an entire orchestra and its conductor, that was. "I do see your point, but I'd like to get to know the fiddle first and choose something suitable for it. And me."

Piers felt so sorry for Kathy, clearly torn between her love of music helping her to rise to the challenge but fighting with her fear of making a fool of herself in front of other people. "What about the Sibelius?" he offered calmly and rationally. "You can play that one with your eyes shut. And I'm sure we can find time for a run-through as there's a piano in your room."

"Yes," Jean-Guy approved, thankful to see that the musician in Kathy was winning out over her nerves. He wished he'd thought of it first. "The Sibelius, as you play it so well. And, as Judy says, it's not for a public concert."

"Oh, the Sibelius would be perfect," Judy approved. "I'll just ring through to our librarian and ask him to bring the music to my study for you so you can have a run through with your pianist before the performance. Anyway, come along and have some lunch." She had hoped to be seen walking through the corridors next to the celebrated Jean-Guy Dechaume but somehow found herself with the pianist who kept her occupied answering his questions mostly about the history of the School.

Silently blessing Piers for occupying Judy, Kathy put her hand through Jean-Guy's arm as they walked behind the other two and asked him softly, "Just what the hell have you signed me up for?"

"Wasn't my idea. Judy just kind of bulldozed her way into it. Are you OK to run through the Sibelius with the orchestra?"

She snuggled against him. "So long as I play with them before you do as I can't compete at your level."

They exchanged a kiss without even slowing their pace. "You'll be fine. There should be time for a quick run-through before Piers has to leave. And just think how envious Emma will be."

Kathy made sure she sat next to Piers for the lunch as Jean-Guy was engrossed in conversation with the other eminent musicians at the table with them and she wanted to sit quietly and get her mind in order. Piers, as he so often did, sat silently beside her and waited for her to speak.

"Do you think I can do this?"

"Of course," he replied. "And I'm not just saying that. I know that to Jean-Guy it's just another gig, but I can understand it's a big deal for you. But, honestly, don't worry about it. Just concentrate on making Emma envious."

"It's funny," Kathy mused as she thoughtfully ate her quiche. "Emma was always going to be the soloist. I hated it."

He spotted the tears in her eyes and discreetly passed across a clean tissue. "Yup, you're just like me. Hate the limelight. Why the hell did we ever let them persuade us to make idiots of ourselves in Yorkshire?"

Grateful for his support she mopped her eyes and gave him a gentle slap on the thigh under the table. "As I remember, we weren't the ones who made idiots of ourselves."

"True. You going to eat those olives?"

"Nah, I only like the green ones."

"Philistine," he said fondly and ate all the black olives off her plate.

Back in the hotel suite, Kathy took the Guarnerius from its case and played it in while Jean-Guy busied himself with the coffee machine and Piers flopped on the sofa but did have the manners to be pretending to look through the piano score of the Sibelius.

"Good violin," Jean-Guy approved. "Anyway, perhaps you should have your run-through now as Piers has already told us twice that he has to get in his statutory rest as he is flying tomorrow and we can't keep him here for ever."

"Too bloody right," yawned the man on the sofa. "You two have got to get yourselves all tarted up for your supper tonight and much as I might want to laugh at you dressed up like a penguin and its mate there is no way I'm hanging about long enough to get dragged along too. Ready then, Piglet? Do you want to run through top to bottom or just pick out a few bits?"

"Run through," she said decisively and waited while her accompanist got settled and they checked tuning. They started out perfectly but she made a mess of the first movement cadenza and nearly screamed in frustration. "I can't do this!" she declared. "I'm not a bloody soloist. I don't want to be one. They can have their violin back."

Jean-Guy was genuinely baffled. "It is just a thank you to the orchestra for the loan of the instrument. They're not expecting a concert level performance from you. Come on, just go from the two bars before the cadenza. We all know you can play this."

"Yes, I know," she snapped, nerves and anxiety coming out as anger. "I can play the bloody thing backwards in my sleep when it's the three of us and the cats."

"I don't understand," Jean-Guy admitted. "You have played many trio concerts with us now. You are an excellent violinist and the Sibelius is well within your capabilities. It is just you and an orchestra. They are musicians too and won't judge you."

Kathy didn't trust herself to speak. She shoved the violin into Piers' hands and threw herself face down on the sofa, hating herself for being so infantile but not sure she could explain what she was going through.

Jean-Guy looked from her to Piers and was genuinely surprised to see the other man was almost glaring at him.

"That was a bit bloody insensitive," Piers told him. "That poor cow is in full panic mode and you just don't get it."

"No, I don't," Jean-Guy admitted and sounded as bewildered as he felt.

"Come off it. You saw the state she was in for Yorkshire. Piglet isn't good at getting outside her comfort zone and this is about as far out of it as it would be if you were about to go and do a flying trapeze act in a circus." He paused. "You can't do a flying trapeze act, can you? Piglet, get your behind back over here and take this bloody violin from me before I drop it."

Kathy trailed back to the piano and did as he had asked, somehow remembering that this man was trained to help people who were too terrified even to get into a plane. "Sorry."

Piers pulled her onto his lap as the piano stool wasn't big enough for two. "No, don't apologise for being afraid. Is there not just a bit of you that wanted to be a soloist?"

"No, not really."

"Piglet..."

"Not any more. Maybe once, when I was a teenager and we all believed we could do anything. But I've learned over the years that I'm not good enough."

"Yes, you are," Jean-Guy tried to reassure her but Piers looked at her more sternly.

"OK, so can you think of this as just a bit of fun? Trying out one of your teenage dreams to see if it fits? I know how you feel. Standing backstage at Annette's gig the other week I was beginning to wonder if I shouldn't have tried to put incontinence pads inside those bloody trousers."

The idea made Kathy smile in spite of herself. "Those trousers were so tight I think the pad would have shown."

"Depends where I put it," he told her with a roguish smile. "Now, if I said to you that you could tell Judy you're not doing it and it wouldn't matter to her, does that make you feel better? Or do you want to have a go at it after all?"

Kathy thought about that and realised she would hate herself more if she let this opportunity go. "I suppose you're annoyingly right, as you always are. Yes, it's just a bad dose of stage fright. But can I borrow one of your incontinence pads, just in case?"

Piers ignored Kathy's boyfriend standing right next to him and kissed her on the nose. "Don't think they'd fit a runt like you. But don't you think stage fright in so many ways makes us perform at our best? Now please get off my legs before you break them and let's finish off this practice unless you think you know the piece well enough and don't want to."

"Just quickly," she requested and felt a lot better. "Just so I can hear what the violin sounds like."

Piers looked at his watch. "We don't have time for all of it. Let's just go through the last movement. You've got to start getting ready to go out soon."

"Sure you won't come with us? We can always hire you some evening dress to wear?"

"Not a hope in hell," he laughed.

Kathy oddly missed Piers once he had gone. She was used to the way he would go away, either on his regular flights or on-call but she was restless at the function that evening although her chat with Piers had prepared her more for her performance of the Sibelius. When they got back to their hotel it wasn't that late so Jean-Guy calculated time zones and told her to ring the Prof and tell him about the new violin. Petr Mihaly was delighted to hear about the Guarnerius and agreed wholeheartedly that Emma would be extremely envious. Kathy was consoled to learn that Audrey was being her usual self and not moping around anywhere but something still bothered her.

The next day was a delicious whirlwind of music at the Juilliard and her run-through of the Sibelius with the renowned New York Philharmonic Orchestra where she stood, as she had once dreamed she would, in front of an internationally famous orchestra and prepared to play a concerto with them. There was a part of her that wished Emma could have been there to witness it and she wondered if she dared rack up a huge phone bill in the hotel and ring her friend that evening. But she stood quietly in front of the orchestra and played the Sibelius perfectly from memory, without fuss, and in her mind as the Guarnerius sang so beautifully for her, the raven flew and circled the almost empty auditorium, listening to her, willing her on and guiding her as it had done so often before. Performance over, the orchestra all gave her a lovely round of applause and agreed it was great to hear the Guarnerius being played. The rehearsal conductor and the leader shook her hand, but then she was left to sit in the auditorium while the orchestra got on with the serious business of rehearsing with their esteemed guest soloist. Kathy sat peacefully in her seat and watched the rehearsal; there were a few other people in the stalls seats too and she guessed they were interested teachers from the school as this first rehearsal was closed to the public. She sighed happily and wished Piers could have been sitting next to her just to share in the joy of the occasion. But although it hadn't been as bad as she had been dreading, it had helped her to realise there was no way she was ever going to be a soloist in a proper concert.

She sat in the auditorium again that evening while Jean-Guy enchanted his American audience with his performance of the Shostakovich but he came to sit with her for the second half of the programme and they listened to a perfect Beethoven Symphony. It was lovely to catch a yellow cab back to their hotel that evening and to fall into that enormous bed, both of them tired and happy, full of the sights and sounds of New York.

The day after that was a free day in their timetable and it didn't matter that all they wanted to do was a gentle spot of sightseeing and some shopping in Macy's. Thankful Jean-Guy wasn't playing that night they dined in a small restaurant close to their hotel and talked about the next day. Piers was due in on the morning Concorde and they guessed he would go to his hotel first to shower and change and then come to meet them at theirs. Working on times, they estimated he would get to them about midday, or at least in time for some lunch. Then they all had to be at the Juilliard for the masterclass at 2pm. That was scheduled to last two hours and then Jean-Guy had to be back at the Lincoln Center by 7.30 to get ready to play the Elgar that evening.

Before they went to bed that night, they ordered breakfast in their suite for 9.30 the next morning thinking they would then be ready for Piers when he turned up later.

They barely seemed to have started on their breakfasts the next morning when the phone rang in their suite and Kathy, her mouth full of that last of her eggs Florentine, let Jean-Guy take the call.

He was smiling as he turned back to her. "Apparently Captain Buchanan is on his way up."

"Oh. It's not like him to use his title. Oh well, I doubt if he'll want any of our breakfast."

"Me neither, but we can always ring down for some more." Jean-Guy didn't bother going back to the breakfast table as less than a minute later someone knocked on the door of their suite. They were both surprised when Piers breezed in still in his uniform with his hat tucked under one arm and a pot of food from a Chinese takeaway in his hands.

"Hi," was the cheerful greeting. "Don't mind me, just carry on with your breakfasts."

Kathy and Jean-Guy both wanted to smile as their unexpectedly early visitor took off his shoes, nonchalantly sat cross-legged in the middle of their unmade bed and started wolfing down Chinese food. They had no idea anyone could use chopsticks so fast.

Kathy went back to her eggs. "Odd sort of breakfast," she remarked.

"Breakfast? You joking? This is supper. I've done a night flight to Helsinki and back while you two were snoring your heads off. Concorde was the end of my working day not the beginning."

"So when did you sleep last?" Kathy asked. "Want some coffee? They've sent us up a huge pot."

"Please. Sleep? I don't remember sleep," he laughed.

Jean-Guy poured some coffee into one of the cups on their breakfast table and took it across. "Here, we'll share the other cup. We were expecting you to go to your hotel first and change."

"Thought about it, but then I thought you don't want to be hanging around here all morning waiting for me so I came straight here from the airport. I've left my luggage at reception downstairs. So when I've finished my supper and you've told me what I'm supposed to be doing, I'll go to my hotel and sort myself out." Food finished, Piers slackened his tie and settled back against the pillows to drink his coffee. "So what's the plan?"

Kathy and Jean-Guy both thought he looked incredibly tired and realised he was probably running on adrenaline by this time.

"The plan," Jean-Guy told him, "is that I will ring down to reception and ask them to bring your luggage up. You can then shower and change here and we can all head out together. From the look of you if you go back to your own hotel now you will fall asleep standing up for the next six hours and we have to be at the Juilliard by one thirty."

"I'm fine, really. But I like the idea of not having to schlepp half way across the city and back just to get changed. Thanks."

The other two watched and, as they had known from experience he would, Piers put the coffee cup on the bedside table and closed his eyes. Within moments he had tipped sideways on the bed and it was obvious he was fast asleep.

"Incredible," Kathy whispered to Jean-Guy. "That man has absolutely no body clock whatsoever. What shall we do with him?"

"Well, I'll get his luggage sent up, you throw a blanket over him, we'll write him a note and then I think it'll be safe for us to go out and leave him for an hour or so."

Jean-Guy had been to New York several years ago. He had come across to the city heavily chaperoned by his parents and officials from the Czechoslovakian embassy and he had had no time to explore the city. Now he wandered the streets with his arm around his girlfriend and drank in the sense of freedom that still felt new to him when he stopped to think about it. Together they had a stroll round Central Park, found a coffee shop for a late elevenses and finally headed back to their hotel at about midday confidently expecting to find Piers still asleep.

To their surprise he was up and dressed in what Jean-Guy called 'presentable' clothes, and running through his part for the Dvorak when they went into their suite.

"Thought you'd still be asleep," Kathy told him kindly.

He shrugged and sorted out some troublesome quavers. "Nah, probably slept for about an hour. I'll be fine now."

"How do you do it?" Jean-Guy asked. "How do you eat supper in the morning, sleep for an hour and then go through a day? If I don't get my eight hours at night I'm a wreck for three days."

"Habit really. You get used to snatching sleep on long flights. I'm sure I'll crash out tonight though."

"Aren't you coming to hear Jean-Guy play the Elgar tonight?" Kathy asked.

"Sure. We've got Annette tomorrow haven't we?"

Kathy had almost forgotten. "Yes, she wants to do a street shoot in the morning when the light's better, then you're on the runway in the evening. Same choreography as last time?"

"No idea, I think she's scared I'll chicken out if she tells me too much. She was muttering dire things about dyeing my hair green which could be interesting at work if it doesn't wash out again. When do you play the Prokofiev?"

"Day after tomorrow. So if you're not completely worn out walking up and down a runway tomorrow night I'd be grateful for a run through with you before the gig."

"Sure it'll be fine. I'll be glad to get home after all this lot and do sod all for best part of a week though. Don't suppose you've heard anything from Sarah at all?"

Kathy shook her head. "No. So far as I know she and your eight children are all fine and healthy. I always leave the Prof our contact details in case there's an emergency."

He half smiled "'Eight children'. I still can't believe it and I was there when the last five arrived. It sounds slightly immoral somehow. Isn't it time you two started producing?" he finished, giving them a quizzical look.

"We're working on it," Jean-Guy almost growled.

Piers' gaze flicked to Kathy but she kept her eyes on the floor. "Piglet?"

"Not up for discussion."

Piers realised she still hadn't told Jean-Guy what had happened to her with her ex. "So, where are we off to first? I don't care where we go so long as I get at least one hot dog off a street stall. And a bag of roasted almonds in Central Park."

"You'll get indigestion," Kathy told him, grateful he hadn't said anything indiscreet and feeling a bit mean for snapping at him. "Sorry, didn't mean to bite, but can we not talk about kids right now, please?"

"OK, but don't do what Chantal and I did and leave it too late to find out if there are any problems."

Kathy caught the look he shot her and hoped Jean-Guy hadn't seen it too. "Regrets?" she asked, to keep the topic away from herself.

"Sometimes. I don't like to think of the life a mixed-race child would have had at that time. But, no point chewing over that old piece of cud. It didn't happen and that's it."

Kathy looked at him and saw how tired he was and she had caught the bitter edge to his voice. "We're giving ourselves until my twenty ninth," she told him before he could make any barbed comments. "And we'll name the firstborn after you."

A ghost of a smile flitted across his face and was gone. "Not if it's a girl, I hope?"

Jean-Guy looked at the pair of them and felt yet again they were cutting him out of something deeply intimate they shared. "So, hot dogs and almonds," he reminded them briskly. "If we're going to eat we'd better go as we don't have much time."

The other two exchanged a glance and realised they had been lost in their own little world again and they were going to have to be ever more careful.

So they all ate hot dogs and pretzels off street stalls and shared a bag of roasted almonds in Central Park, ignoring the looks they got as they carted a cello and a violin in a broken case round with them. It was a cool day for late March so they had needed their coats but the sun had been shining and they arrived at the Juilliard ready for their masterclass with Jean-Guy apparently in a much happier mood now they were safely back in his world.

It was Judy again who took charge of them and even she was bubbling with excitement. "Come and say hi to your students," she invited, "and then you'll need to decide which order you want to tutor them in."

Kathy and Piers were impressed with the way Jean-Guy took charge of the masterclass and recognised some of the Prof's teaching tricks in the way he helped the students get over some of their problems with the work.

Kathy and Piers didn't have much to do in the masterclass but although Kathy was sitting at the front next to Jean-Guy, Piers was more towards the back and trying really hard to maintain his concentration. His mind was totally distracted by a fly walking along his keyboard and he idly wondered how Audrey was getting on.

"Piers!" yelled Jean-Guy's voice. "Are you even awake?"

"Sorry, miles away," he said, realising the entire room was now watching him.

"And that," Jean-Guy laughingly told his pupils and audience, "is what happens when you have a working airline pilot as your pianist. Piers, please concentrate for the next five minutes and just take us from rehearsal mark A to the key change."

He flicked through the score and found the bar then looked across to Jean-Guy for the cue to start. An almost imperceptible nod from the man in charge and he ran through the bars with the violinist and cellist from a trio of young students before he was stopped.

"Thank you," Jean-Guy said to him and gave him an odd look but he didn't say anything, just went back to his teaching.

Kathy looked across to the man at the piano and realised his concentration was totally shot. She thought she had seldom seen him look so tired, and had the ridiculous idea that maybe he really could play the *Dumky* in his sleep.

They concluded the class with a quick run through of the last few minutes of the Trio from the quirky Lento Maestoso to the end but it wasn't their best performance and Jean-Guy was far from happy. When they had finished playing and while the audience was still applauding, Kathy wasn't surprised that Jean-Guy had a few discreet, but sharp, words with the pianist which were clearly rebuffed with a curt reply and a black look. Kathy put the Guarnerius away and looked across first at Jean-Guy who was now surrounded by students and audience all asking him questions and then at Piers who was wearily quietly running through the exercises he always did at the end of a practice session. She went and sat next to him on the page turner's chair.

"Still awake?" she asked softly.

"Not really. You played well. Great violin."

"It's too good for me."

He stifled a yawn. "Don't be silly. He was within his rights to bollock me for that crap playing but he didn't have to be so bloody rude about it. I know I messed up."

Kathy realised some ruffled feathers needed soothing. "I'm betting you shouldn't have done that round trip to Helsinki. I thought you didn't need the money so much now Annette's paying you God knows what to walk around in her designs."

"Helsinki was an easy one. I didn't mind. It was the first officer's maiden commercial flight after training and I was only on board as the safety pilot so didn't actually take the controls. The one scheduled to go with him had called in sick that morning so they put me on instead."

"And before that was the flight you did going back from here when you left us?"

"Um, not really."

"What the hell have you been doing?"

He sighed. "Bit of a cock-up with the on-call. They had me flying too many hours and now I'm just shot. Fortunately I was with Mick and Dacre on the flight here and we could work together if one of us was dead."

"You're an idiot."

"I know. But I honestly hadn't worked out the hours until I was writing up my log. I've been going straight for thirty six hours with sixteen flying hours and only two off."

"Jesus! No wonder you're tired."

"But it gave me an idea." He smothered another yawn. "I think you need to learn to fly."

"What?! Are you completely out of your tree?"

"Hear me out. I don't like being a passenger, Jean-Guy doesn't travel too well in cars and ships so if we can train you to fly with me then we can hire our own aeroplane for any trips like this one and it'll make life a lot easier. It's not going to happen overnight but I was having a bit of a chat with the new boy before the flight and he was telling me his sister is also a qualified commercial pilot but the only airline willing to take her on was Dan Air. Bloody waste of a qualification so I threw away some of my down time having another go at the bosses. Got me bloody nowhere as it always does, but I'm not going to give up. You'll have to learn privately so it won't be cheap. I can't help you out as I'm not qualified to teach PPL. Something for you to think about?"

"Why can't Jean-Guy learn?" Kathy asked while her mind reeled to think this most qualified of pilots would, in a way, be prepared to trust her with his life. She was flattered he even thought she could cope with flying a plane.

"He can't even drive a car. And you're a good driver so I don't see why you shouldn't be able to handle an aeroplane. You don't have to do anything fancy, but we'll need two pilots if we're going to hire a jet and it really would be the ideal solution."

Kathy's mind was still whirling when Jean-Guy and Judy came across to join them. "Problems?" Judy asked brightly.

Piers closed the lid of the piano and got to his feet. "Not at all," he assured her, but didn't sound very friendly. "Right, I'm off to get some sleep at my hotel and you two need some space so I'll call for you later."

Judy watched him leave the room. "Did I upset him?"

"No, honestly," Kathy rushed to reassure. "He's just tired." She gave Jean-Guy one of her nicest smiles. "And what he said made a lot of sense so maybe we should do the same and go back to our hotel for a while?"

To her relief, he gave her a bit of a hug and a grateful smile. "Good idea."

In the solitude of their room, Kathy knew she had to find out. "Are we OK?"

Jean-Guy looked faintly startled at the sudden brutality of the question. "I thought so. Why? What's wrong?"

"I don't know," Kathy admitted and just stood in front of him without touching. "First there was that awful mess with me being so dramatic over the Sibelius, then you gave Piers a right telling-off just now and he's gone off to his hotel in a strop. I just feel as though we're all falling apart." She could not have expressed the relief she felt when he wrapped gentle arms round her and kissed her softly on the mouth.

"Kathy, I hope we are more than OK. Yes, maybe I spoke to Piers a bit more sharply than he deserved but you both know what I'm like when I am at work. I will apologise to him when I see him next. And I think maybe I need to apologise to you too."

She looked up into his dark eyes and saw how sad he looked. "Me? Why?"

He tightened his hug. "Because I didn't understand how you felt."

Kathy caught the sub-text. "And Piers did?"

"Yes," he admitted reluctantly.

She took him by the hand and led him across to the bed so they could sit side-by-side. "Did you believe what he said to me to make me feel better?"

"Well, yes, didn't you?"

"Not completely. As long as we've known him he's told us lies. Sometimes just little ones, maybe not actual lies just half-truths. Ages ago, when the three of us first went to Suffolk the Prof warned me off him and I like to think I've got better at spotting his little tricks." She gently squeezed his hand. "Piers will never do anything to split us up unless one of us lets him know he can. And I'm not going to firstly because I love you far too much and secondly because I think Sarah would lock him in the stock room and throw away the key before she ever lets him go."

Kathy settled happily into her seat in the auditorium that evening. She had put on her Laura Ashley dress with her Orenburg shawl and thought Piers looked very presentable indeed in his dark grey suit and subtly patterned tie. The rest of the audience made her feel a bit shabby as her dress had, after all, been in the sale, but she put the shawl round her shoulders which made her feel better. Piers looked a lot brighter for a few hours' sleep and they read the programme together not paying much attention to what was going on until a gentleman they didn't know interrupted them by leaning over from the seat in front.

"Hi, good evening. Compliments of Kerryanne McDowell but would you care to join her in her box?"

Kathy and Piers looked up like two startled rabbits. "Pardon?" Kathy asked thinking he couldn't mean her.

"Ms McDowell, the novelist, would like you both to join her in her box for this performance." He nodded up towards a box in the first tier and the two followed the line of his gaze and there was Kerryanne, looking just as glamorous but a lot wealthier than she had last time they had seen her.

"Want to?" Kathy asked Piers.

"Sure, why not. I've never been in a box before."

So they followed the gentleman into the box where Kerryanne gave them both a very formal kiss on the cheek suitable for the public place then the three of them sat at the front of the box with Piers in the middle and the gentleman behind.

"Friend of yours?" Piers asked.

"He keeps an eye. How are you both?"

"We're OK. How are the novels coming on?"

"Good. I'm negotiating the film rights to a couple of them. Have you read any?"

"Don't think they've made it to the UK market. Maybe I'll buy a couple while I'm here. You're looking well."

"Thank you. How's the family? Any more kids?"

"No."

"Oh, sure, I remember now. You told me you'd been to see the surgeon."

"Yes I did. And that's not an invitation."

Kathy thought that was a very strange conversation especially as it was followed by a rather frosty silence. She sneaked a look at them but they weren't even looking at each other. Neither had made any attempt to make physical contact but there was something in the atmosphere between them which she couldn't work out.

Kerryanne looked down into the stalls for a few moments watching the audience filing in now the bell had rung. "So this is the famous Jean-Guy whose folks I met?"

There was a slight smile in Piers' eyes. "It will be. Second piece in the programme, just before the interval."

The enthusiastic New York audience welcomed the leader and conductor onto the stage and Kathy settled back in her seat, enjoying the sensation of being in a box in the Lincoln Center watching the New York Philharmonic. But a bit unsettled by that exchange between the two former lovers. She had been convinced Piers and Kerryanne were still an ongoing item but now she really wasn't sure. Intuition told her that Kerryanne was still hopeful but Piers hadn't the least intention of obliging her. Which she found odd as Kerryanne was really a very beautiful woman, and that dress of hers didn't leave much to the imagination.

The audience yelled even louder for the soloist when he came on to play the Elgar and had them spellbound from the first chord. Kerryanne joined most of the audience by leaping to her feet as soon as the music was over, whooping and clapping and making such a racket Kathy thought Piers might be needing his ear plugs again.

Kerryanne sat back in her seat. "Hey, he's real good. I've ordered a bottle of champagne to my box, I hope you two will join me? It's been so good to see you."

"Um, thank you," Kathy said, trying to remember the last time she had drunk champagne. "But we ought to go and meet up with Jean-Guy, he's expecting to sit with us for the rest of the concert."

"Oh, OK," Kerryanne leaned back and spoke to the gentleman behind her. "He'll go fetch Jean-Guy and bring him back here. And he'll get something for you to drink too," she added to Piers.

"Please tell me it's going to be water? I really don't like champagne."

"It'll have water in it. Frozen water. I remembered it's your favourite."

The champagne and canapes were brought to the box along with a bottle of frozen vodka and soon after that a slightly surprised Jean-Guy was escorted in by Kerryanne's gentleman companion. Jean-Guy had changed out of his white tie and tails into something more suitable and gave Kerryanne his most charming smile when they were introduced but was clearly wondering what was going on.

He settled next to Kathy, both of them with their champagne and smoked salmon and gave her a gentle kiss. "So how was it for you?" he asked with the funny little smile that meant he knew exactly what he was saying.

Kathy could not have said how thankful she was that his odd mood had passed and this was her tired but euphoric post-concert Moly come back to her. "Perfection," she told him and kissed him back. "Have you any idea where the loos are?"

"No, but I'll help you find out if you like?"

The two slunk out of the box and into the crowds milling around. "What's the matter?" he asked her.

"There's something odd between those two. What's he said to you about her?"

"Nothing. I mean from what I've learned he doesn't want to get involved with her now he is married and I think perhaps he is afraid she won't behave herself." Jean-Guy just stopped short of saying he had no idea how Piers could resist that woman in the semi-translucent gold dress that he was finding it very hard not to stare at.

"Probably. I wouldn't have put her down as a classical music lover. Maybe it's just she remembered your name from when she and Piers worked together and she's curious to meet you."

"Ah. So she saw my name in the programme listings, guessed you two could be with me and is hoping her former lover will oblige her?"

"Honestly I have no idea. They've had the oddest conversation. Maybe I should say he's being faithful to Sarah and resisting temptation."

Jean-Guy thought to himself that Kerryanne McDowell was one temptation he would find very hard to resist. But he didn't say anything. He jumped as the jostling people pushed them close together and Kathy sneaked a hand inside his waistband.

"Just so long as she doesn't go for you, since you're still live and dangerous."

He blushed and fished her hand out but glad she could still treat him like that. "Stop it," he told her, and tried to sound as though he meant it. "Do you think it's safe to go back there now or do you really want the loo?"

"I think I've just seen the queue for it. I can wait."

They were delayed on their walk back to the box by several people all asking the famous soloist to autograph their programmes for them which he did and Kathy realised that when they were in this world she was going to have to get used to sharing her lovely Moly. She felt quite proud of him. More champagne and canapes and an exquisite Brahms symphony later, Kerryanne's personal limo dropped Kathy and Jean-Guy off at their hotel and they wandered off to their suite feeling mellow and so deeply in love they wondered why they hadn't thought to sink most of a bottle of champagne before.

"Think Piers will be safe with her?" Kathy giggled as she settled with Jean-Guy in their bed.

Jean-Guy wrestled his imagination away from that seductive honey blonde with her plunging neckline and split skirt. "I think his marriage vows have had it. In fact I wouldn't be surprised if he turns up without his ring on tomorrow. He's done all Sarah wanted him to, so why not? He deserves to have what he wants once in a while."

Kathy couldn't quite stop giggling. "He'll be asleep before the limo's dropped him off at his hotel. That and all the vodka he and Kerryanne got through. I don't think I've ever seen him drink so much unless you count the Christmas eggnog."

There was no reply and she looked at the man in the bed next to her. Tired from his busy day and just a bit tipsy, Jean-Guy Dechaume had fallen fast asleep.

Jim Steinman – *Bad for Good*

They were having breakfast in the hotel dining room by seven o'clock the next morning as they were due to have Annette call for them at eight, when a bright-eyed Piers joined them at their table and started systematically eating the blueberries off Kathy's waffles.

"Sleep well?" Jean-Guy asked him and noticed that the wedding ring had indeed gone from Piers' finger.

"Best part of seven hours straight in a bed that didn't cripple my back for once. You have no idea how much better I feel."

"Didn't you have breakfast at your hotel?" Kathy asked as he finished off the blueberries and started on the sliced banana.

"Yes, but it was nowhere near as good as this place. I just like blueberries."

"Well you're the only person I know who does," Kathy told him, not totally sure she believed him. "And where the hell is your wedding ring?"

"On the chain with the alert tag. I haven't had a wild night of passion with Kerryanne and flushed it down the toilet if that's what you're thinking. You know Annette doesn't allow the ring on her shoots."

"So where's Kerryanne now?" Kathy asked feeling very curious. She just managed to salvage the last piece of banana for herself.

"Staying somewhere in the city I would imagine. She and her whatever-he-is gave me a lift back to my hotel and then off they went. But she's asked me to meet her at her publisher some time tomorrow. She's going to get back to me with the details."

Kathy snatched her plate away before he could get the redcurrants too. "Just go and get yourself something to eat," she told him. "The Juilliard's picking up our bill so you might as well."

She and Jean-Guy looked at each other as Piers did as he was told for once and came back to their table with quite a large bowl of fresh fruit which, to their unspoken delight, he polished off with no trouble at all.

Annette and her crew arrived promptly at eight and the photo shoot took place round the edges of Central Park. Kathy couldn't help thinking of her first shoot with Danny in a freezing cold St Albans when the two models had had to get changed behind discreetly placed screens but this time, to her relief, there was a small caravan for the models to use although they still all saw each other's underwear. Annette had learned a lot about designing for the smaller woman after that first attempt and although she had been pleased with the results she had realised that just scaling down her usual designs didn't work, at least they didn't work on Kathy, and this second collection managed to show the petite, blonde model as alluring and sophisticated at the same time rather than someone wearing her big sister's cut-down clothes. Kathy loved the clothes Annette had designed for this collection even if she was shooting her autumn and winter collection on what was actually quite a warm day. It made a change from sitting in a skimpy white dress on a cold, damp log and huddling against Danny for warmth.

Annette looked at the three of them as they stood round sharing a bottle of water between shots. Jean-Guy was still that lovely mix of little boy lost and urban trendsetter in his smart jacket and trousers, but she really wasn't sure what to do with the other two. She so wanted to pose the two of them together. Kathy was in boots that weren't very high-heeled and her bright blue woollen dress and white mohair coat suited her so well with her long hair artistically twisted on top of her head and fixed with a blue pin and Annette watched as the dressers experimented with various scarves and shawls and looked to her for approval but nothing was quite right.

"Lose the mohair," Annette eventually decided and looked across at Piers who was looking particularly gorgeous in a dark grey jacket which owed some of its look to the military uniforms of the nineteenth century and she suddenly realised what she needed. "Piers," she instructed. "Put your jacket on Kathy. No, not properly, just put it across her shoulders as though you're trying to keep her warm."

Kathy felt the weight of the jacket on her and guessed Piers had probably been very hot in it. She instinctively pulled it closed across her chest.

"No!" Annette yelled at her and all three models jumped. "Just let it hang or it looks like a bin-liner on you." She sighed. "Thank you. Now go and stand with Jean-Guy over there under the tree and pretend he's whispering sweet nothings in your ear." Annette watched the two of them get organised and let the photographer take over for a few minutes while she worked out what to do with the other model who had got bored by now and was sitting on a nearby picnic table with his feet on the bench seat. She hated his day-job haircut so much she had got the longer wig on him and for this shoot she had given up with his ears but had clipped a silver ring to his right nostril which he had grumbled about but put up with. "Got it," she said more loudly than she had intended and the man sitting on the table looked at her enquiringly.

"Is it contagious?" he asked mildly.

"It ought to be," she told him. "You can go and get changed. I've done with you for now."

"Oh, OK."

"Don't look so smug. You wait until this evening."

Kathy had only one more dress to wear for that particular shoot and she loved it more than all the others put together. It was bright blue again, fairly plain but with a pewter grey trim and it was cut a lot lower at the front than she was used to but the skirt wasn't correspondingly trashy. The whole effect was extremely tasteful and she knew she would choose that one when Annette asked her which one she wanted to keep. The white mohair went back on her and also a pair of white boots with heels so ridiculously high she was nearly the same height as Jean-Guy which he found very strange as he stood next to this beauty and tried not to peer down the front of her dress but there was a chain on the neck as part of the design and he really wanted to know where the ends of it were attached. He wasn't allowed to get too close to her as the photographer wanted to get a better shot of the dress but as Piers was done and finished, it was only him and Kathy in the caravan so he was able to satisfy his curiosity.

"Keeping that one?" he asked.

Kathy saw the gleam in his eye. "Want me to?"

"Oh, yes."

She gave him a loving kiss on the lips. "I'll wear it to your next gig."

"Can't you wear it tonight?"

She smiled as she realised he hadn't seen a fashion show before. "Tonight I shall be in as few clothes as I think I will get away with and I will probably have ear plugs in." She saw he was now extremely puzzled. "It's going to be a bit hot and noisy."

"Oh, OK," he said, not totally sure he believed her.

New Yorkers were used to such things as fashion shoots going on in their streets and didn't pay much attention to it. Annette and her crew had got it down to a fine art and the whole thing was over by lunchtime. Once all her models were back in their own clothes and the van had packed up, Annette took the three of them for some lunch in Macy's restaurant where most of the other diners seemed to be office workers grabbing a quick meal and who didn't care that there was an international fashion designer and three of her latest models sitting at one of the side tables.

"What are you two up to this afternoon?" Annette asked Kathy and Jean-Guy as she finished off her iced mocha.

"Well, Jean-Guy is recording a radio show pretty much as soon as we get back to the hotel and then we were planning on doing some trio work," Kathy replied absently, still fascinated to think she, of all people, was sitting in Macy's restaurant and next to her in a paper carrier bag was an exclusive Viola design dress of bright blue with a pewter trim and she was going to be wearing it to a concert at the Lincoln Center tomorrow evening while the love of her life enchanted his audience yet again with his cello playing.

Annette hadn't failed to notice that the well-known cellist hadn't passed totally unrecognised even on the streets of New York and she vaguely wondered if she ought to catch him and Kathy for a shoot with their instruments as well. It wouldn't do her own publicity any harm to be associated with the musicians after all. In the meantime, she had more pressing matters to deal with. "Just the two of you?" she asked. She looked at Piers who had claimed he was still full of breakfast and was just drinking a large glass of iced black coffee. "You know you've got four hours in make-up tonight, don't you?"

"Four?" he queried. "You told me one."

"Changed my mind after watching you this morning. Got to get you away from that middle-aged pilot image you've got. Your own mother won't recognise you when you go down that runway tonight."

He looked at her suspiciously. "You're not going to pierce my nose are you?"

She just laughed. "Not today. Got something way more dramatic lined up for you."

By the time they had taken up their seats behind the press at the end of the runway, Kathy and Jean-Guy were all too aware that they, even in their Viola outfits, were small fry when mixed in with the glitterati who surrounded them. Rich and famous people wanting to buy the fashions before anyone else could and parade them at their next A-list event. As one of the smaller houses, and a non-native one as well, Viola was the second house on and Kathy and Jean-Guy had already decided they didn't want to see more than that as it was incredibly hot and noisy in the function room of the hotel that was staging the show.

Kathy had told Jean-Guy what to expect so neither was surprised that they didn't see Piers on the runway with Annette's other models. Kathy was pleased to see Scott had come across but Danny hadn't so they guessed Olga must have recently had her baby. The second male model was a very handsome black man and the two in the audience were appalled by some of the remarks they overheard. It didn't help that one of Annette's female models was at least part Chinese and the other an older but still stunning Native American woman who only that morning had made the fashion designer's coffee for her in Macy's.

"Won't she lose sales using those models?" Jean-Guy hollered in Kathy's ear so she would hear him above the din.

"Do you know what? She really doesn't care. I love that about her. Her attitude is that if people don't like her models then that's their problem. She can still sell enough to make her own fortune and pay them a decent fee into the bargain. Here we go, keep an eye on the back of the stage."

Jean-Guy did as he was told and looked towards the column of darkness. Kathy was a bit surprised that only Annette was standing at one side so she guessed the canny designer wasn't going to run the exact same show she had in London. Before that blinding spotlight came on, the commentary which had been running throughout the show told the audience:

"Final showing for Viola. A lot of questions asked since London and so please give a great NYC reception for what may be the new face of Viola or may just be something from your dreams. Or nightmares. Ladies and gentlemen: Samildánach."

"Who?" Jean-Guy mouthed at Kathy but she, not having a clue either but guessing it was something Gaelic, just shrugged.

Kathy didn't know the song that blasted out through the sound system but there were no heart-stopping bass thumps as it started quietly and the blinding light came on more slowly but there was a unison blend of gasps and cheers as the lone, pale figure was fully lit. He was already wearing the coat and this time the trousers were a dark grey. He raised his head as the lights came up, showing off the black and glinting dark red jewellery round his neck, although his eyes seemed to be closed but Annette had been right, even those who knew who it was didn't recognise him.

The raven-black tousled mane was even longer for this showing than it had been in the morning and had been shot through with dark red and blond streaks and something like raindrops glittered in it too. There was a blood-red stone on a leather braid visible through the carefully arranged fringe on his forehead and set perfectly between brows that had been painted into more of a scowl. He kept his eyes down as he walked along barefoot, each step carefully choreographed with the increasing mania of the music. His identity was hidden behind make up that included a wide, straight black line from the bridge of his nose to his chin and disguised the line of his lips which Kathy found unsettlingly erotic. The glittering stars were in the tips of his ears again and the ornate septum hoop sparkled silver against the black stripe down his face. But the other two knew what had taken most of the four hours as the coat was open revealing what looked like a new tattoo where the artist had outlined the edges of the model's rib cage and there, seemingly emerged from splintered bones and rising up through the sternum, was an exquisitely drawn raven with blood-red eyes and mantled wings. Kathy caught hold of Jean-Guy's hand when she saw that drawing and her mind went back to the huge bird on her balcony nearly six years ago. All that long while, the raven had been protecting her and as Samildánach stopped at the end of the runway the ascending guitar chords accompanied the words:

You can hide away forever from the storm
But you'll never hide away from me

and Kathy knew that he would never let any harm come to her again. She looked hard at his face but couldn't see any emotion behind that make-up. Then as if aware of her gaze he suddenly looked up and Kathy was pretty sure she was among all those who gasped out loud. Annette's stylists had loaded in coloured lenses and Samildánach stared unblinkingly at the cameras of the frantic media with irises as scarily blood-red as those of the nascent raven on his chest. The coat for this show was a deep red that emphasized the chilling red eyes and the inserts were a dark charcoal grey which the model showed off as he had done before in the dramatic swirl as he turned to walk back up the runway. This time his carefully choreographed walk was accompanied by some impressive pyrotechnics as the final bars of the song built up with a series of high guitar notes and drum rhythm and he shed the coat himself barely three paces from the spotlight as the vocal ended, and a few black feathers fell with it. He stepped into the light with his back to the audience and with the last roar of the song his right fist punched up into the air and as if by some kind of enchantment there was a wing of black feathers all along his arm. Then in the abrupt silence the light snapped out and all was pitch darkness again.

Kathy dug her nails into the palms of her hands as the audience went wild all round them but she couldn't speak. All she wanted to do was take Samildánach in her arms then into her bed and caress the raven on his chest while he lay next to her in perfect contentment. She couldn't remember the last time any man had got her so hot. Jean-Guy could hear the comments of the audience and he could also feel the heat of Kathy next to him so he nudged her and nodded towards the exit door. The two wormed their way out into the lobby where the show was being relayed via huge TV screens to even more people and it was a relief to get into the comparative peace and cool of a taxi that took them back to their hotel.

Kathy was calming down a lot by the time Jean-Guy shut the door of their suite behind them but she was not expecting him to stand with his back against the door, not even coming over to her for a hug.

"Well?" he began. "Do you want to change your mind now?"

She reached out for him but he stepped aside. "I don't know what you mean."

"Yes you do. Have you ever been to bed with a married man?"

Suddenly she realised where this was going. "It's not what you think. OK, I admit it, he looked really hot up there and, well, maybe I thought some things I shouldn't. But he and I have never slept together."

Jean-Guy paused. He hadn't been expecting that. "What? Not at all? But you have known him a long time and you are so close to each other."

Feeling as though she was fighting to save her relationship, Kathy tried again to touch him but again he stepped away. "I first met Piers in the corner shop soon after I moved in with Emma back in 1978. I thought he was a policeman. We exchanged the normal pleasantries you do with someone you see fairly regularly but don't even know their name. For all I knew at the time he was married then anyway. We just exchanged a few casual words in the shop."

"And now you are in love with him?" was the surprisingly cold question.

"No! Well, yes, but not like I am with you. Please understand. I'm sure you look at other women sometimes and wonder."

Unable to deny the charge, Jean-Guy got defensive. "Maybe. But I don't share houses with them. I shouldn't be surprised. He has everything else so why shouldn't he have you too? I'm going to bed. Don't wake me up if you decide you don't want to sleep on the sofa."

Kathy gasped with the shock of that. "But…"

"He will join us for breakfast like he always does and in front of him I will ask you to choose. Please have your answer ready."

Kathy watched him stride off to the bathroom and couldn't find any words to say. Stunned and miserable she crashed down on the sofa and buried her face in a cushion so he wouldn't be disturbed by her tears.

They were sitting in a frosty silence in the hotel restaurant when Piers joined them the next morning at their breakfast table. He sat silently with them for a few moments and made no attempt to steal the fruit from their plates.

"Can I explain something to you?" he asked Jean-Guy quite levelly.

"Such as?" came the growl from the man who, now the time had come, didn't want to hear Kathy making her choice.

"Such as I don't want to sleep with your girlfriend."

Jean-Guy wouldn't look up from his plate. "Why not? You have everything else in life."

Piers suddenly grabbed the other man by the wrist hard enough to make him look up and see the unexpected fury in the cornflower eyes. "Let me guess," he began sarkily. "She got the hots for Samildánach last night, you got in a strop and made her sleep on the sofa."

"I…" Jean-Guy started, but he wasn't allowed to continue. He snatched his wrist back but at least didn't look away any more.

"You absolute bloody idiot. What Piglet fell for was every single bit of marketing House of Viola threw at her last night. Every little bit of that charade was designed to make rich women get so steamed up with sexual desire they spent thousands of dollars trying to buy just a little bit of the fantasy. Everything from the crystals in the wig to the bloody tickly toe ring was part of the act. I'm not telling you what they paid me for my part in it but House of Viola had made probably a hundred times that amount in sales by the time I went to bed last night. And, yes, it's none of your bloody business but I went to bed alone. You have no idea how many hours Annette and her crew spent drilling me in how to walk, how to stand and, for Christ's sake, even how to bloody breathe when I was at the end of that bloody runway. It was hard-nosed blatant marketing and it was aimed at every woman and probably a lot of the men too."

Kathy didn't dare say a word but she could see that Jean-Guy was almost squirming by now and she felt a bit of an idiot herself. Certainly the man in the unironed shirt and scruffy jeans, although remarkably handsome, was nowhere near as arousing as Samildánach had been last night.

"So, Jean-Guy, what you need to do now is take Piglet back to bed, where she should have been last night as I have no doubt she was pretty bloody ripe for some of your best fantasies, shag her witless and then tell her you're sorry you ever doubted her. I have never met anyone as faithful as your Piglet and if you doubted her for one second then it just goes to show that Annette knows how to sell designs and that is why she's the one with the millions in the bank."

Jean-Guy finally looked at the woman sitting opposite him. "Well, now I feel like a fool."

Kathy couldn't have expressed how relieved she felt to hear that. When she had said such things to Jean-Guy he hadn't believed her. He had thought she was trying to justify her lust for another man. But now that man had said sex had nothing to do with it. He had been paid to do a job, he had been trained and drilled in what was expected of him for the fee he was being paid and he had performed his duties as best he could. A tiny part of her almost wished it hadn't all been marketing and that maybe, just maybe, there had been some hope for her and Samildánach. But then probably so did nearly everyone who saw the model live or in the photos that were all over the morning papers. She looked at the worried man sitting opposite her, and leaned over so she could give him a loving kiss. "Yes, but you're my fool. Now do you believe me?"

"Yes," he admitted and began to hope maybe there was time to take her to bed after all.

Piers swiped a blueberry off Jean-Guy's plate and gave him a wicked smile. "You mean to tell me I didn't manage to turn you on last night too?"

"No you bloody didn't."

Piers rolled the blueberry into his mouth with his tongue. "Damn, I obviously wasn't trying hard enough. Not even a little bit?"

Jean-Guy could feel his face getter redder and redder by the second. "I... I maybe was jealous of you. You looked very beautiful in all your make-up and jewellery. But I didn't want to have sex with you." A thought occurred to him and he had to say it. "Anyway, I have seen you naked. You're not that pretty."

There was a sound somewhere between a squeak and a snort from the annoyingly handsome one and all three were wheezing with laughter all over again such as only they could.

"Just shut up," Piers pleaded and poured himself a drink of water from the jug on the table. "So, we're all good again, are we?"

"We are," Jean-Guy reassured him and he took Kathy's hand. "And I do owe you a very large apology."

"You can apologise properly later," Kathy said, thankful they seemed to have ridden out that particular storm. "I think I owe you one too for being such a sucker I got taken in by Annette's marketing wiles." She had to smile at Piers. "Mind you, you were amazing, and I can believe it took Annette hours to turn a scruffbag like you into that creation last night. Have you seen it's in all the papers? Annette seems to have set New York on fire first of all by using the League of Nations for her models then sending out

Samildánach. All the papers are full of who he is. One of the Celtic gods I believe. Commonly known as Lugh."

Piers ate the blueberries off Kathy's plate too. "Yup. Not sure I'd call him a god but an important figure in Celtic mythology certainly. His animals are the raven and the lynx. Pity mine's a panther but it's some kind of a big cat and most people can't tell the difference."

"And that raven tattoo?" Kathy asked. "Is it real?"

Making sure nobody else could see, Piers discreetly undid a couple of buttons on his shirt to show them the red-eyed head of the raven. "Sarah is going to kill me, but when I saw the design drawn on I agreed the guy could get his needles out. There were two of them working flat out, one each side just to get it done in time. Bloody hurt too, right on the ribs like that."

"How the hell did Annette get you to agree to that?" Kathy demanded and was a bit regretful as Piers did the buttons up again.

"The only other option was some kind of paint but that didn't look right so she asked if I'd mind. Needless to say she remembered I'd said I didn't care if I got covered in ink so long as it doesn't show at work. Bad feeling that since she spent all that money she's going to be running Sammy out a few more times before she's done with him."

"But unless she's going to specialise in men's coats with wings I can't see what she'll do with you now," Kathy pointed out.

"No, nor can I but she's the one with the ideas, I just take the fees to make them real for her. Anyway, if you two haven't got any plans to go upstairs later on, please can I book one or both of you for this afternoon? Kerryanne rang me at the hotel very late last night as she wants to meet me at her publisher's at two. Apparently she has a proposition for me."

"And how would it help having us with you?" Jean-Guy asked. "You have got me curious now."

"Two reasons. One is that if this is going to be a business meeting I'd like a witness or two. And secondly I don't want that bloody harlot trying to get the trousers off me like she did in the back of her limo the other night."

"You mean you and Kerryanne..." Kathy began.

"No," he cut in flatly. "She got me two years ago before I married Sarah and it's not going to happen again."

Jean-Guy had never met a man so unwilling to give in to his physical desires. "What is the matter with you? Even your wife says you can have lovers if you want them."

Piers suddenly went on the defensive. "I just don't want them. OK? Meeting's at two so I'll call by and pick up whichever one of you wants to come with me. Now, are we doing anything with the Shostakovich this morning or can I go across to Tiffany's and get something for my wife?"

"Go," Jean-Guy told him. "I have some serious apologising to do first of all. But be back in a couple of hours. And it's Prokofiev, not Shostakovich."

With understanding restored, Jean-Guy decided he would rather take a rest in his hotel room to be fresh for his concert that evening as he had to perform the *Sinfonia Concertante* which was the most demanding of the three works he was doing in the series. So the other two caught a yellow cab to the offices of Kerryanne McDowell's publishers and somehow they weren't surprised by the opulence of the building as soon as they stepped into the elegant foyer.

The meeting was held in a conference room that would have accommodated a full symphony orchestra and an audience although all it had in it was a very polished table and chairs and lots and lots of bookcases. Kerryanne introduced her companion as Rachel representing her agent and the publishers were represented by a middle-aged man who instructed them to call him Dom and who gave the impression he was going to be a tough negotiator.

They all sat at one end of the shiny table with Kerryanne and Rachel at one side and Piers and Kathy on the other while Dom sat at the head. Each place was laid with a notepad, pen and a glass for water and there were two cut-glass carafes of iced water between them all. Kathy poured some water for Piers and herself while taking in as much as she could so she could describe it all to Jean-Guy later and she looked across at the women opposite which was how she noticed the necklace Kerryanne was wearing. There was something very familiar about the red stone and black leather braid and she lifted her eyes from the necklace to Kerryanne's face and caught the other woman's smile.

"Were you there last night?" she asked.

"Sure was. I must admit I wasn't expecting to buy from Viola as they're too extreme for my taste but when I saw who was modelling this, how could I resist? I was too late to get the coat and was told in no uncertain terms that the model wasn't for sale." She blew Piers a kiss across the table. "It still smelled of you when I put it on."

Somehow Kathy wasn't surprised when Piers' reply wasn't quite cold enough to freeze helium but not far off it. "Still got the tattoo as well."

It seemed, Kathy thought, Piers was quite well aware of Kerryanne's agenda for him and she couldn't help wondering why he wouldn't oblige. But the tone of his voice gave her a good idea of what had happened in the car the night of the Elgar concert.

Kerryanne caught her breath but she was just as frosty with him. She gave him a filthy look. "Right. Can we get the business out of the way now? I need you to listen to this."

She put a small cassette recorder on the table and pressed the start button.

After a few seconds what sounded like Piers' voice was heard on the tape. "Narsarsuaq, this is Speedbird 446 requesting emergency landing permission."

An accented man's voice replied crackling a bit with static. "Speedbird 446, what the hell are you doing in the air? All flights have been grounded."

"We've got caught in the storm. Repeat, we are requesting emergency landing permission."

"Speedbird 446, we have blizzard conditions, bad windshear and volcanic ash cloud. Landing permission denied. Proceed to Reykjavik; they have snow but no ash."

Piers' voice still sounded perfectly calm. "We won't make Reykjavik. We have instrument malfunctions and worsening weather. We have to put down now or we'll be lost in the storm."

"Speedbird 446, there is no chance in hell you can land here. Put out your mayday and try for Reykjavik."

There was a silence on the tape for a few moments but Kerryanne didn't spool through the static.

"Sorry, Narsarsuaq, but we're out of options and now starting our descent for final approach."

"Speedbird 446, we have refused you landing permission. It isn't safe for you to attempt to land here. Continue towards Reykjavik and put out your mayday."

"We won't make it. At least with you we stand a chance. Can you see our lights?"

The voice of the Air Traffic Controller suddenly sounded weary and despairing. "Speedbird 446, confirm we can just see your lights. What is your number of souls on board, please?"

"One hundred and eight passengers and seven crew."

The voice was then heard to mutter quietly, "No chance in hell. God rest those souls."

Piers leaned forward and stopped the tape. "Where the hell did you get that?" he demanded furiously of Kerryanne.

She wasn't deterred by his anger. "I've written a book featuring that landing and I've got two major film companies fighting over the rights before I even go to print. Unfortunately it seems I have to get permission from you before the publication can be released as we need to use your exact words."

"And if I refuse? That's just half of it. You can't have got the CVR." He saw the look on Kerryanne's face. "How the bloody hell did you get your hands on the cockpit voice recorder as well as the air traffic one?"

"I have my contacts," she told him flatly.

Piers guessed she had got most of her information from the enquiry papers and she certainly had the contacts to read those. But he tried one last protest. "There were, as you just heard, over a hundred of us on that flight. I can't speak for all of them."

"We're not asking you to," Dom interrupted, sounding tetchy. "We have already contacted the other two flight crew members whose voices are audible on the cockpit recording and informed them of our plans and they have agreed to receive a fee for the rights to their identities and words being used in the film. We aren't identifying any of the passengers or cabin crew as Kerryanne has created the main action round them as fictional characters. Although she liked the idea you had a trainee stewardess on board and that is in as a minor theme. I'm sure you are aware she writes crime thrillers and your flight is, for the most part, merely the setting for a fictional story. Mr Hollander and Mr Belmont will each receive a lower fee that I cannot disclose. But which they will lose if we have to fictionalise the crew too and I think they would be a bit upset if you took that away from them."

Kathy could feel the rage coming off Piers like a physical force which was so unlike him. She shot her hardest look at Kerryanne but she was just smiling quietly, certain of her triumph. "Can I take Piers outside for a couple of minutes, please?" she asked. "I'm sure I can persuade him to listen to reason."

Kerryanne's confidence seemed to slip a little but she wasn't going to back down. "Of course," she agreed. "But don't keep him out there too long, we're all busy people."

Kathy and Piers went into the outer office where neither of the two desks had anyone working at it so Kathy hoped the staff were out for a late lunch together and wouldn't be back any time soon. "OK," she invited gently. "Talk to me." She looked at the furious man who was leaning his forehead on a filing cabinet and she physically backed away two paces when he banged his fist hard against the cabinet then spun to face her and she could have sworn there were cold sparks coming off him.

He spoke quite slowly but Kathy could tell he was barely controlling the anger and the hurt bubbling just below the surface.

"She used me," he almost spat. "Seduced and beguiled me and pillow-talked me just to get a bloody story out of me. Do you know what? I was stupid enough to believe she wanted me as a co-pilot on that trip to Moscow after we met during the mess with Marianne. The hell she did. She'd got half a story from somewhere, bribed Mick and Dutchman somehow but they weren't enough for her. So then she got her gunsights on me."

Kathy felt very brave as she put her hands on Piers' arms. "It's OK to feel like that," she consoled. "I kind of understand. It's how my ex made me feel. Sweet words and flattery, nice things for you like knitting the shawl for me, but it wasn't real. And now you feel violated. Just as I did."

To her relief, he gathered her into a hug of gratitude. "I don't know what to do," he admitted.

Kathy looked into his troubled eyes. "Well, you don't do what I did and run away. You stand your ground and screw that bitch for every cent you can get out of her. Ask flat out what they offered Mick and Dutchman then stick a zero on the end. Or, if that's not enough to satisfy you, whatever they offer you just double it. They need your consent for her plans to go ahead from the sound of it. The power is yours. Don't you ever forget that. I wish I'd had your power when the ex left me on the floor like he did." She took his face in her hands as she had done so often before. "Come on, we can do this together. You stick up for yourself. We're going back in there with guns blazing and coming out smelling of roses. If that's not mixing my metaphors too much."

"How can I?" he asked, clearly still angry. "She's the one in control. Has been the whole time."

"No," Kathy said sharply. "That's just what she wants you to believe. Like my ex did with me." She hadn't taken her eyes off his face and saw the first trickle of blood from his nose. "Oh, hell, now you've got a nosebleed. Hang on, there are some tissues on the desk."

Kathy parked him on the edge of one of the desks and shoved a fistful of tissues into his hand. "Sit. Calm down before you bleed from anywhere else." She got some iced water from the dispensing machine so she could perform some rudimentary first aid on his nose which was bleeding quite heavily by this time.

An impatient Kerryanne came out of the conference room to find out what was happening, hoping those two hadn't just bolted and found Kathy holding ice cubes on

Piers' nose while he was mopping his face with some bloodied tissues.

"What the hell happened?" she demanded. "Did you hit him or did he fall?"

"It's only a nosebleed," Kathy said too angry herself to be scared by the other woman's temper. "I just can't stop it." Ignoring Kerryanne she said to Piers, "Put your head back a minute and open your mouth." She had a good look as best she could. "Damn. It looks as though you're bleeding from the back of your mouth but it's going down your nose. That's why this isn't working. Here, suck an ice cube or three. You've got two minutes then I'm calling the paramedics."

He mumbled something unintelligible through a mouthful of ice.

Kerryanne stepped closer to them. "What the hell is going on?" The tone of her voice was the one a USAF officer would use to bollock the other ranks on the parade ground.

Kathy wasn't sure she could bring herself to be polite to this woman who, it seemed, had so lightly and carelessly used her friend for her own ends, so she carried on ignoring her and looked at the wall clock for two minutes. "Feeling better?" she asked Piers.

He gulped a bit as he swallowed what was left of the ice. "Yes, thanks."

"Good. Let me have a check. Yup, all stopped. But your mouth doesn't look too good at the back. Just be careful and don't let that other one wind you up like that again. You have to pay the paramedics here, you know that don't you? Ready to go back in? Oh, for pity's sake, you look as though you've done ten rounds with Mohammed Ali. Go and find the gents and wash your face."

"Just across the corridor," Kerryanne told him. She watched him leave the office and gave Kathy a grudging smile of respect. "I assume you mean me by 'that other one'? Is he sick?"

"He has been," was all Kathy was prepared to say and hoped she had got away with how she had referred to the bestselling author. Although she hadn't meant to be polite and there was no way she was going to apologise. To her relief, an apology didn't seem to be expected.

"What is it? Mouth cancer?" was the surprisingly compassionate question.

Kathy didn't trust this woman and knew it wasn't up to her to tell the whole truth. "No, nothing like that. But just back off a bit will you."

"Excuse me? Did a little squirt like you just tell me to back off?"

"Yes, I did. You've treated a dear, sweet man horribly and you should be ashamed of yourself. Just think of me as the mongoose to your snake."

"Jesus. Feisty little thing aren't you?" Kerryanne remarked but there was a definite note of respect in her voice. "And, trust me, there is nothing dear or sweet about that guy but I can see why he loves you so much."

Kathy's conversation of last night was still raw in her mind. "No he doesn't. Not like you're implying."

"I'm not implying anything. He would kill to protect you and you'd do the same for him. One day, I hope, you and I will be able to be friends."

Kathy looked at this glamorous woman and a small, treacherous part of her hoped so too.

Piers wandered back in looking a lot cleaner. "Sorry about the drama," he said briefly to Kerryanne. "Happens every so often."

"What happened to you?" Kerryanne asked and her voice was much softer.

He smiled in that way he had but didn't answer her question. "Right, I'm ready for you and your little schemes now so shall we all go back in?"

They resumed their places at the huge table and Dom glared at them all. "Mr Buchanan, our offer to you for the rights to your words on that recording and permission to use your identity for the purposes of Ms McDowell's work is two million dollars. Which is more than we are offering your colleagues as yours will be a more dominant character in the dramatization. Needless to say you are not allowed to disclose anything of this agreement to anyone except Ms Fairbanks as your witness and to any nominated legal representative you may choose to appoint. We will not be putting these negotiations through your agent and they are due no percentage fee of any agreed sums. What do you say?"

Piers remembered Kathy's words of advice. "Four. Six if she's put my character in any bedroom scenes."

Dom gave him a filthy look. "Your character goes nowhere near any bedrooms. But you want four million dollars for the rights I just itemised?"

Piers was enjoying himself now and he understood what Kathy had meant about the switch of power. He wished she could have had such a chance when she had needed it. Besides which it was getting quite farcical and he couldn't believe such sums of money were being so casually talked about. "Uh-huh. And how the hell did you get that tape? There's no way I can give consent for that, half the conversation is from Greenland."

"Our legal team have dealt with all that, it's not your concern. We just need you to consent to your name and

Kerryanne's interpretation of you being used in the book and the film. Two and a half and that's the final offer."

"I'll agree to two and a half if it's pounds sterling." His smile was pure mischief, thinking none of this would ever happen. "And I want Danny Tarling to play my part."

"Hold on there," Kerryanne cautioned. "He's one of the hottest stars around at the moment. There is no way we can promise we'll get him especially as it's not a lead role. Much as I would like to."

"So," Dom clarified, thinking what a coup it would be to get the rising British actor on the cast. "You want two and a half million pounds sterling in fees, and Danny Tarling to be contracted to play your character if at all possible?"

"Yes."

Dom looked at this man and his instincts told him that his adversary would lose the fees rather than give in. Some bartering was called for. "Danny Tarling would be a good pull for the box office," he agreed. He knew what the bosses had budgeted and they were nowhere near that ceiling yet, "OK, I'm a fair man and I have to admit it would be a hell of a mess if we don't get your consent. This is my final offer. We'll honour our offer of two and a half million pounds sterling and up it to a full three mill if we get Danny Tarling as well."

Piers looked at Kathy and saw the smile in her eyes. "Oh, you'll get him. He's a personal friend of mine."

Dom knew when he had been outwitted and had a grudging respect for the other man now. "Good. Three million pounds sterling and Danny Tarling's name on the contracts. Will you settle for that?"

"Yes," Piers said, trying to sound all cool and calm but feeling as madly excited and confused as he guessed Kathy was from the way her hand was shaking in his under the table.

"Agreed. If you'll all excuse me I'll just get my secretary to make the final amendments to your agreement and it can be signed here today. Ms Fairbanks can be your witness. And we'll get on to Danny Tarling's agent right now."

To Kathy's vast amusement Piers looked totally poleaxed. "What?" he asked faintly.

"I said 'agreed'. Or do you have any other terms you want to negotiate?"

"Um, no. Thank you."

"Good. Right, I'll go and get the preliminary contracts for you to sign, Or would you rather your legal representative checked them first?"

"If the terms are clear enough I'm happy to sign, but I want a clause in that I can raise a legal challenge retrospectively and that it will be covered by English law. Because, as I'm sure you've worked out, I don't have an American attorney so it's no good stitching me up in US law."

Dom knew when he was beaten. "We have similar clauses for our international clients. I'll get your contract amended before this initial signing."

Kathy admired the cool thinking of the Wing Commander and was so happy to have witnessed his ultimate victory. It made her feel a whole lot better in herself that she could look Kerryanne in the eye and tell her, "I've got Danny's phone number if you want to see if he's home? He should be there this time of year as he's more likely to be away filming in the summer."

"You have a hotline to Danny Tarling?" Kerryanne asked incredulously.

"Oh, yes. I've known him for years," she said airily, enjoying that the upper hand was, just for a few moments, hers. "It was me who introduced him to Piers. I can ring and ask him now if you like?"

"If you're speaking to Danny Tarling about portraying a character in my book, I want to be there too," Kerryanne announced.

Kathy was in a way relieved that Piers wouldn't be alone with the harlot, as he had called her, and she assumed the silent Rachel would behave herself with him as the other three went out of the conference room.

Negotiations finalised, they went back to the room to find Piers standing by the window looking at the sights of New York while Rachel was still at the table going through a diary and making notes.

"All sorted," Dom announced sounding very satisfied, having calculated his own company's profits from this deal. "Mr Tarling has confirmed to Kerryanne personally that he will take the role and he'll notify his agent. Your fee, Mr Buchanan will be wired direct to your bank account and I will need the name of your legal representatives so we can send them copies of this and all future agreements. They will all go by overnight mail with a notification of mailing by telex. You and your crew members are now officially signed as our technical advisors and must not speak or communicate in any way with any party whatsoever about any of this or all agreements are null and void and compensation will be payable by you. This is your preliminary contract to sign, the full agreement will be sent first to your legal representative who may wish to raise further conditions which we may be willing to discuss if necessary. Who will be representing you?"

To Kathy's admiration, Piers had his answer ready. "Sir Giles Delaney QC. He'll be acting on my behalf in all future negotiations. Can you give me your direct line number and his chambers will contact you?"

Dom silently handed over a business card and Kathy could see the resentful respect in his eyes that he hadn't fazed or outwitted this opponent in any way.

Kathy and Piers left the offices of the publisher and managed to find their way into the nearest coffee shop where she ordered a large mocha and a lemon cake and Piers stuck with his iced black coffee but gave in to temptation and had a blueberry muffin on the side.

"What the hell happened in there?" he asked her and his voice was almost shaking.

"I think you just became a multi-millionaire. I can't believe it either."

He had that lovely smile back on his face again now. "So if I went to bed with Kerryanne and now she's paid me all that money, does that make me some kind of a tart?"

Kathy loved his sense of humour. "Oh, yes. But I'll let you calculate your nightly rate on your own. Not sure I want to know." She could see he was already doing maths in his head and tried to divert him as it really was too gross to think of her big brother like that. "Are you sure Giles Delaney won't mind?"

"Not at all. I rang him while you were gossiping with Danny. I got the impression there's nothing he'll enjoy more than a good battle with that lot."

"Must say, I think you're right." She smiled and was pleased to see him actually eat the muffin. "You do realise you can give up your day job now and you won't have to fly Concorde ever again."

"No, I won't, will I," he realised. "No more 2am pager calls to go to the back of beyond. No more dossing in hotels and forgetting what home looks like. I don't get it. All I ever did was land a broken aeroplane in a blizzard. I was just doing my job."

"No, what you did was to have the courage, or maybe just the sheer bloody-mindedness, and the skill to save over a hundred lives. From what I can gather from Mick's storytelling and that recording, anyone else would have taken the advice to try for Reykjavik rather than risk Narsarsuaq and would have perished in the storm." She took a drink of her mocha and missed the ones Alison made. "It's going to change your life, you know that, don't you?"

Piers gave that a bit of thought too. "I hope not. I've only just about got it sorted out to a good place. Come on, drink up as that boyfriend of yours is going to want another run through of that blasted Prokofiev before tea. And I don't care how much I get paid, I'm not bailing out on you two. Audrey would never forgive me."

Kathy couldn't have expressed her relief at those words. Piers was still her friend and always would be, no matter what happened to him. "True. Come on then. Which one of us is going to give the good news to the dictator?"

Piers finished his coffee and raised his empty glass to her. "Oh, that's one for you, I think. Don't you?"

Kathy paused as they got up to leave. "So, what did your maths tell you?"

"About what?"

"Your nightly rate. I saw you working it out."

He looked faintly astonished that she would ask. "I'm not telling you that."

"Why not?" she wanted to know, feeling the happiness bubbling up inside her at his expression.

"Because you're pretty bloody good at maths yourself and quite capable of doing a simple multiplication to work out how many nights were involved."

"True," she had to admit and let him open the door for her.

Laughing together at the sheer absurdity of this latest turn of events, the two friends walked out of the coffee shop onto the bustling streets of New York.

Jean-Guy listened in silence as the other two, with much laughing and poking fun at each other, told him what had happened at the publisher that afternoon. He was in a way thankful they had had the manners to wait until he had had a run-through of the Prokofiev with Piers in the hotel suite and then they had told him. He was pleased for Piers but the first thing he said was a more selfish:

"So you don't need to play with the Dodman Trio any more? And you certainly don't need to be my accompanist?"

Piers was still at the piano and he thankfully took the cup of tea Kathy gave him. "Truthfully, right now I don't know what I'm going to do. As Piglet pointed out I certainly don't need to carry on flying. I've never needed to play trios." He fell silent again. "I don't know. I'm all in just such a muddle right now."

Jean-Guy thoughtfully sipped his own tea and looked across at the woman who had settled herself quite comfortably on the sofa and idly picked up a magazine of knitting patterns she had brought back with her. He knew perfectly well that although her eyes were looking at a picture of a very fashionable black and white sweater, her ears were tuned in to every word that was being said. "What do you want to do?" he asked calmly.

"I don't know. I'd welcome your advice."

Jean-Guy looked at the man at the piano. So perfect to look at and yet surprisingly lacking in self-confidence right now. This wasn't the beautiful man who had stood at the end of the runway last night and had made all the audience desire him. This wasn't even the man who could so calmly handle a supersonic jet airliner. This was someone whose life had suddenly switched direction and he was struggling to cope with it. "OK, but this is just my opinion, right? For now I would carry on as you have always done. Carry on flying your Concorde and playing your music. Over time you will learn to adjust to what has happened to you and you will find your own way forward."

Piers hadn't been expecting that. "Sounds sensible," he agreed. "Not at all what I was thinking you'd say, but sensible."

"Back in the summer of 1980 I was a Czech cellist who had been lucky and got a lot of work. The critics, and my mother, told me I had a natural talent. I just thought I worked hard. Then a French orchestra took me over the border and suddenly I was free. Like you are now. You are free to have the life you want. I had to walk. I walked through the autumn and a lot of the winter and while I walked I was able to think about my freedom that I had. I was no longer just a Czech cellist. I was a defector. I was stateless. I had nothing. For you now, in a way, you have everything. But you have to do the same walk I did and learn to live with what has happened."

Kathy thought that was such a beautiful way of expressing it. She had often thought Jean-Guy spoke almost poetically sometimes but maybe that was what happened when you hadn't started to learn English until you were twelve. Or maybe just what happened when you were simultaneously translating from the Czech in your head as you spoke.

"Have you got any annual leave lined up?" she asked. "I'm sure you could go for one of your long walks and get your head round it."

"I can't take any for a while. I've used up a hell of a lot of it already and my flying hours are right down. Plus the fact they've not long released the lines so I'm all booked up for the next three months anyway." He finished his tea. "But I like the idea of that." Just for a moment he paused and looked at the other two. "Either, or both, of you like to come with me?"

Jean-Guy couldn't imagine anything worse. He had few good memories of his walk across France and couldn't think why anyone would do such a thing for the pleasure of it. Then he looked across at Kathy and saw the look on her face.

Kathy didn't know what to say. Part of her could think of nothing better than spending her days walking with her closest friend but she knew Jean-Guy wouldn't want to do it and she wasn't sure it was something she should do without him.

"Think about it," Piers offered. "Both of you. I don't mind if neither of you comes or you both do. Right, Jean-Guy, are we done with Prokofiev for now?"

Jean-Guy had to smile. "What do you think? You are the one who tells us when we have played too much and need to stop."

"True. You can't perfect perfection, can you? Play it tonight like you did just now and you'll bring the house down."

"Thank you. I think you are perhaps my sternest critic and if that is what you think then I am satisfied. Kathy, why don't you get your violin out and we can play a little trio music until it's time to get ready?"

Piers checked his watch. "Jesus! Is that the time? I'd better be off to my own hotel and get myself sorted out. Sorry, too much talking. Meet you back here in about an hour and a half. At least I won't get bothered by Kerryanne tonight."

Kathy and Piers left Jean-Guy at the stage door that evening then went to find their places in the auditorium. They had got no further than the foyer and couldn't believe their luck was so far out when they saw Kerryanne had turned up for the last concert in the series but this time she was talking to Annette Delaney.

"Shall we pretend we haven't seen them?" Piers hissed in Kathy's ear.

"Too late," she realised as the two women turned and saw them.

"I'm not getting in a box with her again."

"That's fine, we've got our tickets."

There was no sign of Annette's husband nor of Kerryanne's gentleman companion as the two who had been chatting came to greet the couple who had just arrived.

Kerryanne gave Piers a kiss on the cheek and said laughingly, "I gather nobody is supposed to know it was you on that runway last night. Good luck keeping that a secret. That Samildánach is quite a celebrity now."

Piers moved slightly, subtly away from her. "Yes, maybe he is. But I'm not and that's how I want to keep it."

Kerryanne half-laughed. "Oh, I've already had Annette telling me that anyone who leaks your alter ego is likely to be sued by Viola for every last penny they've got. I've got no vested interest in announcing your identity to the world. It's just another secret about you that I'll keep."

Kathy saw the look Piers gave her and was glad he never looked at her like that. It reminded her that this was one man who had been trained by his family in how to do some less-than-pleasant things to people. She tucked her hand through his arm again. "Come on, let's go and find our seats," she said gently.

"Good idea," he agreed. Suddenly he smiled, that lovely smile that was going to make millions for House of

Viola. "You haven't met my bodyguard, have you?" he said to Kerryanne.

She took the joke. "Oh, I have. I met her at the publisher this afternoon, remember? You've made a good choice. What does Sarah think of you two?"

Kathy bridled at her tone. "What do you mean? Piers and I are just friends."

"Sure you are, honey," Kerryanne smiled. "If that's what you say you are."

"Give it up," Piers advised Kathy. "She's never going to believe us no matter what we say. Maybe see you ladies in the interval?"

"Won't you join me in my box again?" Kerryanne tried.

Kathy had her reply ready and didn't notice she still had hold of Piers by the arm. "Oh, no, thank you. We've got seats in the middle of the stalls where the acoustic is so much better. I find boxes can give you a rather lopsided impression of the orchestra."

"Well done," Piers muttered in her ear as the two walked away to the entrance to the stalls.

Kathy gave him her best innocent look. "I have no idea what you're talking about. It's perfectly true."

"Of course it is," he agreed and gave her a quick hug to his side.

Kathy could feel Kerryanne's eyes boring into her back as she walked with Piers into the stalls and out of sight of the other two. Somehow she had a bad feeling Kerryanne McDowell didn't like losing.

Bedřich Smetana – *Piano trio in G minor, Op.15*

"It was awful," Kathy said to Emma as she chatted on the phone with her oldest friend. "I honestly thought that was it for me and Jean-Guy."

"Kath, I saw the photos in the newspapers and I wanted to rip the clothes off him. What the hell was it like when he was standing there in front of you?"

"I've never known anything like it. I tell you, if he'd so much as looked at me the right way I'd have thrown myself at him. But I think he'd probably have called me a tart as he does, and just thrown me straight back."

"Good. You'd be an idiot to ditch Jean-Guy to run off with a married man so much older than you. I mean, I know you've had at least one fling with a married man in your career but I thought you were settled now."

"I am. Piers just got all sensible again and explained that the whole image is all about marketing and by making me get the hots for him it just proved it worked. Apparently Annette's raking in the money now she's run out dear old Sammy as we all call him. She'll be using him quite a lot until he's past it."

"Wow. Bags me a seat right next to the runway next time. But I'll need you next to me to tie me down."

"Silly," Kathy said, grateful as ever to be chatting with her oldest friend who knew all her grubby little secrets. "He won't have you. I honestly have never met a bloke who has turned down so many women in his life. And quite a few men too if what he says is true."

"But the three of you are all OK now, aren't you?"

"I think so. Jean-Guy's sorry for having a go at me anyway."

"Silly sod. And what did Sarah think of the new tattoo?"

Kathy nearly laughed. "She hasn't seen it yet. He stayed on in Earl's Court as he wasn't even officially on holiday for those few days while we were in New York and we haven't seen him since."

Emma sighed dramatically. "You mean he's not going to be available for me any time soon?"

The two started giggling uncontrollably at the very idea of such a thing but Kathy was interrupted by Audrey racing into the kitchen and setting off the three-minute warning.

"Oh, got to go," she said. "Looks like the man of your dreams is about to walk through the door. Thank heavens for an efficient cat or he might have caught us talking about him."

"Oh, let me stick my tongue down the phone and lick his ear," Emma pleaded laughingly. "Just you let me know next time he's stripping down to leathers and feathers."

"Will do," Kathy promised and hung up just as the subject of her conversation stepped into the kitchen,

"Oh, hi," he greeted her a bit suspiciously as he had heard the phone being hung up and she was definitely laughing about something. "Have I missed anything exciting?"

"Oh, no. Just me and Emma."

"Glad I did miss it in that case. Just looked in for a long weekend as I came across the parts for the Smetana in a second-hand shop in the Charing Cross Road and I know Jean-Guy's been looking for that for ages."

"Oh! Well done. Want to start playing now or do you want tea or something first?"

Piers helped himself to a glass of water. "This'll do me for now. Meant to be here for lunch but was longer at

Giles' chambers than I thought I would be. Never mind. Contracts all finalised now." He handed a paper bag across to her. "Right, I'll just go and dump my stuff upstairs and you can go and make Jean-Guy very happy. Or have you done that once already today?"

Kathy caught his teasing tone. "Once? You underestimate me."

"Go on, hop it, you tart. Thank Christ you picked the other one. I'd never keep up with you."

"Going to see Sarah this time round?"

He pulled a face. "Um, probably not."

"You are such a wuss. You could aways undress in the dark."

He gave her one of his lovely smiles. "Oh, no, that wouldn't work, would it?"

"Why not?" she asked and then realised he had caught her out again.

"The undressing is one of the best parts of it, isn't it?"

Kathy had to laugh with him. "And you called me a tart?!"

"Yup, but right now I'm not sure I'm ready for the reactions. I'll maybe pick a time when Alison isn't in the house."

Kathy felt ridiculously sorry for him. "Go and put your things in your room and I'll give the music to Jean-Guy. Maybe one of us should be with you when you strip off in front of your wife."

Piers was already heading towards the stairs with Audrey tagging along behind. "Just shut up. You're not helping."

They played the Smetana after tea and the Prof didn't even pretend he wasn't listening but came and sat on the piano stool again so he could be page-turner and general advisor. Not that the Dodman Trio needed his advice much these days. He never tired of listening to them and how the three would work together as one musician.

"Excellent!" he praised them as they closed the trio in style. "Do you have any idea when you will play that one out? It doesn't seem to need much work on it and it has been a while since you ran out anything new."

Jean-Guy almost sighed. "We don't have any bookings as a Trio until we go back to Germany next year. Kathy has a couple of gigs with the Strettos coming up very soon, I am busy with my orchestral work and then we have to work on *The Planets* ready for Christmas."

Kathy wished Jean-Guy wouldn't mention her playing with the Strettos quite so casually. To him it was a chance for her to extend herself as a musician and he knew she had been working hard to commit their repertoire to memory but she had found it difficult. She didn't often play without music and she felt as though someone had snatched away her security blanket by making her stand up and play even the most basic of Haydn quartets without the music to prompt her. She knew it was no worse than someone like Danny having to learn lines for a film or a play. She had to know her own notes but also the cues and harmonies of the other players in the group and that was what she couldn't practise on her own or with Jean-Guy. He helped her as best he could by filling in the cello part for her but she still felt she wasn't ready for it.

"Ah, yes," the Prof remembered. "When are you off to Sweden?"

"Too soon," she mumbled and didn't want to think about it.

Piers half-laughed. "And when exactly might that be?"

"Wednesday next week. It's only for a couple of days and I'll be back on the Friday."

"Oh, OK. This is a practice session is it?"

"Yes. Just running through their more basic works. They won't want me for the *Lithuanian* for a couple of months and I'll have to go back to Sweden for a week or so in May so we can work on that and I'll be doing my first concerts with them. For them it's local as it's in Uppsala and Helsinki but I haven't played in either place and I'm not sure I'm looking forward to it."

"Uh-huh. Want a lift?"

Kathy felt an odd surge of hope run through her. "What do you mean?"

"Next week. I'm not flying for a few days so we can hire something from the club and I can be your chauffeur. If you want that is."

The relief Kathy felt surprised her. "You can do that?"

"Sure. I'll give Pete Finch a ring and see what's available for us. We can go straight to that airstrip we saw and it'll save you messing about having to get to Heathrow or wherever and then find your way up from Stockholm. You coming too?" he asked Jean-Guy.

"Ah, no. I have some sessions with the BBC next week. Can you just hire a plane like that? It would help Kathy a lot to have someone with her."

"I'll see what I can do. Can't make any promises until I've made a few calls and I'll have to watch the flying hours as it'll be between Concorde runs. But, why not? You'd do the same for me, wouldn't you, Piglet?"

She hadn't forgotten his suggestion that she should learn to fly. "You're not going to make me fly it are you?" she checked. "I never know with you."

"Not this time," he laughed. "Have to get you a few lessons first. Let me go and see what I can organise. Who were you booked to fly with?"

"SAS."

"Oh, that'll be fine. Give me your ticket and I'll get them to refund it next time I'm at work."

Kathy gave him her best smile. "So useful," she told him happily. "Not just a pretty face, are you?"

"Hmm," was all he said. "Flattery won't get you anywhere."

Kathy wasn't sure whether she was scared witless or madly excited as she sat in the cockpit with Piers and watched as he so expertly checked over the controls before turning to her.

"Right, Piglet. I haven't forgotten my idea so your job for this flight is to watch and to think if it's something you may be able to do. OK?"

She looked ahead as he pressed a few more buttons and the twin propellers of the blue and white plane whirled into life. "I can't fly a plane."

"Not right now," he agreed as he followed the directions of the man on the ground who sent them off to the runway. There was nobody else flying that day and Kathy couldn't help comparing it to the bustle of Heathrow and the take-off queues that Concorde was allowed to jump.

"Pity we can't fly there in your usual plane," she offered faintly and instinctively clutched her seat as Piers put a bit of throttle through the engines ready for their take-off run.

Piers almost laughed. "Could you imagine it? Poor Concorde would be in the next field before Dave in the control tower had seen her coming." He looked across and saw what she was doing. "Piglet, let go."

Kathy clung on even harder. "No. I hate this bit, it's too scary."

"I'm not going anywhere until you put your hands on the instrument panel. Just don't press anything. And it's not scary at all once you know what's going on. Now, let go and I'll explain it all to you."

Kathy managed to put her hands on her thighs. "Will that do?"

"For now," he told her with one of his smiles. "Now, just watch ahead and I'll explain it all to you. Ready?"

"As I'll ever be," she admitted and her voice wobbled.

Kathy almost forgot she was shut in a very small metal box with the man who had got her so hot and bothered when he was on another kind of runway in New York. This was the man who could teach people to fly Concorde. And not to be scared of aeroplanes when they were in them as a passenger. In spite of her fears, she found it oddly calming to listen to the cadences of his trained voice as he explained to her exactly what the plane was doing as they whisked down the runway and then up into the air in one of the smoothest take-offs she had ever known.

"Right, that's your worst bit over," Piers told her and adjusted their course slightly so they were heading for the beacon they needed. "I'm not going to spoon-feed you with what's going on all the way across to Sweden, but do you think now that maybe it's something you could do?"

"I, um, think maybe just a little thing like this. I'll never know how you dare fly big things with people behind you like that."

"Oh, I started out on machines even smaller than this one."

"Did you have to have lots of lessons before you got your licence like I did with Danny?"

He laughed then. "From what I can gather your lessons came with benefits. Mine were with an absolute bastard of an instructor. He'd flown Spitfires in the Battle of Britain, switched to Coastal Command and learned to fly bombers. The joke was that if you put wings and an engine on a bathtub, he could fly it."

Just for a second, Kathy caught a glimpse of that young RAF trainee pilot learning to speak with an English accent and no doubt fired up with enthusiasm for this new skill he was being taught. She couldn't imagine ever getting that excited about flying a plane. She hadn't even liked driving at first. "Which is what he taught all of you to do as well?" she checked.

"Certainly did. Anyway, have a look down out of the window."

Kathy hadn't dared take her eyes off the clouds in front. "Why?"

"Because we're at our maximum altitude, not even half the height of a standard airliner and so far below Concorde you wouldn't even see her when she overtook us."

Kathy forced herself to look at the ships below them and felt her stomach heave. "It's like the worst rollercoaster in the world," she pleaded. "Promise me you're not going to fly upside down on this trip?"

He laughed gently. "No, no aerobatics this time."

Kathy's stomach got used to the idea and she watched a yacht go pelting past a slower cargo ship. "It's funny up here, isn't it? It's like our own little world. There's nobody to bother us." She decided perhaps she could get used to the idea after all. "Maybe it's something I'll do one day but I can't imagine it's cheap. And, well, as you know, Jean-Guy and I keep hoping I'll get pregnant fairly soon. And I don't think it'll be too smart an idea to try to learn to fly if I'm expecting, do you?"

He looked across at her then as such an idea had never occurred to him. "Do you know what?" he asked, "I wouldn't have a clue. Airline doesn't employ women pilots."

"No! Why on earth not?"

"No idea. I flew with quite a few when I was with Air France, including a couple on Concorde when we were testing her and I don't think any of them were pregnant at the time. But it's the same with the RAF. Whole pool of pilots they're just not tapping into."

Kathy hadn't even thought of such a thing but something suddenly made sense. "Ah, so I'm to be the pawn in your game of promoting British women pilots?"

"Yup," he laughed. "Told you before, I reckon you'll be good at it. And you don't want to fly commercial anyway so we can soon get you your PPL if you work at it."

"My what?"

"Private Pilot's Licence. There are a couple of ladies at the Club and I'm sure they'll welcome you with open arms."

"I'll think about it. Maybe. But not right now. Have you ever asked Sarah if she wants to learn to fly?"

He did laugh then. "You must be bloody joking. She's too shit-scared even to get in an aeroplane. Of any size."

"Oh, how ironic. Are you going to let her go on one of your courses?"

"Difficult topic. I know she's scared but she doesn't know I know. But it's got to be a bit obvious over the months we've been together."

Kathy began to think maybe learning to fly could be quite a good idea. "Tell you what, if I ever get a licence I'll take her for a flight. How's that?"

"Hold you to that. OK, make sure your belt is secure as we're coming in to land in about ten minutes."

Kathy was oddly disappointed and realised she had spent the entire flight so busy watching the traffic on the North Sea and thinking about flying, she hadn't had any time to have any carnal thoughts about the man sitting so close to her. She wondered if he had done it deliberately. "Oh, I've quite enjoyed our little flight."

"Any time, Piglet. Just let me know. But I'll want some lifts in return."

"Give me time to think about it," she laughed. "I have no idea what Jean-Guy will make of such a mad scheme anyway. He thinks I'm quite potty enough as it is."

"And I bet he doesn't know the half of it. Now, hush, let me concentrate."

Gisela had driven to the airstrip to meet them and when Kathy saw the car she had brought she almost shrieked in delight. "Oh, my God! She's got Danny's old Escort. That's the car I passed my test on. Can't believe he's kept it so long."

Piers was shuffling through the paperwork he had to deal with and looked ahead through the windscreen to where a madly grinning Gisela was standing next to a dark blue car. "Ask her nicely and she may let you drive it to the farm. Right, come on, we've got to show our travel papers and pay the landing fee. Then you and Gisela can get gossiping. I sometimes think you're worse with her than you are with Emma."

"Never!" Kathy declared. "Emma knows far too much about me and my past." She suddenly felt a whole lot better about this trip and she was smiling as Piers let her get out of the plane first.

The other members of the Stretto Quartet noticed at once that Kathy had a new violin and told her that it was no more than she deserved. They held their first rehearsal on the Wednesday afternoon as Kathy didn't feel at all tired after travelling in her own private plane. It had all been so much easier than going via the big international airports she began to wish she could afford a private plane every time she travelled. But her pilot had borrowed a map and gone for a walk while she played music with the others. Olga, she was told, had taken both her children to visit their grandparents in Russia and wasn't expected back for at least a month. Danny, it turned out was also away as he was filming another series as Alan McKenna which meant he wouldn't be back until about a week before his wife was due to return with their children. Because both Danny and Olga were away, the apple store where they lived had been given over to Kathy and Piers for their stay. They didn't mind. It had two perfectly good bedrooms, a bathroom with a lock on the door and a well-stocked kitchen. In fact, they were happier on their own in the apple store than they would have been in the farmhouse as the guests of Berit and Per along with Kristian and Agnetha.

They played Haydn for that first run-through and Kathy felt a bit self-conscious standing in the first violin spot without any music to hide behind. She wasn't used to playing standing up for so long either as she was an ensemble player and by the time they stopped in the early evening, she wasn't sure she'd be able to cope with rehearsing the *Lithuanian.* They were due to rehearse some more after their evening meal and Gisela told Kathy to try and bring Piers across as they still had the piano and it would be good to play some quintets for a while. None of them would try to play those from memory but it would make a change for them all.

Kathy was still on a high when she went across to the apple store and had to give Piers a hug of greeting as he was obviously preparing them a meal which smelled delicious.

"Get off, you daft woman," he told her and fended her off with a fish slice. "Good rehearsal?"

Kathy flopped onto the sofa and leaned back so she could watch him in the kitchen. "Oh, one of the best. They're such a good quartet I can't believe they'll let me play with them. Mind you, I don't think Samuel said one word during the whole afternoon but he's one heck of a violinist. I don't know why he won't play first."

"Maybe the same reason you don't want to be a soloist?" Piers asked mildly and checked on whatever it was he was cooking in the oven. "Cup of tea?"

"There's tea?"

"Oh, yes. If there's one word of Russian I learned back in 1981 it was the word for tea. I thought it was only the English who drank so much of the stuff but it seems the Russians could give them a run for their money. Also some things with Swedish writing on which I'm not going anywhere near. Even if they do look like rice and flour."

After their fish supper, Kathy and Piers went back to the practice room where the other three Strettos were having a heated debate about something. Kathy was quite surprised to hear even Samuel was joining in. She knew Gisela could talk enough for the two of them, and she knew Kristian could be forceful in his opinions when he wanted to be, but she had never thought Samuel would get so animated. She had no idea what the conversation was about as they were carrying it on in Swedish and it stopped so abruptly when they realised their guests had arrived that Kathy could only assume they had been talking about her.

"Problem?" she asked and sounded as anxious as she felt.

It was Gisela who tried to pretend it was no big deal. "Um, yes and no."

"Can I help at all?" Kathy tried, wondering if they were going to tell her to go home and now she had done a proper rehearsal, hoping they wouldn't.

"I don't know," was the reply she hadn't been expecting. Gisela glanced at Samuel and Kristian but they just nodded as if telling her to go on. "You see, you played so well with us this afternoon, we're thinking maybe we should ask you to join us permanently."

Kathy could scarcely believe what she was hearing. "What? But where would that leave Olga?"

"It's complicated," Gisela said shortly. "But I can see you've brought our tame piano player along so let's play some quintets for a while and then, oh, I don't know. Yes, I think we'll just put all our cards on the table as the old cliché puts it and let you decide."

They played quintets for an hour or so. The Strettos were more than happy with their violinist and temporary pianist and each privately thought how wonderful it would be to keep the five of them together for at least one concert.

Kathy's mind was mulling over what Gisela had said even as she looked at the notes in front of her and played them so perfectly. She had never played with such a prestigious group as the Stretto Quartet. They had made themselves quite a reputation now on the classical music circuit in spite of the fact they were all young players, although critics were divided on what they thought of the *Lithuanian.* Some of them said it was good to see a string quartet breaking the mould and showing they weren't just a load of stuffy, upper-middle-class kids playing the same old same old that other quartets had done for decades. Others took the totally opposing view that string quartets should stick to what they were supposed to do and if they wanted to be a bit avant-garde then they should go no newer than Schoenberg or a bit of Max Davies.

At the end of a perfect Brahms quintet, Gisela looked at Samuel and Kristian and said abruptly to Kathy, "OK, I think it's best if you two go and talk about this between yourselves. Ring Jean-Guy if you want to, I'm sure Danny can afford the phone bill. And please don't worry about Olga. She spends more and more time back in Mother Russia these days and even her husband can't help feeling it's only a matter of time before she dumps him completely and runs back to Mum and Dad."

"That's a pretty drastic thing to do," Piers pointed out.

Gisela closed her eyes for a moment then told them the brutal truth. "Olga isn't happy. She married Danny honestly believing he would move to the USSR with her and take with him his uncle's famous viola. He has been a few times. Seems to get on well with her parents. But there's no way he would ever move out there permanently. So Olga is stuck in limbo. The UK won't grant her any kind of Leave to Remain until she shows some sign of wanting to commit to life there but while she's forever swanning off to Russia that isn't likely to happen. The last time Danny applied for a visa to go with her for a month or so, the British refused him permission to go there even though the Soviets had said he was more than welcome."

Kathy looked at Piers. "This is all beyond me," she admitted.

"Sounds like a right mess," he agreed. "But basically, what you have to think about is whether you'd want to be a full-time Stretto. Presumably that would mean giving up your ensemble work and probably even moving out here. No idea how that would affect Jean-Guy. But you mustn't worry about what the rest of us will do. Decide what you want to do if it comes to it."

"That's one hell of a decision."

"It is."

"Can we go for a walk and talk about it?"

"It's dark."

Gisela had been looking from one to the other. "Take a big torch and just go up the road a bit and back again. Don't wander off into the woods but you'll be safe enough on the road."

"Safe from what?" Kathy asked, suddenly anxious.

It was Kristian who told her in his soft, accented English. "We are quite remote here and over the years I have lived here we have seen bears and wolves. Just once a lynx. Lots of wild pigs and elks. But the animals run away from people." He saw the nervousness on Kathy's face. "You will be fine. They are no trouble."

Kathy wasn't convinced but, partly reassured by the teenager who had grown up there, she let the others get them organised with outdoor clothing and the torch then off they went. Turning right out of the gates as Berit had recommended as that took them into the more remote areas of the surrounding forest and meant they were more likely to see the animals.

For a while they walked in silence. Kathy had her hand tucked through Piers' arm and she was relying on his hearing picking up any sounds of wildlife around them. The road was unlit and deserted and Kathy couldn't help feeling a bit spooked. She wasn't used to anywhere being so dark and so quiet. Even in Suffolk there was the light from the power station and always the sound of the sea. Suddenly Piers stopped walking and she stood next to him wondering what he had heard. Just on the perimeters of the torch beam they saw a large, grey cat cross the road and go into the forest to their right.

"What was that?" she murmured to him.

"No idea. Didn't Kristian say they have lynx round here?"

"Can we go back now? I'm not used to all this wildlife."

"Nor am I," he pointed out to her. "Come over here a minute."

They went to the side of the road where there was a wooden fence wide enough to sit on so they sat side-by-side and Piers snapped off the torch. Slowly, Kathy's eyes adjusted to what little light there was from the moon and she found she was listening for the slightest noise around her. In the depth of the forest what sounded like a small herd of ponies was on the move so she guessed they were the elk Kristian had mentioned. Sitting in the dark, surrounded by the sounds of the natural world round them, Kathy knew what she had to say.

"I can't stay. It's so beautiful here but I don't belong."

"What do you mean?" Piers prompted gently.

Seeking reassurance, Kathy tucked her arms round him and leaned on his shoulder. "This is your world. I can see you camping out here in the middle of the forest and you'd probably find a wild pig in your sleeping bag by the morning with a couple of lynxes keeping your feet warm and a she-wolf making sure you didn't come to any harm."

"What the hell are you talking about?"

"You're part of this. I'm not. I can't live out here. I need the bright city lights, even just the sound of the sea. I couldn't ask Jean-Guy to move out here. Even living in Stockholm and commuting out here for practice would have its problems."

"You would get used to the environment. How do you feel about it musically?"

"I'm not good enough."

"Piglet…"

"No!" she interrupted. "I'm not. Doing all that memory work is so hard." She stole a sideways glance at the man perched next to her on the fence but he was looking across the road and not at her.

"Do you want to put in the hard graft to do the memory work? The Strettos have quite a reputation on the circuit and it wouldn't do your professional reputation any harm to be able to put that on your CV." She didn't reply to that and he turned slightly to look at her to find she was almost staring at him in the low light. "Piglet? Are you having some kind of trance?"

Kathy had been wondering how any human being, man or woman, could be as beautiful as that man sitting next to her on the fence. That was the face that was going to make Annette a fortune and she couldn't look away. What she wanted to do right now was grab hold of him, take him into the silent forest and make love with him until they were both too exhausted to move. She reached up to touch the side of his face but he caught her neatly by the wrist.

"Right, that's it. Back we go. Hypothermia is obviously setting in," he said rather brutally and got off the fence without offering to help her down.

She felt as though her emotions were being put through a mangle and she craved physical comfort but he stepped away from her when she tried to take his hand. This, she realised, was the man who had had a lot of women trying to seduce him and, so far as she knew, only two had succeeded. First there had been the woman whose name she didn't know who had brought about the end of his marriage and then there had been Kerryanne.

"Oh, for Christ's sake, get off the fence. Literally and figuratively," he said sharply and gave her arm a tug.

Kathy staggered a bit as she landed on her feet and for no reason she could fathom, she started to cry.

"Piglet, no, not the water works," he pleaded.

"I'm sorry," she managed to gulp. "I don't know what's the matter with me tonight. You've got enough problems of your own without me trying to load mine onto you as well."

He tucked his hand through her arm and switched the torch back on so they could walk back to the farm. "Don't you think you've answered your own question?"

"How do you mean?" she asked.

"If having to learn to play with the Strettos is a 'problem' in your mind then maybe you shouldn't do it?"

"But I want the challenge musically."

"Do you?"

"I think so."

"Think so?"

They walked on in silence until the torch beam picked out the gates of the farm.

"I like the idea of being a dep but I don't want to play full-time with them. I love my crazy life half in Suffolk and half in Earl's Court. I don't want to move to Sweden."

"There you go, wasn't so hard, was it?"

"Well, actually, yes it was. Have you decided what you're going to do yet?"

He didn't reply until they were back in the apple store. "Yes. I'm like you. Right now my life is in a good place. I can clear the mortgage on the house, sort out something for the kids. But what the hell would I do all day if I wasn't flying or having Jean-Guy bully me over the music? I can't just sit on my arse and look at the scenery."

"I'm sure Jean-Guy will be very glad to hear that. Now, are we going to have a cup of tea before bedtime?"

He gave her an odd look. "Definitely."

"What's that funny look for?"

"Don't you think maybe you should tell the others what you've decided or I know you and you won't sleep tonight worrying about what they'll say."

Kathy paused and looked at the man sorting out mugs and tea bags for their drinks. It still didn't feel right to see him doing such domesticated things when he looked like he did and had the job he had.

Piers glanced up from what he was doing. "Piglet, are you doing that weird trance thing again?"

"I don't know what I'm doing," the unhappy Kathy confessed.

Piers finished off their teas. "Come on, come and sit on the sofa and tell your big brother all about it."

"No."

He hadn't been expecting the blunt refusal and it threw him rather. "OK, fair enough. But is there anything I can do to help?"

"I need to speak to Jean-Guy."

"Right. Got you. I'll take my tea to bed. Drop by to tell me the results if you want to."

"Thank you. Sorry. I just can't think straight with you standing in front of me."

He knew this wasn't the time to be flippant with her. But she really did have this uncanny knack of saying something that ought to be such a compliment but left him feeling vaguely as though he had been mildly insulted. He had no idea how she did it but he always found it rather fun. "Talk to you later," was all he said.

"Oh, now I've upset you."

"No you haven't. Jean-Guy is your boyfriend, he's much more of a musician than I am. He'll be able to talk this through with you with a better understanding of the implications than I ever will."

"You know me too well," Kathy told him and her voice was more bitter than she had expected.

Piers gave her a lovely smile and headed towards the door. "Talk to him."

"Yes, I will. But maybe…"

"No, Piglet. Do it right now. I can see your brain is in overload just thinking about it. I'll say goodnight and leave you to it."

"Yes, thank you," she said with her mind already forming the sentences she was going to say. "See you in the morning."

She heard him going up the stairs then looked across at the phone which was on one of the kitchen cupboards. She knew Jean-Guy was in Earl's Court that evening as he had a concert and she calculated he would probably be home by now. No doubt tired, but in his usual post-concert mood. Still not convinced she was doing the right thing, or even what the right thing was any more, she lifted the receiver and dialled the London number.

It never occurred to Kathy to check the time when she had finally finished talking with Jean-Guy but it vaguely impinged on her that the apple store was equipped with very handy night lights. The thought flitted through her mind that it was probably something Danny and Olga had set up when they had a tiny baby in the house and needed to get about in the middle of the night to look after her. She was much clearer in her mind as she pushed open the door of Piers' room, somehow expecting him to be sitting up in bed and reading, waiting for her to let him know how her chat with Jean-Guy had gone.

Just for a split second she caught him sleeping but the sound of the door disturbed him and he lifted his head from the pillow. "Piglet?" he asked, sounding half stupid with sleep.

"Sorry," she whispered. "Didn't realise it was so late. Off to bed now. See you in the morning."

The head thudded down again and he didn't say a word. Kathy looked at him as he lay there, stretched out in the bed, totally relaxed with the covers pulled up to his chin and his eyes closed. Suddenly she realised where her thoughts were going. She pulled the door shut and bolted off to her own room and barely took time to go to the bathroom before shooting into her own bed and hunching up with her own covers nearly over her head. For that moment, when he hadn't quite woken up, all she could imagine was taking those few paces across his room, lifting up the bedcovers and getting in there with him. Snuggling up against him, feeling his warmth and his love. Her hands would get to caress the raven at last. She had to do it. Not sure whether she was madly excited or frightened witless, she went back to the door to the other bedroom and got hold of the handle.

"Don't even think about it," came Piers' voice from inside.

Kathy wanted to laugh now as she suddenly saw her own behaviour as quite ridiculous. "Don't flatter yourself. I've talked myself dry and I'm going to make some tea. Just wondered if you wanted any?"

"It's two o'clock in the morning. Just, just go away."

"Sorry. 'Night."

"Good night," was all he said but she could hear the smile in his voice.

The next day it poured with rain all day but the Stretto Quartet spent their time in the practice room working hard to introduce their new violinist to their repertoire. Piers had been with them for the discussions which started straight after breakfast and they all agreed that Kathy had made the right choice when she explained how she had spent literally hours on the phone with Jean-Guy and eventually the two of them had worked out a solution. Kathy was going to stay with the Strettos while Olga was on her maternity leave but although she was incredibly flattered they had asked her to go full-time with them, it wasn't something she wanted to do.

She missed out the bits where Jean-Guy had tried to persuade her that they could manage living in Sweden; he had argued gently that it wasn't impossible for them to stay in London and she could go across to Sweden as needed. But he had finally had to accept that the woman he loved beyond reason just didn't want the musical prestige of playing in the quartet for the next years of her musical life.

"I hope you'll understand," she finished her explanation. "Jean-Guy finally saw my point of view. I'm so incredibly flattered to have been asked, but, in a way, I don't want to commit to just one group. I like being totally freelance, nobody has priority over my time and I know you're going through a quiet patch because you knew Olga was going to be taking time out but when you really get going I wouldn't have time for anything else. I'll always be more than happy to come and be part of your quartet but on the other hand I like to know that I can also play with other groups. If Jane rings me up to ask if I can do a gig that night because someone's pulled out then I've only got my diary to look at. I won't mess anyone else up with what I decide to do."

It was Kristian who answered her first. "I can understand. But the Strettos are not quite like that. I play in another group, Samuel often has rank and file in orchestras to do. Gisela is the only one of us who doesn't play with anyone else."

"But it's all based in Sweden," Gisela had to agree. "Yes, I can take your point. You're probably booked solid in the UK anyway for the next couple of years and I can see it would be a logistical nightmare. But at least we have you for a while so best we all get back to work. You staying?" she asked Piers.

"No chance. You'll only want me to play quintets with you," he laughed. "Nope, there's a perfectly good piano in the house which Berit has said I'm more than welcome to use. And I have a sneaking feeling a certain young soprano may want another coaching session unless I'm much mistaken. See you all for lunch."

Piers left the other four to their practice and dashed off through the rain back to the main house.

Now she had made her decision, Kathy was glad she wasn't going to have to uproot herself and move to Sweden, or even spend the next few years virtually commuting between two countries. But she spent most of the morning wondering what Gisela did when the Strettos weren't bringing her in any income. It seemed rude to ask. But she really wanted to know.

Eventually when they decided to break for lunch, she asked flat out, hoping Gisela wouldn't be offended.

"Oh, it's nothing exciting," Gisela rushed to reassure her. "I'm not some international woman of mystery. I trained as a civil engineer before I decided music was a lot more fun so I've also got a job translating very boring, technical papers and books from English to German and the other way round. Suits me as I can sit at home to do it. And if I get really bored then I also make bags and purses which I sell through a shop in Uppsala. So, not as exciting as your music, but it earns me a living."

"Wow," Kathy said, impressed. "Must be incredible to speak languages so well you can do that."

"Sometimes. But ask the others and they'll tell you I'm a whole lot happier just playing my viola."

"Do you play the violin as well?" Kathy asked as they paused in the doorway of the practice room, waiting for a particularly heavy downpour to pass.

"Not any more. Like most viola players I started on violin. Switched to viola when I was about twelve and never looked back. Danny's quite the exception as he doesn't know one end of a violin from the other and absolutely refuses to learn."

"Well, with his family tree are you really surprised?"

"Not in the slightest," Gisela laughed. "Right, that's it. Too hungry to care. Going to make a dash for it."

It was still raining the next day when Kathy and Piers flew back to Ipswich. They chatted on music and the weather and Kathy began to doubt again whether she wanted to learn to fly as the little plane was buffeted by the crosswinds and the windscreen wipers struggled to keep the screen clear. The members of the flying club had been waiting anxiously for the blue and white plane to come back and had half-expected the pilot to ring from Sweden to say he was delaying the flight. But the pilot knew he had to get in his statutory rest before taking Concorde to New York and wasn't going to risk infringing any aviation laws, so they arrived back only fifteen minutes after their expected time and those watching from the club lounge had to give the pilot a round of applause as that plane landed so neatly and was brought to the shelter of the hangar.

Kathy had seen what the people in the lounge were doing but thought it best not to say anything. She was looking forward to seeing Jean-Guy again and getting back to what had become her familiar life. It had been a very odd experience sharing the apple store with Piers and she was glad now that he had told her to go away and hadn't let her into his room. They had exchanged what were probably their darkest secrets, but she knew they both still held things in their past they weren't going to share with anyone, not even each other. She knew he wouldn't hurt her physically, they would each defend the other to the bitter end but there was still some kind of barrier between them. Being shut in a small plane and then sharing the apple store with him had brought them physically very close and she knew now that part of her would always want more from him than the fraternal love that was all he seemed to want to offer. He gave no clues that he wanted to share the ultimate intimacy with her. Or if he had, she had missed them. He could tease her and tell her, even in front of Jean-Guy, that he had missed his chance with her. As he let her get out of the little aeroplane first, she regretted more bitterly than she ever had before that she had missed her chance with him. At least for now.

It was well into May before Sarah found out her husband had a new tattoo and she wouldn't have found out then if Eithne hadn't thrown up over her father and he, without thinking, mopped her face with the front of his shirt which had just been covered in sick anyway. Sarah screamed at him and tore his shirt in her anger so she could see what he had done and then he quietly and resolutely walked out of the house without saying a word. She had screamed loudly enough for her mother to hear her upstairs where she had been doing some sewing that evening and her mother went downstairs to find Sarah angrily pacing the floor of the back room and swearing she didn't want to see her husband ever again, while Alison looked on and didn't make any attempt to change her mind.

Sarah's mother eventually calmed her daughter down and persuaded her that she couldn't try to control Piers like that. They had agreed right from the very beginning of their relationship that he was free to come and go and do as he pleased, even to the extent of taking lovers if he wanted to. All he had had to do was provide her with a family and he had fulfilled his side of the bargain. So a contrite Sarah rang the farmhouse the next morning when she was over the worst of her temper and was told by an apologetic Kathy that Piers had already left for London.

Kathy had taken the phone call in the kitchen. She hung up then looked at the three men at the breakfast table, one of whom was twirling a platinum ring round his wedding finger.

"Well, you've made your wife cry. How does that make you feel?"

"Serves her right," was all he said and the others could tell he meant it. "I was expecting fireworks, but, bloody hell, I never even knew she knew language like that. Just over a bloody tattoo. Anyway, I really must be off. Will I see you two in London any time soon?"

"Not to stay for any length of time," Kathy told him. "But we'll be in and out as we usually are."

"OK, well, I'll see you both when I do. No idea when I'll next be back here." Piers got to his feet and to the relief of the others, he shrugged with a rather sad smile. "Oh, what the hell. I'll call her tonight."

As it always did, the farmhouse seemed quiet once he had gone. Audrey sat in the middle of the kitchen floor and looked at the back door as if waiting for it to open again and bring her human back to her.

"He'll be back, Audrey," Kathy tried to console the little cat. She was suddenly rather annoyed with Sarah for the way she had treated Piers. "I'm going to go and see Sarah."

"Don't get involved…" Jean-Guy started then saw she had picked up the album of photos Annette had given them. "Ah. Good idea. Want me to come too?"

"Yes please. You'll do this so much better than I could. People never take me seriously at my size."

Jean-Guy gave her a hug. "Trust me, you in a temper is not something anyone would dismiss lightly. I was so glad it was Piers you shouted at last year and not me."

Kathy returned the hug. "Silly. Why on earth would I ever shout at you?"

Somehow Sarah wasn't surprised to have a visit from Kathy and Jean-Guy. They weren't as angry as she was expecting so she took them along to the back room where there were babies and toddlers all over the place.

"How do you manage them on your own?" Jean-Guy asked curiously as Catherine grabbed him by the leg and started chewing his trousers.

"Just fine. It's no worse than being a childminder and Alison helps in the evenings. The health visitor's still keeping in touch and the doctor is always asking for updates on the quins. How's Piers?"

"A bit upset," Kathy said brutally sarcastic. "What did you think he'd be? I'll keep an eye on the brood for you and let Jean-Guy show you the photos."

"Photos?" Sarah asked warily, realising that maybe Kathy was very angry indeed but hiding it well. She had a bad feeling that an angry Kathy wasn't someone she wanted to meet.

"A fashion shoot the three of us did in New York," Jean-Guy explained kindly.

Sarah relaxed a bit. "Oh, OK. I liked the last ones I saw."

"Let's go to the kitchen," Jean-Guy invited her. "It's a bit quieter out there."

The two went out to the kitchen where Jean-Guy slapped the photo album on the table and opened it to the photo of Samildánach at the end of the runway with his blood-red eyes glowing in the flash guns and his face unrecognisable behind the make-up. The deep red coat had fallen open so the raven was exposed to the world on his pale skin and it could still make Jean-Guy remember how Kathy had reacted to it. But he had looked at the photo with the model explaining to him how it was all so carefully posed and staged and he had to admit that Annette certainly knew how to milk an audience. He wasn't quite sure how a bisexual woman would feel about the character of Samildánach and he was rather gratified that she looked at it for a while and he could see from her eyes that the image was having quite an effect on her too.

Sarah sat at the table and looked up at the man standing on the other side of it. "It looks like someone out of a movie. Please tell me that's not him?"

"Then I would have to lie to you. That is who you have married. Just look at him. I have heard it said he was paid nearly seven figures to be dressed up and tattooed like that and if the design had just been drawn on with ink he would have sweated it off half way down the runway. It is hot; the music is so loud he wears plugs to stop his ears from bleeding. He does it to give you and your children a better life. He lost his first love and it nearly destroyed him. He loved her so much he tried to join her in death. Luckily for you, and your quins, he failed. And you, like a petulant child, don't like his tattoo?"

Sarah couldn't look at him. "He knows I don't like them. I'd rather he went out and had an affair with someone like I've said he can."

Jean-Guy just managed not to lose his temper with this woman who seemed to be deliberately missing the point. "Did you even hear what I said? Listen to me. Open your ears and your mind. I am going to tell you things he didn't want you to know but Kathy and I think you should. Not just because you're his wife but because we hope it will help you to understand him. He drank industrial bleach to go and be with Chantal. He burned his stomach, his throat and his mouth. He has damaged the membranes in his nose and has had to have hours of dental work to repair the enamel on his teeth. Has he ever told you he was awarded the Queen's Gallantry Medal for refusing to let over a hundred people die in a storm? No. And I bet he hasn't told you that story has now been written as a novel and a film script and what he has been paid for his identity, his recorded conversation and his technical knowledge to be used. He flies Concorde to New York and back because he wants to, no longer because he has to."

Sarah felt as though Jean-Guy was raining physical blows on her body as well as her mind. She had had no idea but deep inside was an inconsolable sadness that the man she had married hadn't felt able to tell her.

Jean-Guy hadn't finished with her yet. "You need to make up your mind what you want to do. He has fulfilled all his side of his deal with you and all I am asking is that if you have any compassion it will be you who breaks the marriage and offers him the chance to be free because he won't. He will see that you and the children are provided for."

Sarah tried to protest. "He's always been free to go any time he wants to." She looked again at that dramatic photo and remembered the feel of the only man she had ever allowed into her bed. "I don't want him to go. I love him more than I think he could understand. I don't know what to do."

Jean-Guy flicked over a page of the album to where Samildánach was standing with his back to the audience, butterfly tattoo exposed to the skull, right fist punching the air and the raven's wing iridescent in the lights. "Tell him."

"Jesus!" Sarah breathed. "He doesn't even look real."

"He is very real and he is hurting. He doesn't want to lose you either. It has taken the two of you a long time to realise you love each other and now you must acknowledge it to each other. You have imposed your rules on him yet will accept none of his." He put his head on one side and looked at the miserable woman at the table. "Tell you what, why don't you get a tattoo? Then the rest of us will look after the kids for a night or two and you can go and visit your husband in his London home. If you love him as much as you think you do then you must show him or you will lose him."

"Me? Get a tattoo?"

"Yes. Go part way to meeting him on his terms. He has gone many miles to meet you on yours. For what? To have you shout at him over a drawing that won't wash off because, oh yes, it's not what decent people do?"

"I've never been to London," she whispered. "I wouldn't know where to go."

Jean-Guy was pleased to see that Sarah finally seemed to be preparing to fight for what she didn't want to lose. "I'm sure Kathy will give you a lift to Ipswich. Then you can catch the Underground Circle Line from Liverpool Street to Gloucester Road and then all you have to do is walk for about five minutes and you are at his house. I will give you a map." He let that much information sink in for a while. "May I suggest a butterfly tattoo? And put it somewhere only your lovers will see it."

Kathy and Jean-Guy soon found out that looking after eight children for three nights and two days was one of the most exhausting things they had ever done and they didn't know how Sarah and Alison managed it. They couldn't remember the names half the time, got the feeds in a muddle and thought the mucky bottoms would never end. But they did it, and solemnly pledged they would never, ever have more than two children.

It was with a profound sense of relief that they put the infants into various papooses and prams and transported the whole lot of them back to their mother in the village.

Sarah was looking happier than they had seen for a long time.

"Good few days?" Kathy asked unnecessarily.

"The best. He took me out to Heathrow so I could see where he works and I've met Annette now as she called round at the house to talk dates with him as he wasn't answering her letters. He was a bit down when I arrived but he cheered up a lot while I was there. We didn't see any of the tourist things but that didn't matter. We can do that any time. Westminster Abbey isn't going to go anywhere, is it?" Sarah had hugged all her children while she chattered. "And you two have been so lovely looking after this lot for me."

Kathy could sense that all was well again between husband and wife and she hoped this time it would be for a long time. "And have you got over the shock of the tattoo?"

"Mine or his?" she smiled. "Yes to both. That raven is so dramatic, I think Annette is going to pose him topless in all her shoots from now on." She held out her left hand. "He's bought me an eternity ring too," she told them and Kathy saw the narrow, elegant band of diamonds and platinum nestled between the other two rings Sarah wore.

Nobody, except perhaps Alison and now Piers, knew where Sarah had had her tattoo but Kathy knew she had definitely had one as she had gone with Sarah to the tattoo parlour and had helped choose the simple butterfly design. But then Sarah had gone into another room with the tattooist and all Kathy had heard was the buzz of the needles. She had almost been tempted to have one herself.

There was a slight smile on her face as she asked the other woman, "And what did you give him?"

Sarah looked almost embarrassed. "He, um, explained to me again about his joints as I nearly dislocated his shoulder one night. And I felt so bad to think I had been hurting him all this while so we spent a lot of time working out ways round it…" she stopped abruptly and blushed a deep shade of scarlet, but then continued almost brazenly. "And I told him now I know what to do he'll get it all over again when he's next up for the weekend. Are you two staying for some tea or going home to rest?"

"Rest!" they chorused.

Arnold Schoenberg – *String Quartet No.2, Op. 10*

In spite of what Sarah had promised her husband, he still hadn't been back to Suffolk by the time Kathy was getting ready to return to Sweden at the end of June for her first concerts with the Stretto Quartet and the Prof and Jean-Guy were getting quite worried about her. It had taken a while but eventually they had learned the whole story of her time in Sweden from the invitation to go full time with them to her behaviour towards Piers which she was now so deeply ashamed of she was glad he hadn't been with them since he had brought her back.

Jean-Guy had been so proud of her when she had rung him to tell him she had had that invitation to join the Strettos he had struggled to accept her decision not to take up the offer. She couldn't have said he was disappointed in her but he was certainly puzzled that any musician would turn down such an opportunity. He had spoken to the Prof about it but the older man just said placidly that it had to be Kathy's decision and they shouldn't try to persuade her to do anything she didn't want to do. Remembering how her ex had forced Kathy into many decisions she hadn't wanted to make, Jean-Guy had backed off although he felt he would never understand. It hadn't helped that Piers was never in the house in Earl's Court when they were although there were signs that he had been in and out so they weren't worried about him. The Prof had even made a discreet phone call to those he worked for, but they said he was busy with his airline duties and what he was up to was nothing to do with them.

It was a beautiful summer morning when Kathy joined the Prof in the kitchen and she stood at the open back door for a few moments just enjoying the view of the garden. It looked quite respectable that morning as Jean-Guy had wrestled with the ancient mower and cut the grass yesterday.

"Looking forward to Sweden?" the Prof asked her as he handed her a mug of tea.

Kathy smiled as she sat at the table. "Funnily enough, yes. I'm so much easier in my mind for knowing I'm not doing it full time. Do you think I'm mad? I'm pretty sure Jean-Guy does even though he's trying to be understanding about it all."

"Jean-Guy is a soloist. He has different work patterns from you."

"Ever the diplomat," Kathy had to laugh. "Pity he can't come with me but he really is horrendously busy at the moment." Her regret that Piers couldn't be with her again hung in the air like a silent sub-text even though part of her reasoned that he wasn't likely to want to after the way she had treated him last time.

The Prof was about to ask her if she wanted any toast when Audrey came pelting out to the kitchen and raced round and round the table, yowling at the top of her lungs so they both knew that could only mean one thing.

"Oh!" Kathy exclaimed and hoped she didn't sound as relieved as she felt. "That must mean Piers is on his way. I hope he's been alright." She almost envied Audrey who hurled herself at the man who walked in through the kitchen door and clung to the front of his shirt, purring like mad that her human had come back to her.

"Bloody airline," was his greeting as he dropped his holdall on the floor and sat at the table so he could take his mug of tea from the Prof. "Thanks, Prof. Bet you lot thought I'd abandoned you."

"We were starting to wonder," Kathy smiled but didn't try to touch him. "What have they been up to with you."

Piers necked the tea and immediately looked a lot better. "Bastards have had me out at Shannon doing some more of their bloody training. They trained me to do the work when they were breaking me back in last year. I just know the buggers are pushing me more and more towards training work. Even worse, I've picked up rumours that they've got me in mind for line training and a whole load of stuff that's more admin based. So, I'm afraid I got a bit, um, bolshy and said if they don't put me back as flight crew then I'm going back to Air France. That made them think. They know full well I've got an open invitation to jump airlines any time I choose. And I still might." He gave the Prof a glare as if daring him to say anything about any ulterior motives the British might have for keeping him in this country.

The Prof wasn't going to provoke that one. "So what did you agree?"

"They saw my point of view. Eventually. So I'm now on two weeks leave then back to my usual lines at the start of July. God that bloody training is hard work. Has its rewards but I swear if I have to do one more loop over the Atlantic I'm going to keep going until I hit the eastern seaboard." He looked at the woman sitting so quietly at the table. "All packed up for Sweden?" was all he asked.

"Dreading it," she said without thinking.

"Second thoughts?"

"No, not really. But this is for a couple of concerts not just mucking about in the practice room."

"Want me to fly you across again?"

Kathy had no idea how her relief lit up her face. "I'm going tomorrow. Can you do that at such short notice?"

"If you'd like me to," he said simply. "I can soon ring the club and see what's available."

Kathy couldn't resist giving him a hug and if the Prof hadn't been there would have given him many reassurances that this time she would behave. "That would be lovely, thank you! It's been so long since we saw you, we were beginning to think you were deliberately avoiding us."

He unhooked her arms from behind his back. "Not quite. Just not been worth trying to get out here from Ireland between training weeks. Managed a couple of stopovers in London so I could bollock the bosses for keeping me out there, but that was all I had time for." His smile was more ironic that humorous. "Having always sworn blind I'd never be a teacher, the sods turned me into one and I hate to think how many hours I've spent in that bloody aeroplane while my students got their heads round it all." The smile became a half-laugh. "I suppose the problem is that I was trained on her nearly ten years ago now, in French as well, and I've forgotten what it's like to be a learner. Been an interesting experience. But now they've given me these couple of weeks off before I go operational again so, yes, if it helps you, I can be your chaperone."

"Chaperone?" Kathy echoed.

"Oh, yes. Danny's back there, along with a wildly jealous Olga."

Kathy's spirits crashed again. "But, if Olga's back, why have they asked me to carry on with them?"

"Because she's still on her agreed maternity leave and this is just part of the agreement you thrashed out with them back in September. She had her baby on Valentine's Day this year, they've called him Dmitri Ivan so Danny gets his D name and she gets her Russian one and she's adamant she's taking her full six months off so she won't be playing with them again until August at the earliest but having had my ear bent by Danny on the phone one evening I'm pretty bloody sure she may not be with them even then. She's got work piling up in Russia and it's all getting a bit political for me so I'm staying well out of it and I'd recommend you do the same." Piers looked up as Jean-Guy joined them in the kitchen. "Ah, the man himself. Are you coming to Sweden with Piglet? I'm available to be chauffeur again if you want to hitch a lift."

Jean-Guy was pleased to see the other man had finally rejoined them but there was a warning bell ringing very loudly in his brain now it seemed those two were off on their own again. "Sadly not, I have bookings for the next week. I was going to go down to London tomorrow and stay in Earl's Court until they are all done as they are all London-based. I had hoped to catch you there so we could do some work on our repertoire."

"I've got two weeks off work," Piers offered. "So I can look after Piglet for you this week and deal with you next. In fact, if you've got any new works lined up I'll take them with me and look at them while we're away."

Jean-Guy really hoped he could trust those two to behave themselves this time. Kathy had admitted how close she had come to breaking that trust he had in her. But Kathy had been so miserable lately and now here she was smiling again, so he began to have his doubts. "Yes, I have a couple of new works I would like to try," he admitted cautiously. "Will you have time to look at them?"

"Oh, yes. We'll have Danny and Olga in residence so Piglet and I will be in the main house so even if I can't get to the Steinway in the practice room there's a perfectly good upright in the house I can use while they're hard at work in the barn."

A tiny bit of relief started to dilute the scepticism Jean-Guy had been feeling. "Ah, now I understand. You are looking to do some flying in a little plane which is quieter than your Concorde and you also want to avoid Olga while you are there."

Piers smiled glad to see the other man wasn't going to start making snide comments about not messing about with his girlfriend. "Yup, pretty much. Right, I'll go and ring the flying club because if they don't have a plane for us then I guess I'm just giving you a lift to the airport."

Kathy had to give Jean-Guy a hug, thankful he had decided to trust her with Piers after all and determined she wasn't going to overstep anything with him this time. "I wish you were coming too. I have a bad feeling Olga won't be too happy to see me there."

"She was the one who suggested you for these six months," Jean-Guy pointed out. He smiled into her eyes and tried to think of a way he could lure her back upstairs right now. "But I can see you might like a bodyguard if Olga is around and at least we know Piers knows how to use a gun if he has to."

Piers got up from the table and put his mug in the sink. "If that bloody Olga is there I think she may be the one needing the bodyguard if she doesn't behave herself."

"Just remember," Kathy told him lightly, "she is married to a former Army marksman."

Piers gave her a lovely smile. "Ah, yes, but I was trained to fight the British Army. They don't scare me."

Kathy ignored the cold shiver than ran down her spine and she hoped it wouldn't come to a showdown between Piers and Danny. "Just go and hire us a plane," she told him. "Your war is over now."

He went off to use the phone in the hall but the others could have sworn he muttered quietly, "My war is never over."

Piers managed to hire the blue and white plane again and they left Ipswich airfield on a calm, sunny morning the next day. Kathy was ready for it this time and looked all round her as they took off and settled to their cruising height and speed.

"I'd love to sit with you in Concorde one day," she sighed. "You take off so fast and go so high so quickly it's nothing like this little plane really, is it?"

"Not at all," he had to agree. "Maybe one day we'll wangle you something but even if you're in the jump seat you won't see much. Just get bored by the chat between us at the flight deck as you won't understand much of it. What are you playing with the Strettos on this trip?"

"Oh, just some Mozart, Haydn, the old standards really." Kathy was momentarily distracted by a flock of gulls flying below them. "And I asked Sarah's mum to make me some more summery concert dresses too. I love the ones she made me back in the autumn of 81 but it's June now and I'd look a bit silly in dark red."

"You'd never look silly in anything," he told her loyally.

Kathy was expecting him to say something else but she looked across and realised he was watching the gulls too but far more keenly than she had.

"Bloody birds," he said half to himself. "Problem with this bus is we have to go at such a low altitude we're more likely to hit the sodding things. Really don't like birds."

"Guess you're not getting a pet parrot any time soon then?" she asked lightly, not wanting to think of what might happen if one of the gulls did hit either propeller on the plane.

The gulls went on their way and she could tell Piers had relaxed again. "No bloody chance. Fortunately most birds have the sense to avoid the noisy thing in their air space but every so often we get an idiot that wants to have a closer look. Or does the whole Icarus thing and gets too close so they get sucked in."

"Silly bird," was all she said and shuddered inwardly thinking of the mess and chaos that would create.

Gisela again met them at the airfield but this time didn't let Kathy drive the old Ford Escort to the farm. "Bit of a problem," she said flatly as soon as she had driven from the airfield. "We nearly stopped you from coming but if we're careful it should all be alright."

"Oh? What's up?" Kathy asked and hoped this wasn't going to be a waste of time.

"Danny's daughter has gone down with measles so we've slapped the whole four of them in quarantine in the apple store. Have you two both had it?"

"I have," Kathy said. "I think I was about six and I caught it off my little sister who brought it home after her first day at school."

"Me too," Piers said from the back seat. "My sister brought it home from school too. Bloody sisters. I don't remember a thing about it as I can't have been more than two."

"I kind of vaguely remember it," Kathy offered. "They told me it had affected my eyes and I had to wear glasses for a few years. Well, I was supposed to but I didn't. Horrible things with round pink frames. No way was I going to be seen in public in those."

Gisela cut across the chat even though she loved the way those two old friends would gossip away like that. "Well, that's a relief at any rate. Good. Now, the other thing is, as you know, you said you don't want to join us long term. Which is fair enough, it's totally your decision and we all respect that. But it does mean we have been holding auditions and it looks as though we may have found ourselves a Norwegian violinist who will suit us."

Piers' attention sharpened. "So does that mean Olga's definitely going?"

There was a bit of a pause before Gisela replied. "Yes, and no. She has made it quite clear that she wants to spend more time with her family back in the Soviet Union. In a way I can see why as the fiddle she plays belongs to the State and they get a bit twitchy if she's away with it for too long. There is no way on this earth she will ever do what Jean-Guy did and defect. The British won't offer her any sort of residency while she keeps going home to Mum and Dad so it's all a bit difficult. She had hoped you would join us which would free her basically to become a freelance violinist with most of her work in the Soviet Union while Danny goes and does his film work in the States. So, no, we're not asking her to leave but she will almost certainly drift away from us."

"Hence the Norwegian violinist," Kathy agreed. "What's she like?"

"He. Harald. Nice bloke. We've spoken on the phone after we heard his audition tape but he's got a lot of work at the moment and we're still trying to find a mutual date when he can come across to us. Annoyingly he's based up Trondheim way so not like he can just pop across for the day."

"Interesting dynamic in your *Lithuanian* then," Piers commented. "Bet you're looking forward to climbing all over a strapping young Norwegian in the third movement."

Gisela roared with laughter. "Never seen the bloke. He could be four foot nothing with a peg leg and terrible body odour for all I know."

Kathy had to laugh too but she couldn't restrain her sigh. "I wish in a way I could come and join you all but I don't see how it would ever work out."

Gisela glanced across and gave her a brief smile. "Oh, you'll always be our first choice of dep, don't worry. I think Danny's a bit disappointed as it looks like he's not going to get the chance to swarm all over you on a public stage." Thankful the man on the back seat was only a friend, she asked curiously, "Why did you and Danny split up anyway? He always sounds so regretful that you ever did. Not that he even mentioned you before we saw you in Yorkshire but now you feature a lot in the conversation."

Kathy hadn't been expecting that and almost resented the question. But she realised the other woman was just curious. There was no malice in it and unlikely to be any repercussions. "Oh, well. It was one of those things I suppose. We shouldn't have done it as he was my driving teacher but, I don't know, somehow it just kind of happened. I couldn't even tell you which one of us started it now."

"Well he always swears blind it was you."

Kathy was very aware that Piers was sitting on the back seat and no doubt storing all this information. "It might have been. I wasn't in a good place when I took it in my head to learn to drive. Only picked that driving school as I'd seen them round and about where I lived and I suppose it was someone in the office who booked me to Danny." She had to smile. "I always remember when I turned up there for my first lesson, absolutely terrified and they told me the name of my teacher and said that he was out with another pupil but wouldn't be long. So I sat and waited and he was at least fifteen minutes late then he walked in through some kind of back entrance with the tallest old lady I had ever seen in my life. He was a bit behind her and she was definitely taller than him. I'd say at least Piers' height if not taller. Then this skinny bloke with the long brown hair and a fag in his face looked from her to me and said 'I'll be needing to adjust the seat then'. And that was how we met."

"Love across the handbrake?" Gisela laughed.

"Hardly," Kathy snorted. "My first lesson was only half an hour as that was all I could afford and we finished up having a blazing row and him telling me I'd never pass the test in a million years if I didn't learn to concentrate and stop trying to kill the pair of us. He had a filthy temper on him in those days."

They had reached the farm by this time and Gisela parked neatly next to Danny's bright red Saab. "Oh, he still has but he doesn't let rip on us any more. How on earth did you go from that to where you got to?"

There was a silence as Gisela had turned the engine off. "It was funny," Kathy remembered. "I'd decided to learn to drive as that was one thing my abusive ex had forbidden me to do. So it was one of the first things I did. That and stop cutting my hair. And when Danny started bollocking me I just yelled straight back at him. It felt so good. It felt as though I was free at last. I could shout at this man and all he did was start to laugh. He didn't try to tell me I was stupid, didn't smack me or anything. He just laughed. He really didn't care that I'd just given him a mouthful of abuse. We got on famously after that. I mean, he was careful not to get up to anything with me while we were on our lessons and I must have had five at least before he asked me out. But it was after the lesson was over and we were standing in the car park at the back of the driving school. He wasn't the first man to ask me out after I'd run away from my ex but he was the first one I accepted."

"It was very brave of you to agree from the sound of it," Gisela said softly.

"Well, almost. He'd got tickets for that night's Prom concert and it was one I wanted to see as they'd got Itzhak Perlman playing the Beethoven concerto and I'd been planning on joining the queue for the gallery with Emma anyway. But Danny had got tickets. It was years later I found out that his uncle had been friends with one of Perlman's teachers and they'd met in the past so he pulled a few strings and even got us backstage to meet him."

"Wow. Quite an impressive first date."

"Oh, yes. Emma was seething jealous for at least a month. Anyway, I can see Berit in the doorway and she's probably wondering why we're all still sitting here."

"Yes, she probably is," Gisela agreed. "Even though she knows you and I could talk the hind legs off a donkey. Anyway, Piers, just to warn you, Agnetha wants to ask you something so make sure you get left with her and Berit at some point because she sure as hell won't be on her own with you."

Piers got stiffly from the rather cramped back seat of the car and crunched his right hip back into place. "And what does she want to ask me?"

"I have no idea. She won't even tell Danny so it's unlikely to be more Schubert. I'd guess she wants you as an accompanist for something but no idea what. And was that you making that bloody awful noise?"

"That was him," Kathy agreed. "I'm only glad he can't crack his fingers. I hate it when people do that."

It was a bit odd at the table for lunch that day. Danny, Olga and their children were in quarantine in their house, Gisela had gone to join Samuel for their meal which left Kathy with Piers, Berit and Agnetha. Kristian was still at college and not due home until two o'clock and his father was at work so it was just the four of them. Agnetha kept looking at the one man at the table but she didn't speak to anyone and Kathy really wanted to know what the girl was going to ask. But she was expected in the practice room at two o'clock when Kristian was back, so she had to go with her curiosity unsatisfied. Gisela's comment about accompanying made sense as she realised the borrowed piano was still in the practice room although it had been rather unceremoniously shoved to one side and had instrument cases on top of it.

They just had a quick run-through that afternoon, ready for their concert that evening, and had finished by three thirty. The four of them were talking about the venue for that evening when they were interrupted by the arrival of Piers and Agnetha. Kathy was astonished that Agnetha would even cross the yard in the company of a man she barely knew but she looked relaxed and was almost smiling about something.

"You lot finished?" was Piers' rather abrupt greeting. "We'd like to use the piano. Piglet, do me a favour and send Danny across would you, please? We've all had measles anyway and I can't do this without an interpreter."

"What are you going to be doing?" she tried.

Piers just gave her a filthy look. "Tell you later. Maybe. Go on, hop it."

Kathy did as she had been asked, thankful Danny had seen her approaching his house and had come outside to find out what she wanted before Olga put in an appearance. But as the men were manoeuvring the piano into a better position, Gisela invited her across to the stable block for a cup of tea and she knew she couldn't really refuse.

The two women had just got comfortably settled in the living room of Gisela's home when Samuel and Kristian came in to join them and the four resumed their chatter about the music and what they would be playing that night.

By the time Kathy and Kristian had to go back to the main house to change for the concert the lights had been turned on in the practice room and they could see Piers was indeed accompanying Agnetha but the old barn was well sound-proofed and they couldn't hear anything. Kristian stopped and watched for a while.

"She is singing in German," he offered in his accented English that was more fluent than Kathy had somehow expected. "From the faces she is pulling I think it is more modern than Schubert. Yes, now she is angry about something."

Kathy looked too and she could quite clearly see that the young singer was getting agitated about something but the accompanist was staying perfectly calm and the onlookers could tell he had persuaded her to work on some troublesome bars for a few minutes.

"Much as I could watch all night," Kathy mused, "I really think we'd better get going."

"Yes," her companion agreed. "Maybe after tonight she will tell me. She has been asking for weeks if you were coming with Piers again so we knew she wanted something."

The two resumed their walk. "And it wasn't something she could ask any of her tutors at college?"

"It seems not. It is all very mysterious."

Kathy's first concert with the Stretto Quartet was one of those musical experiences she knew she would never forget. She wished either Jean-Guy or Piers could have been there to witness the perfect music and be proud of her for not forgetting any of her notes. She felt a bit of a fraud standing in the first violin spot but as the sweet sounds of Mozart's *Dissonance* quartet came to her ears time and again she wished the moment could have gone on for ever.

Four tired but happy musicians were just packing their instruments away when there was a knock on the dressing room door and Piers came in.

"Good show," he complimented them. "Thought the first violin was a bit dodgy though."

"How did you get in?" a delighted Kathy wanted to know and she just restrained herself from giving him a rib-crushing hug she was so pleased he had witnessed her debut.

"Um, walked up to the box office and bought a ticket?" he laughed.

"No, silly. I mean how did you get here? We all came in Gisela's car."

"Borrowed Danny's Saab. Anyone want a lift home in it?"

There was a bit of a hush in the room. "You did what?" Gisela asked.

"Borrowed the Saab," he repeated as though it was obvious.

"But he doesn't let anyone near that car."

"Ah," Piers had to smile. "Trade-off is he gets to drive my Aston next time he's in London."

"Yup, can't compete with that," Gisela had to agree. "So, go on. We're all dying to know. What did Agnetha want?"

"Oh, she just wanted to run through some Schoenberg with me. Did a pretty good job of it in the end." He saw the way the others were looking at him. "It's something she's heard Roisin do on record and thought I'd be able to help. And, yes, it was something she performed when I knew her but I wasn't her accompanist for it. Just her rehearsal pianist. Oddly enough I quite liked it back then so I didn't mind running through it today."

"Are you giving us a riddle?" Kristian asked curiously. "Or are you going to tell us?"

"Nah, I'll let you all work it out. Coming, Piglet? Kristian, do you want a ride back with us? We'll get there in half the time it'll take those other two in that old rust-bucket."

"Yes, thank you. That would be good."

All the way back to the farm, Kathy racked her brains trying to solve the puzzle Piers had given them. She spared a few moments to admire the way he could handle the unfamiliar car on the dark Swedish roads especially as it was a left hand drive but her mind was more absorbed in the music.

"Oh!" she suddenly yelped and Piers narrowly avoided swerving the car into a hedge. "Schoenberg. Second string quartet. Has a soprano singing in the third and fourth movements."

"For Christ's sake, Piglet. Don't yell like that when I'm driving."

"Sorry. But I am right, aren't I?"

"Yes you are, you little witch. Agnetha wanted to know what I thought of her singing before she asked all of you if you'd perform it with her one day." There was an odd sort of snuffling sound from the back seat. "You OK back there?"

"Yes," Kristian croaked. "I don't know words in English to tell you. She has had so much courage to do that. It will be an honour to play with her."

"I thought it was brave of her too," Piers admitted as he swung the car up the drive to the farmhouse and barely slackened his speed. "Told her she needs to work on it for a bit before it's ready to run out with you lot but I think she'll get there. Quite a leap for her to go from Schubert to Schoenberg like that."

After a light snack, a drink and some chat with Kristian's parents, Kathy followed Piers up the stairs to where they had been given rooms opposite each other on the top floor under the eaves. Finally she felt she could give him that hug and a soft kiss on the cheek.

"Thank you for coming tonight," she said.

"My pleasure. Jean-Guy will be annoyed to have missed it but we couldn't leave you on your own for your first night out with the Strettos, could we?"

"Sleep with me tonight," she heard her voice whisper seductively.

He stepped back from her as though she had slapped him. "Whoa. No. That is a very bad idea. What the hell's got into you tonight? I thought you wouldn't do that to me this time."

Kathy hadn't realised she had spoken aloud. She put her hands to her face and felt herself go scarlet with embarrassment. "I am so sorry. I didn't mean to say that."

"Well you did say it," he pointed out coldly. "And I just wish to God you hadn't." With that he turned on his heel and firmly closed the door of his room behind him.

Kathy shot into her room and flung herself face down on her bed. She could feel her whole body was shaking, and confused thoughts of shame, embarrassment and desire ran round and through her until she couldn't think straight. She really wished she hadn't said that to Piers. Her behaviour had been bad enough last time and now she had made it even worse. The day after tomorrow she had to get in a very small plane with him and he had to trust her to behave herself. He had sat with her in a layby on the A12 and explained how women would offer themselves to him and how he didn't want it. Now she had gone and done that very thing. There would be no rest for her now until this was resolved. She took a deep breath, rolled off her bed and resolutely crossed the landing.

She tapped almost nervously on the door. "Ratty, please let me explain?"

There was a silence from inside his room and she was just wondering if he had gone to bed already when he opened his door a crack and half his face looked at her. "What?"

"Can I come in?"

"Do I need to call a witness?"

She realised he meant it. "No."

He stood back and let her in.

It didn't help her state of mind that he was clearly in the middle of getting ready for bed but he pointedly buttoned up his shirt again. "Go on then. Let me hear what you've got to say for yourself."

She stood in front of him and knew she was pleading to save their friendship. "When I play music I put, and I'm sorry if this is a cliché, but I put my heart and my soul into it. Maybe you do too, maybe you don't. Playing music, especially such as the sounds I heard tonight, can, no do, make me very emotional. Sometimes I walk off a concert platform and all I want to do is go home and cry. Sometimes I want to go down the pub and get drunk. And just sometimes, like tonight, my soul wants to feel another human being with me. I want to be in someone's arms, to feel loved and to love them back. You came to listen to that concert tonight out of love. Not the kind of love that means you want to get into bed with me, but the love of a friend or a brother. And I, like an idiot, let my heart over-rule my head and let out my inside feelings. I don't want to go to bed with you. Not you specifically. But tonight's music has made me miss Jean-Guy and I suppose you just got in the way."

He didn't speak for what seemed like ages to the tortured Kathy. "Thank you for your explanation," he said, oddly formal. "It's helped me to understand. But please don't do it again."

She looked up at him and was relieved to see he was smiling now. "OK, I won't," she told him.

"Good. Because next time I might not walk away and that would create one hell of a mess. Now, go to bed and have lots of filthy dreams about Jean-Guy." He watched as she turned to go to her room. "Has he asked you to marry him yet?"

Kathy spun back to face him and felt as though her heart was about to leap out of her rib cage. "What?" she breathed.

He gave her one of his lovely, wicked smiles. "Nothing. Just curious."

"No you're not. What has he said to you?"

"Nothing," came the protest but he was laughing at her now.

Kathy grabbed a towel lying within reach on a chair and fondly smacked him on the arm with it. "Tell me."

Piers grabbed the towel before she could hit him with it again. "OK, he told me the other week that you'd once said you'd never get married and he was just asking if I thought there was any chance you'd ever change your mind."

Kathy let go of the towel and didn't know which emotion was winning out. Part of her was madly excited at the thought of having Jean-Guy as her husband, but a far larger part of her couldn't let go of the memories of last time she had been going to get married. "What did you tell him?" she hardly dared ask.

"I told him the truth."

"Which is?"

"That you changed your mind a long time ago."

She looked into the eyes of this beautiful, broken man and knew it was true.

Wolfgang Amadeus Mozart – *Sinfonia Concertante for violin, viola and orchestra in Eb, K 364 (320d)*

Having found out that the two visitors had already had measles, Danny slipped out of his quarantine the day after Kathy's concert with the Strettos and joined the others in the practice room.

"Who let you out?" Gisela laughed when he came in to join them.

"I was going bloody stir crazy in there," he replied perfectly seriously. "Any news on Harald getting over here?"

"Looks like sometime round the end of October," Gisela told him. "Any reason?"

"It's just that you're running out the *Lithuanian* next month and I didn't know whether you still wanted me for that or not. My agent has just asked me if I can take on a late booking for some modelling work and it would mean I'll be unavailable for the gig."

"Probably pays better too," Gisela agreed. She shrugged. "Sorry, can't promise you anything. He may just pick up his fiddle and play everything we throw at him. He's been sent a copy of the score for it and he reckons he knows most of the other things we play as he's done chamber work for years. If I were you I'd take the modelling gig. If it comes to a crisis then I guess Kathy and I can work out some steamy lesbian moves to get the audience rioting in the aisles."

Kathy looked at Danny, then across to Gisela and hoped that wasn't going to happen. To her relief, the other woman howled with laughter.

"Don't worry, Kathy. There's not a chance in hell I'd do that with you. On stage or in private."

"Good," Danny said, rather more forcefully than the others had been expecting. "Anyway, where's our tame piano player gone?"

Kathy had scrabbled some of her wits back together by this time. "He's not that tame. Gone off for one of his walks so we won't see him until it's dark. Probably not even then if he's taken a torch with him."

"Damn. I was hoping to make use of him and you're off again tomorrow,"

"What do you need an accompanist for?" Gisela asked curiously. "Or isn't it his piano playing you want him for?"

Danny gave her a filthy look. "Olga asked me to ask him if he could run through the Mozart *Sinfonia Concertante* with us. She's been asked to play it in Minsk about Christmas time and hasn't looked at it for years. So I said I'd run through it with her when we have time and she's not so daft she hasn't worked out we've got a potential rehearsal pianist with us for a couple of days."

Kathy couldn't help noticing that Danny hadn't said who was going to look after the children while he played duets with his wife.

They all looked round as the door to the practice room banged shut as the wind caught it and a distinctly windblown Piers came in. "Bloody hell it's blowing a sodding gale out there," was his greeting and he pushed the rain-soaked hood of his coat down his back which only added to the puddle he was making on the floor. He wiped the worst of the rainwater off his face with his fingers and realised all the other people in the room were looking at him. "What? Haven't you ever seen anyone get caught in the rain before?"

Kathy was quite convinced Piers, having got so wet, was still a bit damp when he sat at the piano that evening and watched Danny and Olga get ready to play their duet. The Strettos had had an easy gig that day. Just a short lunchtime recital in a church in Stockholm and after the full concert yesterday it had been an almost relaxing occasion in the end. And Kathy had loved what she had seen of Stockholm. She wasn't surprised Piers had asked her to be page turner and she was quite looking forward to hearing Danny and Olga play one of her favourite duets. Berit had gone across to the apple store to look after Sally and Dmitri, the others all had things to do so it was just the four of them in the practice room. Kathy guessed Danny had told his wife she had to be nice to the piano player who was doing her a favour after all as she was perfectly pleasant to him and remembered his wife's name and to ask after all his eight children. She didn't even make any comments about their Gaelic names even though her Russian tongue clearly struggled to pronounce them.

Kathy hadn't played many duets with Jean-Guy but they had often played through their trio parts together without the pianist when he was away and she had always rather enjoyed it. They made a good partnership musically as well as personally and she loved to hear the way her Guarnerius would mix its sound with his old cello and the two of them would make lovely music. Then, more often than not, playing together would lead to a session in bed while the music still ran round in her head and became part of their lovemaking. She sat quietly next to Piers while Danny and Olga started their practice session with a heated debate on timing and dynamics before either of them had even played a note. Eventually Olga shouted something in Russian at her husband and Kathy wondered why he didn't storm out of the room judging by the look on his face. But he just grumpily tucked his viola under his chin and the two string players glared at the pianist as though the delay in the start was his fault.

To Kathy's unspoken admiration, Piers didn't even acknowledge the looks the other two were giving him. "Do you want me to play the whole introduction?" he asked politely. "Or just give you a couple of bars in for your start?"

"You play everything," Olga told him as though he was an idiot. "I need to remember introduction. Or are you not able to play it?"

Kathy heard Piers catch his breath and his voice dropped several degrees of Fahrenheit. "Yes, I can play it. Just didn't know what you wanted."

"Then play it," Olga snapped at him.

Another sharp inhalation and Piers deliberately looked across at Danny. "Tempo as per the score?"

"Yes. Thank you," came the reply from the man who was now clearly wondering why the piano player was still sitting there and hadn't gone flying out of the room in a rage.

Kathy made sure she gently touched Piers' arm in gratitude as she turned the first page of his music. She knew he was putting up with the way he was being treated just so she could hear the duet being played. She had told him enough times that it was one of her favourites but she had never played it on stage as it was a bit too close to a solo work for her comfort. That and the fact she hadn't known a viola player good enough to do it with her as that had been before she knew Danny had had the operations on his hand. They had even tried it once with the viola part missing but it sounded lopsided and they hadn't played it again.

Neither pianist nor page turner was surprised that the soloists didn't even make it to the end of the first movement before they exploded with a spectacular row in what sounded like very profane Russian and Olga, as expected, went storming out of the practice room leaving her violin behind on one of the chairs.

Piers had stopped playing when the shouting started and he looked at the viola player. "Well, I thought Jean-Guy and I got argumentative enough, but that was pretty damned impressive. Did she cast slurs on your playing or your parentage?"

Danny had to smile at the other man who didn't seem the slightest bit fazed by the squabble. "Both." He looked over at Kathy and his smile widened. "Well, she's left her violin behind, want to take over where she left off?"

Kathy remembered how once she had been in love with this man. "Can we start from the beginning again?"

"Best you check with the orchestra."

Piers sighed loudly and turned his music back to the opening. "As it's you," he told her.

Kathy gave him a brief hug of gratitude and was about to get to her feet when he put his hand on her arm.

"Just be careful," he said to her too quietly for Danny to hear.

Kathy didn't give Piers' caution another thought until she and Danny had played the piece right through. She had kept one eye on the door in case a very jealous Olga came back but it was still just the three of them in the room as she and Danny brought the piece to a beautiful close and she wished the two of them had played duets during their dating days. They had been standing quite close together while they played and she felt him lean towards her and land a soft kiss on her cheek.

"Sleep with me tonight?" he whispered.

Kathy had barely had time to register those were the exact words she had said to Piers last night when, with a suddenness that made the two soloists jump, the lid of the piano was banged shut far too hard.

"Got any spare fags?" Piers asked Danny very sharply and the other two realised he had heard what had been said.

"Yes, of course," Danny almost bleated and he caught Kathy's eye. "Sorry," he said to her, not trying to pretend he hadn't said anything. "Don't know what came over me."

Kathy looked at the man at the piano and just for a brief second she hated him. It seemed the raven had gone beyond protecting her and was now smothering her. She opened her mouth to protest that she was a free and single woman and she could sleep with whoever she liked but the coldness of his eyes stopped her. She may not have been married but the man still standing too close to her was. And he had a very volatile and jealous wife who she could quite believe would be capable of physical revenge.

"It's fine," she said and tried to smile. "Forgotten already."

Piers didn't quite frogmarch Danny out of the practice room but he made him walk quickly and neither spoke a word in Kathy's earshot.

She carefully put Olga's violin back in its case and paused a moment just to look at it. She had never been that close to a Stradivarius until she had played that instrument in Yorkshire and she couldn't help thinking how she preferred her Guarnerius.

"It's good violin," came Olga's voice next to her and Kathy jumped.

"Sorry, miles away. Yes, it's lovely. Hope you don't mind my playing it? Danny said it would be OK and I think he wanted to run through the whole piece this evening while Piers was available."

"I think maybe he wanted chance to stand close to you and remember how you used to be. He has told me two of you used to be lovers."

"A long time ago," Kathy said calmly, hoping Olga wasn't about to launch into some kind of tirade while they were alone together.

"Yes, I know. He is my first."

Kathy couldn't believe the other woman would take her into her confidence so easily. She wondered why Olga would do something like that and waited to hear what would come next.

"KGB told me to marry him so he would move to Soviet Union and bring his uncle's viola with him. We were friends but we had no love for each other."

Kathy suddenly felt rather sorry for her. "Jean-Guy and I started out as friends. So did Piers and Sarah."

"Yes, I know. But Piers and Sarah can't be together and you and Jean-Guy had only silly wedding here back in autumn. Has he even asked you to marry him properly?"

"Not yet. It doesn't bother me. We love each other and we're going to stick together now."

Olga sniffed. "Maybe. Anyway, I have told others that they don't need you any more. I can take over until Norwegian violinist is available. So when they do *Lithuanian* next time I will have Danny again. Not you."

Kathy felt as though the other woman had knocked all the breath from her body. "So that's it? I've been fired from the Strettos? Just because you thought your husband fancied me? You can't do that."

"It is done. So you can go home tomorrow now and I don't expect to see you here again."

The hot tears stung Kathy's eyes and she bit her bottom lip to stop herself crying. "Can I speak to Gisela about this, please?"

"If you wish, but she will support me. Goodbye, Kathy. I wish it could have worked out for you."

"No you don't," Kathy heard herself say to the retreating Olga but she said it very softly and got no clue the other woman had heard. The tears were running from her eyes when someone came into the practice room and she hoped it wasn't Olga come back to torment her any more.

"Here, Piglet, blow your nose and then let's get out of here."

Kathy looked up into Piers' eyes. "You've heard then?"

"Oh, yes. There's a balloon the size of Yorkshire going up out there. That bloody bitch has told me what she's done and she did it in front of all the others. Not quite sure which one's going to kill her first so I left them to it. Right, we're going to get you out of here just as soon as we can. Danny's on the phone right now but it looks like we can't take off until the morning as there's nobody at the club right now. I've no idea how they're all going to handle it. Don't give a shit. Nobody treats you like that and gets away with it. If they don't want you any more then screw the lot of them. You sure as hell don't need them either. You're my first priority right now and I'm guessing you don't want to hang about one minute longer than you have to. How long will it take you to pack your bags?"

Kathy blew her nose on the clean tissue he had given her. "About two minutes the mood I'm in. And, no, I don't want to hear what happens next. Because I know. She'll worm her way back in until they've got Harald with them."

"Must say I have to agree with you."

The two looked round as someone else arrived but it was only Danny. "Sorry, you won't get take off clearance until the morning now. Good news is that they can have someone there by 5am to get you sorted. Will that suit the other end? Can't imagine Ipswich is that busy."

"Ipswich will be fine. There'll be someone there by the time we're in their airspace."

Danny looked at Kathy but made no attempt to persuade her to stay. "This is my fault," he started.

Kathy cut in before Piers could agree with him and the two of them had a full-scale argument. "No. It's not. Not really. Olga saw me as a threat to her music and her marriage."

"Don't be so bloody magnanimous," Piers snapped but more at Danny than her. "What time can we leave?"

"Four thirty be OK?"

"We'll be ready," Kathy told him.

There was a short pause. "I, um, I really am sorry."

"So you should be," Piers fired back. "Why the hell don't you just dump the bloody bitch? We've all seen the way she treats you."

"Leave it," Kathy told Piers and caught hold of his arm. "Come on, let's go and get ready for the morning. Haven't you got a flight plan or something to work out?"

Neither of the men said another word but Kathy remembered Berit's warning about those two as she and Piers left the practice room in a silence so cold it would have frozen helium. As she crossed the yard next to Piers, Kathy was convinced she was being watched from the window of the apple store but she didn't care. She put one arm round him as they got to the door.

"Thank you," was all she said.

Kathy arrived at the farmhouse while the Prof was just settling for a peaceful breakfast with his coffee and the paper. Jean-Guy was half disturbed by what sounded like the back door slamming shut then he was woken fully when the

Prof came into his room and told him to come downstairs immediately as Kathy needed to talk to him. Panicked and anxious, Jean-Guy almost ran down in his pyjamas to find Kathy at the table, her hands shaking as she tried to drink a mug of tea and he could tell from her body language that she was absolutely furious about something. At first he could only assume Piers had upset her but the truth, when she told it to them, was far more shocking.

"I mean," she finished. "It's not like I haven't lost jobs before. But this time it was personal and I'm finding that so hard to accept. How Piers held it together and didn't go and strangle that horrible woman I have no idea. I think Danny's pretty upset too. He didn't say a word all the time he took us to the airstrip. And the flying club weren't very happy either as they had to send someone along really early so we could take off. Oh, it was all such a mess. I suppose it didn't really hit me until we landed back at Ipswich in the small hours. We just had to leave the plane and come back here as the flying club hadn't woken up yet. Piers said he'll ring them later this morning to explain."

Jean-Guy realised something. "Where is he anyway?"

"Gone to be with Sarah and the kids. He said he didn't trust himself not to let the Prof hear some of his worst language if he stopped off here. I think Sarah's used to him by now."

"I don't know what to say," Jean-Guy finally admitted. "If it helps you then I will join in your, what is your word? Boycott and I won't have anything to do with the Strettos either." He could hardly bear to look into her huge blue eyes now swimming with tears of rage and regret that her musical opportunity had ended that way and he didn't know what to do for the best. What he wanted to do was take her to bed, comfort her physically and ask her to marry him. But he had been wanting to do that for months and somehow the perfect opportunity never presented itself.

"Thank you," Kathy managed to say. "That is very sweet of you but I don't think you need to worry about that as there is no way Piers or I will go anywhere near the Octet and that's all you're likely to do with them."

Jean-Guy knew that was true but he didn't like the brutal way she said it. He didn't like the way it sounded as though Piers and Danny had been there for her when he had been innocently stuck in Suffolk with no idea what was happening. Above all he wasn't sure she would accept him any more if he did ask her to be his wife. Except Piers and Danny were both married men. It gave him a headache just thinking about it.

"What else can I do for you?" he asked simply.

Kathy looked at her adorable Moly with the worry lines etched on his face and fell in love with him all over again. "I don't know," she admitted. "I just don't know where I go from here. Is it just the Strettos who don't want me any more or am I now blacklisted on the whole circuit?"

"Oh, no," Jean-Guy rushed to reassure her. "I'm sure it's nothing like that. It was Olga being spiteful with no good reason. I'm sure that the others will manage to persuade her that she was totally in the wrong and if we give it some time then it can be sorted out."

Kathy pounded her fists on the table. "But I don't want it sorted out!" she almost screamed. "They treated me like that and I'm not going to forgive them. Ever. And if you can't understand that then I don't know I can forgive you either."

Jean-Guy looked at the Prof as they listened to the sounds of a furious Kathy running up the stairs and then the door of her room slammed. "Is that it?" he asked the Prof weakly. "Has she dismissed me as the Strettos seem to have dismissed her?"

The older man could only think of one solution. "Give her some time to think it over and get some rest. Then when it is a more civilised hour for most people I suggest you ring Sarah's house and ask Piers to come back here. I would like to hear his side of this story too."

"You mean he's the best one to help her? Again. Why the hell did she choose me two years ago? She would have been much better off with him."

"No she wouldn't," the Prof told him calmly. "Now that sounds as though she has gone into the bathroom so I suggest you go and get dressed while you have your room to yourself and then the four of us will sit down calmly and rationally later today and talk this through."

"I don't think Piers is one for the deep conversations, do you? He is always afraid we will ask him questions he doesn't want to answer."

"Very true," the Prof had to acknowledge. "What was that new piece of music you had sent to you the other day?"

Jean-Guy returned the other man's artful smile. "Ah, yes. The cello arrangement of Bartok's viola concerto. Yes, I think you're right and maybe I need to call on my rehearsal pianist as I would like to run that one out at my next series with the BBC Symphony."

Kathy still hadn't put in an appearance, having taken a very long bath and then gone to bed, by the time the innocent Piers turned up at the farmhouse and helped himself to some coffee. To the relief of the other two men, he seemed perfectly calm and in control as he always did but they didn't like to think what was going on in his mind.

"What's this music then?" he asked Jean-Guy.

"Oh, you will hate it. Bring your coffee through. Can you stay for lunch?"

"Yes, thank you. I've still got enough of my two weeks' leave yet to be at the mercy of this dictator for the next few days."

"I will be gentle with you," Jean-Guy promised as he led the other man out of the kitchen. "For a while at least."

Piers followed Jean-Guy into the sitting room and was surprised Kathy wasn't in one of the chairs doing her knitting. "Piglet not out of bed yet?" he asked and sat at the piano, assuming Jean-Guy's lack of reply meant his guess was correct. He flicked through the score he had been given and wished Jean-Guy didn't like the discordant moderns so much. "Couldn't you have picked something with a tune to it?" he queried lightly and waited for the sarky reply. Not a sound came from the renowned cellist so Piers looked up from the music to see the other man was just standing beside the piano and looking at him with an indecipherable expression on his face. "What? What have I done wrong now?"

"You have done nothing wrong," came the sad admission. "But I think I may have."

Kathy's temper slowly faded in the comfort of the farmhouse with its music and its cats. She was sorry Piers had had to go back to London so soon and she hoped he had a lovely on-call without being paged as he wasn't due to pick up his Concorde lines for another three days. Every time Jean-Guy tried to talk to her about what had happened she told him quite truthfully that she didn't even want to think about it. She had other work lined up, the fact none of it had been cancelled told her that it was only Olga who had been so mean to her and she was going to concentrate on the bookings she had rather than regret the ones she had lost.

She knew her playing wasn't the reason her services had been dispensed with so abruptly, but in spite of her brave words her confidence had still taken a bashing and she was almost reluctant to pick up the other bookings she had. But she had a nice one at the end of the month, just a long fortnight since her rude dismissal, and she travelled to London to join Jean-Guy who had already been there for a few days almost looking forward to it. This was a chamber orchestra she had played with many times before, most of the players knew each other and it was always a happy gathering when they first got together for one of their concerts. They had a rehearsal on the Friday afternoon and the concert on Saturday evening then Kathy had planned to stay on until the Monday morning when Jean-Guy would have finished his London engagements too so the two of them could avoid the Sunday engineering works on the railways and the Prof had said he would pick them up at Ipswich.

She arrived at Liverpool Street just after lunch time and joined the queue to buy an Underground ticket. The queue wasn't long but she was eager to get home to Earl's Court as it seemed to have been ages since she had been in London and playing music in a concert. Piers was now back on his regular work schedule with his Concorde runs and one on-call a month, but the airline still liked it when Captain B was on-call and he didn't often get away with a shift. Sometimes he was away for best part of a week if he was on a long-haul and his lodgers had noticed that since he had gone back to work after losing Chantal, he was more and more reluctant to be away from home for so long and he only ever bid for the New York Concorde lines now even if he couldn't avoid the longer flights when he was on-call. He had once talked about not renewing the other type-ratings he held but he hadn't done it yet and his lodgers couldn't help wondering if there was something in the background that kept him type-rated on the planes he didn't want to fly any more.

The man at the head of the queue was obviously struggling to understand the ticket clerk's West Indian accent and those behind him were getting a bit impatient now. Kathy looked round her and was convinced that was Piers a few people ahead of her in the queue. His black hair was more brown in the harsh lights but there was no mistaking that perfect profile as he looked irritably round the ticket hall. He caught the glance of the petite, blonde woman behind him and there was a slight pause as their eyes locked. Kathy realised that wasn't Piers. It was a man about the same age, or maybe younger, but his eyes were more green and his hair was definitely brown but the similarity to Piers was striking. The same slightly round face and eyes and the same incredible cheekbones. The stranger was looking at her as though he knew her from somewhere too which was a bit disconcerting because she was certain now she didn't know him. The man at the window finally got his ticket and moved away so the queue shuffled forward and the stranger looked away so he could sort out some change to buy his ticket.

Kathy puzzled about that all the way to the house in Earl's Court. She had felt that odd sensation she had had when she had first seen Piers in the corner shop. It was as though the stranger in the queue would have leaped to her defence if she had needed it. And he had appeared to recognise her too. Which was even more peculiar. She shrugged as she opened the car port door and stepped into the kitchen.

"Oh!" she exclaimed on seeing who was sitting at the table. "Wasn't expecting to see you here."

Danny got to his feet to greet her with a soft kiss on the cheek. "Sorry. Got a voiceover job in London and Piers said I could stay for a couple of days. He and Jean-Guy aren't back from their lunchtime gig yet I'm afraid. Can I make you some coffee?"

"Yes, thank you," she said warily.

"Glad to have caught you," was his blunt comment as he made her a drink and handed it to her. "I wasn't happy about the way you left Sweden and that's putting it diplomatically."

"No, nor was I," she snapped. "Sorry, probably not your fault."

"None of us knew what the hell was going on. Olga told us that she'd told you basically to piss off and leave her husband alone and by the time I'd finished bollocking her, Piers had made his plans to get you out of there and the temper he was in I felt I had no choice but to take you to the airfield. I'm so sorry it ended like that. And, no, it wasn't my idea. Or anyone else's idea apart from her. Didn't do her any good as the other three ganged up against her and told her that she wasn't needed to play with them so she's buggered off back to the depths of Mother Russia for a few weeks and the Strettos have had to reschedule a couple of gigs as they had a feeling they knew what you would say if they asked you to come back so soon."

Kathy took a couple of welcome sips of her coffee while her mind processed what Danny had told her. "Would they ever want me back?" she asked barely above a whisper.

"The three of them would come over here and kidnap you if they thought Jean-Guy would let you go. Please don't let what that conniving cow did to you put you off from working with the Strettos again. We've still got the Octet to get organised."

"It's not going to work is it?" Kathy asked him but they both knew the answer. "There is no way I can ever play that Octet while Olga's in it. And I know Piers wouldn't want to either. And probably nor would Jean-Guy the mood he's been in since it all kicked off."

The wretched Danny had nothing to say to that. "I can't apologise enough," was the best he could offer.

"For what? For having such a bitch of a wife? For being such a wuss you just took us to the airport and didn't fight a bit harder for me to be allowed to stay?"

"Don't," he almost pleaded. "I feel it's my fault anyway. Why the hell did I proposition you like I did? What we had was good but it's been over a long time and we've both moved on."

"That's not what you whispered in my ear," she retorted, still angry with him and having managed to convince herself that maybe it was his fault.

"I know. I don't know why I did that. I suppose it was just you, and the music and…"

Kathy suddenly felt sorry for this miserable man. "I know. I do understand. Only the day before I'd said those very words to Piers. It's just that he told me to get stuffed by himself without the need for an avenging wife."

Grey eyes looked into blue and the two old friends exchanged wry smiles. "Forgiven?" Danny asked hopefully.

Kathy held out the hand that wasn't holding a mug. "Forgiven."

Danny gave her a quick kiss on the cheek. "Thank Christ for that."

"Oh, I don't think we could ever not be friends, could we?" She looked hard into his eyes. "But you haven't exactly broken up with Olga either, have you?"

"Sometimes I'd like to but it's not easy with the kids and the politics and…"

Whatever else Danny was going to say was interrupted by the arrival of Jean-Guy and Piers through the car port door and before Kathy could tell Danny he had to do what was best for himself, she was enveloped in a hug by a delighted Jean-Guy.

"I'm so happy you two are friends again," he told her.
"Yes please, Piers. I would like some coffee."

"Was I offering?" came the light-hearted comment from the man already working the machine.

"How did it go?" Kathy asked and let Jean-Guy give her quite a heady snog.

"My accompanist just gets better every time," he laughed.

"Cheeky sod," Piers replied as he handed the exuberant cellist a mug of coffee. "If only I could say the same about my soloist."

Much as Kathy loved to listen to those two hurl insults at each other, she totally forgot Danny had been about to say something to her as she remembered the man at the station. "Have you got a brother?" she suddenly fired at Piers.

He paused with his mug of coffee halfway to his lips. "What kind of a question is that? You know I haven't. Why do you ask?"

"I saw a man in the ticket queue at Liverpool Street and he just looked so much like you it was uncanny. But then I saw it wasn't you as his hair was more brown and he had funny eyes kind of not quite green or grey. But just the shape of his face and something about his nose made him really look like you." Kathy looked at Piers and if she hadn't known better would have sworn there was almost a look of panic in his eyes.

"When was this?" he asked and his voice was a bit too casually curious.

"Not that long ago. When I got here just now. It was one of those funny things as he looked at me as though he knew me too. But he was a total stranger."

"Did you hear where he bought a ticket to?"

Kathy was surprised to be so questioned. "Well, no. He was a few people ahead of me."

"And could he have heard where you travelled to?"

"No idea. He'd gone into the crowd by the time I got to the front of the queue and I wasn't paying him any attention."

Piers' gaze flicked to Danny for an instant and Kathy got the distinct impression he didn't want this conversation to continue in front of him, but then he suddenly smiled. "Hmm. Pity I can't ask my mother what she got up to in the past. Anyway, if you'll all excuse me I'll go and get out of my concert clothes and then I'd better eat something."

"I'll make you both some sandwiches," Kathy offered. "But first I'm going to chase you up the stairs as I want to get myself a cardigan."

"You'd never catch me with those short legs," he teased her but he didn't say anything else as the two of them went up the stairs. He paused on the first floor landing and waited for her to speak.

"You know who that man is, don't you?"

Piers' smile was wry. "I don't know him, but if it's who I think it is then I know of him. Can you keep the other two downstairs for a few minutes while I make a phone call?"

"Of course. Who do you think he is?"

"Can't say. But the man I'm thinking of is, or rather was, one of the Prof's lot and maybe I'm just paranoid but I'll make a quick call and check."

"Oh, OK. Leave you to it."

"Thanks, Piglet." He watched her turn to go back downstairs. "And, Piglet?"

"What?"

"Don't forget your cardigan."

Kathy went back down to the kitchen, pulling on her beige mohair cardigan as she went but only Jean-Guy was in the kitchen.

"What have you done with the other one?" she asked.

"Gone out to work. He says he'll be back by teatime as this is just a preliminary run through with the production team and the actual recording is tomorrow. It's for some advert or another so the whole thing will only last about thirty seconds. But do you have any idea what he's being paid to do it?"

"No idea at all."

Jean-Guy almost laughed. "Put it this way, I think I may be in the wrong job." He sobered abruptly. "What's upset Piers?"

"Nothing that I know of."

"Good. Is he on his way back down to us?"

"Couple of minutes to change if he doesn't fall asleep on his bed." Kathy was starting to feel unsettled herself now. "Why?"

"Danny asked me to ask you something and I'd rather Piers was with us when I did it."

Kathy closed her eyes for a few seconds, she had thought it oddly coincidental that Danny should be in the house and guessed maybe his voiceover job had been a convenient excuse for him to be there. "What's going on?" Jean-Guy didn't reply so she grabbed his sleeve and towed him to the staircase door. "Come on."

"Where to?" he asked, hoping it might be their bedroom.

"I want to find out what the hell is going on round here."

The two of them went up the stairs in time to hear Piers say, "OK, thanks. If you wouldn't mind checking for me and let me know?" He hung up the phone and looked round as the other two came into the sitting room. "Don't tell me, Piglet's curiosity got the better of her?"

"Something like that," Kathy had to admit.

Piers gave her one of his lovely smiles. "Sorry to disappoint you but I was just checking with the Prof as I can't find a piece of music and may have left it in Suffolk."

Kathy knew he was lying but his face was guileless and she also knew he wasn't going to tell her any secrets. "How very careless of you. And how very unlike you."

"Do you have a minute?" Jean-Guy interrupted and the other two both paid him attention. "It's just that, um, yes, Danny does have work to do in London but he has also come as the peace envoy."

"I'm not doing that bloody Octet," Piers cut in quickly. "At least not while that bloody Olga is part of it."

"Just hush a minute," Jean-Guy told him. "No, it is not about the Octet. It is about Kathy. Now, as we know, Olga told you to go." Jean-Guy caught her hands and tried to speak calmly. "From what Danny says there has been the most enormous row among them and now Olga has run away to her parents in Russia. They don't know when she will be back but they are certain she will be. Their violinist Harald still has commitments although he is winding them down now, and they have one big gap in their programming before he can join them permanently. He won't be living with them as he has family near Stockholm and he will commute so it seems Danny and Olga won't have to move out of the apple store." He knew he was at risk of babbling now so he paused and Kathy guessed what was coming. "They have a performance of the *Lithuanian* scheduled and they don't want to cancel. It is in September so Olga should have been back with them but they have told her they don't want her but they originally thought she would be which means Danny is booked to do it. He turned down a modelling job for Chanel or Gucci or someone to do it so he has lost that booking now but I don't think he has regrets and, and now I don't know where I am going with this."

Kathy loved the way Jean-Guy would get himself in such a muddle when he was trying to say something important in English even now, but she got the main point of what he was saying and her first instinct was to refuse flat-out to have anything to do with that group ever again. None of the other Strettos seemed to have fought for her to stay but then she didn't know what might have been happening in the background over there.

"What's so special about it? They've cancelled others," Kathy pointed out, while somewhere deep inside her that old flame of excitement was starting to burn as it hadn't done for quite a long time in her professional life. She saw the way Jean-Guy looked at Piers and realised they both knew the answer to her question. "What?" she persisted.

She could tell Jean-Guy was having an effort to keep his voice calm as underneath his words he was madly excited about something too. "It will be the Australian premiere. They are doing a short tour of south east Australia and the *Lithuanian* has been heavily advertised so they need a violinist who knows them and who knows the music. And, no, there is no way they are asking Olga. Basically she is now fired from them as you once believed you were."

Kathy hadn't been expecting anything as momentous as that. An Australian premiere. With the Stretto Quartet. While she was still getting her thoughts in order, Piers said to her, "Don't rush your decision, Piglet. We all know, that kicking you out was purely Olga's idea. I've spoken to Danny about it since he got here for this visit and the others are just as furious about it as you are."

"I don't want to go back," she said out loud but her voice wasn't as certain as her words.

"I'm sure you don't right now," Piers replied gently. "Just think about it."

"It hurt, getting thrown out like that," she started to rationalise as she looked for a way round this.

"Yes, I know," Piers sympathised.

Just for a second, Kathy hated him and turned on him furiously. "What the hell do you know about it? Have you ever been chucked out of something you loved doing? No, didn't think so. So just shut up, butt out, and all the rest of it. What are you laughing at?"

"Piglet, you have no idea how much the pair of us love you when you get in that mood. Now, listen. Give me a minute, OK?"

"OK," she agreed grumpily, curiosity overcoming temper, and a lovely warm feeling inside her at the way he had said those two both loved her like that.

"Once upon a time," he began with a smile on his face, "they asked me to try out for the Red Arrows. That's kind of the flying equivalent of the Strettos. So I bit their arm off to have a go. Bloody months of training, hours of practice flying. And just as I thought I'd got the hang of it the buggers threw me out."

"Because you weren't good enough?"

"No, because of something I couldn't control. Just like you. It's not your fault Danny couldn't contain himself. Bloody hell, you did the same to Jean-Guy in Yorkshire, remember?"

Just for a fleeting moment, Kathy wondered if she had done the same to him too, but then she looked at the blushing Jean-Guy and returned Piers' smile. "You told us they didn't want you because you kept being sick."

"That was the official reason they gave. It was partly true. I don't have the best digestive system for spinning round in circles and going upside down but the bald truth was I didn't fit in. Wrong social background. And that's not including their thoughts on my wife at the time."

Kathy was genuinely appalled. "They can do that?"

"In those days, quite easily. Yes, I was an officer. In fact I outranked some of the other pilots but that didn't matter. They gave me my marching orders and sent me back to my squadron. So I know exactly how much your pride is hurt."

"It's not really the same though, is it?"

"In a way. It was the officers in charge who wanted me out, not my fellow pilots. In fact two of them said that if I got thrown out then they'd go too. Which is exactly what Kristian told Gisela and Samuel. He said that they asked you very nicely to reconsider, or he was off to have his career without them."

Kathy thought of the quiet young man who had stood next to her to watch Agnetha sing and then had sat in the back of the Saab and listened to the chatter of those in the front. She did wonder if maybe Agnetha had told Kristian that she knew Kathy was a victim as she had been. It would explain his understanding. "Kristian did? I'd never have guessed that. I'd have understood it more if you'd said Gisela."

"Put it this way. If you say once and for all there is no chance you will ever go back to them then it could well mean the end of the Stretto Quartet. Which is more than I ever managed with the Red Arrows so all respect to you. Best I ever managed was when Concorde was formation flying with them for a flypast over London. The bosses gave me the gig and I had some fun with those RAF buggers during practice. Infantile I know, but made me feel better after all those years."

Kathy's tumbled mind was temporarily distracted. "And did those two pilots leave? The ones who said they would?"

Piers paused in the way he did when he needed to collect his thoughts. "One of them did. And there were fifty more queuing up to take our places."

"That was nice of him."

"Unexpected. We didn't even like each other all that much. He was some toffee-nosed git from the upper classes but he stuck to his principles, I've got to give him that."

"What happened to him?"

"Bastard got a promotion, became my CO and probably one of the best friends I ever made in the RAF. Taught me a hell of a lot about being in charge of a Group. Not that I ever made it that far. But you're doing it again and side-tracking us. Go and play your rehearsal, just think about what you want to do and then put those other poor sods out of their misery."

Anton Webern – *String Quartet, Op. 28*

"I really don't know how you do it," Emma remarked to her oldest friend as the two sat on the sofa in the farmhouse sitting room and shared a bottle of white wine. "I mean, you always were one for getting yourself into scrapes but, honestly, can't you just be dull and boring like I am now?" She caught Kathy's glare. "And that wasn't meant to be a sarky comment on your lack of babies. I'm sure you'll get round to it when you've stopped tearing all over the world with a violin under your arm."

"Maybe," Kathy said vaguely and finished off her third glass, feeling the alcohol starting to numb her tired mind. "Not sure I want any now."

"Oh, don't be so silly," Emma told her crisply. "You do know Jean-Guy has put off a couple of his gigs so he can go to Australia with you?"

"Yes," Kathy mumbled, knowing where this was going.

"Would he do that if he didn't care about you? I mean, we're all used to him now and I think we tend to forget just what a big gun he is in the music world."

Kathy poured the dregs of the bottle into her glass. "Yes, I suppose we do," she agreed wistfully. "I mean, look who I share houses with now. One of the big names in classical music and a bloke who flies bloody Concorde. Not exactly what we thought we'd end up with, is it?"

Emma really wanted to laugh now. "Now that is very true. I think we thought we'd be the big guns and Concorde wasn't even flying in those days."

"He told me how he got thrown out of the Red Arrows. Made me feel a bit better anyway. And this time I'm sure he was telling me the truth for once."

"Oh? Don't tell me, he wouldn't do as he was told."

"No, funnily enough his RAF record is almost exemplary."

"Almost?"

"He won't give us the details. But apparently it was something to do with a penguin and a visiting Air Marshall."

"Do you wish you'd chosen him?"

"As a boyfriend? No. He's happy with Sarah and I hope Jean-Guy and I will get over whatever it is that's wrong with us at the moment."

"He still hasn't asked you then?"

"No."

Emma knew when her oldest friend didn't want to talk about something but she wasn't going to let this go so easily. "So why don't you ask him?"

"Because right now I'm not sure he'd accept. I'm not sure I'd accept him if he asked me tomorrow. I don't know. Something's changed somewhere along the lines and I don't know where we're going any more. He's away so much with his work I sometimes wonder what he's up to half the time."

"Well, fairly soon you're all going to Australia and I'm trying really hard not to hate you right now. I assume the pair of you are still sleeping together?"

"We're still sharing a bed," was all Kathy was going to admit even if this was Emma who knew all her mucky little secrets. "I've talked to Sarah about how she copes while Piers is away but she's married to him, she's got Alison and even though she can kind of understand it's not the same for her."

"And in Australia?" Emma persisted.

"Oh, it's all a bit odd as apparently Agnetha has asked to come too so she's going to be sharing a room with Gisela, and Kristian and Samuel will be sharing the other one. It all seems very odd. I've no idea why she'd want to do that."

Emma had heard all about Agnetha. "Well, I'm guessing the others asked her if she'd like to so she's not stuck in the middle of a Swedish forest with Kristian's parents and a minor war going on between Danny and Olga. But what will she do all day? She's not even an instrumentalist."

"No idea. Gisela spoke to Jean-Guy about it for ages as he'll pretty much be her chaperone while we're playing. He seems happy enough to do it."

Emma didn't make any remarks about most men in their thirties would probably be delighted to look after a sixteen-year-old Swedish girl who was quite a pretty little thing from the sound of it.

"He's so sweet. He looked after me at the beginning when he knew what Richard had done to me and I think he's half terrified he'll scare her away and half proud she trusts him enough to hang out with him."

Emma looked at her oldest friend and was consoled to see the love in her eyes. She tapped the modest emerald engagement ring which was all Derek had been able to afford for her. "Ask him."

The summer started to cool towards autumn and Kathy got ready to fly out to Australia with the Stretto Quartet. They hadn't asked her to come out to Sweden again but the three had travelled to London a couple of times to practise with her and it had worked out well with Gisela and Samuel in the room on the top floor opposite Piers, and Kristian upstairs in the one usable attic room. They had even managed one session on the *Lithuanian* when Danny had been in the capital for his work and they all had great hopes for the Australian premiere of the contentious work. Nobody mentioned Olga but Danny told Kathy that the children were back in Sweden so she assumed the mother was too but nothing was said.

Now matters had been resolved with the playing members of the Stretto Quartet, Kathy had no regrets about her decision to go back to them. The musician in her was looking forward to going to Australia as she had never travelled that far before and her curious mind always liked to see other countries. Considering the miles they would be travelling, they weren't going to be away for long but she still packed and unpacked her suitcase a dozen times before she was happy. It was going to be early spring in Australia and she was glad Sarah's mother had made her some more suitable dresses to wear. One day, she told herself, she would step onto a stage in full Viola outfit. But in the meantime, the dresses Sarah's mum made were perfectly good enough and at least they fitted her just as well as Annette's clothes did.

They were flying out on one of Piers' Concorde days but he was on the afternoon flight for once and didn't need to be at the airport as early as they did but he drove them in anyway and stayed with them all the way into the departures lounge. The other four were coming to Heathrow direct from Stockholm, they were due to meet up in the departures lounge and Kathy hoped nothing would go wrong. She was grateful Piers knew the right people to ask to check the inbound Stockholm flight was on time and, so far as anyone could find out, all the passengers who should have been on the plane were safely on board.

Kathy was quite aware that the handsome pilot was getting the usual admiring looks but she just stood next to him without touching and looked at the planes buzzing about the airport.

"It's a long way. Australia," she offered at one point.

"Yup. I wouldn't like to fly all that way," was his not-very-helpful reply.

"But you have."

"Not in one go like the passengers do. Honestly, you'll be fine. They'll be feeding you meals and turning the lights on and off to make you go to sleep so you won't have a clue what's going on by the time you get there. And you'll get a quick look at Singapore on your way there and back."

"And that's supposed to make me feel better?"

Piers watched critically as an incoming American Airlines pilot made a bit of a dodgy landing but he guessed that the pilot might not have landed there before as the airline hadn't been coming to London for more than a year. He turned back to Kathy. "Stop panicking. The Stockholm flight touched down an hour ago so you know they're here somewhere. I expect Gisela's dragged them all off for a proper English cup of tea. You'll be fine once you get going. And there you are, that looks like the rest of your lot just coming to join you."

Kathy looked across and saw the welcome sight of the other Strettos plus Agnetha walking across the concourse to join them. Danny would be flying in direct from the States, had promised himself a stopover in Hawaii and would be with them just for a couple of days so he could adjust to the time zones, join in the performance of the *Lithuanian* and then fly off again. Kathy was glad she wasn't doing such a quick turnaround for her visit. She was looking forward to seeing Australia now and even more because she was doing it with friends. As she watched the other musicians coming across to join them the thought jarred into her mind that maybe Jean-Guy would propose to her while they were away. Something was still holding him back. Then again, she thought and tried not to smile, maybe she would just take a deep breath and ask him instead. The worst he could do was refuse and after the knocks she'd had recently that would be a minor setback.

Piers joined in the greetings with the other Strettos but didn't hang about to chat with them. "Best be off," he said as soon as he decently could. "Briefings to go to and aeroplanes to check."

Kathy gave him just a small hug as he settled his hat on his head and put an identity card round his neck on a lanyard. She hadn't seen that before and felt almost maternally proud when she saw it rather unsubtly declared him as *Concorde Crew* on one side. She guessed it was something all air crew now had to do at the airport and she began to understand his grumbles about all the rules and regulations coming in these days.

"Have a good time," he wished them. "Bring me back a souvenir."

Kathy watched him go, striking as ever in his captain's uniform and turning heads as he strode through the concourse with the sure steps of a man in his home territory.

Gisela nudged her with her elbow "Bit of alright isn't he?"

"Hush. He's spoken for."

Gisela smiled fondly at Samuel. "Aren't the best ones always?"

For Kathy, her trip to Australia with the Stretto Quartet passed like a dream. Her days were spent in beautiful, demanding music and her nights in the company of the man she loved more than any other who had welcomed her back into his arms now she had found her way forward and in many ways she blessed him for giving her the space to reach her own decisions without sex getting in the way. Jean-Guy deliberately kept a low profile during the visit although he couldn't pass unrecognised in the classical music world. Several people asked him if he was there with his wife and it took a few days for the group to realise that people assumed he was with Agnetha as the two of them spent a lot of time in each other's company while the others rehearsed or played their concerts.

Kathy was delighted to watch the shy Agnetha slowly get used to the company of the famous cellist and the terrified, abused child began to blossom into a more confident young woman. The Stretto Quartet hadn't been to Australia before but they weren't being too adventurous with the travelling and were performing in Melbourne, Adelaide and Sydney with plenty of time between gigs and the *Lithuanian* was only being performed in Sydney on their last night in the country.

They were playing the Webern Quartet for the first half so the audience wouldn't have the transition of a traditional work to the more jarring Orlov composition and Gisela played the first half with them. They all changed into different clothes for the second half and Kathy laughingly let Jean-Guy check her outfit to make sure she wouldn't show anything she shouldn't when Danny threw her to the floor in the third movement. Jean-Guy waited with them in the wings of the stage just before the second half started and Kathy sensed he was in a bit of an odd mood. She saw Gisela looking at her with a huge smile on her face and she wondered what the other woman knew. It seemed unlikely Jean-Guy would take her into his confidence about any marriage proposal plans. Then those waiting in the wings heard the roar from the audience when the change of viola player was announced and she understood what had amused Gisela so much.

"Next time, huh?" Danny said to Gisela as he passed her backstage so he could walk on between Samuel and Kristian, with a grinning Kathy taking the lead as the first violin and thinking maybe she was getting just a bit too obsessed with the idea of marrying Jean-Guy.

Jean-Guy was very quiet as he settled next to her in their bed that night and she cuddled into his arms, determined to enjoy their relationship as it was. It had been very odd having the weight of Danny on top of her on the stage that evening. He had felt a heck of a lot heavier than he had when she had been in bed with him. But he had also been on stage, his professionalism meant he stuck to the choreography and the pair of them had got quite a cheer from the enthusiastic Australian audience who had soon shown they were far from offended by what was going on.

"Well?" she asked Jean-Guy. "Did I do alright?"

She was not expecting him to brush the wayward hair off her face and give her a soft kiss. "You did so much more than alright. I am so in awe of you I don't dare touch you."

Kathy looked into his dark eyes but there was no sign he wasn't being serious. "What? This is me. The one who has the crises of confidence until you and Piers talk some sense into me. Please feel free to touch."

He nuzzled his face into her neck in that familiar gesture that meant the start of their lovemaking but not this time.

"Are you quite alright?" she asked when he hadn't made any progress for a few minutes.

"Yes. I'm sorry. I watched you with Danny tonight and I need to make sense of it in my head."

Kathy couldn't believe what she was hearing. She was settled now in her own mind and couldn't accept that Jean-Guy was going to start all over again with his uncertainties. "But, but you were there when we first tried out the moves. You've seen us rehearsing. Why is it now so different?"

"Because tonight he meant it."

"No he didn't."

"Kathy, I know what I saw. Now, if you don't mind, I am very tired and tomorrow we start that long flight home so I would like to get some sleep."

She lay quietly beside the man she knew perfectly well wasn't sleeping and she wished she could afford to ring home and talk to Piers or to Emma. It had all been so clear just a few very short hours ago when she had waited to go on stage. Now it was all in a muddle again.

Her work with the Strettos was the last Kathy had for a while as she knew she would come back tired, and Jane had managed to juggle her bookings so she had the rest of September off. Jean-Guy went back to his hectic schedule, still without proposing marriage to her and Kathy got ever more confused as the month dragged to an end and she thought of how Piers had told her of the Earth settling down for the short days of winter. She felt she had a lot in common with the Earth that year. All she could see ahead were the dark days with nothing to remind her that the wheel would turn and the world would wake again in the spring. Eventually, as October came in cold and crisp, Kathy told the Prof she needed to do some early Christmas shopping and she went to Earl's Court with Jean-Guy hoping to catch Piers between flights so she could find out if he knew what was going on.

They arrived on the Thursday as Jean-Guy had a rehearsal on the Friday morning with the concert on the Saturday and their landlord got home in the middle of Friday afternoon in an exceptionally foul mood. He could barely bring himself to be civil to the other two before stomping off up the stairs to the top floor so he could get some sleep. He had been away for just over a week and the other two knew he had been on a special Concorde flight to Nadi

International in Fiji with stopovers in Singapore and Dubai. Kathy was quite glad that concert and rehearsal bookings were keeping Jean-Guy in London for a few days and she was in the kitchen reading the newspaper when Piers put in his appearance the next morning. He looked as though he had just got out of bed as he hadn't shaved yet, his hair was in a mess and she just knew he wasn't wearing anything under that dark grey bathrobe.

"Sleep well?" she asked and watched as he made himself some coffee as the machine was still switched on.

"Had better nights," he said grumpily and was clearly about to go back upstairs.

"Just sit a minute," she asked him. "What's the matter? You in trouble with the bosses again?"

He half smiled. "What do you mean 'again'?" he asked lightly. "Don't you know my bosses love me most of the time? No, it's not my job. Well, it is, but not the airline one."

"Oh," was the best Kathy could offer as she realised what he meant. "Can you tell me anything about it?"

"No, not really. Bastards hunted me down in my hotel in Dubai. They brought Kerryanne with them and set her to work on me too."

Kathy was appalled that anyone would do anything so under-handed even if it was a recruitment drive for the sake of national security. "Goodness. Well, I suppose it was nice for you to see her again."

He did smile then and finally sat at the table with her, carefully making sure the robe was decently closed. "One way of putting it. It didn't end well. I told them that I've got my day job with the airline, I can just about find time to play trios with you two, but there is no chance in hell I'm going to do any work for them ever again. So they raked over all the muck about how I hadn't coped with Chantal and then they tried to tell me that I wasn't fit to fly and, well, let's just say it maybe wasn't the most diplomatic thing to do to say some of the things I did in a posh hotel in Dubai. Which meant I got snitched on to the airline, which was a major bollocking when I got back and a fine deducted from my salary."

"Can they do that?"

Piers sighed and put down his coffee. "There are things in the background I don't like. Yes, the airline can reprimand me if I misbehave in public while in uniform, but I wasn't in uniform. It was a stopover so the crew could get in their rest period before the next sector of the flight."

Kathy waited but he didn't say any more. "Which means?"

"Which means the bastards are keeping an eye on me and it means I'm still too far on their radar for my liking. I just hope they aren't looking at you too."

"But they can't force you to go and work for them, can they?"

Piers finished his coffee and got up to fill his mug with water. "Don't think so. But I have a bad feeling that sooner or later I'm going to find out. I'll have a word with the Prof next time I see him but I don't know how much he knows these days. He's a wily old boy and I don't know exactly how involved he is in all this. Way more than I am, I'm sure of that. Anyway, to more pleasant things. It feels as though I haven't seen you for days and it's been months since I managed to get out to Suffolk, so what's going on in your world? I saw the crits for the Strettos in Australia so I'm guessing you don't regret your decision to help them out until Harald is available."

"No, no regrets. In fact I'm glad you put your sensible hat on and talked me into it." She looked up and realised he was watching her closely.

"What's the problem?" he asked.

Kathy didn't know where to start and barely noticed he had sat back at the table with her but hadn't hitched his robe up properly and she had a lovely look at the leaping panther on his shoulder as well as the head of the raven on his chest. She kept her gaze unashamedly on the red eyes of the bird. "It's me and Jean-Guy."

Piers waited but she didn't elaborate. "But the pair of you are rock solid."

"Are we?"

"Well, I thought you were."

She told her story to the raven. The whole story of how Jean-Guy had been more and more reluctant to make love to her. She had even wondered if he was becoming attracted to Agnetha and had fallen out of love with her but she knew that wasn't the problem with him. She jumped as Piers reached across the table and lifted her face by the chin.

"Piglet, has it maybe occurred to you that he's a bit frightened of you?"

His touch was cold as it always was and she looked straight into his eyes. She remembered Jean-Guy's remark about being in awe of her after the *Lithuanian* concert but she hadn't taken him that seriously at the time. "No, I must admit it hadn't. I mean, he's one of the big names in the music world. Why would he be scared of me? What on earth do you mean?"

"Look at it from his point of view. He met this woman who had been through the worst thing possible. Your self confidence was at rock bottom, you had no pride, no sense of self-worth and you just got through each day at the time as it hit you. And now a couple of weeks ago you were on stage on the other side of the world and doing things with a film star that a hell of a lot of women can only dream about. You're not the person he met at Emma's wedding. Hell, I'm not even sure you're the same person who walked up to me in the pet food aisle and asked where the bread was. He's got to get his head round what you've become. Piglet, no, not the water works. Not before breakfast. Oh, for Christ's sake. Stop wiping your nose on your hands. That's a disgusting habit. Here."

Kathy took the piece of kitchen roll he gave her but still couldn't stop crying. "I'm sorry," she eventually managed to say. "I don't know what's the matter with me these days."

"Well, I've got a bloody good idea but I'm not wading into that one."

She looked up into his eyes but if anything he looked sad and regretful. There was no laughter in him any more and she knew just what that felt like. "Seems we both don't know where we're going from here."

He lightly touched her cheek." Seems we're both going to have to fight bloody hard to get to where we want to be. Or, in my case, don't want to be."

Just for a brief second, Kathy allowed herself the luxury of resting her face on his hand. "Our little army of two," she mused. "What should I do with him?"

"Truthfully? I'd give him a couple of weeks. You're settling back into your ensemble work, he's all over the place doing his solo stuff and I'm sure he'll realise that it's still the same you he's got with him."

Kathy caught one last glimpse of the raven as Piers got to his feet and pulled his robe round himself more tightly. "He's got until Christmas. If he hasn't asked me to marry him by the time we go to bed on Christmas Eve then I'm bloody well asking him," she announced.

Piers gave her one of his lovely smiles. "Just don't ask me to be bridesmaid, huh?"

Piers heard the phone ringing as he got out of his car and shivered as the freezing November air bit through his uniform jacket. He knew he didn't stand a chance of getting into the house and up the stairs before whoever it was rang off so he didn't hurry. But the phone kept ringing so he ran up the stairs and grabbed the receiver.

"Hullo?" he asked suspiciously as it suddenly occurred to him this could be a very unwelcome call from certain offices in Whitehall.

"Piers, good. Petr Mihaly. Are you coming here for the weekend?"

"I can do. What's happened? Is Sarah OK? And the kids?"

"Yes, please don't worry about them. I have had a letter and I would value your opinion on it."

Piers still wasn't sure this wasn't a recruitment drive. "From whom?"

"When are you flying again?"

"Tuesday, but it's the early Concorde run so I'll have to be back here Monday evening latest."

"Good. Get in your car and come, please."

"Just one thing," Piers started, sensing the other man was about to hang up. "Is it a music letter or one less welcome?"

"Musical. Very much so."

Realising he wasn't going to get a night in his London home as he liked to do, Piers showered and changed then climbed back into his car and drove out to Suffolk. He got there late at night so although Audrey came to greet him and the Prof hadn't locked the door, there was no sign of the other two.

"Where are they?" he asked.

"Gone to bed. Thank you for coming. I know it's late and I promise not to keep you up much longer. Would you like a drink of anything?"

"Tea would be good, thanks." Piers took the sheet of paper the Prof gave him. "Can't read this, it's not even in English."

"Translation on the back."

Piers flipped the sheet over and read the few brief lines. "Bloody hell. What do you think he should do?"

"I don't know. That is why I called you in. You are much closer to him as a musician and as a friend. Should I even show it to him?"

"Yes. Because I wouldn't mind betting Jane's got a copy of it too. It'll take her a bit longer to get a translation of it but she won't be long in calculating her commission. He'll want to accept. No doubt about it. Want me to talk to him about it?"

"Maybe after he has read it. But I will show it to him tomorrow and I hope you'll be there when I do."

"I'll offer to run through the Smetana with the pair of them. That always puts him in a good mood."

Both Kathy and Jean-Guy were delighted that their pianist had turned up unexpectedly. They knew, or had guessed, that he didn't come to Suffolk so much these days as Alison had made sure he was made to feel unwelcome when he went to see his wife, and it was a lovely treat to have him there. He had had a good night's sleep in his bed with nothing but the sound of the sea to lull him to sleep and the other two were even more delighted when he asked them if they fancied playing some trios that morning. He artfully steered them round to agreeing to the Smetana and the three settled down to some serious work on the piece while an ecstatic Audrey sat on top of the piano and purred so loudly they could hear her in the quieter passages.

The Prof sat in his study and listened as the sounds of his homeland sang through the house that had been his home now for nearly thirty years. He looked at the letter in his hand again and wished he didn't have such a sense of foreboding about it all. He knew Piers shared his doubts but wasn't going to say them out loud unless Jean-Guy looked like being unreasonable. It was certainly a very remarkable offer considering the cellist had run away from his home just over three years ago.

On the face of it, it was a perfectly harmless letter. It had come from the Symphony Orchestra in Prague, addressed to Jean-Guy via the British Embassy, and a copy had gone to his agent. The orchestra invited the renowned cellist to return to the land of his birth to give a series of recitals in Prague. One would be with the orchestra itself and for the other they proposed a more intimate cello and piano recital or, if he preferred, they would be happy to welcome the Dodman Trio to Czechoslovakia. They were offering a short stay of just those two nights but if Mr Dechaume was happy to be in Prague then there would be no problems if he wanted to extend his stay as audience demand was expected to be very high. The proposed date was just under a year away in the September of 1984 and the letter carried many assurances that Mr Dechaume, as a British citizen, would at all times be offered the protection of a visiting foreign national.

The Prof listened to the trio, played together by those three and knew that by the time of the proposed visit they would have it to perfection. It would be for two nights and three days. It could be the chance for Jean-Guy to meet with his parents again. So why did it feel so wrong? In spite of his brief chat with Piers last night, he so nearly screwed up that letter and threw it away but as Piers had pointed out, Jane would already be calculating her commission and working hard to make sure there were more than the proposed two concerts. The trio came to an end and he knew what he had to do. With a heavy heart, he went into the sitting room where there was the usual lively post run-through discussion going on.

"I'll go and make the coffee now," he announced and caught the eye of the man at the piano. "But before we go to the kitchen, Jean-Guy I would like you to read this letter."

So Jean-Guy read his letter first to himself and then read the translation out loud but didn't ask the others for advice. His head told him it would be foolish to go, but his heart was already back in Prague. Everything tumbled in his mind from the realisation the other three weren't sure what to say, to the knowledge that the time had come for him to take a huge step forward. He was ready to go back now. But only if he had the strength of the woman he loved with him to make him remember where his home was and where he now belonged.

"It may not be without risk," the Prof cautioned him after he hadn't spoken for a while. "There is a good chance your parents will be allowed to see you, but we must none of us forget the lengths the Soviets went to and if you go, you must all accept that they may well try again."

Kathy looked at the man she loved and knew he would go. The pull of his homeland was too strong and all she and Piers could do was go with him and try to protect him in any way they could.

"I want to go," Jean-Guy admitted and nobody was surprised. "And I'm sure we can work out a way to make it as safe as we can." He looked at Kathy and knew this was the time. After all the misunderstandings and fractures over the last year or so, there was only one solution. It may not work, but he had to do it. Right now. "But there is one thing I need to know before I will agree to go." The other three looked at him as he reached across and took Kathy's hand in his. "Will you make me happy and take me there as a married man? A properly, legally married one?"

After all her doubts and worries, Kathy hadn't been expecting that and she felt a fleeting moment of sheer blind panic, then she looked at her dear, sweet Moly and heard again that call of the raven but this time it wasn't telling her to run. She closed her fingers round Jean-Guy's hand and smiled at him through her tears of happiness. "Just name the day."

The story continues in *Pagan Sonata*

Printed in Great Britain
by Amazon